BLACK STAR

BLACKTHORNE LEGACY SERIES - BOOK ONE

LISA DOUGHTY

Black Star

Written

By

Lisa Doughty

February 2nd, 2017

Copyright © 2017 by Lisa Doughty

All rights reserved.

Edited

By

Diane Fournival

PUBLISHER'S NOTE

This book is dedicated to my husband Steve.
He is the love of my life.
He puts up with every crazy whim I have
and encourages me to see them through.
This book is the result of that encouragement.
Thank you for making all my dreams come true.

PROLOGUE

British Virgin Islands, 1723

"What I have to tell you will change our futures forever."

"Surely you exaggerate, Jon."

"I have to remarry."

"Jon, I know these last six months without Felicia have been difficult for you. I can't begin to imagine what you are going through..."

Henry Francis Hastings, the current Earl of Huntington, looked at his friend he'd known since childhood, Jonathon Patrick Warrington, the fourth Marquess of Blackthorne. He looked ragged and frazzled. His black hair was peppered with gray, more than when Henry saw him last. He looked as though he'd lost weight and his light blue eyes had lost some of their luster, he clearly was in distress. Despite that, he was still an impressive figure with his six-foot three-inch height and muscular frame at age of forty-eight. To marry while still in mourning for his wife would have the gossip's tongues wagging all over London. Henry understood the impact of scandal on one's life. He was very familiar the effect of scandal on a family's name and reputation. He had to leave London because of such a scandal. His family will be a victim of his actions for years to come. He tried to make sense of what his friend was trying to tell him.

"Slow down, start from the beginning. We will reason this through together."

"You don't understand. I *have* to remarry. I was found in a...compromising situation, one I have no recollection of doing. I am sure I was set up. You will be, too, once you know who the woman is."

"Who?" he asked, his stomach dropping. He knew the answer. There was only one family that had cause to do something so heinous.

"Penelope Verny," he said. Disgust riddled his voice and he hung his head.

"Good God, what happened?" Henry asked, a feeling of dread racing up his spine.

"I should have known better than to accept an invitation to Verny's soiree, but Lord Davenport was due to attend. I had been petitioning for his support in the House of Lords for the southern trade routes. I knew that swine Ivan Verny would try to persuade Davenport to give the routes to his company. The invitation felt odd, but I couldn't take a chance and leave Davenport in Verny's slimy hands. I had to go, to intervene if necessary."

"I would have done the same." Henry interjected.

"I rode two hours to his estate in Penbury. Once I arrived, I found out that Davenport had declined the invitation. I had originally planned to stay for dinner and depart early the next morning. Learning this, I wanted to leave immediately but I didn't want to raise suspicion of my motives so I decided to stay with the plan. That disgusting chit Penelope made eyes at me all night. After dinner, the gentlemen retired for brandy. I was never so relieved to get away from her. I gutted down one glass of Verny's cheap brandy, instantly felt dizzy, and retired to my room. I must have passed out, because the next thing I knew, Verny was bursting through the door. Penelope was there, lying next to me, naked. Verny started yelling, she started screaming, and before I knew it, the entire houseful of servants filled the bed chamber."

"That low lying scumbag! He must be desperate to try to get away with something like this!" Henry said, livid.

"I agreed to marry the chit, to avoid a scandal. The company can't afford rumormongering. My seat at the House of Lords is precarious at best, because of the fleet's loss of the *Bounty* and *Windseeker*. Both frigates were carrying the crown's cargo at the time. I decided to do some digging, and found out that Verny Trade is failing. Three of their biggest frigates have been sunk or seized by pirates. Also, Verny has lost more than the company is worth at the gambling tables. I believe the timing of Verny's collapse and my ships' demise is no coincidence. However, I have no proof. I need time to quietly investigate the matter. Until I find out what happened, I feel we need to do everything we can to safeguard all we have worked for." His voice shook at the end of his explanation.

"Do you think you were drugged then? I wouldn't put it past Verny."

"Without a doubt. I detest that wretched creature Penelope and I know I never touched her." Jon said adamantly, and took another fortifying swig from his brandy. "Brace yourself, it gets worse. I wouldn't have spent a month on a ship in winter to tell you that. I would've sent a missive."

"You mean there's more? More than you were drugged and defrauded into agreeing to marry the vile daughter of our biggest competitor?"

"She claims to be with child." Jon's expression was one of a defeated man. "Verny is vowing to say I raped his daughter if I don't agree to merge our two companies and make his fictitious grandchild the heir to fifty percent."

"Good God, all we've worked for... all these years...," Henry whispered. "If the company has to assume Verny's debts, we'll be back to square one. Does he know I'm your silent partner?"

"No. I would never reveal our arrangement, drugged or not. That's why he demanded fifty percent instead of a third. He knows I would never give him a controlling interest. He's scum, but not stupid." Jon swallowed what was left in his glass. "I'll marry the chit, but afterwards, she will be locked away at my country estate. I will have my staff watch her. I expect a miscarriage to be announced in due course. Then, I will petition for an annulment. I can't stand to look at her. I feel as though I'm disrespecting Felicia." He wiped a tear.

"He's crazy to think you would agree to give any shares in the first place!"

"The fact is, he can't demand something that I don't have."

"What do you mean?"

"I intend to abdicate my title and ownership to Sy." Jon said determined, but resigned.

Henry was astonished. "What? Sy is not ready for that responsibility. He has yet to complete his first commission, much less run an entire fleet! What of our partnership? That will change our entire arrangement."

"It's the only way I can think to keep Verny out of our business. It will protect Sy's and Raven's inheritance, your shares, the title, estates, everything. Even if there is a child and it turns out to be male, he won't be in line for an inheritance or title unless Sy has no heirs. To that, I have an idea to ensure that Blackthorne Shipping will remain ours, but I need your agreement. That's the true reason why I'm here."

"You don't need my agreement to abdicate. I appreciate you asking, but a simple contract for my shares will be binding," Henry stated.

"Not if something should happen to Sy. It could be contested. The legal battle alone could hold us up for years. We need an indisputable family bond, one that will guarantee an heir for Sy." He paused. "I propose we sign a marriage contract for Sy and Rhea."

"Rhea! My daughter's but fifteen, almost sixteen. She is not ready to be a Marchioness." Henry thought about his Rhea. She was so young and innocent, following her brother around, trying to be on her brother's crew and earn a mark of her own just like the men, she is a tomboy, not a lady. "Rhea was not raised in society. She is...different, has ideas of her own. She wants to be on a deck of a ship, not in a ballroom. I have to admit, she's a better seaman than most of the men, so I humor her. Her mother does not and insists on etiquette lessons, but Rhea's most resistant. She is not nearly ready for such a title and all the responsibilities it entails. Have you discussed this with Sy?" Henry stated, bluntly.

"Sy is bitter. Our relationship is strained at best. He is angry about my upcoming marriage and doesn't believe that I was forced to marry. Sy feels I have betrayed his mother's memory. Shortly, he will be leaving for his commission. I'm hoping his time at sea will cool his temper. This will give Rhea time to mature, and you will be able to prepare her for her role as Marchioness.

I suggest we tell neither Sy nor Rhea of this for now. I propose a marriage by proxy. I will continue my investigation quietly. If I can find proof that I need to end all this, we can tear up the contract and the children will never know. But, if Verny and Penelope persist or try something else, they will have no legal recourse. Everyone's safe."

"You certainly have put a lot of thought into this, but I

worry that we may be setting our children up for unhappy futures. They barely know each other." He was silent for a few moments. "Given the circumstances, I agree it's the best course of action."

"Thank you," Jon said, relieved. "It is my sincere hope that we will never have to act on the contract. I must find the proof I need and remove that Verny scum from our lives forever."

"They can easily dispute the marriage contract." Henry pointed out.

"They can try. But, they can never dispute the marks. Since Sy will receive his mark for a Blackthorne commission, I can add the appropriate marriage coordinates designed into his insignia to seal the marriage. Only you and I will know of that portion of the seal. The problem will be how to get the mark on Rhea?" Jon stated, rubbing his chin.

"Leave that to me. I'll see it done." Henry knew just how to accomplish the deed.

"I don't trust these vermin. I wish there was more I could do to protect Blackthorne Shipping. I know Verny is behind the disappearance of the *Bounty* and the *Windseeker*. Once they realize their plan has failed, they will retaliate with a vengeance. We could lose more of the fleet." Jon said, raking his hand through his hair. "Their actions prove how desperate they are."

"There is one thing that can be done..." Henry intimated.

"What?" Jon asked, puzzled.

"It's time for the Black Lyon to come out of retirement."

CHAPTER 1

Caribbean Sea, 1727

SHE WAS FAST, impressively so. She had the wind and could out run him but were slowing. Why? He was being toyed with, that's why. Letting him close in was a fatal mistake. Two leagues and the ship would be in range of his long cannons. This captain, if it was who he thought it was, was not a fool. Maybe it wasn't him, and he was on a fool's chase? What was he missing? Was it a trap?

"Folsom! What do you see man?" he bellowed up to the crow's nest.

It was dangerous to climb the mainmast to the crow's nest at full sail. He would climb himself, but he would not fit in the small nest on the foremast. At six foot, five inches the nest was too small for him to balance and hold his spyglass. He needed two hands for his spyglass since it was larger than most. It was custom made to his specifications, therefore it could see farther and sharper than the typical captain's spyglass. The price for the extended view was that the instrument was long and heavy. Others who attempted to look through it were forced brace it on something solid to keep it steady. He was strong enough to hold it to his eye, although not for an extended time. The extra range it afforded was invaluable. He could see the crew of another ship and anticipate their next move. He could tell if they were setting up to turn or run, then maneuver his ship in range of his bow cannons. This advantage had won him many a vessel and made him a dangerous adversary on the high seas. Anticipation won the battle every time.

Today was different. He couldn't get a clear picture of this ship. The image was somehow blurry and distorted despite his clear line of sight. She had cut and run once he came roaring up her flank. She pulled away so fast he thought there was no hope of catching her. In frustration, he ordered an extra jib, hoping to catch more wind and close the gap. The *Breakneck* groaned in protest, listing to a dangerous pitch. He was pushing her beyond her capabilities. The crew's tense faces confirmed their concerns as well. He looked at Smith, his first mate and most trusted friend. The look on his face was that of utmost confidence in his captain. This was vital for the crew to see. But when he looked in his eyes he could see the message loud and clear, *I hope you know what you're doing.* It was an unspoken language that came from being friends since boyhood.

With the smallest of nods, he reassured his first mate. Smith turned and shouted an order to the boatswain who followed it without question. They all knew what was at stake if they failed. They needed to catch this ship at all costs. He needed to know if this was the legendary ship, the ship of myths, the one that plagued his company and threatened the very foundation of his future.

Suddenly, she started to slow more, not enough to overtake her, but maybe enough that he could get a good look. Perhaps with the better advantage that the crow's nest granted, Folsom could see something he couldn't.

"Folsom! Report!" he bellowed impatiently.

Folsom wrapped his arm around the mast and brought the glass to his eye. The ship beneath him pitched and swayed. The wind bit at his face and roared in his ears. Fear gripped him with a cold hand. This was his chance to be noticed by the infamous Captain Sy Black. He fought to find the ship on the horizon, the pitch and sway making it nearly impossible. Finally, he found his image on the third try. The sway of the vessel made it difficult to keep it in focus but he knew there would be hell to pay if he had nothing to report. No one, and that meant no one, survived the captain's wrath if they did not complete an order. Trembling, he focused on the image as best he could. Why could he not make it out clearly? He had never had such difficulty before. He could see it, but no detail was clear.

"Ne'er seen the likes o' her before, Cap! Canna tell for sure but she looks to be full sail. The crew looks ta be standing and watchin' us. No' a one scurrying abo't. We'll catch 'er in no time! She looks two and one and a half leagues and closing, Sir!" he shouted down over the wind.

"What do you think Smith?" he asked his first mate. "I don't like it. Something doesn't feel right. Why let us gain after pulling away so easily? Something's amiss. What am I missing?" Before Smith could answer the captain looked through his spyglass again. "Folsom is right, I can just make out the silhouettes of the crew standing frozen, as if waiting for an order." The sun flickered on something. What was that flash? Another spyglass? The captain scanned the ship intently. He tried refocusing, then he saw him, holding a spyglass looking straight at him sizing him up! There was a white halo of hair that moved and flowed around the figure reflecting the sun. Then he knew for certain, it was his foe.

"It's the White Lyon! We pursue! All steady, ahead full!" he shouted, in a tone not to be disobeyed. "Folsom, tie off your safety line and get down here now!"

The crew sprang into action. Orders were being shouted and men ran to comply. He could feel the adrenaline filling his veins. We've got him! If he wanted a fight, he'd bloody well get one.

"Let me look!" Smith grabbed the spyglass. He could not hold it with the captain's ease. He propped an elbow on the rail to help hold the glass. He found the ship through the eye, just as he was focusing, a brilliant white flash blinded him.

"Ahh!" Smith screamed, jumping back and dropping the glass. It rolled to rest at the captain's feet. The captain stood shielding his eyes from the blinding light. Instinctively, Smith turned away from the searing blaze and saw the crew panicking. Some of the men were screaming and covering their eyes. Others were hitting the deck and covering their heads. The ship was completely engulfed in brilliant white light.

Then it was gone. As fast as it appeared, it disappeared.

Smith got to his feet. He rubbed his eyes in an effort to stop the spinning white dots. He looked at the captain, he was still standing at the bow, peering in the direction of the ship they were pursuing. Anger radiated from him, and Smith instinctively took a step away. He rubbed his eyes again and tried to focus on the sea. The ship was gone!

"Graahh! What the hell just happened!" the captain bellowed, at no one in particular. He picked up the spyglass, held it to his eye, and scanned the sea. Another roar of anger escaped before he kicked the rail.

"Jones! You have the helm! Pursue full speed toward the flash and find that ship! Report in a half! And it better be news I want to hear!"

"Aye, Captain!" Jones replied, loudly.

He ran up the stairs to aft deck, took his post, and yelled over the rail. "Ya heard the Cap' men! To yer stations! Do yer job or ya'll be dancin' with Jack Ketch 'fore I'm done with ya!" At his threat the men scrambled to their stations. No one wanted to face the hangman's noose.

"Smith, Hap. My quarters. Now!" the captain ordered without looking back to see if they followed. Smith helped Hap to his feet and they followed the captain, who was storming down the stairs to his quarters. He had to turn sideways and duck to fit his height and shoulders through the door.

He sat behind his desk. The wall of large paned glass windows flooded the cabin with light and cast a backlit shadow on his face, making him appear dark and threatening. He was a terrifying figure; dressed in black from the scarf that held back his long black hair, to the polished boots that covered from knee to toe. He wore his shirt unbuttoned from neck to navel, allowing one to see the sculpted muscles of his chest and abdomen. He radiated power and strength. And he was furious. He would look like the devil himself if it wasn't for the piercing, sky blue eyes now centered on the gentlemen who followed him in.

Smith was a frequent visitor to the captain's quarters. He had known him since their days at Eton and was comfortable following him into his private sanctuary, often joining him there for the evening repast. He was no longer intimidated by the captain's size or demeanor. At school, that scowl and intimidating physique often proved to be an asset. He was a fiercely loyal friend and, although it was never spoken aloud, they knew they would give their lives for each other. Hap, on the other hand, was not at all comfortable in the captain's presence. Few were.

"What the hell was that!" Anger and frustration were evident by the way his fist came down on the desk. It was a wonder the legs were not broken and the desk top reduced to splinters. The loud bang made both men jump.

"Now Sy, none of us have seen that before, except Hap here. All we've known is the myths and legends about the White Lyon. I didn't believe them, but now that I've seen it for myself..." he said, in an even voice, trying to diffuse the captain's anger. The captain stood so suddenly that his chair went flying and hit the wall. Smith wondered how the furniture survived his friend.

"Ships don't just disappear! What was that light? There has to be a logical explanation for all of this and I'm going to find it!" the captain spat angrily.

He righted the chair with more force than necessary. Then, he silently stared out the large window with his legs spread apart and his hands clasped behind his back. The stance emphasized the muscles in his back and arms. There was no denying the strength that he emitted.

The silence was deafening. After a moment, Smith elbowed Hap, gave him a look, and jerked his head in the captain's direction. It was a clear signal for Hap to say something.

"I tried to warn ye Cap'n. T'was just like before. 'Tis the way of the White Lyon. Comin' as if'n a star from the sky and gone 'ike one 'ust the same. There's no way'n to see 'im comin' or goin'. No one can get close ta 'im to get a look. Ask anyone Cap'n. Anyone 'ats tangled with White Lyon loses, 'es a ghost or a sea wizard fer sure!"

"Hog wash!" The captain crossed the room in a few short strides and looked at Hap. Hap was a seasoned sailor. It showed in the lines in his face and his sun leathered skin. As were most seasoned sailors, he was superstitious. When something couldn't be explained then it became supernatural, a legend of the sea.

"I don't believe in sea monsters, ghosts or wizards. There is always a logical explanation. I will figure it out and find the White Lyon!" Sy's voice was deadly serious. "Tell me all you know."

CHAPTER 2

*S*he knew she was in trouble. There was no getting out of or delaying the coming lecture. She knew she had taken an unnecessary risk, but she hadn't been able to stop herself. Now there would be hell to pay. She saw him stomping up the path to her cottage as she stood in her favorite spot in the world. The small knoll where her cottage sat had the best view of the cove and the sea below. It was a hike from the docks, but it was worth it. It gave her privacy and solitude. The steep and rocky path that led to her small sanctuary was the only way to get there. The birds and animals along the route would sound the alarm if someone was approaching giving her plenty of time to walk out front to see who was coming. She didn't need to check who was coming this time. She knew it was Jat.

Jat was the only person that would, or could, question her decisions. He was the only person she would discuss

LISA DOUGHTY

them with besides her brother, Titan. Jat had taught her everything important in life, including everything she knew about the sea. He taught her how to read the weather using the clouds and the waves, to navigate using the stars, and how to fight and defend herself using the Tiano tribal methods. She owed him much, though he would never think so.

Titan, her older brother, found Jat drifting at sea, dehydrated, and starving on a small raft made of logs and vines. His tongue was cut from his mouth. It took her mother three painstaking months to nurse him back to health. A first, it was as if he had lost the will to live. He would not attempt to communicate with anyone. He only stared at the ceiling, refusing to eat. She visited, leaving a small toy on his bed. It was a poorly constructed bird she made from twigs and feathers. At eight, she had no experience making anything, but tried constantly. She was too curious by half about how to build things and how things worked. Titan, her older brother, was annoyed by her incessant questions, often pleading to his mother to make her stop following him around. So, when Jat picked up her haphazard bird and examined it, she peeked at him to see what he would think. He examined it with interest, turning it at different angles, trying to figure out what it was. Finally, he motioned for her to come closer. He linked his hands together and made a motion of a bird flapping its wings.

"Yes! Yes!" she nodded enthusiastically, her blond curls bouncing around her face, "It's a bird!" She copied the

18

motion to confirm. She smiled a beautiful wide smile and he grinned back.

"Oh, you're awake. Good. Now I want you to eat everything on this tray." Her mother talked to him as if he understood every word, as she set the tray on the table.

"Rhea, you shoo now and leave this boy be!" The tray had porridge, broth and biscuits. She looked at Jat, motioned as if eating, then screwed up her face and stuck out her tongue. He smiled and his shoulders shook.

"I said shoo Rhea, I mean it!" Her mother pushed her to the door and closed it. Rhea ran to the kitchen. Being ignored by the kitchen staff was normal. She stayed close to the wall and grabbed a couple rolls from the freshly baked batch. Next, she went into the pantry and gathered a small piece of ham and a chunk of cheese. Using her skirt as a satchel, she walked by the fresh baked tarts, absconding with one as she rushed by. Running up the back stairs, she peeked down the hallway and saw her mother leaving Jat's room. Rhea let herself in once the coast was clear.

"I don't know what you eat where you come from but this is good food from here." She dumped her booty on the bed. "I gotta go, got my lessons now, uck!" She made the same face she had made about her mother's food tray. "Can I come back?" She stared at his face with anticipation.

He looked at the food dumped haphazardly on his bed then at her face, with an anxious expression. He nodded slowly, not sure what he just agreed to.

She squealed and clapped her hands.

"I'll try to come back later if I can, eat well!" She mimed eating while she said it. "Bye!" She waved and he waved back.

She finally had a friend of her own. She wasn't able to go back to see him that day. When she went to her bed chamber that evening, the bird she had made for him was on her bed. It was perfectly formed, with a tail added for realism. Tears sprang to her eyes and she wanted to run to his room and thank him, but just as she started towards the door, her governess swept in followed by servants with buckets of warmed water and a tub. It would have to wait till tomorrow. She would make him a dog next. There were lots of dogs in the village and she was sure she could do a better job on a dog.

As the years passed, they developed a language of their own.

What started out as toys evolved into small boats, then larger boats they could sail in the pond. She tried to share her accomplishments with Titan, only to be patted on the shoulder and told what a good job she'd done in an absent-minded manner. If she was too insistent he took her back to Jat and asked him to take her away. Jat understood the hurt and rejection she felt from her brother. He would always crouch down and motion to her that it didn't matter, that they would make a bigger, faster one next time. He never failed to make her feel better and bring a smile to her face.

Rhea knew that was not be the case today. She could see the anger in every step as he came up the path. She turned to look at the sea. She stood, legs apart, breeze in her face and hand grasping the hilt of the small cutlass tucked in the back of her belt. She knew what was expected of her and she would do it.

~

"HALT! STATE YOUR INTENTIONS," she commanded, once he reached the top of the path.

Jat stopped. She wasn't facing him. He smiled, despite his anger. Command respect, control the situation, and catch your opponent off guard if possible. He had taught her well. Too well. She knew he couldn't talk unless she was looking at him to see his sign language. To move would be disrespectful and there would be consequences. He had no choice but to wait. She knew he would either calm down or increase his anger. Either way, she would have the advantage. His heart swelled with pride.

He took a deep breath and waited. Rhea was an impressive sight, without a doubt as she stood looking over the sea as if she owned it. What a beauty she had grown to be, with a thick cascade of white blond tresses falling down her back. It was no wonder she had the nickname of White Lyon.

He took a deep breath, crossed his arms, and tapped his foot. He studied her since she had her back turned. Wearing her usual, a white peasant top tucked into brown leather pants and black knee high boots did not deter from her female form. The wide black belt that buckled at her stomach had straps that went over her shoulders then crisscrossed at her back to help support the weight of the weapons it held. Her hands were crossed behind her and concealed under her mass of hair, which reached well past her derriere. He knew she had two pistols and a small cutlass on her belt. He had no doubt that she was holding onto the hilt of her cutlass. Trust no one, not even him, he taught her. She was proving that she had learned her lesson well.

Rhea was much too beautiful for her chosen profession. At five foot and six she towered over most of the women in the village. Her body was toned, strong and well-proportioned. She walked with a confident stride, just as any man who held her station would do. That would be enough to set her apart, but it was her uncommon coloring that truly made her special. Her hair, which she refused to cut or queue, was always unbound and flowing down her back. It was a light golden color, streaked with platinum strands from spending hours in the sun making it almost white. Her facial features were delicate, like her mother's, with high cheek bones, a slender nose and perfectly arched light brown eyebrows. But it was her eyes were undoubtedly her most exquisite feature. They were like no others he had ever seen. They were a turquoise, truly turquoise like the Caribbean Sea, with a dark blue, almost black, rim around the iris. They were framed with jet black lashes, in stark contrast to her hair. The effect was mesmerizing. It was hard not to stare.

He thought back to the first time he saw her peeking above the mattress at the foot of his bed. Her curly white hair, shorter then, bounced around her shoulders as she waited to see what he would do with the toy she had made him. Those turquoise eyes were so expressive he could tell what she was thinking without a word spoken. He knew right then and there that all that his suffering had led him to her.

She was taller than most women, yes, but that was where her advantage ended. Tall but slender, she had no weight to throw behind a punch. Fighting with her fists would be a disadvantage for her. Therefore, they had concentrated on knife skills. She was also proficient with pistols, but that only allowed for two shots, which would buy time, but not enough to survive if attacked. He had taught her the Tiano warrior way of fighting. It was perfect for her. Bring your enemy close. Let them think they have the advantage, then strike when they do not expect it. It took nerves of steel to perfect. It took patience. Waiting was difficult in a fight, waiting too long could cost you your life.

RHEA TURNED SLIGHTLY and looked over her shoulder. The breeze coming from the ocean caught several strands of hair and blew them across her face. She shook her head to get them to return to their place. Jat was tapping his foot, a clear sign this strategy was not working. She realized that she had better speak her peace before she lost her small advantage. She turned her back to him again and looked at the ocean then down to the cove and saw the people going about their business, not sensing the turmoil happening just up the hill. A woman ran and jumped into the open arms of a man coming down the gangway of the *Star*. Was that Alona and Pax? When did that happen? She didn't know they were together.

Rhea was proud of what she had built here with her brother and Jat. It had been three years since her Uncle Harry had left the small island to her. Her uncle Harry used the island primarily for the natural resources to re-stock his ships with fresh water and various indigenous fruits. The occasional wild boar was hunted and the meat cured for the long voyages. The cove, which was the top of a volcano at one point, was basically landlocked by a reef. The entrance was completely obscured to passing ships by two overlapping land masses. The channel into the cove was blocked by a coral reef. If you did not know where the entrance was you would miss it. Her uncle found it by exploring the island on foot, *Paradiso* he named it. In his day, he moored his ships at sea and rowed into the cove by longboat.

It was beautiful, with three fresh water waterfalls cascading down the cliffs. It was her idea to drop large rocks on the reef to break it apart and clear a channel. Rocks bound by chains were dropped repeatedly to break apart the reef, it was painstaking work, but after a year a narrow channel was opened. That changed everything. Two small frigates could then be moored in the cove, bringing building supplies and other materials to develop the island. Over the next two years, docks, a small village, and two small warehouses were built, along with a small shipyard where they constructed the *Star*. They were now a full-fledged community with families starting. Soon babies would be born here.

"I know what you're going to say, but I had to see it." Rhea could hear him approaching behind her, he was done waiting. She tightened her grip on the hilt of her cutlass. Was this to be a test, then? She turned abruptly. "I didn't let them close enough to see anything. As it was, I didn't get but a glimpse myself. Look…" She waved her hand to the hustle and bustle below. "Everyone's back safe and sound!"

Rhea looked into his eyes. He was disappointed, she could see it, and her heart sank. She could take his anger, but not his disappointment.

"Jat, please, overall, it was a successful mission, was it not? We were to be a diversion and we diverted. Titan no doubt did his job and is on his way to father. I just wasn't expecting it to be *him*." She sounded dejected. "The rumors are true. He's built a galleon to rival the *Star*. Did you see how fast it was? Once he figures out his ballast is off…" She looked at the ground, she needed time to think. *He* was back and time was running out. She needed a plan, and quick.

Jat started motioning, clearly agitated.

"I am not changing the subject! If you've told me once you've told me a thousand times, *'know your enemy as well as you know yourself.'* How am I to do that if I am not able to at least see…" he cut her with his motioning.

"It was the vessel I wanted to see. I have no idea what

you are insinuating!" she shouted, trying to sound indignant. Why did she bother? He knew her too well. Rhea looked at the ground in a rare moment of vulnerability. She was trying to see *him*. Curiosity got the better of her. The rumors were of him were impressive. He was quickly becoming a legend of his own. She wished she didn't hate him so. She would love to meet him...again.

Jat lifted her chin to look at him. He motioned to her in a gentle and caring way.

"What do you mean he is not my enemy? If not, then what is he?"

With a look of regret, he put his hand to his forehead, then brought it down to clap his other hand. Tears welled in her eyes, making them look a deeper blue. She would not let them fall, ever! Not because of *him*!

"Husband? Ha!"

SHE STORMED INTO HER COTTAGE. Jat took a deep breath and sighed, before he followed her. He leaned against the door jamb, watching her storm around the room. Her cottage was small with a table, two stools, and a fireplace carved into the side of the hill. There was a pot of stew bubbling over the low fire, supplied by Jat's wife no doubt. A curtain was pulled back and secured on a hook on the wall that lead to another room, which contained the most unexpected furnishings. He cringed at the sight. There was a large canopy bed, complete with green velvet curtains, a gift from her brother. It engulfed the room, leaving only enough space for a small ornate chest. He felt a twinge in his back as he remembered helping bring that monstrosity up the steep, narrow path with six other men. There were some things he would never understand about her people, like a need for such a large bed. He would burn that bed before he'd help carry it anywhere again.

She went to the cupboard and withdrew two small bowls. She slopped stew in before dropping them on the table. Then, she retrieved a loaf of bread and slammed that on the table. Two cups filled generously with wine followed. She looked at him, irritated, then nodded at the stool, not understanding why he hadn't sat already. She had to know he had already eaten. He could not wait to get off the *Star* to see his wife Liana. He ate with her, amongst other things, seeking her advice before coming to talk with Rhea.

"You know what you need to say. I don't need to tell you," Liana advised. She was right and he would this time, come hell or high water. He sat, forcing himself to relax. He picked up the hunk of bread she practically threw at him, and dipped it in his bowl of stew. He took a small bite, while waiting for her to say something. It was delicious. Damn, his wife cooked good. He was a lucky man.

She stabbed her bread in the stew, but didn't take a bite. She shoved the food away and put her palms to her eyes. "Damn and blast, Jat, I just want to put this behind me and move on. Why was *he* here after three years? He will ruin everything!"

She looked at Jat, as he sat patiently, waiting for her to begin.

This was humiliating to talk about. Rhea sighed and decided to get the conversation over with.

"Alright, I was avoiding the subject. What do you expect me to say? I haven't seen him since I was a girl of only ten years. He avoided me at all costs then, calling me 'Minx' and spending all of his time with my brother. I barely remember much about him except that he had jet black hair and light blue eyes. He left for school with Titan and has never been back. Now all Titan does, is brag about him and his accomplishments. It's like salt in an open wound every time his name is mentioned." She looked up at Jat, desperation in her eyes. "What am I to do now? I was tricked into this marriage. I was lied to when the markings were made. How could my parents do this to me?" Rhea grabbed her cup and stared aimlessly at the red liquid. "Why is he here after all this time? Three years! Not a word from him! Three years, Jat! Do you know how embarrassing that is?" He looked at her with a straight and unreadable face. He knew she wasn't done and there'd be no reasoning with her till she was. "It's nothing like you and Liana, Jat. It's obvious he doesn't want this union either, or he would have come for me. Instead, he's chasing the wind to the other end of the world. Well that is just fine with me! I have work to do. He can just go back where he came from!"

She looked at the marking on Jat's arm. Liana's had the same design on hers joining them in marriage. She remembered the day well, she was so happy that he had found her. They looked at each other with such love; something she would never have.

Rhea thought she had lost him when he took a boat and a small crew in the middle of the night. She couldn't believe he had left her. Jat returned three weeks later, with Liana. He told her he couldn't tell her about his plans or she would have insisted on coming along. He was right, she would have, even stowed away if she needed to.

He had gone back to his home island to get Liana. He wasn't going to wait any longer, knowing Liana's fate was surely worse than death. He had lost his tongue trying to protect her when he saw the chieftain's son raping her in the jungle. She was beaten so badly that she was hardly recognizable. He knocked her attacker out with a rock to the back of his head. When he carried Liana's lifeless body to the village and placed her in front of the Chief, he did not believe that his son had committed the heinous act. He imprisoned Jat and cut out his tongue so he could never speak of it again. The next morning, they exiled him to the sea on a small raft with no water and to certain death. Jat knew that the village would consider Liana soiled. If she survived the beating, she would never be accepted, would be shunned, and would live on scraps to survive. He knew the chieftain's son would be sure she would die of starvation, if he hadn't killed her already. Jat snuck into the village at night, carried her back to the boat, and headed back before anyone was the wiser. Nearly starved and filthy from living in the jungle, she was barley aware that Jat had taken her. He nursed her on the boat. Unable to speak, he tried his best to tell her she was safe and going to a place where she would be accepted. Four months later they were in love, exchanging marks as husband and wife. Today she carries his child. The first for the island and their new community.

Rhea's mark showed her commitment and devotion to her crew. She spent years trying to earn her place amongst her brother's motley crew, and when she was finally marked it was the happiest day of her life. She was surprised and elated that her father recognized her hard work after objecting for so long. At sixteen years old, she wasn't going to question his decision to agree. In deference to her mother's wishes, her mark was on her thigh instead of the typical place on the upper arm for all to see. That way when she returned to England it could be concealed from polite society, who would not appreciate the meaning.

Her mark was a circle with the front half of a prancing lion in the middle. The outer ring had symbols that indicated the date and coordinates of her induction. No two markings were alike because of these coordinates. When she married, her coordinates would be added to the mark of her husband and his to hers. The mark was for life, therefore, so was the brethren of the crew and the marriage.

She had endured all the rituals of being marked, as embarrassing as it was. Marks were made by inserting a needle in the skin then applying ink to stain the skin permanently. Once done, the skin was raw and sore. That was when each member of the crew slapped the mark in acceptance of its new member, bonding them as brothers. The redder that mark, the stronger the bond. She stood as the crew lined up to show their acceptance. She cut one leg from her pants, stood with her legs braced apart, and stared each man in the eye as they came to slap her mark. As a show of respect none held back because she was a girl. Her mark was bright red and small droplets of blood were oozing when Titan walked up to her. Her eyes were glassy with tears but she did not let them fall. He looked in her eyes as he slapped her mark hard. He said the words:

"As Captain of the *Rogue* I accept you as a brother. From this moment on I will give my life for yours if needed. You will be given no favor. You must follow orders without objection and with haste. You will never steal from your brothers. You will never be a traitor to your ship or its crew, even if you must give your life. You will treat all women and men of association with honor and respect and protect them as your own. From this moment on you will never abandon your brothers unless life has left their body, for they will do the same for you. To these terms do you pledge yourself?"

With tears in her eyes she replied loudly for all to hear, "Aye, Captain, I do!"

He slapped her mark again, harder than before. "As Captain, I expect unconditional loyalty and will give it in return. I expect no one to give more than I am willing to give myself. To show your loyalty you must do the same to me and the others. Walk the line."

She looked at her brother's face and could see a mixture of pride and trepidation. He raised his sleeve to reveal his mark of induction. She stared into his eyes as she slapped it twice, as hard as she could. He gave her a nod. She looked at the long line of new brothers, each raising their sleeves to receive the slap of loyalty. With a quivering lip, she walked the line, slapping each mark as hard as she could. Once she slapped the last mark, her hand stinging, shouts rang out and she was hefted up on the men's shoulders and paraded into the village. She had never felt as wonderful as she did at that moment.

Unbeknownst to her at the time, that was also the day she was married, to Sylvester Evan Warrington, heir to the Marquess of Blackthorne, known to all as the infamous Captain Sy Black.

CHAPTER 3

"**W**here is she?" Titan yelled to Jat, as he jumped to the dock. Just as Jat was beginning to point, a loud explosion and a plume of black smoke blew through the windows of the warehouse at the end of the dock. They knew immediately it had to be Rhea. Titan's heart jumped into his throat.

"Bloody hell! What was that?" Titan shouted. They both took off running. Titan was the first to burst through the door. Jat collided into Titan's back when he came to an abrupt stop because of the black smoke billowing out the door preventing him from entering. Titan tried to focus. No flames were visible, just the haze from the residual smoke.

"Rhea! Otis!" he called out, frantically, when he heard laughter. Laughter? Relief flooded him as they ran toward the sound. Otis and Rhea, their faces and clothing black and their hair smoking. Titan immediately started patting Otis's head, because it was smoking the most.

"Hey, hey cease and desist! You're going knock me unconscious for goodness sake!" Otis tried to fend off Titan's blows.

"What the hell was that?" Titan shouted, at no one in particular. Jat was helping Rhea to her feet. She tried to brush as much of the black from the front of her shirt, to no avail.

"Answer me, damn it!" Titan asked, exasperated.

His hands were still shaking when he looked around the room. The walls and windows were blackened by the blast and a few small items were toppled, but everything else was intact. He was amazed that the windows had survived and were only covered in soot.

"What?" Rhea and Otis yelled in unison, their ears ringing from the blast. They looked at each other for a brief moment, then started laughing hysterically.

"What in damnation is going on here? You could have killed yourselves or burned down the village!" Titan's anger was growing by the minute. Both of them laughing like goons wasn't helping.

"It's alright, Titan, we just have to adjust the amounts a little. No one's going to die. Otis has it under control, don't you Otis?" she said, louder than she realized, patting Titan's shoulder. She looked to Otis and gave a small sideways nod towards Titan, indicating for him to say something. Otis's eyes widened in understanding.

"Oh, surely, just a small adjustment will do the trick. It's amazing, simply amazing! We should be able to increase range considerably. I just need to think on the matter some. Yes, yes, this is going to be revolutionary! Yes, yes..." He started mumbling to himself as he walked away in deep concentration, his fingers reaming out his ears.

"You see brother? Don't fret, just a small adjustment is needed, that's all." she yelled at Titan, totally ignoring Jat's scowl. She patted Titan's shoulder again condescendingly, then started guiding both he and Jat toward the door. Titan looked at Jat, who looked as confused as he was. Why were they so happy? Didn't they just blow themselves up? What caused the explosion?

"Why don't you go down to Maggie's and get yourself a drink? I suggest the cold ale. It's so much better cold, Titan! You simply must try it. Otis has devised a way to run it through tubes and make it as cold as the sea in winter. It's incredible! I'll join you in a few minutes. I just need to help Otis reset. Alright then, say hello to Maggie for me..." She practically shoved them out the door and closed it, leaving both men looking bemused.

"How many days have I been gone?" he asked, looking at the door and then to Jat. Jat raised two fingers.

"That's what I thought. Unbelievable. Two days and I've lost all control of her again." He hung his head, dejected. "Mother's going kill me. I have to bring her home, and when she sees the hellion Rhea's become, I'm done for." Titan sighed, resigned. "Suddenly, getting a drink is a sound idea." He looked at Jat, who was wearing a smirk.

"I don't know how you do it, keep up with her all the time. Join me?" Titan gave Jat a strong pat on his back. They both smiled and turned toward the road that led to the village. "The man's a marvel, cold ale through tubes? This I have to see. So, what do you think they're up to now?"

Jat shrugged and motioned with his hands.

"You are right about that! I'm sure we will find out soon enough!"

❧

"THAT WAS AMAZING! What did you call this stuff?" Rhea picked up a small glass vial containing an amber liquid. Otis came running over.

"NO! It's way too volatile to be handled like that! I'll take it." He put on gloves made from blankets, took it from her and placed it gently back in an empty slot in a wood box full of similar vials.

"It's nitroglycerin. In liquid form, it will explode with the slightest movement. It's a miracle the ship that brought it here didn't blow itself to smithereens. We have three boxes of a dozen vials each. If I can break it down to a solid, it will be much more stable. I need to do some calculations, but I think with a few adjustments to both the cannons and the formula we will be able to considerably increase the firing range." He looked down at his desk, searching for something.

"That is amazing! Simply amazing!" She repeated very excited about the prospect. "What will you need? Make a list and I will give it to Titan to fulfill. When do you think we can test it?" She looked at Otis with childlike excitement.

He looked into her beautiful eyes, the black smudges on her face emphasizing their unusual color. Otis shook his head to stop from staring. Even covered in black soot she was extremely appealing, and the fact that she didn't know how beautiful she was only added to that appeal.

He'd never forget the first time he saw her. She was like a white rose amongst the thorns of burly seamen that made up the crew of the *Rogue*. She seemed right out of the sun with her white blond hair glowing. He thought he was hallucinating. After three weeks in the hole, it took time for his eyes to adjust to the daylight and when they did, her beautiful face came into focus. Pax and Toothless Tom dragged him to the top deck. He thought for sure that he was to be thrown overboard until he saw the angel from the sun. She ran up to him yelling at the men that were dragging him then unceremoniously dropped him on the deck.

"Pax, Tom, what did you do to him?"

"It weren't us, swear! We found him like this, locked up in the hole. We brought him up here to get a better look at 'im." Pax proclaimed, Tom nodding in agreement vigorously behind him. "We ain't hurt 'im none. We just bringin' 'im for the Cap to look at."

"Take him to the *Rogue* and put him with Doc. We'll see

what Titan wants to do with him." She walked away, barking orders to the men who scurried to do her bidding.

Doc wasn't a real doctor but was the closest they had so he was called Doc. Doc had some training from the war and had extensive experience with herbs and healing remedies. He also talked nonstop. He learned all about the crew and the ship from Doc's nonstop chatter while he fussed over him. It was three days before he saw his angel again. She entered the infirmary with a giant of a man who leaned against the door jamb, crossed his arms in front of his chest and glowered at him. It was obvious he was protective over the lovely young woman. They shared the same unusual eye color, so he assumed they must be related.

"How's he doing, Doc?" Titan's booming voice filled the room. Rhea had sat on the stool next to his bed. He tried not to stare at her but couldn't help himself. She was mesmerizing. Dressed in men's clothes, complete with belt, britches and boots she must be used to people staring at her. But it was her bewitching eyes, her face framed by white blond tresses falling freely about her shoulders, that held him. Those eyes were so full of compassion he couldn't find his tongue. She put her hand on his arm.

"He'll live." Doc replied dryly. "Be outta here in a day or two." He sounded disappointed. Otis guessed that he didn't have too many people who put up with his endless chatter.

"I am Rhea. This brooding gentleman behind me is my brother, Titan. Don't let his gruff demeanor scare you. He's that way because he's the captain of this vessel and it's expected." She said the last part of her last statment in a whisper.

"I heard that. Rhea, why don't you go back on deck. It's obvious he lost his tongue because of you." He looked past Rhea to Otis and said, "You'll get used to her, she'll be annoying you before you know it." he chuckled.

"Titan! You'll give him the wrong impression of me," she said, looking over her shoulder at him, then gave Otis a wink. It was utterly charming. He couldn't help but smile at her. "How are you feeling? Are you up to telling us your name and your circumstance? Why were you in the hole?"

"My name is Otis McGregor, madam. I feel much better due to Doc's excellent care, thank you. I am more than willing to answer any questions you and the captain may have. But first can you please tell me where we are headed? What happened to the ship I was on?"

"It was dispatched." Titan replied curtly. "We dispatch all vessels conducting human trafficking. Why were you on it?" Otis knew better than to lie, this man was not to be trifled with. Besides, he had nothing to lose. Anything was better than where he was going.

"I was condemned to the Americas. I was to be an indentured servant since I had no way to pay for the damage I caused at my last place of employment. I was put in debtor's prison for a time. I tried to escape several times and return to my home in Scotland. The last time I was caught they removed the toes on my left foot so I couldn't run anymore." He moved the blanket aside and showed them his left foot.

Rhea gasped and put her hand to her mouth. "I was sold to a factory in America and shipped out. The guards told the crew that I had made multiple escape attempts, so they threw me into the hole. My best estimation is that I was down there for three weeks."

"What kind of damage did you do to your last employer?" Titan asked in a matter of fact tone.

"I was a scientist, one of my experiments went awry. I accidentally blew a hole in the laboratory wall." He looked down embarrassed. "Nobody was hurt and I know what I did wrong. It won't happen again." He peeked up at Rhea's face. There was no judgment there. He gave her a tentative smile. She smiled a big toothy grin back and his heart skipped a beat. Who could ever get used to that? A portly gentleman came up behind Titan and quietly said something to him.

"I'm needed on deck. Rhea are you coming?" She waved him off without looking back. "Doc, you leave this room while she's here and you'll answer to me, understand?" he said gruffly before he turned and followed the other gentleman.

"Aye, aye, Cap." Doc replied, loud and clear. Rhea rolled her eyes.

She scooted her stool closer to his bedside. Rhea held out her hand with a pair of spectacles in them.

"Are these yours? she asked.

"My glasses! Oh, thank the lord above!" he exclaimed, excited. He put them on and turned back to Rhea. She was looking at him intensely, as if she were expecting something.

"Madam, to where are we sailing?" Otis said, to break the silence.

"Paradise." She gave him another heart stopping smile. "You're a scientist? How interesting."

From that day forward they talked every day. She had a smart mind behind that beautiful face. She was completely devoid of vanity. She pulled her weight with the crew and they treated her just as any other. She climbed the mast faster than the other seamen and knew every knot as well. She took her shift just as though it was the most natural thing to do. She was also full of intelligent questions. Once he was strong enough to walk on deck, Rhea walked with him. They talked of the ship she wanted to build; she even showed him her drawings. He helped her perfect her designs and added a few ideas of his own. It was evident that the crew was fiercely protective of her. Eyes were on them every moment they were together. They made sure their weapons were clearly visible to Otis, some even going as far as massaging the hilt of their cutlass when they knew he was looking. The message was clear: touch her and die. At forty-two what did they think he was going to do with this young girl? He could be her father. There was no romance in their friendship, not an inkling of it, but he didn't care as long as he could look at her every day. She was his angel.

A few weeks into their journey they were forced to stop. The rudder shaft had splintered and the vessel was adrift. Titan, his first mate and chief engineer were arguing about the best way to repair it and limp home. Rhea immediately got Otis to look at the problem. Within the hour, they were underway. He fashioned a brace from items in the hull to repair the shaft. The chief engineer scratched his head and looked at the contraption, clearly impressed.

"Would've never thought of that, good job." He slapped Otis on the back, nearly knocking him to the ground. "Come have a look at this over here, can't wrap my brain around this problem and was gonna handle it in port. Maybe you can think of something?" For the remaining week, he resolved several problems aboard and improved maneuverability in general. The day before they were to arrive at the island he was marked and inducted. With pride and self-confidence, he walked the line though he just couldn't bring himself to slap Rhea's mark as hard as he did the others. That was three years ago. Now he had a home and lab of his own. Rhea's voice snapped him back to the present.

"I have to go to Maggie's and catch up with Titan. I wonder why he's back so quick, I didn't expect him for three more days. I hope there's nothing amiss at home. Give your list to Titan or Jat and I'll see it done." She talked over her shoulder as she walked to the door.

Otis watched her exit, her hair swaying back and forth in rhythm with her hips. It should be illegal for women to walk like that!

CHAPTER 4

*R*hea ran up the path to her cottage. She needed
to change her shirt and wash her face before
going to Maggie's. A bath in the waterfall and pond behind
her cottage would be preferred, but there wasn't time. If she
didn't get to Maggie's quick, Titan could very well be too far
into his cups to tell her why he'd come back early. Her mind
was racing with possibilities and she would worry all night
thinking the worst. It better not be about *him*. She'd had
quite enough anguish over *him* already.

Rhea still smelled of smoke when she strolled into
Maggie's, but she didn't care. Titan and Jat were sitting in
the far corner with their chairs leaning against the wall,
boots on the table. Both of them had their legs crossed at the
ankles as if they didn't have a care in the world. The place
was bustling. The cold ale must be a popular, indeed.

Every face was familiar. The only way onto the island was

on one of their ships. Only the crew and their families were allowed to settle on the island. The community had doubled in size over the last few years. What a diverse group they had accumulated. All were rejects for one reason or another. All had been recruited for their special talent, which they shared with the community. All of them were fiercely loyal, and bore the mark of the White or Black Lyon.

Rhea smiled and nodded to the people sitting at tables as she walked by. She stopped in front of Titan, feet braced apart, arms crossed in front of her chest, and tried to look intimidating.

"Why are you back so quickly, is something amiss?" she asked.

"It's good to see you too Rhe-Rhe!" He used her childhood nickname to irritate her. It worked. "I'm glad to see you didn't burn off all your hair. We wouldn't be calling you the White Lyon without your signature mane, now could we?" He smirked, and hit Jat with his elbow. Well, at least he wasn't angry. She kicked his feet off the table, forcing his chair forward with a thud.

"I'm serious, Titan! Nothing would keep you from your favorite whorehouse unless something was wrong." She grabbed the closest chair, spun it around, and sat on it backward. Jat raised an eyebrow.

"Oh, stop Jat! You both can see the door. I will know by your faces if something happened behind me." He wasn't appeased, but gave in. He knew she wouldn't sit with her back to the door if they weren't on the island and let it go.

"Are mother and father alright?" Concern laced her question.

"Right as rain, both of them." He picked up his mug and took a long draw.

"Was the Red Dragon spotted then?" she inquired, referring to the pirate that often raided her father's fleet. Until the White Lyon had come along, that is.

"Nope." He raised his hand to hail Maggie to the table. He watched Maggie fill the pitcher from a contraption in the wall. She brought it over and set it down on the table along with a mug for Rhea. Titan reached for the pitcher as if he was ignoring her. Rhea lost her patience completely when she realized Titan was purposely stalling to be irritating.

"Titan!"

"Alright, Alright! I'm just running' a rig on ya, sis' nothing's wrong, I'm to bring you home that's all," he said, with a rakish smile.

"What? Why?" Her face paled. This couldn't be good.

"They didn't tell me any specifics, just to go get you and you're to leave the *Star* here. Aunt Magda is visiting, I'm sure that's all it is." He poured a mug of ale and slid it to her. "My guess is mother doesn't want Aunt Magda to see you acting a pirate. Better break out a proper lady's dress," he said, with a chuckle.

"Oh, ha ha, you're so hilarious. I can't go home right now and you well know it. The *New Star* will be ready to launch soon. What Otis and I are working on now will need to be tested at sea..."

"You forget I have no control over this," he interrupted. "Are you suggesting I tell father no? Are you refusing to go home?" he asked.

"No, I'm not refusing.... I'm delaying," she answered, in a tight voice. She avoided meeting Titan's eyes.

"What's really bothering you Rhe?" He leaned forward and put his hand on her arm. "Are you worried about running into that Lieutenant Riley? If he were to come within a hundred feet of you he wouldn't ever walk right again!"

She looked at his face and saw the love there. If only that really was the problem. He thought she still loved the hand-some lieutenant, and she would continue to let him think that, too. It was precisely that lieutenant who had inadvertently brought the truth of her marriage to light. He courted her hard and fast, for he had limited time in port at Nevis, the island where she grew up. Young and naïve, she had allowed herself to trust the first gentleman that had treated her like a lady. She had dreams of moving to England as his wife and starting a family. She wanted to forge her own path, and not be in her brother's shadow any longer. As the second son to an earl, he planned go back to England at the end of his tour where he had a job at the naval offices. She was shocked and hurt when her father refused the proposal from the lieutenant. When she confronted her father, and told him she would run away with him if he didn't agree, he was forced to tell her that she was already married. He showed her the wedding contract that proved she had been married for eighteen months. Her fate had been sealed.

Desperate, Lieutenant Riley snuck in her window and tried to convince her to leave with him that night. When she tried to explain that it was impossible, he became violent. He grabbed her hands with one hand and covered her mouth with the other. He forced her to the floor. She could smell the liquor on his breath.

"I will have you as mine. I will make you mine now, and there will be no choice but for you to come with me!" he growled in her ear, as he forced his knee between her legs. She forced herself to relax. He took it as permission. "You'll like it, I promise." He lifted his hips up to move between her legs, a fatal mistake. She brought her knee up hard. He made a guttural sound she had never heard before. It was half scream, half gasp for air. He rolled off, clutching between his legs. She was up in a flash and grabbed the knife from under her pillow. She had been such a fool to trust him. Jat was right, never ever trust anyone. She ran back to him, straddled his chest, and placed the knife to his throat. That's when Titan burst through the door. She leaned down to a mere inch from his face.

"You will never touch me again," she hissed, between her teeth. "Do you hear me?" Titan was there, pulling her off him and reaching for the knife. He was yelling, but she couldn't hear him. She was blinded by rage. Pax and Tom ran in as Titan pulled her into the hall.

"Rhe, did he hurt you? Did he…touch you?" He grabbed her chin and forced her to look at him.

"No," she whispered, and dropped her eyes. "I stopped him before he could…"

Pax and Tom came out of her room, carrying the tied up and unconscious lieutenant. Bruises were becoming visible and one of his eyes was starting to swell. It was obvious that the boys got in a few licks before he passed out. Her father and mother came scurrying down the hall, pulling their wrappers on as they ran.

"What's happening here?" His question was directed to Titan.

"This guttersnipe tried to rape Rhea, father!" Titan's face was red with rage.

"He's about to be lost at sea, sir," Pax stated, as if it were decided. Their mother gasped. Pax and Tom started moving out to complete the deed.

"Halt!" her father shouted. "You cannot just throw him in the ocean, boys. He a son of an earl. If he disappears there will surely be an investigation, which will lead directly back to Rhea. She will be ruined in the very least!" he stated.

"Father, surely you don't mean to let him get away with this, he almost raped her!" Titan was enraged.

"Certainly not! We will take him to his superiors. There are laws that govern a sailor of the Navy. I will ensure that he is punished or, by God, there will be hell to pay. I am not without influence. Justice will be done. Give me a moment to grab my cloak." He turned to her mother. "Take care of Rhea, dear." He touched her face tenderly and went to get his cloak.

"It's all over now." Rhea's mother put her arm around her daughter's shoulders and pulled her back into her bedroom. "I'm here for you darling."

Sobs came, as the gravity of the situation hit her. Her future was gone. The man she thought she knew almost raped her. She was married without her consent, without even a courtship, to a man she'd last seen when she was a child. She felt as if everything was spinning out of control. Well, no more! She would control her life from now on. She'd be damned if she would meekly accept this situation. She would build a world of her own.

Now, the truth was, she knew she was out of time. She knew now that *he* was back, her fate had been sealed. Her father would make her honor the contract. She had hoped for enough time to prove that she was more valuable than an object to trade off in marriage. It was too late.

BACK AT HER mother's house, Aunt Magda was sitting on the settee, talking as if this was not a life changing moment for Rhea.

"You will need a new wardrobe dear," she said, sipping her tea. "We must leave as soon as possible. A new wardrobe will take time."

"She has several dresses that are current Magda. I make

her update the styles every year. They are made of the most unique silks and materials. Absolutely beautiful too," her mother exclaimed, then said, under her breath, "Not that they ever get worn."

"There are not many balls on *Paradiso*, mother," she replied, sardonically. Her mother ignored her remark turning back to her sister.

"I can't thank you enough Magda, for taking on this task. We know the position we are putting you in. This couldn't have come at a worse time. With the new plant opening, we won't be able to get away for months. We don't know how we will be able to make it up to you," Carla said to her sister.

"It's my pleasure, truly. Chester and I never had any children so this is actually a dream of mine. It will be fun to escort Rhea around as if it's her first season. Even if the circumstances are a bit unusual, I will do my best to make it seem like a normal coming out." she said, with an enthusiasm that annoyed Rhea.

"Why you want to be a part of the farce is beyond me, Aunt Magda. This all seems so unnecessary. The deed is done. Announce it in the papers and be done with it, I say." Rhea said, irritated.

"That would cause quite a scandal, my dear, for you and for the Blackthornes. That is precisely what we are trying to avoid. It must seem as though you met in a normal manner, had a courtship, and were married as you should have been dear." her mother said.

"Don't you want a wedding Rhea? Most girls dream of a wedding their whole lives." Aunt Magda asked.

"The thought of wedding someone who obviously doesn't want to be wed to me is not a very romantic picture, wouldn't you agree?" Rhea pointed out.

"I remember the boy to be quite tall and handsome. You are very beautiful Rhea. Maybe you will find an attraction for each other?" her Mother interjected.

"Mother! That is not helping." Rhea said, appalled.

"Well, maybe just an accord then." she amended her remark.

"If he wanted an accord or anything else he would have come here a long time ago." she replied, emphatically. This was going from bad to worse. There had to be a way to talk father out of this, Rhea thought to herself.

"Where's father? I've been waiting over an hour." she said, irritated.

"He's with your brother, preparing for your trip. Titan's not happy about his circumstance either. He has been blind-sided worse than you, so keep that in mind. At least you knew this day would come eventually. He found out that he's become the Earl of Huntington just this week. It's time both of you to stop this running around the high seas and attend to your duties." she said, in a motherly tone she recognized from childhood.

"Taking over father's title and his seat in the House of Lords is hardly the same as a marriage to a man who doesn't want you, mother. Wouldn't you agree?" Rhea snapped.

"Your father would return if he could, you know that Rhea." Her mother replied sadly. "We have little choice in the matter. Besides, it's time to stop all this...this business of running around on high seas for months at a time." She waved her hand in the air irritated.

"Back to her wardrobe. Does it include shoes? Aunt Magda asked, trying to change the subject and stop the escalating argument. "What about her hair? It will take a seasoned ladies' maid to style that large mass of hair. Will I need to find one when we get back?"

"No. I'm bringing Liana and Jat. Liana can do my hair. I don't want some old biddy begging me to cut it. This is going to be a miserable enough experience, thank you!" Rhea sighed and plopped herself down on a chair in dismay.

"You are overreacting, my dear. All young ladies can't wait to go to town and have their first season. It will be good to take a break. You have done nothing but work over the last few years. You could go and try to enjoy yourself." her mother pointed out.

"Mother, you keep saying that as if this is going to be a fun experience. I am already married, but I have to parade myself around as if I'm not. I have to dance and act happy. Pretend to be courted by a man who doesn't want anything to do with me, then go through a farce of a wedding. What kind of person thinks that is fun?" Rhea asked.

"I think you are missing the impact of not doing it. Your brother needs this seat in the House of Lords and you need him to be there, for *your* businesses. It is imperative that society believes this alliance is real. Business is conducted by status and reputation, which are built in social circles, at balls and dinner parties, may I point out. For us to continue doing the family business, *your* business, this must be done in a way that looks genuine. The marriage must look natural. Lord Blackthorne has as much to lose as we do. He will want to do his duty. I don't think it's going to be as bad as you think." her mother tried to convince her.

"Try to make an adventure out of it dear. Once it's over you can come back, at least for a long visit." Aunt Magda reasoned.

Her father and Titan came through the door. They bowed to the ladies and Rhea rolled her eyes.

"Father, may I speak to you in private? It will only take a minute and I've been waiting for you for over an hour." she asked, impatiently.

"It won't do any good Rhe. I already tried." Titan said sarcastically.

"This is your fault Henry. You let them traipse around the seas endlessly, now they don't want to do their family duties." she scolded her husband.

"Enough, all of you! Rhea come into my study now." He walked out before anyone could say another word.

Rhea hastily followed him, thinking of what she was going to say. Once in the study, he gave his daughter a big hug. At first, Rhea was shocked by the affection, but then she put her face against his chest and let the tears flow. Henry rubbed her back as she let it all out. Once it was clear that she was composing herself, he pushed her away and looked down at her beautiful face. His little girl.

"Rhea, I want you to know that I never wanted this situation to come to pass. I was hoping with every fiber of my being that we would be able to find a way to make this an easier transition, but it wasn't meant to be, and now we must honor the contract. That is the way of it. The marks have been made. It must be done. For both you and Titan." he explained, before she could say anything.

"But father, haven't I proven myself as more valuable here than what you could receive by any marriage contract?" she asked, in a small voice.

"I think the bigger question is why do you think you have to? You don't need to prove your worth to your mother or me. We love you unconditionally. What you have done is amazing, but it doesn't release us from our obligation. Our word and our honor to keep it, is bigger than any one thing, without them we are nothing. You have to honor the contract just as Lord Blackthorne does. I have every confidence that you both will find a way to make this situation work, if not as husband and wife, then as business partners." he said, in a softer tone.

She looked at her feet because she couldn't look at his face. He always had a way of disappointing her and making her feel confident at the same time. She resigned herself to the situation.

"I will do my duty and go through with this marriage

farce, but once I do, may I return? I want to finish my work." she asked.

"That will be between you and your husband. You are always welcome home, of course. We have indulged you for a long time, and will continue to do so, in order to maintain what you've accomplished. It is time for you to do your duty for your family. Can you do that?" he asked.

"Yes father." she sighed.

He kissed her forehead. They walked to the door. Titan was leaning against the wall outside, waiting for her. Her father went to the parlor to talk to his wife.

"Well? Did you get us out of it?" Titan asked, jokingly.

"No," she said, and narrowed her eyes. "We are off to London, big brother."

"Damn, you were my last hope."

CHAPTER 5

"Ships don't just appear, then disappear!" Sy stated, clearly frustrated. He took a healthy swig of his rum. He sat behind the desk in the captain's cabin aboard the *Breakneck*. Smith stood, looking out the large glass window.

"Well, it disappeared and we haven't seen it since. It's been six weeks. We have been to every den of iniquity, paid good coin to the lowest of lows, only to discover that nobody else has seen it either. Not a word or rumor even. What self-respecting pirate doesn't brag about his exploits?" Smith grabbed the bottle to refill his glass.

"One that doesn't want to get caught." Sy chuckled sardonically. "I've tried everything to lure them out of whatever hole they are hiding in. I increased the bounty on their heads by double and planted rumors of gold on ships along the northern trade route, but they bite at nothing." Sy slammed his cup down, spilling his rum, soaking the papers on his desk.

"He's cunning that's for sure. He appeared out of nowhere to join leagues with the Black Lyon, terrorized the trade route for a year then disappeared. The only good thing about the situation is that it looks like they have run off the Red Dragon in the process." Smith took a gulp of his rum. "Do you think they might be related? White Lyon, Black Lyon, that can't be a coincidence, can it?" Smith asked.

"I thought of that, I can't reason it out. If they are relations, then why doesn't the Black Lyon disappear in the same fashion? They would rule the seas if they had a fleet of disappearing ships. Plus, *pirate* is a generous description to give these Lyons. From all that I have discovered the White Lyon has never boarded another ship. He appears beside or behind his prey only to disable or to draw the gun ships away from the real target. Then the Black Lyon scoops in and takes his bounty. There are times he leaves the ship and crew unharmed yet other times he burns the ship to the ground and sets the crew adrift. I can't figure what they are about? Have you ever heard of pirates setting a crew adrift? Why not just kill them? Why take a chance they'll survive?"

"Have you talked to any survivors?" Smith inquired.

"No. Only to those who found the small boats. The crew always seems to kill each other off. Survival of the fittest I suppose." Sy paced back and forth across the cabin having to duck under the large beam in the center each time.

"Well, it's going to remain an unsolved mystery for a while since you've been summoned home."

"Summoned is right. Damn the old man, I wish he would leave me be. I have goals of my own and I'm close, too. The *Breakneck* has proven to be a worthy design. If I use his connections in the House of Lords to solicit investors, we could start the Blackthorne ship building division. I don't want to ask him for money again, I want to do this on my own."

"I would think he'd be happy to expand Blackthorne, but I respect that you want to do it on your own. It's commendable." Smith raised his glass in a salute to Sy. "Well, there are other benefits to returning to London, for you at least."

"And pray tell what would that be? Debutant balls?" he joked.

"The widow Willoboughy for one." he pointed out.

Amelia Willoboughy was married to the Earl of Willoboughy who was twenty-five years her senior. He died just eighteen months into the marriage. She was left with a lucrative allowance and a stepson almost her age. Amelia was a wonderful distraction for a time. At first, he was flattered by her attention. Limited to debutants and ladies of the evening for his experience with the fairer sex, Amelia was different, she was as coy as society demanded but as experienced as those in the profession.

It started as a flirtation, long forbidden kisses stolen during social events and balls, that quickly turned to a liaison. Amelia encouraged him to try new things, entering their sexual interludes with wild abandonment. Sy learned a lot about a woman's body, thanks to her, and even more about his own. At first, their meetings were secretive and he looked forward to them, excited for the adventure of it, then Amelia became territorial and jealous. At first, she would hover, taking his arm as if staking her claim, and talking down to other ladies of the *Ton*. He started to see the real Amelia emerge with her cynicism. He couldn't abide her rumormongering, a form of bullying in his opinion, to keep the other ladies from showing interest in his direction. It became obvious that she was posturing herself to be the next Marchioness of Blackthorne.

In the end, she became too much for him, demanding of his time, as an escort and in her bed. He broke it off shortly before receiving his commission, using it as a perfect excuse to end the affair.

"That's over. I would not be interested in a reconciliation." he stated. "She is too taxing for my taste."

"Well I, for one, enjoy Emily at Madam Pricilla's. I hope she is still there after all this time. I intend to make her my first stop once I settle back into my room at the family townhouse." Smith said, filling his glass once more.

"I might join you, if my appointment with my father doesn't totally spoil my mood." It had been a long time since he'd had the company of a woman. Smith's suggestion had merit.

Sy looked at his friend. He wasn't exactly a big man but he was above average. Two years at sea was hard work, earning them both a great deal of muscle and strength. They were no longer the green boys they were at the beginning of their first commission. Both of them were competent seamen and proficient fighters, essential to their chosen profession. They let their hair grow long, mostly out of necessity. Not only was there no one to tend to it but it was easier to queue when needed. He wondered how the ladies were going to react to the change in their appearance.

Smith was the third son to the Earl of Danbury, so there was little to no chance of inheriting the title. Sy thought back to the first time they met. He walked around the corner of Eton hall to find Smith surrounded by three upperclassmen intent on hazing him. He had been gangly in his youth, but nonetheless was trying to keep his attackers at bay.

Sy never liked or participated in hazing of lowerclassmen. Having gone through the process himself the year before, he thought it a useless exercise, an excuse for the upper-classmen to abuse their classmates with no consequences. Unlike the others, he didn't take the abuse for long. When he had reached the end of his tolerance, he fought back. Even though it was four against one, he still managed to break two noses and one arm before the fourth ran away. Having proven himself a formidable opponent, he was left alone and earned a reputation of someone to avoid at all costs. He was so irritated by the whole process he would often stop the abuse to others if he came upon it, like he intended to do for Smith.

He was about to intervene when he noticed that Smith

actually had some skill at fighting. He parried punches and landed a few of his own, although not effective enough since he was weak from fighting off three aggressors simultaneously. Sy was impressed by his fortitude. Smith wasn't backing down, despite the odds against him. Sy had respect for the young fellow. Then, one of them sucker punched Smith in the back and he fell, they proceeded to punch him while he was down. At that cowardly move, Sy saw red and jumped in the fray. He easily flung one assailant against the wall, knocked him unconscious denting the plaster. The others recognized Sy and one of them immediately ran off without a word or look back. Busily concentrating on pummeling Smith, the third was unaware that his friends had been dispatched. He screamed like a girl when Sy lifted him by his jacket collar and flung him against the wall next to his friend, denting the wall again. He recovered quickly and limped away before Sy could do any more damage. Sy helped Smith up and took him to the school infirmary. He visited him every day during his recovery and they had been inseparable since.

The dents in the wall made during that fight remained there as a reminder of what happened to those who dared challenge Sy or Smith. To his knowledge, the dents were still there, but the story behind how they were made had become greatly embellished. Needless to say, no one dared to challenge Sy or Smith again.

Sy graduated Eton and left to earn a commission, Smith followed, believing that would be a better opportunity than continuing his education. They earned their marks together, refusing an elevated rank because of their titles. The long voyages allowed them to dream of building a faster, more efficient gunship, which would be a desired commodity. Sy discovered quickly that Smith had a keen mind for ship design. He found a kindred spirit in Smith, one that wanted to earn his way in life and not rely on his luck of birth, as most of the titled tended to do. When their commission ended, they decided to take another, this time on a gunship. They studied the ship and worked their way up in rank. At the end of their second commission, Sy was unanimously voted Captain on the gunship *Outrider* in the Blackthorne fleet. Smith was promoted to first mate.

Sy petitioned his father to look at the designs for the new gunship. Although he hated to do it, he asked his father for a small portion of the Blackthorne shipyard to build the *Breakneck* and the balance of the money needed above what he earned on his commissions to fund the project. He knew his father readily agreed as an olive branch to their strained relationship. Determined to make it clear that this was a business proposition, he and Smith worked day and night to perfect the *Breakneck*.

The day that the *Breakneck* launched his father was there, but stayed in the background, letting his son have the moment. Then he promptly asked him to guard the *Dogwind* merchant ship on their next voyage. The *Breakneck* was all they imagined it to be. It still needed a few revisions, but for the most part was faster, lighter and efficient so it required less crew to sail. Sy felt redeemed, and couldn't wait to return to his father to report its success.

Then they were attacked by the Black Lyon. Just as Sy was ready to close in and test the *Breakneck's* mettle in battle, the White Lyon had come up on his flank. He had no choice but to give chase, the perfect chance to prove that the *Breakneck* was the fastest ship on the sea. He would've been a legend, damn his ego and his pride. The White Lyon had disappeared in flash of light and the *Dogwind* limped home damaged, divested of its cargo by the Black Lyon himself. His wild goose chase across the seas to catch both Lyons had been fruitless. Now he would have to go back and face his father, a failure. His Father couldn't deny that the *Breakneck* was efficient and fast or that building more ships like it would be an excellent business. He had to rely on those points in their upcoming meeting, not his failure protecting the *Dogwind*.

"You know, it may be time to let things go, Sy. I don't believe your father will be as critical as you think. He has done nothing but try to repair your relationship and support your endeavors." Smith said, as if he could read his thoughts. He took a pull from his glass, hoping he wasn't overstepping. "At least that's what I see. I don't think catching the Lyons would have changed his opinion of you or this ship. But what do I know?" he added, as a buffer.

Smith was right and Sy knew it. He was holding on to his anger for his own benefit. If he stayed angry with his father he wouldn't have to focus on his mother's death. The unbearable pain of her passing still consumed him. He would never forgive himself for not being there for her and his sister, Raven. He was on his first commission when she took ill and couldn't get home in time. Guilt swelled in his chest, still raw from the loss. He didn't like the feeling of helplessness and lack of control. Anger was easier. He pounced on a reason to be angry with his father and be able to leave home where the memories were too painful. Even now, the thought of returning home was giving him anxiety. His father, who was always close to both of his children and put them first in his life, remarried just six months after his mother's passing. Sy felt betrayed and his mother's fading memory disrespected. He couldn't believe his father, a pillar of a man, could have been duped as he claimed. Truthfully, he didn't want to deal with any of it, neither his mother's passing nor another woman walking the halls of his home. For this reason, he couldn't let his anger go. Plus, now he would always have to deal with Penelope. He had never loathed another person as much as he loathed that woman.

"You don't have to deal with Penelope Verny. I do." he pointed out to Smith.

"Good point, I tend to try and forget about that vile woman all together." Smith agreed.

"Unfortunately, I have no choice. Makes it hard for me to forgive when I have a constant reminder such as her." Sy filled his glass again at the thought. Yes, it was comforting to hold onto his anger. "I intend to go in and face the consequences of my failure and get back to chasing the Lyons as quickly as possible. If I stay for any length of time, my father will be widower again and have a son in Newgate prison."

"Well then, we must make it the highest of priorities to visit Madam Pricilla's. With either possibility, we may not have another opportunity for a long time."

CHAPTER 6

*S*y stormed into the foyer of his father's townhouse two days later, his irritation obvious. He practically threw the cloak he carried to his father's butler, Watson.

"Where is he Watson?" He knew he was being discourteous to the faithful butler. He had worked himself into quite a rage in the short carriage ride from his townhouse. He'd only been in London one night and he was already desperate to leave. The stench was worse than ever and the heat was stifling this time of year. That was compounded by the many of layers of clothing that he was required to wear while in town. He wanted to get back to his ship, back to sea, back to his hunt.

He hadn't seen his father since he launched the *Breakneck*. That parting was strained at best. Now he was summoned from across the ocean like a lad in short pants. He swore to himself; he was going to keep this meeting brief and to the point. He would not allow himself to lose his temper.

"Welcome home, my Lord. Your father is in his study but is currently occupied with a guest. He shouldn't be but a moment. He is expecting you, I will tell him you have arrived. May I suggest you wait in the parlor with his other guests. Shall I announce you?"

He was the same old Watson Sy remembered, never losing his composure or showing emotion on his face. Even when Sy put bitters in the prim and proper butler's tea, he controlled his expression and drank the entire cup as if nothing was amiss. He was older now, his hair completely gray and balding. His attire was impeccable as always.

"That won't be necessary Watson." He gave him a rakish half smile by way of apology. Watson knew how rare that smile occurred and was appeased.

"As you wish, my lord." He folded Sy's cloak over his arm and walked away, presumably to tell his father that he had arrived as Sy walked the short distance to the parlor doors. He hated London, such pomp and circumstance just to enter a room. He opened the parlor door and had to duck slightly to fit through the frame. He stopped short of entering, stunned at the unexpected sight in front of him.

She had her back to him looking up at the family portrait of Sy at age eight standing next to his mother with his little sister Raven in her lap. Her head was cocked slightly to the side as she examined the family picture. Her light blond hair fell like a waterfall of waves down her back, well past her derriere. She had a large amount of it pinned on the top of her head in an intricate design of curls and braids. The style wasn't in fashion but he could tell that there was no way to keep the entire heavy mass up on her small head. She wore a dark blue day dress with short capped sleeves which amplified the light color of her hair. Her dress was form fitting without the unusual number of petticoats popular amongst most ladies, allowing him a good glimpse of her slim figure. She wore a wide belt at her waist that accentuated the curve of her hips. She was taller than the average lady, but even so, the top of her head would only barely reach his shoulders. He found her extremely appealing from behind and wished she would turn around.

"She was very beautiful was she not?" she asked out loud. He scanned the room to see who she was talking to but saw no one.

"Yes, she was." he answered.

She twirled around and gasped at the sight of him. His heart skipped a beat. She was beautiful. Her face was delicately featured with high cheek bones and gently curving light brown eyebrows. Her figure was even more appealing from the front with ample breasts emphasized by the cut of her neckline. Her skin was a lovely golden color. But the most intriguing thing about this creature were her eyes. He knew he was staring, but the color was so unique, like nothing he'd ever seen before, and her eyelashes were jet black like a frame around them.

Breathe, move you nitwit, do something besides stare at her like a dumbstruck fool! he chastised himself.

"Excuse me, madam, I didn't mean to startle you." He moved further into the room and stood his full height, willing himself to look away, but couldn't.

"My lord!" She gave a quick curtsy. "My apologies, I thought you were my aunt."

IT'S WAS *HIM*. In the flesh, standing not eight feet from her. Not in her mind or in her dreams, but right here! Rhea's heart started slamming in her chest. She was sure he could hear it from across the room. He was so much larger than she had remembered. No, he was an absolutely mammoth of a man. He had to have three inches on Titan. He was dressed in black from his boots to his jacket except for his white shirt and haphazardly tied cravat. His shoulders and arms were thick with muscle, barely contained in his jacket. His hair was as black as his clothes and tied at the back of his neck with a piece of leather. She couldn't tell how long it was, just that it fell past his collar and out of sight. His eyes were a clear blue color, like the sky, and they felt like they were penetrating through her gown. She felt goosebumps forming on her arms under his stare. It felt like a caress as his eyes moved down then back up, pausing at her chest for the barest of seconds, then locking eyes with hers. She wasn't sure what to do, she wasn't expecting to meet him today, like this.

"She is visiting your father," she said awkwardly. "My aunt, that is…is visiting your father, my lord," she added, stumbling through the sentence.

"You have me at a disadvantage, madam, have we met?" Sy took a few steps closer. "I'm sure I would have remembered making your acquaintance." he said, with a rakish smile.

"Are you serious, my lord?" Was he flirting with her? Teasing her? Anger welled up inside her. "Surely you haven't completely forgotten me?" she said angrily. "Under the circumstances, I would think you would at least have an inkling…"

"And what circumstances might that be?" he interrupted. What an arse, to tease her on such an occasion, as if he didn't know!"

"It is impolite to tease such, my lord. Are you seriously saying you have no idea who I am?" She stepped closer to him and stared directly in his eyes taking his measure. Suddenly, she couldn't breathe, not sure if it was anger or the close proximity to him. He was devastatingly handsome with those piercing blue eyes which were emphasized by his black lashes, brows and short beard trimmed neatly to hug his jawline. Butterflies started fluttering in her stomach when he too took another step closer also.

"If you could tell me your name, madam, it might jog my memory, and clear up any myst…"

"I am Lady Rhea Hastings, my lord." She cut him off to show her annoyance.

She watched his features for a reaction. All the years she had waited for this very moment. The anticipation of what he would say about their circumstance had all come to this second. She held her breath. If she hadn't been staring at him so intently she would have missed it. His eyes widened slightly and his rakish little smirk dropped but a fraction. In a flash, he closed the remainder of the space between them until he was towering over her, their toes almost touching. She had to crane her neck to continue looking him in the eye. She slowly reached behind her back and put her hand on the hilt of her knife tucked in her belt. She could see Jat coming out of the shadows behind him and made a small gesture with her hand for him to stand down.

"Hello Minx."

THE SCENT of jasmine greeted him as he approached her. He took a deep breath, enjoying the feminine aroma. He could see the swells of her breasts rising and falling in irritation. So, this is Titan's little sister. He remembered her, she was always a little spitfire, which explains her irritation, it was just like her to be angry that he didn't recognize her. It also meant she's totally off limits. He was downright disappointed. Regret flooded him. It was best to be polite and excuse himself quickly.

"It's been a long time. You have grown into a..." He dipped his eyes and took a long lingering look one last time. She was magnificent, a pity he was never to see her again. "Beautiful young woman." He sounded almost sad.

"And you, my lord, have grown very...very... ah...big."

Sy couldn't help himself but smile bigger at her feeble attempt at an insult. Her cheeks turned pink with embarrassment and frustration. The color only added to her appeal, he felt the urge to kiss her.

"And you know what they say about the big ones." she continued with a smirk, and renewed confidence.

He lowered his face so that it was just a few inches from hers. Damn, her eyes were beautiful.

"What do they say, my lady?" he asked sarcastically.

"The bigger they are, the faster they sink." she said, without backing away. He was used to his size intimidating even the most hardened sailor and here was this girl – no, certainly not a girl any longer – a woman, standing her ground against him. He felt a pang of excitement and the urge to kiss her doubled. He could feel his member thickening at the thought.

"Something I have yet to experience...Minx." he said quietly, almost a caress, using her nickname in a teasing tone. Her eyes dropped to his mouth making his eyes drop to hers. They were full and slightly parted, ready for him. If he were to lean forward just a fraction their lips would touch. An overwhelming urge to reach out and pull her against his chest overcame him. He envisioned throwing her over his shoulder and taking her upstairs to one of the bedrooms and…

"Ahem! My lord, your father will receive you now." Watson said loudly from the open doorway.

Rhea's eyes dropped to the floor and she stepped back slowly. He felt as if the air was sucked from the room as she left their close proximity. He wanted to pull her back. Moreover, he wanted to excuse the butler and everyone else to see where this conversation would go. He didn't want to move from his spot or for this moment to be over. He closed his eyes and backed up a step reluctantly.

"Thank you, Watson." He gave Rhea a slight bow. "It was a pleasure to see you again, my lady." He turned to walk from the room. Without breaking his stride, he looked toward the shadows where Jat was standing. "Hello Jat." he said, before he exited. Rhea let out the breath she was holding.

∼

"WAS THAT LORD BLACKTHORNE?" Aunt Magda asked as she entered a moment later. "Oh my, what an imposing figure he is. My dear, I have news from his father."

"He doesn't know yet." she said forlornly before her aunt could say it.

"Why, you are right! Lord Blackthorne told me that today will be the first time his son will learn of the marriage contract. His father seemed so sad and concerned for his son.

It was heart wrenching, really. How did you know?" She looked at Rhea puzzled.

"I need to think, shall we go?" Rhea stated and started to walk out of the parlor.

Now she was more confused than ever. All this time she thought he didn't want to honor the contract, that he didn't want her. Now he was to be blindsided. Anger and self-pity were threatening to consume her. How could her parents do this to her? Judging by his reaction to her today, so cold and aloof, he would surely protest the contract and she would be forced to face a new rejection. She wanted to go home, needed to go home. She was useful and respected there, had a life and purpose. She was done being a pawn and needed to take control of this situation. Determination to get home and back to her work was the foremost priority now. She had to think, needed to be alone, to reason this out in her mind.

"But Lord Blackthorne wanted to meet you and surely Sylvester will want to speak with…"

"We just spoke, Aunt Magda. I have to leave, please no arguments, ok?" Rhea pleaded, and exited the parlor to halt further discussion. She had to get out of there now, vowing that she would not lose her composure here, in his house.

CHAPTER 7

The study door was open. Sy could see his father standing behind his desk, his back to him. When he ducked though the door frame, his father turned to look at him. He could see the trepidation on his father's face. He was searching Sy's face, trying to determine if he was still angry. He was.

"Hello, son." His deep voice was familiar, comforting somehow, and his anger cooled a bit.

"Father." He gave a slight bow to show respect and to help ease the tension. Anything to get this over with as quickly as possible. "I received your summons, what couldn't wait? I was closing in on the pirates that attacked the *Dogwind*."

"It is not necessary for you to apprehend them, son. It has been months, surely a father can request an audience?" he replied, sounding disappointed and sad.

"Father, I would prefer this meeting be as non-confrontational as possible. We have had disagreements in the past and I would prefer to leave them there. Surely you didn't call me across the ocean for a visit? You requested that I join the Blackthorne fleet as a gunship and protector, which I was doing. It takes time, father. These pirates are devious. There are a lot of hiding places in the islands. I also discovered that the Red Dragon is not responsible for most of the plundering of our ships. It is actually the Black Lyon, aided by the White Lyon." Sy strained to keep his voice even.

"The White Lyon? I thought the White Lyon was a myth, tall tales from superstitious seaman?" he asked.

"I saw the White Lyon with my own eyes. I assure you he is not a myth. He is up to some sort of trickery. I have yet to figure it out, but I will. So, if you don't mind father, I would like to leave and continue my pursuit as soon as possible. Please come to the point of this meeting." he said, gruffly.

"I see time has changed nothing." he sighed. "I'm afraid this meeting will undoubtedly make things worse for us, then. I just ask that you hear me out before you pass judgment. I want you to know my actions were made to protect you and your sister."

"When have Raven and I ever been a priority to you or influenced your actions of late?" Sy angrily pulled the knot out of his cravat, it suddenly feeling tighter around his neck, and walked over to the tray that held a crystal decanter of brandy and glasses. He poured a healthy portion of the amber liquid then drank it all in one swallow. He closed his eyes and tried to reign in his temper. Then refilled his glass and went to lean against the fireplace mantel.

"What has happened now? What action of yours could possibly require my presence in London?"

"I have abdicated my title to you."

Sy swung around to face his father, spilling his brandy in the process.

"Why in the hell would you do that?" his shock obvious.

"Actually son, you have been the Marquess of Blackthorne for some time. I abdicated before you left for your commission. I have been working as surrogate in your absence. I had to protect you and your sister's inheritance. I had no other option." He went to sit in the chair behind his desk. "I was going to tell you when you returned from your first commission but you didn't come back. Then again after your second, but you were still angry. You asked to build the *Breakneck*. I knew it took all you had to ask me for the space and funds. I knew it was important to you. I hoped that in a way it might help mend our relationship. I was afraid this news might put another wedge between us and I couldn't bear that."

"If that is true, then why now?" Sy asked, still reeling from the news.

"There are many things you don't know regarding the family business son. It's time you do. I'm not sure where to begin..." He rubbed his temples, trying to organize his thoughts.

"Why don't you start with why you were forced to abdicate?" Sy suggested, impatiently.

"As I stated before, it was to protect your inheritance. I had to be sure that my new wife and the vermin she's related to would never have an avenue to get their grubby hands on it. They may have forced me to marry that wretched woman but I'll be damned to hell before she gains from the union."

"No one forced you to be intimate with her father."

There it was. The reason for the divide between them. Sy felt betrayed and his mother disrespected. His father sighed and stared at the desk. It was an old argument but one Sy would never let him forget.

"Son, I swear to you, one day you will see the truth of the matter. Until that time, my priority is to keep Blackthorne Shipping protected for you and your sister's future. By abdicating my title and all its holdings, including Blackthorne Shipping, Penelope had no right to any of it. She instantly became the dowager with rights only to the dowager townhouse and a small allowance on which to live. Of course, she greedily scooped up what she could but has constantly complained that the funds aren't enough to maintain the lifestyle of the acting Marchioness of Blackthorne. To appease her, I have supplemented her, now and again, so she would leave me alone. She is a vile woman, not discreet with her liaisons, parades her lovers in public, and has lavish parties. She spends every penny she gets and uses the family name to influence the members of the *Ton*. I cannot wait to rid myself of her."

He paused and looked at his son, but did not find any sympathy there.

"I cannot prove what I am about to tell you, but I am certain that the Vernys are behind the loss of the *Windward* and the *Bounty*. I have suspected for some time that the Vernys were in league with the Red Dragon and the pirating of our cargo. The pirate seemed to know which ships to attack and to which port they were headed. At first I thought I had a mole in the offices. Then Verny Shipping purchased two new frigates even though the company was on the verge of collapse. I did some checking and discovered that they were financed by an overseas investor. The coincidence was too much to ignore. So, I sought protection for our fleet from an off-shore resource, and started planting false information about freight and its destinations. It wasn't long before the Red Dragon took the bait, proving at least a part of my suspicions."

"What off-shore resource has been protecting Black-thorne? They surely didn't come to our aid with the *Dogwind* when the Black Lyon attacked." Sy said, adamantly.

His father gulped, and Sy could tell he was apprehensive about what he was going to say next.

"Actually son, the Black Lyon is the off-shore resource. He was to apprehend the cargo and bring it to our overseas offices to be distributed. Our plan was to outmaneuver the Red Dragon so he would move off our trade routes and go to an area where there was less competition. It was Hunting-ton's idea. I must say that it has worked, too. We have not lost a ship or a life since the Black Lyon started his campaign. He has also divested the area of human traffickers, burning their ships to the water. They avoid the area at all costs. As you can imagine, it was important that no one knew of our alliance so only Huntington, myself, and now you are privy to this information." He looked at Sy's stunned face, waiting for the tempest to rain down on him.

"Who is he father?" Sy said, in a tight controlled voice.

"I do not know. I did not want to know, to protect myself from any further association. You must not pursue it either, son. That is the other part of the reason I called you home. You must let it go, for the protection of the Blackthorne name and title." Sy's mind was reeling.

"Then I ask you this. If your marriage to his daughter benefits them, why would he want the loss of the ships? That seems counterproductive, doesn't it?" Sy questioned, barely holding on to his temper.

"Not if he gains my seat in the House of Lords because of incompetence. The timing of the death of the Earl of Chamberlain four months ago, which leaves an open seat, and the ships' disappearances, can't be ignored. Verny is behind this, I know it. If Verny gains one of the seats he could very well block our trade rights, especially if he can make me look incompetent and unworthy to the crown. There is a lot Verny doesn't know about Blackthorne Shipping. I have an ironclad way of stopping him from obtaining either seat. Unbeknownst to Verny, Chamberlain was also a surrogate for his brother-in-law who has yet to claim the seat. Verny thinks there are no heirs to the Chamberlain seat. The Chamberlain vote was the swing vote. He was also an ally, which enabled us to obtain the majority of the trade routes for the Crown."

"This makes no sense father. Even if I were to take your seat it would not solve the issue. It's the swing vote that is needed."

"That is true. The brother-in-law in which Chamberlain surrogated for is my silent partner. He runs the overseas office for Blackthorne Shipping. His son will take the seat and secure the vote. To this point, he has been fulfilling another important role for the company."

"Why won't this partner fill the seat, why his son? Why me? You both could work together to secure the routes."

"My silent partner is the Earl of Huntington, son." He waited for his reaction.

Sy knew that Huntington left England in a cloud of scandal. He was accused of kidnapping the daughter of the Marquess of Trenton. The Marquess did not approve of the match with Huntington. He had the Duke of Stratton's son in mind for his daughter but before the match could be announced his daughter disappeared with Huntington. As result of the union they had a son and a daughter. Sy had spent a few summers with the Huntington's in his teens and attended Eton with their son, Titan. Now that he looked back on the situation it made perfect sense. His father and the Earl also went to school together. It would have been a perfect business arrangement for Huntington to open the overseas offices and avoid the scandal while Sy's father ran the London offices. Huntington would never be able to take the seat back himself, but Titan, his son with the proper connections could.

"I remember the ridicule that Titan received because of the scandal at Eton, father. I intervened on his behalf but I think that legacy will follow him. How will he be received at the House of Lords even with my support?" he asked.

"The seats are bonded by marriage." His father looked away, but Sy could see the pain on his face.

"Marriage? Titan married?" Sy was confused.

"No son, his sister, Lady Rhea Hastings has married." He said softly. His voice gruff with emotion.

Sy felt as though he had been punched in the gut. That beautiful women belonged to someone else. Why did he care? She was off limits to him anyway. Wait a minute, if Rhea was married and it bonded the families then...

He looked at his father's face. "Who did Lady Rhea marry, father?" he asked, but he knew there could only be one answer. His father had betrayed him again.

"Now son, arranged marriages happen all the time. I had to protect you and your sister. I did what I felt best. You are untouchable now. They have no power over you or what you decide to do with Blackthorne Shipping. I have settled an annual sum on Penelope to keep her away from us. Your sister will have her full dowry when her time comes. I will live on my salary and other small investments. You are in complete control this way. Can you not see the security for all in this plan?" he pleaded.

Sy was pacing like a caged animal throughout his father's

litany. He yanked the tie from his hair. He had the feeling of being trapped and needed to feel free of something. The jacket came next, discarded on the ground. He walked over to the chair and kicked its leg but that wasn't satisfying at all. He picked up his discarded brandy glass and stormed over to fill it. He filled it to the brim only to carry it over to the mantel and place it on top untouched. Then he sat down and put his hands over his face. He needed to get ahold of himself so he could process this information. He took a deep breath and tried to relax.

"Let me be certain that I understand the situation correctly." He took a deep ragged breath before continuing, hoping it would calm his temper. "I am now the Marquess of Blackthorne. I have been married, by proxy I assume, to Lady Rhea Hastings without my consent. I am expected to attend to your seat at the House of Lords. I have a silent partner in overseas offices, who are also my in-laws, that can't return to England because of scandal. Oh, I am also responsible for my younger sister, including her dowry, till the time she is to marry. Have I left anything out?" he said, sarcastically.

"Well, there is one more detail to discuss."

"What more can you possibly do to me, father?"

"No one other than Rhea, Rhea's parents, her Aunt Magda, myself and now you know of this union. They have brought Rhea back to London under the ruse that she will be coming out this season. We need for you and her to meet, court, and get married in front of the *Ton* as if it were a natural union. It is important that a public courtship happen for your marriage to have credibility in the House of Lords. The union must be above reproach. Then Huntington can take his seat as a brother-in-law to a Marquess. No one will be bold enough to question his position. It will nullify a potential scandal if your union is a love match."

"This is a nightmare! I have a life of my own, father. Now I have to pretend to court someone I'm already married to? What am I going to do with a wife, father?" He stood and started to pace again. He stopped abruptly. "You say Rhea knows? How long? Was she a part of this?"

"No, she was as oblivious as you were. She found out by accident, not sure when exactly, but her father was forced to tell her. We had planned to tell you both together, let you know each other before we announced the match publicly. Now circumstances have forced our hand. I must warn you son, Rhea isn't favorable to this situation either. Her aunt assures me that she is a lovely girl and just needs time to know you, but she's apprehensive. As I'm sure you are." He tried to be reassuring but this was an unmitigated mess.

Sy stood up, grabbed his coat, and started toward the door.

"Where are you going?" his father asked stunned.

"Home," Sy stated simply.

"Don't you want to discuss this further?" Sy slowly turned back to look at his father.

"This morning I was Captain of my own ship, in control of my future. Now I am a Marquess, a husband, a guardian and no longer in control of my own life. Oh, and lest I forget, in league with the very pirates that I have been chasing relentlessly these past months. Excuse me father, but I am terrified of what you will say next." He stormed from the room.

His father walked over to the mantel and picked up Sy's full glass of brandy. Tears formed in his eyes. Aunt Magda was now his last hope. He had no choice but to pray that she knew what she was doing.

CHAPTER 8

*R*hea paced in front of the open window, dressed only in her chemise. The evening was a stifling hot with no breeze at all. She couldn't sleep. Between the heat and her encounter with Sy earlier, sleep was impossible. This is ridiculous, she thought. If she were at home or on the *Star* she would just confront the problem head on. She would speak with the person in question about the issue face to face. London was an enigma to her, so many rules of etiquette to follow. She didn't understand polite society. In order to speak to Sy she would need to make an appointment, wait for a chaperone, and then exchange polite fripperies instead of direct conversation. How did these people get anything done? She would have had ten things done in the time it takes her to dress in the morning! She couldn't wait that long, she'd go insane. She needed to get home as soon as possible. She was already feeling guilty about Jat and

Liana. Liana was three months pregnant and wanted to return home to have her baby. They needed to beat the winter storms, otherwise they would be stuck here till spring.

That settles it! Rhea was a Captain, Sy was a Captain. She would just go to him and reason out the situation, man to man. After all, this wasn't either of their doing, right? He couldn't blame her for wanting to discuss the situation rationally and form an exit plan. Grabbing her garter and knife from her trunk, she slid the lace garter up to her thigh and then slipped the knife in it. The thought of putting on a corset and a dress in this heat seemed odious, so she decided against it, and pulled her boots on instead. A small pistol was next, she loaded it before putting it her boot. She would put her cloak over her chemise and keep it on during what was sure to be a short conversation.

Rhea knew exactly where Sy's townhouse was located. It was just two short blocks from her aunt's. They had been by it several times since it was on the route to her aunt's townhouse. She couldn't help but look at it every time they went by. She noticed that there was a sturdy looking tree that reached the windows of the second floor. That was to be her target for entry tonight. She couldn't very well knock on the front door and ask to see him. Instead, she would sneak in through the upstairs window and wait for him. That way, they could talk in private and nobody needed to know. This predicament was between them, after all. It was time to take this matter into her own hands.

She wasn't sure what time it was but it had been dark for several hours. Pulling up the hood of her cloak to conceal her hair, she snuck down the servants' stairs and out through the kitchen door. It must have been late because no one was about. She left the door unlocked for her return. It was easy to traverse the back alleys for the two short blocks. She was relieved that she saw nobody on her way there.

The tree, on the other hand, wasn't as simple as she thought it would be. The lowest branch was far out of reach. She tried to jump and catch it but didn't come close. After deliberating for a moment, she wedged herself between the tree and the building, bracing her back against the tree with her feet pressed on the building, she slowly walked herself up the trunk. Her cloak snagged a few times but she easily overcame the problem by wiggling around a little until it released itself. In no time, she could reach the lowest branch and was able to shimmy up to the window. Using her knife, she jimmied the lock open and crawled through.

It was his study. She saw that the desk was uncovered but the rest of the furniture was draped with white cloth. The bookshelves were empty and boxes were stacked around the room. She could smell dust. She crossed the room and cracked the door open to peek in the hall. It was dark, but she could see light coming up the stairwell. She tiptoed down the hall to the next door. It was slightly ajar and light was streaming through the opening. She could see most of the room through the gap in the door. It appeared to be empty so she opened it and poked her head in. Seeing no one, she quickly went in and closed the door quietly. It was his bedroom, judging by the size of the bed. It reminded her of the bed Titan gave her except the drapery was burgundy velvet instead of green. A wave of home sickness assaulted her. It also stiffened her resolve. She shook it off and looked around the room. It was obviously recently prepared for him. Crisp white sheets adorned the bed and the covers were turned back. There were two lit candles, one on each table beside the bed. The room was newly dusted and there was a large trunk in the corner. An oversized wingback chair was placed in front of the fireplace but because of the hot weather there was no fire.

She looked back to the trunk, curiosity eating at her. She wanted to learn more about him. Maybe his things would give her a clue of what he was like. He was her husband, right? It wouldn't be improper for a wife to look inside her husband's trunk. Her reasoning in place, she opened the lid. Every item in the trunk was black. Black shirts folded on one side and black trousers on the other. She picked up one of the shirts and brought it to her nose. It smelled of him, musk and the sea. She closed her eyes and inhaled the scent again. She sighed. How wonderful to smell the sea and him? She jumped when she heard voices and footsteps in the hall. She quickly replaced the shirt and closed the lid quietly. She stood up and faced the door. The voices continued, but she couldn't make out the muffled conversation. Damn and blast, why didn't she leave the door ajar? She looked down at the trunk and took a guilty step away from it. Then she realized that she now stood next to the bed. Drat, she didn't want to appear that she was giving him an invitation. She was about to step closer to the fireplace, a neutral spot, when the door handle began to turn. She panicked and frantically looked around for a place to hide. The door started to open. She crouched down and slid under the bed. What was she doing? It was too late. He had already stepped into the room. She would look three times the idiot if she came crawling out from under his bed.

Sy walked in, and paused a moment, then watched his booted feet as he crossed the room. He stopped at the end of the bed. Oh lord, he knew she was there! Then the bed creaked above her as he sat on the bed. One foot disappeared, followed by a boot dropping to the floor. She almost screamed at the loud thud it made. She covered her mouth in the nick of time. A naked foot appeared as the other foot disappeared, followed by the other boot. The bed creaked again. A white shirt fluttered to the floor. Then black trousers pooled around his ankles before he stepped out of them. Was he naked? Oh God! What had she done to herself? Now she was really stuck. She would have to wait till he fell asleep and try to sneak out quietly. His bare feet padded to the side of the bed. It creaked and sagged under his weight. She heard a pounding sound next and guessed he was fluffing his pillow. Ugh! What a ninny she was. If Jat or her crew knew where she was at that moment, they would never take her seriously again. This was humiliating! She wanted to bang her head on the floor in frustration.

She placed one hand on top of the other and rested her chin upon them to wait as she contemplated her situation. What was it about this man that made her lose all her composure? She'd only met him once, she acted like a simpleton then and now she was hiding under his bed like one. The bed creaked again and the sag shifted, he rolled over. She tried to think of anything but where she was or the possibly naked man above her. She forced herself to think about Otis and the new *Star* she was building. He had to have figured out what to do with new cannon design by now and the third deck must be complete. She turned her head to the side resting her cheek on hands like a pillow and tried to relax. Suddenly, an arm hung down the side of the bed. Her eyes widened and she waited for it to reach for her. It didn't, it just hung there limp. She stared at it wide eyed waiting. His forearm bulged with muscle and veins. His hand had long fingers; it looked relaxed. She could see the creases in his palm and callouses where his fingers joined his hand. She wanted to reach out and touch it. Get ahold of yourself, geez!

She heard a faint snore, held her breath and listened. Another snore, this one slightly louder, then another, and another, thank the heavens! She started scooting out the opposite side. Once out, she rolled over and sat up enough to look on the bed. His back was to her but she could see the rise and fall of his chest in even breaths as he slept. His back was uncovered. The sheet was draped over his hips and thighs. His back was all muscle. Lord, he was enormous.

He let out a loud snore, which startled her, and brought

her back to the moment. She went to stand up but then decided she should remove her boots first. She took the pistol out and put it in her cloak pocket. Then she pulled off her boots. The sound of the leather sliding over her feet seemed loud in the silence. She paused and looked at him but he hadn't moved. Finally, she got up, pinched the top of her boots together with her fingers, and started tip toeing towards the door. She looked back to the bed. The candle was still lit on the bedside table at his back but she couldn't make out his features because of the shadows. Knowing it was foolish, she couldn't help herself, she had to look at his face. This may be her only chance. She would never be able to gaze freely at him in public and wanted to commit his face to memory. She had imagined what he looked like a million times, now she would be able to think of him as he really was.

She tiptoed to the side of the bed. Just as she reached his side, he rolled to his back and took a heavy breath. The arm closest to her extended out and brushed against her cloak. She gasped and quickly put her hand to her mouth to muffle the sound. She froze, looking down at him, waiting for his eyes to open. He let out a loud snore instead. She relaxed and dropped her hand in relief.

He was gorgeous! Lying there bare chested, the sheet only covering his hips and part of his thighs. His skin was bronze, everywhere, he obviously didn't wear his black shirts often. He had an expansive chest with well-formed pectoral muscles. It narrowed to his waist and flat abdomen that was stacked with muscles. His chest and abdomen was completely devoid of hair except for a line that started at his navel and disappeared below the sheet. His biceps had to be the same circumference as her thighs. His neck was thick too, in proportion his chest and shoulders. His strong chin had a neatly trimmed beard that connected to a mustache surrounding full lips. Thick black lashes fanned his cheeks. His long black hair fanned the pillow and caught the candlelight light in places. A light sheen of sweat coated his skin, which made it glimmer in the candlelight. He was so handsome he almost didn't look real. She almost sighed, he'd been in her imagination for such a long time, and he was so much better in real life than she imagined him. What would it be like to kiss those lips, his thick neck? She licked her lips at the thought, what she wouldn't give to run her tongue up the side of his sexy neck and taste his skin.

She let her eyes drift down past the sheets to his thighs. They were as muscular as the rest of him and sprinkled with short black hair. She noticed something on his leg peeking out from the sheet. A dark mark of some kind. Her eyes widened in surprise. Was that their mark, the mark that bound them in marriage? How could she forget that fact, he would have a mark that matched hers to seal the contract! It was mostly covered by the sheet. She squinted her eyes and leaned in to get a closer look. Some of her hair came over her shoulder and brushed his leg. She tried to grab it but wasn't fast enough. She looked at his face, he was still fast asleep. She pushed her hair and cloak over her shoulder so it wouldn't fall and hit him again. She took two fingers and pinched a fold of the sheet, then slowly tried to move it so she could see the mark. She was so intent on her task that she didn't realize that her tongue was sticking out of her mouth.

Suddenly, she was flying in the air. Her back slammed down on the mattress. A heavy weight landed on top of her. Sy quickly pinned her hands above her head, his face within inches from hers, his expression unreadable.

"Hello wife."

CHAPTER 9

"*L*et go of me!"

He let her squirm for a minute so she would know that it was futile. He was in control. Her soft body was rubbing his as she writhed beneath him attempting to get out. With only a thin sheet at his waist and her chemise separating them, he could feel every inch of her, especially her nipples rubbing against his chest. She was surprisingly strong for her size. Her long hair was fanned out around her head. She smelled like jasmine and woman, just as he remembered. He could smell her the moment he entered his room, he knew she was hiding somewhere. It wasn't long till he figured out she was under the bed. He decided to have a little fun and wanted to see what she was up to. The little minx hadn't changed much, well, at least not in tenacity anyway. What was she wearing? He could feel every curve of her body under him. No corset, stays or dress, just her chemise and a cloak that was now pinned behind her back. She stopped moving suddenly.

"Are you done?" he asked, sarcastically.

"*Please* let me go," she pleaded.

"I'll let you go when I get some answers. What are you doing here?" he asked, his voice even. She was breathing heavy after her exertion. Every breath she took made her nipples rub against his chest. His cock was thickening involuntarily. Damn, she smelled so good.

"I came to talk to you, my lord," she squeaked out, in a breathy voice.

"From under my bed?" he teased. He gave her a rakish smile. As he stared into those captivating eyes, he felt hypnotized, he couldn't look away. For a moment, he was utterly lost.

"I will explain, if you could please ease your weight a bit...," she squeaked out.

"Oh, apologies." He shook his head to reclaim focus, then transferred both her hands into one of his and used his free arm to lift some of his weight off her chest. Unfortunately, the new position pressed his now fully aroused member at the junction of her thighs. He could feel her triangle of womanly hair through the thin layer of material. He groaned. She ignored it and turned her head to hide her embarrassment. "Is that better?" he asked, in a strained voice.

"It is very difficult to concentrate on a conversation in this position, my lord."

"You are damned right about that!" He laughed, and couldn't resist looking down at the top of her breasts practically heaving in his face. Her breathing had calmed some but they still rose and fell rapidly, he could see her nipples were hard. It was a very enticing view.

"It would be better if you just released me, my lord," she pleaded, and tried to move away from his hardness. She wiggled her hips in an attempt to move away from him, he groaned again as his control slipped a fraction. She needed to get to the point and quickly!

"Just spit it out, madam!" It came out harsher than he meant and it startled her.

"I came to strike a bargain with you!" she rushed out.

They stared at each other for a long moment. She moved her hips again, brushing against his arousal. His member throbbed in need. He had to close his eyes to regain his composure. He knew he should let her go, but when he opened his eyes, she was staring at his lips. He couldn't help it. He dipped his head to taste her neck. She stiffened a little as he lightly touched her skin with his lips then relaxed. She was intoxicating, he knew he should stop and listen to what she had to say, but she was just too alluring. She smelled so good, felt so soft beneath him, he lost his resolve and he had to taste her.

"Bargain you say?" he said against her neck, as he kissed and licked his way down to her collar bone and then started working his way back up.

"Yes...um... if you could just...ah" Rhea sighed with pleasure and closed her eyes as he sucked on her ear lobe. She had lost her train of thought completely, he smiled at the knowledge. His hot breath was on her ear, then his tongue. When he ground his arousal against her lightly, her eyes flew open but she didn't respond.

She was innocent, he was sure of it. Damn she was beautiful. He could see passion sparking in those eyes. She parted her mouth slightly as if she might say something. He took possession of it instead. He started lightly at first slowly increasing the pressure. He swept his tongue over her lips. She opened them a fraction, so he did it again, she moaned and opened for him. He gently tasted her with his tongue, rubbing it against hers in invitation, willing her to respond.

He could feel her body becoming soft and pliable under his touch. When he pulled his tongue out of her mouth she chased it with her own. Their tongues danced in a seductive dance getting to know each other. When he moaned into her mouth she arched up against him in response. Her body had taken over and moved sensually beneath him. He tore his mouth away and she tried to follow but when he licked and kissed his way down her neck again she couldn't help but arch up against him, inviting more. He had to taste her skin, had to possess her now. He continued to kiss and lick his way to the valley between her breasts. Through the thin layer of the chemise, he could tell her skin was soft. When his mouth was on her nipple and he sucked the hard nub into his mouth. She moaned and struggled to get her hands free.

When he let go, her hands went to the back of his head to hold him at her breast. He moaned as she threaded her fingers through his hair and pulled slightly. Sy needed to taste skin. He untied the ribbon on the front of her chemise and slid the fabric over her shoulder to bare the other breast. Once it was free, he kissed his way across her velvety soft skin to the bare nipple. He circled his tongue around it and she pulled his hair again and moaned. He sucked the nipple in his mouth gently. She moved her hips with pleasure and arched against his mouth, a sexy moan escaped her lips. She was so responsive. His erection throbbed with the realization. He needed to taste all of her. He shifted his weight and put his knee between her legs.

Everything changed in an instant.

He felt her tense. He was moving too fast and he knew it. Damn it, he did not want to stop. Truthfully, he didn't think he could. The need to possess this woman was primal now. He returned his mouth to hers to reignite her passion. His kiss was possessive, meant to let her know how much he wanted her. He wanted her response, he thrust his tongue into her mouth searching for it. She started to relax and return his kiss although timid in comparison to before. He tried to slow down. She was innocent and he wanted her to trust him. He needed her to trust him. Her legs spread wider a little. He shifted his weight again to let her. He lifted to judge her reaction.

She reached up with both hands and pulled him down to

her mouth. He slid one of his hands beneath her and squeezed her derriere closer against his arousal, grinding on her lightly. She bent her leg rubbing it against his, until her foot was flat on the bed. She used it to arch her hips against him seductively. He flexed his hips and rubbed his shaft gently against her. A moan of pleasure escaped her mouth and spurred him on. His mouth covered hers once again shattering any thoughts in his head other than the kiss. He put his other leg between hers and spread her legs wider apart.

He had to have her. Bury himself inside her. She was so responsive and innocent at the same time. She was soft and sensual, erotic and he couldn't get enough of her. He reached down to move her chemise out of the way when he felt the knife slip between them and press at his neck under his chin. He stopped kissing and lifted his head slightly trying to pull away from the blade. She kept the pressure on the knife against his skin.

"Stop." she said, with a ragged voice, breathing heavy.

"Now?" he sounded incredulous. He usually had the opposite effect on the fairer sex. This was new.

"Get off me, my lord." She pressed the knife harder against his throat warning him to obey.

He could feel the blade slicing his skin. Did she really think she could hurt him with that puny knife? He could overcome her in an instant and divest her of it, but that would only make her afraid of him. He didn't want that. He wanted her trust.

He wanted her, damn it! He growled and in one smooth movement he rolled them over and pinned her to him, straddling her legs across his lap. He put one hand on her hip, the other on the opposite thigh. Her hair flew like a white curtain around her, half falling down her back and the rest settled around her shoulders or covered her face. To his surprise, she kept the knife firmly planted firmly at his neck. He would let her think she had the upper hand for the moment.

She took her free arm and in a practiced motion she flipped the heavy mass of hair behind her. It settled like a frame around her shoulders and face. Her cheeks were rosy; her lips were swollen and shiny from his kisses. Her eyes were sparkling, full of passion making him want to knock the knife from her hand and kiss her again. She looked absolutely stunning.

"We need to talk, my lord," she said, breathlessly. She didn't seem to notice the neck of the chemise was open to her navel. He was gifted with the most amazing view of her perfect heaving breasts, her nipples shiny from his ministrations.

"We need to finish what we started, madam," he interrupted, as he thrust his hips up slightly rubbing his arousal against her sex.

"Ahhh," she moaned as pleasure surged through her.

He knew the moment when she realized she was straddling his arousal. She tried to slide back a bit and the same sensation racked her body, her hips trembled under his palm and her eyes become hooded. He took advantage of their position and thrust his hips again gently.

"Please, my lord..." she put her free hand on his chest to support herself, perhaps lift herself a bit, but her own primal impulses were taking over. It was the most beautiful thing he had ever seen.

Rhea had never felt anything so delicious in her life! Nor had anyone touched her so intimately before. Every time she tried to move away, a new set of incredible sensations racked her body. At first she was desperately trying to get away and now...she was chasing something... she should stop this, she heard somewhere in the far recesses of her mind. Just one more time, then another, then another, his hands were firm on her hips, moving her so he rubbed the perfect spot. Oh god, what was happening? She gave into it, relaxing against him, and when he stopped moving her, she took over.

"Oh god, please..." she whispered, not realizing she uttered it out loud.

"As you wish, madam."

He watched the lust building in her expression as they rubbed against each other. He kept her pinned against his hard shaft as he moved her hips back and forth slowly with his hands. Watched her eyes as they filled with passion until she threw her head back with desire. She seemed to forget that she was holding a knife to his throat. Each time he pulled her forward it pressed harder against his skin. He could feel small scratches being made by the blade but didn't care. She pushed herself off his chest to arch her back into the movement. He loved her uninhibited response to him, he was getting close to bursting, his erection becoming painful. He thrust his hips up against her as she slid back. He took his hand from her thigh and grabbed the wrist that held the knife and moved her hand from away from his throat. She didn't notice. He took the knife from her hand and tossed it further away. She never stopped moving, searching for her orgasm. He reached up and pulled the string to release her cloak then tossed it to the side, enjoying the full view of her bare breasts.

Her eyes were closed, he was disappointed that he couldn't look in them when she climaxed. He could tell she was close because she was totally unaware that he tossed her knife and cloak aside. Both of her hands were on his chest now. He placed his hand back on her hip and quickened the rhythm. He could feel the wet heat of her seating through the material. Now that her cloak was removed each time she arched and threw her head back her hair pooled on his thighs and her breasts thrusted towards him. It was completely erotic. Watching her take pleasure rubbing against his shaft made him ready to burst but he wanted her climax first. He pressed down harder on her hips then quickened the pace faster still. She started to moan and arched her back, then fell forward, slapping her hands on his chest to brace herself as her climax racked her body. Her hair fell like a curtain closing around him. One more thrust against her and his seed burst on his belly making a wet stain on the sheet separating them. He reached up lacing his fingers through her hair at the nape of her neck and brought her lips down to his. They shared a passionate kiss then she collapsed on his chest.

~

RHEA CLOSED her eyes and let the waves of ecstasy roll through her. It felt wonderful, his skin was soft and slick from sweat against her cheek and breasts. He smelled divine too. Suddenly, the reality of what just happened came upon her in a rush. Her eyes sprang open. She jumped off him and the bed quickly. She turned her back on him in embarrassment pulling her chemise back into place and tying it. Anger quickly took its place. She was not angry at him, but herself. First for acting like a ninny and hiding under the bed then giving into his touch. Get ahold of yourself Rhea! You complete idiot!

"Rhea?"

He said her name with so much compassion that it pulled at her heart. She decided to act as if nothing had happened. She came here to make a bargain and that's exactly what she would do. She squared her shoulders and turned around to face him. Her heart jumped in her throat. He was lying on his side with the sheet draped across his loins. He had one knee bent and he was leaning on one arm. He looked like a pirate, he was so handsome, it wasn't fair! She wanted to run to him and kiss him. What is it about this man?

"Come back here." He raised his hand in invitation.

"I think it's safer if I keep my distance, my lord," she replied.

"Sy."

"Sy?"

"My name, Rhea. Or at least that is what my close friends call me."

"I don't think it would be proper, my lord," she said, trying to sound emphatic.

"Proper? Technically you are my wife and after what we just shared I think proper has been thrown out the window, don't you agree?" he replied, sardonically.

She flushed three shades of red.

"About that, my lor...Sy. We need to talk. I have a bargain for you."

"So, you mentioned. Why do you think you are safer over there?" He changed the subject.

"I can't seem to think properly when..." She paused to think about her answer. "In close proximity to you." She looked down at her hands. Why was she acting so shy? She straightened her shoulders and her resolve. "About my bargain...?"

"Why do you feel the need to make a bargain with me?" He was smiling, he seemed to be enjoying her discomfort. She needed more distance from him to think straight.

"Do you have a robe, my lord...I mean Sy? I'd be happy to fetch it for you." she asked, hopefully. She really could not concentrate while he lay there naked. Then she realized that she was no longer wearing her cloak. And where was her knife?

"No." He said emphatically, looking extremely pleased with himself.

"Where is my cloak?" she asked, confused. She didn't dare mention the knife.

"You don't need it. Answer the question Rhea. Why do you need to make a bargain with me?" His tone was stern and not to be argued with.

He was right, time to get to the subject at hand. She would be fine as long as she didn't look at him. She started to pace beside the bed. She felt better moving around, giving herself something else to concentrate on.

"A bargain, between the two of us, to get us out of this predicament as quickly as possible."

"Predicament?" he asked, even though she knew, he knew exactly what she was talking about.

"The marriage contract of course!" she said, exasperated at his teasing, and threw her hands up. "I know you don't want this marriage and I believe I have the perfect solution for both of us."

"I don't?"

"You don't what?" she said, having lost her place in the conversation because of his constant interruptions.

"Why don't I want this marriage?" He laid back on the bed, propping himself up on the pillows as if he was expecting the conversation to take a while. Did he want this marriage?

"You were forced into it just as I was. Of course, you don't want it." She was getting exasperated again. "Like I said. I have a bargain..."

"I'm not so sure. After what happened earlier..."

"That was a mistake," she blurted out, "It wasn't supposed to happen." It was her turn to interrupt. She needed to get this conversation back on the subject. "I'm trying to tell you I have a plan."

"You don't want to be married to me? I'm considered quite a catch," he teased her.

She looked at him then. It was a mistake. She wanted to scream '*Yes I do!*' and run into his arms. In truth, she had felt married to him for a long time. Rhea knew he was teasing her, but she felt the stab of resentment. If he had wanted to be married, he would have come to her as soon as learned about the contract. But he didn't. He probably spent the entire afternoon trying to form a plan to get out of it, just like she had. Somehow, that thought made her feel even worse.

"I don't want to be married to a man that doesn't want to be married to me," she said, forlornly. "Besides I have my work. Otis and I are so close..."

SY BOUNDED out of the bed and grabbed her by the shoulders.

"Who the hell is Otis?" he asked, angrily. He realized he

was man-handling her and dropped his hands immediately. Where the hell did that come from?

"He's my friend. We work together," she said, shocked by his reaction. She looked away from his naked body, ignoring the desire building in her, she walked over to put the wing-back chair between them.

Damn, he scared her. Sy went back to his bed and covered himself. He needed to find out more about this Otis. He couldn't ask her now that she was frightened. Did she love this Otis? His stomach dropped at the thought. What? Was this woman getting under his skin? He had known her for less than a day, that couldn't be possible.

"What's this bargain you keep speaking of?" He sounded surly again, damn, he needed to get a hold of himeself.

"It's quite brilliant actually." she said, relieved to back on the subject at hand. "We follow the original plan, meet in society, court and get married as propriety dictates. That will secure your and my brother's seats. We will have a marriage in name only. I will go home once the appropriate amount of time has passed. Then you can petition for an annulment. I will not require any settlement from you and you can keep my dowry. In return, you will help my brother make a respectable return to society." She gave him a weak smile.

"Rhea, to get an annulment you would have to prove that there was no intimacy. You will have to remain a virgin, be examined, to prove it to the courts." he pointed out. He had guessed that she was innocent. Did she give herself to this Otis? He had to know, her reaction would tell him..

"I know this, my lord, I mean, Sy." she said, with no hesitation.

Relief flooded him. He suddenly felt very possessive of his little Minx.

"May I point out that, so far, we cannot be in the same room for more than a few minutes without losing control with each other? We have to live as a couple for six months ,then apart for the same, before either of us can petition for the annulment. How do you suppose we will be able to accomplish that? I want you right now and I think you want me too." He smiled his rakish smile.

"I can control myself." She lifted her chin in defiance. He laughed at her.

"The hell you can!"

"I can, too!" she said, insulted. "You are very sure of yourself, *my lord*." she said, snidely.

"Prove it," he stated, simply.

"How could I possibly prove that to you?" She crossed her arms in front of her.

"Come here. Kiss me." *Please,* he thought.

Her eyes widened and her mouth dropped open. She was buggered!

"Distance is the best solution, my lord. We just need to stay away from each other." She backed up a step, to prove her point.

He smiled, he had her. There was no way he wasn't going to touch her again. This Otis guy didn't stand a chance. He stood up, but this time tied the sheet around his waist before he crossed the room. Her beautiful eyes were as large as saucers as he approached. She backed herself against the fireplace and was trapped. He grabbed her chin gently and lifted it so she was looking directly into his eyes.

"I will agree to your bargain, if you to agree to my terms." He leaned closer to her as if he was going to kiss her. Her mouth parted slightly, and she held her breath. She wanted him, he could see it. He dropped her chin, walked to the end of the bed, and leaned against the post. Sy was pleased to see that she was visibly disappointed, enormously pleased.

"My terms are that if we become intimate, in any fashion, before an annulment is possible, we will both honor the contract to the letter. Do you agree?" He looked at her again.

She looked him straight in the eye. "I agree, my lord," she said in a commanding voice, so sure of herself, that it caught him by surprise.

She spotted her cloak on the bed, and made a wide circle around him to retrieve it. She put it on and tied it at the neck. Then she made another wide circle to retrieve her boots. She quickly pulled them on.

He watched her routine with amusement. He abruptly pushed himself off the post. She flinched and he suppressed a smile. He turned, and found her knife on the bed. He examined it for a second and decided it wouldn't do. It was way too short to do any serious damage. He would need to buy her a slightly longer and narrower one. He shook his head. What the hell was he thinking? This knife was just at his throat and he had the scratches to prove it. He tossed it up, caught it by the blade, and handed to her.

"I believe this is yours, *my lady*. May I inquire, how did you get here?" he asked, curious.

She took the knife and, without thinking, lifted her chemise and slipped it into her garter. He groaned at the sight of her shapely leg. She really was magnificent. What she said next jolted him from his thoughts.

"I walked, my lord"

"WHAT? You walked the streets of London, in your chemise, alone?" he said, incredulously.

"Yes, my lord, I can take care of myself." she said, confidently, dismissing his reaction. "Shall I send a note as to which event I will be attending tomorrow night?"

"Why?" he said, still rattled that she had walked there by herself.

"So, we can begin our agreement, my lord," she answered, as if he were a simpleton. "We need to meet and get on with it as soon as possible."

"No." He loved the way her eyes sparkled when she was riled.

"No?" She sounded disappointed and confused.

"No, I do not require a note, I will find you." He stepped closer.

"Oh. Well then, goodnight, my lord." She curtsied and turned toward the door.

He grabbed her arm and pulled her against his chest. Before she could protest, he kissed her. It was a possessive kiss, one meant to dominate, to mark her as his. As soon as she started to respond, he ended it. He wanted her to remember the attraction between them.

"Goodnight, madam." he said, void of emotion. He turned her around and gave her a little push. She walked out and closed the door.

He ran to his chest to get dressed and follow her home. Damn, but his wife had spunk. This was going to be fun.

CHAPTER 10

"If he's not here we should give up for the evening. If you want to make an appearance at the Wessex gathering, we must go now. They have to be well past dinner and brandy by now." Smith pointed out to Sy. "Is this just some kind of stall tactic so you will not have to attend? I know how much you love going to these things." Smith said, laughing.

Sy was beyond irritated. Hell yes, he wanted to go, but only to see Rhea again. He could think of nothing else but the look of passion on her beautiful face as she rubbed her sex against his shaft. He was walking around in a perpetual state of hardness because of his wayward thoughts. He couldn't wait to get there, get her alone, so he could kiss her again. He'd never thought about a woman this much before. He had had his fair share of liaisons but they were to take care of his needs. This little Minx has gotten under his skin somehow, all he could think about was getting Rhea into his bed. Then she'd have to honor the contract. He would have done his duty regardless, had no choice really, but he'd be damned if she was going to go back to this Otis gentleman. Just the thought of another man sharing her bed made his blood boil. Where the hell was her brother? If she wanted him to help Titan back into polite society, then he was going to get that over with quickly. He wanted to get on with the game of seducing his wife.

They had been to four places looking for Titan. They started at *White's* then tried *Brook's,* the other popular gentleman's club. He was at neither and no one had seen him. Next, they decided to try the pubs at the wharf. They had no luck at the *Lamb and Flag* and now were walking into *The Swan.* Sy ducked through the door and scanned the room. It was bustling with dock workers and sailors. When he walked in, the conversation hushed to whispers. He was used to it. He got the same reaction even when he wasn't dressed in his finery.

"Sy! Is that the mighty Captain Sy Black?" someone called, sarcastically. The whispered conversation began again.

Titan. Finally! He wanted to throw him over his shoulder and into the carriage. He suppressed the urge, because Titan didn't know anything about his plans for him this evening. He would have to waste a few more precious moments to explain. Titan stood to greet him. They grasped arms at the elbow and slapped each other hard on the shoulder. Titan looked good. Sy realized he was happy to see his friend.

"I didn't expect to see you so soon. I heard you only arrived a couple days ago. I've heard a lot about you. You've made quite the reputation for yourself!" Titan said, with a hint of sarcasm.

"Really? I've heard nothing about you," he replied, with equal sarcasm. Titan didn't take the bait. He just smiled back, looking like the cat that ate the canary. "You remember Smith." He waved his hand in Smith's direction.

"Of course, of course, how do you do fair Smith? It's been a while. You're still keeping company with this brute I see." They repeated the same greeting of handshake and slaps.

"These are my colleagues, Pax and Tom." He waved to a set of seamen sitting at his table. "These are my friends from Eton and beyond, Sy Black and Smith." Introductions done, he waved at the barkeep. "Pete! Two more."

"I'm afraid we won't have time to share cups this evening and neither do you. I've been looking for you for some time, and now we are late for an engagement," he stated. "Sorry for the late notice. I did send a note to your residence earlier today. My footman returned and told me that you were gone for the day and weren't due to return till late evening. I've been trying to track you down ever since."

"What engagement are you referring to?" Titan asked, and settled in his chair like he wasn't going anywhere.

"At Wessex's place," he stated, flatly.

"You must have me confused with my sister and aunt. I'm sure I didn't receive an invitation." Titan took a long swallow of his ale then belched rudely.

"It is getting terribly late, Sy. Maybe we should call it a night. I could use a cup of ale." Smith said, looking around for a chair.

"Titan, unfortunately, I've been put in charge of introducing you into society. I have wasted half the evening tracking you down. If you don't get out of that chair right now, I'm going to knock you out and drag you to the Wessex's. It's up to you how you want society to see you for the first time. Black eye or no black eye." He snapped impatiently, he'd had enough! Time was wasting and Rhea might leave if they didn't get there soon.

Pax and Tom started to stand up. Titan put his hand up.

"Whoa, whoa big guy! What is this about? What's the hurry? Can't we meet tomorrow?" he asked, completely shocked by Sy's threat.

"No," Sy stated, emphatically.

"I'm not dressed for an engagement, as you can see," Titan pointed out, waving a hand down at his clothes.

"I anticipated that fact, and have clothes for you in the carriage. You can change on the way. Now, let's go!" He walked towards the door. "Don't make me come back in here. You won't like it." he said over his shoulder.

TITAN, Smith and the guys looked at each other in shock.

"We'd better go, I've seen him like this before, you don't

want to mess with him. Trust me." Smith said, and walked toward the door.

"I guess I have an engagement." Titan quipped, to Pax and Tom.

"We can back you up if you don't want to go." Pax assured him, stealing a glance at Sy's retreating back.

"It's alright, curiosity has got me now, I have to see what's got him in a tizzy." Titan downed the rest of his ale. He waved to his chums and walked to the door.

Titan jumped into the waiting carriage. He could see a jacket, shirt and cravat waiting for him. Smith crammed himself next to Sy so Titan could have room to change. As soon as he closed the door, Sy banged on the roof and the carriage took off.

"Are these yours?" he asked Sy.

"No, they're yours, I sent a footman for them. Mine would be too big." he said, with a smirk. He was teasing, in truth, Titan was just as muscular as Sy, but a few inches shorter.

Titan started undressing. There wasn't much room in the carriage with three large men but he had to make do.

"So, what has you so fired up this evening that you would threaten a black eye to get your way? Surely, we could've talked tomorrow. Not that I don't appreciate it, that is." He continued dressing as he asked.

"Apologies. I guess I could've asked nicer but I made the commitment to Wessex for us. I didn't want to start out on the wrong foot." he lied. Well, it was a half lie.

"Thank you... I think. My aunt will be pleased you dragged me along. She practically begged that I chaperone tonight. I sent Jat so I could get out of it." He pulled the white shirt Sy brought for him over his head. "Hey, my sister is going to be there. I bet you won't even recognize her. She's a grown woman now. Pretty little thing, too. Most men are at a loss for words when they first meet her," Titan said, with pride.

Sy's chest constricted at that comment. He remembered his reaction the first time he saw her and had no doubt Titan spoke the truth. He was imagining her surrounded by men at Wessex's, all vying for her attentions. The thought disturbed him. Why was this coach going so damn slow?

"She's a charmer for sure, had my whole crew wrapped around her little finger," Titan continued.

Ugh. Another stab to his heart. He wished he could give Titan that black eye he promised earlier so he'd shut up. His nerves were already standing on end and his comments were not helping.

"I pity the man that marries her," he said, with a shake of his head. That caught Sy's attention.

"Why do you say that?" he asked, trying to act nonchalant.

"She's got a mind of her own, that one. There's no controlling her once she's got her sights set on something. Oh, the stories I could tell you. There are times when I want to hug her and kill her at the same time. Her husband, if she finds one this season, will certainly have his hands full." he said, in an amused tone. He was trying to tie his cravat, with no success. Smith tried to help, but Titan kept slapping his hand away. Finally, Sy leaned over and tied it, a bit too tight.

"Are you trying to choke me to death?"

Just as Sy was about to ask Titan about Rhea, the carriage stopped in front of the Wessex's townhouse. Sy jumped out the carriage and took the steps to the front door two at a time. Smith and Titan had barely stepped out when Sy was knocking on the front door. They both stared at Sy, bemused.

"He is taking this task very seriously, isn't he Smith?"

"Yes, I believe he is."

CHAPTER 11

*R*hea was a bundle of nerves. She kept watching the door, waiting for Sy to arrive. Her heart jumped into her throat every time someone walked in. The whole evening had been complete torture so far. At dinner Rhea sat next to a Lord Dumferys but had no appetite. Lord Dumferys was a nice, older man who had tried to make conversation, but she was too anxious to reciprocate. All Rhea could concentrate on were the empty chairs. Was one of them for Sy? Was he due to arrive anytime? She drove herself to distraction. Her nerves were completely frayed.

She had never been intimate with anyone before. Stolen kisses in the shadows is all she had experienced, with the exception of the incident with Lieutenant Riley. How does one act with a person after such a thing? She didn't know, and couldn't ask anyone for advice on the matter. This was so uncomfortable! How had she let her emotions get away from her again? Get ahold of yourself, she scolded herself for the fifth time this evening. He had agreed to the bargain, she would be free soon, right? She knew she was fooling herself, he consumed her thoughts. Warm, delicious heat pooled in her belly, and lower, every time she thought about last night. She visualized each moment over and over, and could still feel his lips on hers, his sculpted muscles under her fingers. Lord help her, she wanted more of him. He said he would find her, but at this point she was sure he'd forgotten. Obviously, he wasn't affected the same way. Rejection started to creep in again. It's for the best, she reasoned, she was in such a state she would surely do something to embarrass herself. At the first opportunity, she would find Aunt Magda, plead a headache, and ask to go home.

She tried to concentrate on the party conversation. The guests retired to the sitting room. She was on one of the many small settees, facing two young ladies who had been introduced to her earlier. They were both lovely. Lady Lily Belfort was charming, with her blond hair and blue eyes a classic English beauty. Miss Maisy Waterford had a very animated personality that made her big brown eyes sparkle when she laughed. She adored them both but really didn't know what to say to them. Her experience with conversation for the last few years had been mostly with men, occasionally with their women or wives, but none with ladies of polite society. It was clear that they would not be interested in her experimental innovations in ship building, so she decided to do more listening than talking. They hardly seemed to notice.

"You're lucky you are allowed to wear darker colors for your first season. You look so elegant. I've never seen that color silk in any of the dressmakers' shops, not that mother would let me buy it anyway. It's such a unique shade of green. And the style! You are sure to turn the heads of everyone this season!" Maisy exclaimed, with her usual enthusiasm. "You must give me a reference to your dressmaker. My closet if full of pastels, thanks to mother. Why I feel like I'm picking from a patch of posies every time I select a gown!"

"Me too! It's my second season and my mother insists on the same droll colors. I was lucky to get a dark blue riding outfit this season," Lily chimed in. "She feels if I look young, everyone will forget it's my second season."

"Where did you acquire such unique material Rhea?" Maisy asked again.

"Actually, my brother acquired it for me. He's in shipping and..." Rhea tried to reply.

"You have a brother? Does he look like you? I mean, not exactly like you, but like a man like you?" Lily couldn't contain her enthusiasm.

"I haven't thought on it much since he's my brother, but he too has an unusual eye color like mine. He's quite tall and has auburn hair. Most ladies think he's handsome but I wouldn't know because I don't look at him like that." she explained.

"He sounds divine!" Maisy sighed. "Will you introduce us at the Atterby's ball tomorrow night? Just everyone goes to the Atterby's ball. It kicks off the season. Will you both be attending?" Maisy asked.

"I will have to ask my aunt." It was the perfect excuse to ask Aunt Magda to leave. "I will...."

"Goodness, is that Lord Blackthorne? Oh, my heavens, it is! Look Maisy!" Lily exclaimed in surprise, and Maisy nodded. Rhea froze. Butterflies started fluttering in her stomach, her heart leapt in her throat, and her palms started to sweat. She couldn't look. Get ahold of yourself Rhea, she chastised herself.

"Who is that handsome man with him? I don't recognize him..., but isn't that Lord Smith tagging along?" Lily added.

He has people with him? Now she had to look. She turned sideways. Her heart leapt right back into her throat. He looked so handsome. Once again, he was dressed all in black except for his white shirt and cravat. He towered above the gentlemen in the room. Is that Titan? It was. What? Titan said he would rather go to the gallows than attend this affair. Did Sy insist he come? Was he keeping his end of the bargain? Her mind started spinning.

She watched Sy, Titan and the other gentlemen go to greet their host. They were exchanged pleasantries, and Sy was introduced Titan to Lord Wessex. Lady Wessex was practically pulling her daughter's arm out of its socket to present her to Sy. She gave him a girlish curtsy. He bowed, took her hand, and kissed it politely. She started fanning herself vigorously with the small fan hanging on her wrist. Sy waved a hand, introducing Titan and the other gentleman. She curtsied again and they bowed in unison. She started fanning herself vigorously again. Rhea was riveted as they crossed the room toward Aunt Magda, stopping to exchange pleasantries along the way. Titan presented Sy and the other gentleman to her aunt and another round of bows followed. Sy never once looked for Rhea. Disappointment filled her and she realized her suspicions were true. He didn't feel the same way. Hurt pooled in her belly and she struggled to not let it show.

"Who do you suppose that is?" Lily inquired. "It must be one of his shipmates or something. I heard he went on his commission and never came back. There were rumors that he was lost at sea. I guess the rumors were false." Lily sighed. "He was one of the most desirable bachelors back then, son to a Marquess and all, handsome devil too. That certainly hasn't changed has it Maisy?"

"It most certainly has not! He seems so much taller than I remember and look at those shoulders!" she sighed, and collapsed back on the settee. "The sea certainly has agreed with him."

"Maisy, get yourself together, they're coming this way!" She elbowed her friend, who sat up straight as a pin.

Rhea closed her eyes. She knew they were coming to talk to her. Relax. She took a deep breath. Get yourself together Rhea!

"Rhea dear, look who came! Your brother came with Lord Blackthorne," Aunt Magda announced gaily.

"That's your brother?" Maisy and Lily said in unison. They looked at each other, embarrassed, and turned a lovely shade of pink.

Titan couldn't help but chuckle. He saved the pretty young ladies from their embarrassment, "Why Rhea, what have you been telling these lovely women? Ladies, please don't believe a word she said. I swear it's a pack of lies." He took Rhea's hand and helped her up. "Good God, Rhea, you're a vision, you should wear gowns more often!" He kissed her cheek in a grand show of gallantry. She gave him a warning look and wished she could kick him in the shin.

"May I present Lord Blackthorne and Lord Smith? Both are friends from my Eton days."

Smith bowed, but Sy stepped forward and took her hand. He bowed, and kissed the back of her fingers. She felt weak at the knees. She could feel the heat from his hand through her glove. Some of the hairs from his beard penetrated the silk brushing against her skin. Memories of when he took her nipple in his mouth flooded her. She watched in slow motion as he rose to his full height and looked down on her. She just stared at him, dumbstruck. His words broke the spell.

"It's a pleasure to make your acquaintance again, Lady Hastings," he said, and gave her a rakish smile.

Rhea could swear she heard a sigh from the other girls. Again? Surely, he wasn't referring to last night in front of everyone.

"You've met before? Why didn't you say something, Rhea?" Maisy burst out.

Rhea opened her mouth to answer but nothing came out. She was too rattled with memories of their interlude to come up with a evasive response. Sy smiled.

"We met in the islands when she was but a child. I had the pleasure of visiting her family one summer." Their eyes met and she let go of the breath she was holding. "Have you ladies met Lord Huntington and Lord Smith?" he stated, waving to them. He looked back at Rhea, who was still looking at him. He gave her hand a gentle squeeze.

"May I present Lady Belfort and Miss Waterford." Rhea recovered quickly. Titan and Smith bowed, and the ladies curtsied in return. Titan and Smith moved closer to the ladies and started engaging them in small talk. Sy stepped closer to Rhea to give them room. Rhea's eyes went back to Sy's, she couldn't help it. He looked at her and gave her a knowing smile.

"Lord Blackthorne, you have an injury on your neck!" Aunt Magda pointed out in alarm.

"It is but a scratch, Lady Chamberlain. Nothing to worry yourself over, thank you for your concern," he said, without taking his eyes from Rhea's.

"That is such an unusual injury, my lord, does it give you much discomfort?" She looked at it curiously. "How does one come by such an injury so close to one's throat?" she asked, perplexed. She leaned in closer, trying to get a better look.

"It's a result of a very...uh, passionate discussion I had recently. It doesn't pain me at all but does remind me of the experience." As Rhea stared at the scratches on his neck, she could feel her cheeks warm at the memory of straddling his strong body. She could almost feel his firm hands on her hips as he brought her pleasure. Her breathing quickened as a stirring began deep in her belly, her nipples tingled and heat started pooling lower. Thank goodness Lord Wessex made an announcement distracting her from her wayward thoughts.

"If you will all join us in the garden, Lady Wessex and I have arranged special entertainment to get us out of the heat in the house. Please join us outside if you will." Lord Wessex announced.

THE ROOM FILLED with murmurs as the guests started organizing themselves. Smith asked Maisy if he could escort her and Titan extended his arm to Lily then extended his other arm to his aunt. It was then that Sy realized he had never let go of Rhea's hand. He simply tucked it in his arm to cover up the breach in manners, but Aunt Magda noticed.

"This is going to be easier than I thought," Aunt Magda said, under her breath.

"What's going to be easier?" Titan asked.

"Nothing dear, nothing, let us hurry so we can find a spot with the best view. My eyes aren't as good as they used to be." she said, trying to separate Rhea's brother from the couple.

Sy walked slower than the others, a plan forming in his mind. He looked at Rhea and wondered what had her so distracted. The blush on her cheeks extended to the low neckline of her peacock blue dress. It revealed a tantalizing view of the swells of her breasts. She was magnificent. Were other gentlemen enjoying the sight as much as he? A stab of jealousy gripped him instantly, and he pushed the thought to the back of his brain.

"How was your day, my lady?" he asked, hoping she would say something about last night. He wanted to know if she was thinking about him as much as he was her.

"It was busy, my lord. And yours?" her voice was husky and sensual. He glanced again at her breasts and a vision of them naked before him as she climaxed had his member hardening painfully against the fall of his trousers. He had the sudden urge to throw her over his shoulder and find the nearest bed. *Control yourself Blackthorne, you're not a young pup anymore, for Christ sake.*

"It was productive," he stated through gritted teeth. He was very pleased with himself actually. He had gotten through two of the business reports his father sent over without thinking of her, but once he started the third he couldn't concentrate any longer. Finally, he gave up and went to order her a gift, a proper knife. He had deliberated for a long time over how he wanted the hilt designed and was eager to see it done.

He steered her close to a small alcove off the hallway. He needed a moment alone with her. He checked over his shoulder to be sure they were the last couple out before he pushed her gently into the dark alcove.

"My lord, I don't think this is a good idea," she whispered, as he steered her into the dark space. He gently turned her to face him and backed her in further. The back of her legs hit a bench. She lost her balance and grabbed the back of his arms as he drew closer.

"Then don't think," he said, and covered her mouth with his in a fiery kiss.

HIS HEAT and passion consumed her. Desire engulfed every taut nerve in her body. Rhea responded to his kiss with equal measure, seductively rubbing her tongue against his. She put her hands on the back of his neck to hold him closer. He reached down and scooped her up then sat down on the bench with her on his lap, never breaking contact with her lips. Their tongues entwined in a sexual dance. She leaned into him, wanting to feel her breasts against his chest, tilting her head from side to side to taste him fully as she sucked on his tongue. He tasted like heaven. Visions of him lying on his bed, his bronzed skin, defined muscles, and thick neck spurred her need. She had an overwhelming desire to feel his skin against hers. She pulled back and looked at his face. His eyes were full of lust and desire. Hunger, for her.

"Rhea?" he whispered.

She slipped her hands around to the front of his neck and pulled at his cravat, untying it, and slid it off completely, dropping it on her lap. Next, she unbuttoned the top two buttons of his shirt and spread the collar apart. She lifted his chin with her gloved hand. He complied, letting her have her way with him. She looked at the knife scratches she gave him, then back to his eyes. Slowly, she lowered, gently placing her lips on the marks and kissed her way softly along them. He moaned and drew her in closer. She felt empowered by his reaction, so she did what she had dreamed of doing since she first saw him lying naked. She kissed and sucked the length of his neck as far down as his shirt would allow then licked his firm flesh all the way up to his chin with the flat of her tongue. He moaned again, a deep guttural sound, and put his head back to give her better access as he squeezed her waist in encouragement. He tasted so good, salt and musk, and his beard felt soft on her face. A warm, erotic feeling started to build in her belly and loins. She switched to the other side of his neck and did the same. His head was back, braced against the wall, his eyes hooded with passion and his full lips were slightly parted when she finished. She stared at his lips for a second, then slipped her fingers around to the nape of his neck to pull him closer. He moaned when she sucked his lower lip into her mouth. She sucked on it gently, rubbing her tongue along it softly, innocently. He was intoxicating, she wanted more. She covered his mouth with hers once more and rubbed her tongue on his as an invitation. He took total possession of her then, thrusting his tongue into her mouth over and over, with his hands on her back and neck trapping her in his passion. She was consumed by his hunger for her.

Someone laughed loudly outside. Shocked at the sound, she came crashing back to reality. She pulled away suddenly and tried to jump off his lap but he held her. She did it again! What was it about this man? She had no control of herself in his presence. Within ten minutes of being around him she was undressing him in a dark alcove and suckling his neck. She needed to distance herself from him before… she didn't know what. She pushed back and tried to wiggle off his lap.

"My lord, we must stop…I'm so sorry I…we must." She couldn't think of what to say. Embarrassment flooded her and she looked away. She tried to stand up again.

"Wait," he whispered in a gruff, shaky voice. "Let me compose myself."

"Oh, of course," she said, apologetically. She wiggled closer and buttoned his collar, he put his head back resting against the wall with his eyes closed. He gulped a few tomes as she worked the buttons. She reached down and recovered the cravat her lap. She placed it around his neck but didn't know how to tie it.

"I'm sorry, my lord, but I don't…," she whispered. He grabbed her hands gently.

"Rhea, you need to stop touching me now. I will never be able to get myself together if you don't stop," he whispered back.

"If you could just tie your cravat then…"

He put his hand on her hip and pulled her against his arousal. Her eyes widened in understanding.

"I think you should go first. I'll join you in a moment." He poked his head out and checked the hallway. "Go." He practically threw her off his lap. She stumbled, but righted herself immediately.

"Go, I'll be right behind you. Find your brother and aunt." he whispered, from the darkness.

HE WATCHED as she practically ran out to the gardens, stopping for only a second to smooth her skirt. He smiled and started to tie his cravat, he couldn't be more pleased. His relief was palatable, she wanted him, he knew that now for certain now. Her attraction to him was as strong as his was for her. She couldn't help herself, for that he felt as giddy as a schoolboy and ten feet tall. Unfortunately, so was his erection. Good God, that was the singular most erotic experience he'd ever had, without sex. He could still smell her. Rhea and jasmine, a heady scent that would undoubtedly haunt him all night.

He wouldn't have stopped, he realized, he would've taken her right here if they had continued. What was wrong with him? Where was his self-control? Why did he need to know her passion matched his and why was he so relieved about it? He wanted her back here right now, to feel her skin and let her hair down to its full glory. His little minx was going to be the death of him.

Blood hell! Why did he agree to this ridiculous bargain of

hers? What seemed like fun at first, had quickly become torture! She was his wife and he could lock her in his bedroom and make love to her for weeks if he so chose. No, he could never force himself on anyone and he knew it, especially Rhea. He wanted her uncontrollable passion and desire, not compliance out of a sense of duty. Besides, he had given his word, now he had to see it through. What he needed to do right now was to stop thinking about her or he'd be in this alcove all night! He closed his eyes and rested his head back against the wall and thought about the business reports.

RHEA FOUND her aunt standing close to the front of the crowd. Jugglers were just taking their places on the lawn.

"Where's Lord Blackthorne?" Aunt Magda asked Rhea in a whisper, with a knowing smile.

"He'll be here in a moment," she said, not taking her eyes of the jugglers.

"He will have to stand to the side with your brother. Lord Blackthorne and Titan, are too tall to see the entertainment from here without blocking everyone's view. Would you like to go stand with them dear? I'm fine if you would prefer to be with them." She smiled encouragingly at Rhea.

"No!" she shouted, involuntarily, then composed herself and added, "I'd rather be here in the front with you." She gave her aunt her sweetest smile and held her arm affectionately. Distance, she thought to herself, you must keep your distance. She saw Sy walk over and stand next to Titan. He caught her eye, gave her a slight nod, and a knowing smile. Her heart jumped into her throat. She jerked her head back to the jugglers. She heard her aunt chuckle, and wondered what was funny.

Titan nodded at Sy when he walked up.

"Don't plan anything for tomorrow night," Sy said to Titan, without looking at him.

"May I ask why?" Titan replied, sardonically.

"Brush off your formals. You're going to Atterby's ball."

CHAPTER 12

The Atterby's ball. It was the official opening of the season; the event where everyone went to be seen and brush shoulders with the upper crust of the *Ton*. The Prince Regent was known to make an appearance, along with members of the royal court. This was evident by the line of carriages and the crush of people waiting to get inside Atterby House.

"At this rate, we won't arrive till the ball is over." Aunt Magda stated, looking out the window of their carriage.

"We could just go home." Rhea said, ruefully.

Rhea really didn't care about the ball. She was too preoccupied with her situation with Sy. He was going to be there and she needed to keep her distance somehow. There was no controlling herself around the man. She'd never felt such a strong attraction toward anyone before, as a matter of fact, she had never thought about sex before, it was a mild curiosity at best. Sy had opened the floodgates of her sensuality. Now her skin tingled whenever she thought of him. She was walking around like a simpering fool, daydreaming about him, visualizing him naked on the bed, longing to kiss his neck again. Oh, that neck! It haunted her, the feel and taste of it under her lips. Ugh! It was as if he had crawled into her skin, infecting her, she was consumed with nothing but thoughts of him. It frightened her, this loss of control. When he was there she wanted him, when he was gone she yearned for him. If this agony continued, she would give in, lock herself in the bedroom with the man for a month, living out every fantasy she'd had about him since last night. This was just not working for her, she needed to get back to the island. This had to stop. She needed to focus on the task of getting this business over with and getting home. Before he found out who she truly was.

"No need to be nervous about your first ball, dear. You look lovely. Liana has outdone herself. Your hair is a masterpiece. I've never seen you look so beautiful. And that dress, you are sure to turn heads tonight." Aunt Magda exclaimed, in earnest. She didn't say it directly but Rhea knew she was referring to Sy. "Oh, here we are, finally! Are you ready my dear? This is so exciting!" Rhea sighed, please God, give her strength to be in Sy's presence and not make a fool of herself.

∽

SY HAD POSITIONED HIMSELF, Titan and Smith so he could watch the staircase leading into the ballroom. He intended to completely occupy Rhea at this ball. There was no way he was going to let any of these flops and dandies fawn all over her.

Rhea and Aunt Magda were probably caught up in the crush to get in. There had to be three hundred people in the ballroom and at least as many outside waiting to be announced. He wished he could have talked to her aunt and escorted her here, but, unfortunately, that is not the way this was supposed to work. He needed to get through a few of these public events before he could make offer for her. He understood the importance of appearances. No one could know about the back-door deal made to secure their seats. He was impatient though, he wanted this resolved as quickly as possible.

"How's a man supposed to dance with a lady wearing all those petticoats? I've been away from town too long. I'll surely step on a skirt or two tonight." Smith stated.

"I'm not dancing. As soon as I get Rhea and Aunt Magda settled, I'm off to the gentlemen's parlor for cards and brandy. I'm not in the mood for small talk with the young husband hunting females." Titan complained. Sy could tell Titan was just as put out with these events as he was. "Where are they anyway?" he said, clearly irritated, pulling at his cravat.

"Probably stuck in the crush outside. Please remember, Titan, you are supposed to be making a good impression here. This is one of the biggest events of the season. A lot of business will take place tonight. Being nice to a few strategic husband hunting females might open some doors to some influential fathers." Sy stated.

"Yeah, Yeah. Not to worry, I know how to conduct myself. Ah, there they are, finally!" he said, looking at the top of the staircase.

If Sy thought he was over the heart-stopping reaction he had when he first saw her, he was wrong. She was a vision. He couldn't move, he was so stunned. Rhea practically glowed as she stood at the top of the staircase. She wore a Grecian style gown made of sliver silk. One of her shoulders was bare as the front of the bodice gathered to the opposite shoulder and secured with a diamond brooch. She wore a wide belt made of pewter silk covered with clear glass beads which caught the light. Her skirt was swept up and gathered across the front, which emphasized her hips. She wore minimal petticoats making her look statuesque and elegant. Her hair was in her signature half up, half down style, with a ribbon woven through it that matched her belt. The glass beads in her hair caught the light when she turned her head. She wore pewter silk gloves to complete her ensemble. He had no words. She looked unbelievably beautiful, surreal.

Titan chuckled, reached over, and closed Sy's mouth.

"I told you she grew up to be a pretty little thing," he said, teasingly.

"She's utterly enchanting," he said, just above a whisper.

"She has that effect on men in general. Come on big guy."

He slapped Sy's arm. "Let's go get her before she's mobbed. Smith, would you mind continuing to guard this settee for my aunt?" He gave Sy a little shove in Rhea's direction.

"It would be my pleasure," Smith smiled knowingly.

"How do you not worry incessantly for her safety?" Sy asked, as they walked with purpose to retrieve the ladies.

"I do, but believe it or not she can take care of herself. Jat saw to that. At home, she literally has a whole army of protectors. They treat her as their little sister and guard her with their lives. Any one of them would swim through shark infested waters for her. Nobody dares to mess with her. I guess that's why my parents sent her here with my aunt. She'll have a better chance to find a match here, in town." They walked up to Rhea and Aunt Magda.

"Titan, my heavens, this event gets larger and larger every year. I'm sure we are too late to claim a settee. I'm afraid I'll be on my feet all night." Aunt Magda said, concerned.

"No worries aunt, we have secured one for you. May I say, you look lovely this evening. Sister you are a vision, I fear you will not have time to make use of the settee at all. Your dance card will surely fill quickly. You remember Lord Blackthorne." He waved his hand in Sy's direction. "He's come to help get you through the crowd and settled."

Sy bowed to Aunt Magda, turned to Rhea and bowed again. He held out his arm and she took it. Sy felt some of the pent-up tension ease at her touch.

"You look beautiful Rhea," he said, once Titan and Magda were out of earshot.

"Thank you, my lord," she said, looking straight ahead. She couldn't bear to look at him; her heart was in her throat. She could feel the heat radiating between them where they touched.

"I want you to save all the waltzes for me," he stated, his face emotionless. He nodded to someone, and gave the gentleman a rakish half smile.

"That hardly seems fair, my lord," Rhea said, trying to keep her face emotionless as well.

"Fair or not. Nobody waltzes with my wife but me." His tone was final.

She had no chance to reply as they had arrived at the settee Smith was guarding. Titan was settling Aunt Magda on the settee. Smith was staring at her, an astonished look on his face, as she approached.

"Lord Smith, how lovely to see you." She curtsied. He seemed petrified for a moment.

"Lady Hastings, excuse me, you look so lovely this evening I believe you made me lose my train of thought," Smith finally stammered out, bowing to her.

"She does that to people," Titan interjected.

"Titan! You say the most outrageous things." She narrowed her eyes at him, then turned back to Smith. "Thank you for the complement Lord Smith, but I'm sure there will be many lovely ladies here this evening," she said, politely.

"To be sure, but none will hold a candle to you. May I ask for a dance this evening?" he said, with a slight bow.

"I would be delighted. You are the first or, actually the second, to inquire. It's my first ball you see, so I'm not quite sure how the process works," she replied.

She pulled her dance card from her wrist. Sy took it from her. Then he wrote his name in various spots and handed it back to her. She looked perplexed at his satisfied grin, then handed it to Smith. He read the card, his eyes snapped to Sy, shocked.

"Sy, you cannot possibly take the first and last dance *and* all of the waltzes tonight. Why, that wouldn't be seemly for Lady Hastings to dance that much with one gentleman," he said, quietly, leaning in close to Sy for privacy.

"Fine," he said, with irritation, and took the card back.

He edited it, then handed it back. Smith read it, and tried not to chuckle. He added his name and handed it back to Rhea with a bow. He moved closer to Titan.

"Titan, it looks as if you will not be spending much time with your brandy and cards after all," Smith said, in Titan's direction.

"What's that you say?" Titan turned from his aunt at Smith's comment.

"I said, it looks as though you may not have to worry about dancing with those husband hunting ladies you were referring to either. You are otherwise occupied." He nodded toward Rhea's dance card then to Sy, who was looking in the other direction.

Titan took Rhea's card from her hand and read it. He almost laughed out loud when he saw that Sy had crossed out his name for some of the dances and inserted Titan's instead. Had he had fallen under Rhea's spell? The infamous Captain Sy Black, Marquess of Blackthorne, done in by his little sister? Perhaps this evening wouldn't be so boring after all.

"What's all the fuss about?" Aunt Magda inquired. Titan put a finger to his lips and showed her Rhea's dance card. She smiled.

"See, I told you this was going to be easy," she whispered.

"Aunt, I get the distinct impression that you know something I don't. I expect a full explanation."

"In due time dear, in due time," she replied, with a tap of her fan on his arm.

RHEA DIDN'T NOTICE the exchanges regarding her dance card. She was too distracted by the grandeur of the Atterby's ballroom. It had to be fifty feet tall with a balcony that went around the entire circumference of the room with the exception of the tall sweeping staircase where she was announced. There was a full orchestra playing softly by the dance floor. The dance floor was humongous, taking up most of the bottom floor. Around the perimeter were various sets of double doors. Some of the doors led to rooms with refreshments and a gentlemen's parlor, others led out to the expansive gardens in the back. The gardens were lit with candle chandeliers on tall posts shedding candlelight along it's paths. It was overwhelming in its opulence. She didn't know where to look first.

"Rhea!" She heard her name from somewhere in the crowd. Lily and Maisy, who were waving frantically, were crossing the room towards her. She smiled and waved back.

"Rhea! You look stunning!" Maisy lifted Rhea's hands. "Everyone, just everyone, is talking about you. So many young gentlemen are walking up to us because they heard we attended the Wessex soiree with you."

"Yes, they have been asking us to make introductions. We were non-committal, of course, because we wanted to talk to you first," Lily added. "We came to stand with you so everyone will know we're friends. I hope that's alright. Is it alright?" Lily asked.

"Of course," she answered.

"Your dress! My goodness, Rhea, looks like it was made on Mount Olympus by the Gods. Your style is surely to be imitated this season. I know I want to copy both dresses you have worn, so far. I need all the help I can get to be noticed, it is my second season, after all. Would you be offended?" Lily asked. Rhea opened her mouth to answer when Maisy interrupted.

"Yes, I admit I'm green with jealousy, too, you look so elegant. I feel like I should be sitting on top of an ice cream cone in this dress. Mother insisted I wear it," Maisy said, referring to her light-yellow dress with at least ten or more petticoats under the skirt.

Rhea tried not to smile at her reference. They both

looked like they could be served on the dessert tray. Maisy, in her light-yellow dress with matching lace fan and feathers in her hair. Lily was wearing in a light pink gown with full skirts and pink flowering in her coif. She tried to soothe their fears about their appearances, in truth, she was self-conscious about her own dress. She felt like an enigma. She didn't match the current fashion at all. Maybe she should have taken Hilda's advice and added a few more petticoats. She just could not stand to wear them, they were very uncomfortably hot, she was not used to wearing so many layers of clothing. Nothing could be done now. She'd just have to grin and bear it for the evening.

"You both look lovely. The stitching and bead work on your bodice is marvelous Lily, I've never seen such an intricate design before. And that lovely color emphasizes your beautiful brown eyes Maisy," she placated.

"You think so?" they said, in unison. They looked at each other and laughed.

Their presence eased the tension. She never thought about having girlfriends before, she liked it very much. It was such a light and easy friendship. She didn't need to prove anything or feel like she had to measure up. She relaxed, and smiled at her new friends.

"The two of us will surely fill our dance cards tonight now that we have a secret weapon to attract suitors!" Maisy said, with much enthusiasm.

"Secret weapon?" Rhea inquired.

"Why, you, of course," Maisy stated, blatantly. "Look, here they come."

SY AND TITAN watched the exchange between the women from a distance. Titan was amused, wondering what they were talking about. He was not used to seeing Rhea talking to other young women her age and wondered how she was faring. She didn't look like she needed to be rescued. She was smiling and laughing. Rhea really was a beautiful woman. It took getting her away from the island and into a dress for him to see how grown up she had become. He was suddenly overcome with a sense of pride.

Titan glanced over at Sy. He was definitely keeping an eye on Rhea while trying to have a discussion with Lord Humphries. He chuckled to himself recalling what Sy had done to Rhea's dance card. Poor girl wouldn't have a single waltz with anyone other than he or Sy. He was used to other men being protective of Rhea, but this was different. He didn't look at her like a little sister. Had the aloof Lord of Blackthorne fallen really for Rhea? Titan believed he had. He decided to test his theory and walked up to the gentlemen.

"Sy, I noticed you put me down to dance with Rhea for the last dance of the evening?" he asked him, casually.

"Yes, I took the liberty of securing that dance for you. I assumed you would be escorting her home," he said, as if it made perfect sense.

"Good thinking, but as this is Rhea's first ball and her first season, I'm sure she would prefer to save the last spot for someone who catches her eye this evening," he said, and waited for a reaction.

"The hell she will!" he blurted out, before thinking.

Titan smiled, he guessed right, Sy has already fallen under her spell.

"I was only thinking of her safety, Titan. There will be a large crush to get out, and it would be better if she were with you to be escorted out, is it not?"

Sy looked supremely uncomfortable as he tried to recover from his blunder. Titan smiled sardonically, enjoying his friends revealing reaction. Sy's eyes narrowed at Titan and looked as though he wanted to punch him in the mouth.

"If you prefer, I can take the responsibility of the last dance and escort Lady Rhea and your aunt home. Their townhouse is just two blocks from mine," Sy offered.

"That won't be necessary. This evening is turning out to be much more entertaining than I expected. I'll take care of my sister, thank you." He patted Sy's shoulder. "I'm off to get a drink. Would any of you gentlemen care to join me?" he asked, smiling again. Titan was pleased. If there was anyone who could handle Rhea, it was the infamous Captain Sy Black. There was more to this situation though, his instincts were telling him, and he knew exactly who to ask.

"Count me in," Smith answered quickly.

"Me too," Humphries chimed in.

"It's too early for me," Sy stated.

That got Sy a look from both Smith and Titan. Smith was surprised and Titan was smirking as he went over to his aunt.

"Aunt Magda, I am going for a drink, can I bring you back some punch?" he asked, politely.

"Oh, how sweet, yes dear, that would be wonderful. Could you manage a glass for my friend Lady Witherspoon?" indicating the woman sitting next to her.

"Why certainly," he replied, joyfully, then leaned down to whisper in his aunt's ear. "If you can manage to tell me what's really going on with Sy and Rhea when I return."

She just looked up at him and smiled. His aunt was up to something. He would get to the bottom if it eventually.

THE NEXT COUPLE of hours were torture for Sy. Although he danced the first dance with Rhea in an effort to stake his claim, it seemed to make little difference. There was a steady stream of gentlemen requesting an introduction to Rhea. His jaw was starting to get sore from clenching his teeth every time she put her hand on someone's arm to be led to the dance floor. He could barely concentrate on the conversations taking place around him as several lords and ladies welcomed him back to town.

Many inquired if he was going to stay now that he was done with his commission. A few bolder ladies introduced their daughters in hopes they would catch Sy's eye. The whole situation was grating on his nerves, being forced to make polite conversation, when all he wanted to do is keep an eye on Rhea.

The occasional jab from Titan was especially annoying. He had to walk away when Titan mentioned to Smith that Lord Barton would be a good match for his sister. Lord Barton? He was a weasel, complete with a whiny voice and a whistle when he pronounced any word with an 's'! How he could think he was worthy of Rhea? This was going to be a long evening. He needed a drink but didn't dare leave her to these jackanapes, someone might try to entice her into the gardens, and he'd be damned if he'd let that happen.

RHEA, Maisy and Lily were surrounded by a large group of young gentlemen and her dance card was completely full. She didn't know how she could possibly remember all of their names and titles, or how she was going to dance every dance, since she was already fatigued. The room seemed stuffy with all these gentlemen crowding her. Maisy and Lily were in their element. They talked easily with the gentlemen. When one would ask Rhea a question, either Maisy or Lily would answer for her. She was very grateful for their interference as she looked around for Titan, she wanted him to take her outside for a breath of fresh air. Where was he? She tried to excuse herself to ask Aunt Magda where he was, but the throng of men started to object, closing in on her. Suddenly, they all were looking at something behind her. Some of them even backed up a step. The hairs on the back of her neck stood on end. It was Sy, she could feel him.

"Give her some air, gentlemen, the evening is young yet," Sy said, from behind her.

His deep voice sent shivers down her spine and woke the butterflies in her stomach. She resisted the urge to close her eyes and gulp, because everyone was watching her.

"Your brother has gone to the gentlemen's parlor for refreshments. You look flushed Lady Hastings. May I take you out to the gardens for a breath of fresh air?" He held out his arm.

A loud round of grumbles came from her audience. She should refuse and wait for her brother, but rational thought left her as soon as she looked up at his face. Those blue eyes entrapped her, and her hand came up in an unconscious motion of acceptance. Wasn't she supposed to be keeping her distance from him? As if in a dream, he reached for her hand. He tucked it against his bicep and covered her hand with his own. She could feel the muscles beneath his coat flex, it was an extremely possessive gesture.

"Gentlemen, ladies, if you will excuse us," Sy said, with a nod to the crowd.

Rhea turned to speak with Lily and Maisy, but was caught off guard by their expressions. Both were staring at Sy's hand covering hers, as a matter of fact, everyone was staring at them in surprise. She looked to Sy for an explanation but he just smiled rakishly and started toward the garden.

The fresh air felt good. She also appreciated being away from the throng even though the gardens were full of strolling couples. The light from the candelabras was more than ample to light the paths and open spaces. They also created a lot of shadowed areas where the couples could escape. Every now and then she could hear a giggle coming from one of those dark shadows. How she wanted Sy to take her into one of those dark areas but at the same time was frightened at the prospect. She looked at his profile for any indication that he may be thinking the same. His expression was unreadable.

"What do you think of the Atterby's ballroom?" he asked, making polite conversation.

"It's like nothing I've ever seen before, my lord. It's quite overwhelming, actually."

"Are you enjoying your first ball?"

"It's been very interesting, my lord."

"Do you ever think there will be a time when you will be comfortable calling me Sy, Rhea? At least when we are alone?"

"We should never be alone, my lord, but I will endeavor to call you Sy when others cannot hear. Will that please you, my lord?"

"Yes. *You* please me, Rhea. I hope a day will come when you feel that I please you, too." There was silence between them for a moment before he asked, "Why do you feel that we should never be alone?"

"I feel...," she searched for the right words. "I feel as

though we act...irresponsibly when we are in close proximity."

"Irresponsibly?" he asked, in a sarcastic tone.

"You tease me, my lord, but I am perfectly serious. You are a man of experience, while I have none. It is difficult for me to resist the temptation that being alone with you presents," she answered truthfully, embarrassing as it was. She could feel her cheeks turning pink.

SY'S HEART started racing at her confession. He had to touch her, he needed to feel her skin against his. He had the urge to scoop her up and take her into one of the shadowy alcoves, but he swore to himself they would have one evening where he did not pounce on her. He wanted them to start to build a relationship, something more than this undeniable attraction they had for each other. All his pent-up frustration was starting to work on his resolve to leave her be this evening. Her words dissolved the last of that resolve into dust.

Sy clandestinely removed his glove then moved his hand to the top of her glove just above her elbow. He ran his finger back and forth on above of the glove where it met her skin. Her skin was soft and warm. She shivered, and he could feel goose bumps rising where his fingers caressed. He moved her hand further up his arm, and he slowly traced his finger back at the top of her glove. Then slowly, he slid the glove down, sliding his finger against her sensitive skin. Sy steered them around the outside path of the garden. There were couples walking a short distance in front of them. He looked down at Rhea as he rubbed his fingers in slow seductive circles up her arm. She closed her eyes for a short moment, then bit her bottom lip. He smiled, enjoying her reaction. Once he reached the juncture between her elbow and bicep he paid special attention to the crease there, rubbing his finger back and forth sensually in the crease. She quietly moaned, a sexy, sensual sound, and ran her tongue across her lips.

He couldn't take no more. At the next shadowed area, he pushed her in it and cover her mouth with his. She arched against him and put her hands on the back of his head to pull him to her. They shared a lust filled kiss for moment before he pulled back.

"I am not going to be able to do this Rhea. I want you too much," he whispered, and put his forehead to hers.

"What choice do we have?" she said, breathlessly.

She was right, they had no choice but to see this through.

"Come to me tonight," he whispered. "Only we will know."

He stared into her eyes and knew she wanted to say yes. He could see her luscious mouth want to form the word, but she didn't. She looked away and bit her lip. When she looked back at him there were tears in her eyes. He didn't understand her hesitation, surely she could see they wanted each other.

"That is not a good idea, my lord, and you well know it," she whispered back.

He pulled back enough to look at her. He needed to reach her, to convince her that they wanted each other. He knew she could feel it, but was resisting, why?

"We want each other, we are married, there is nothing wrong with it," he pushed.

"I will come to you, I promise, but it is too soon. We hardly know each other. I do not want to make a mistake both of us will regret," she whispered, so faintly he could barely hear it.

He lifted her chin so she was forced to look at him. He wished he could see her face better, look into her eyes so she would know he was speaking the truth and ease her fears.

"I would never regret being with you Rhea," he stated, then sighed. "I'm being impatient. I will try to slow down. Will that please you?"

She looked up to the stars and took a deep breath. He watched a tear escape and streak down her lovely cheek. He rubbed it away with his thumb then held her close, desperate to erase the sadness in her eyes.

"Yes," she said, in a whisper.

"Then let's go have your first ball," he said, in a light-hearted voice. "I am willing to wait for you to be ready Rhea."

He kissed her again. A possessive kiss. She responded, her hands holding him there a fraction longer than he intended. He groaned when she licked his bottom lip and rubbed her thumb along his jaw. This woman was going to be the death of him yet.

~

RHEA COULDN'T LET GO of him. She knew she was giving him mixed signals, but couldn't help it. Each kiss felt like it might be their last. She wanted him to remember this feeling, this feeling of overwhelming desire that he invoked in her. She tried to pull him back when he wanted to end the kiss. No, just a little longer, she licked his bottom lip in invitation. She wanted him to want her not because of obligation or the contract. When he moved closer again, she increased the pressure of her lips on his. He moaned and pulled her hard against his chest. He took over the kiss. It was powerful and demanding, she tried to keep up with him. His hand slid up her side to the top of her bodice. His thumb brushed over her breast and circled her nipple. It turned hard with his attention. He slipped four of his fingers inside the top of her bodice and brushed the hardened nipple with the back of his fingers. Heat surged into her loins at his touch, making her arch up against him. She unbuttoned his coat and slipped her hands inside, sliding them up his chest. Suddenly, he pulled away, groaning.

"Rhea. We cannot do this here. Good lord, you drive me to distraction. We must stop or I won't be able to." he whispered then crushed her to his chest once again. "You are mine and mine alone, remember that." He put his chin on the top of her head as he said it, holding her tight.

Rhea rested the cheek against his chest. She could hear his heart racing like her own. It made her feel powerful, validated, knowing she had the same effect on him as he did on her. She was on dangerous ground, this overwhelming attraction she felt for him frightened her. She felt unable to resist it. Somehow she had to find the strength, they had no future together, once he found out the truth…

"We should go back," he said, though he continued to hold her tight to his body not moving.

"Of course," she replied reluctantly, she slid her hands around his waist under his jacket hugging him to her, she would rather stay right here for the rest of the ball.

Sy leaned back and looked down at Rhea. Her lips were swollen from his kisses and her cheeks were flushed. He kissed her forehead affectionately as he slid her hands from around his waist. Then buttoned his coat and helped her straighten her dress. When he was certain it was safe to leave their spot, he steered her back onto the path. He took the long way back to the ballroom so they could collect themselves before entering the throng of people. As soon as they walked back to their group, a young gentleman approached. He gave a Sy wary glance.

"I believe the next dance is mine Lady Hastings," he stated politely, with a bow.

"Yes, of course." She gave him a weak smile. He blushed three shades of red.

Sy gave her hand a knowing squeeze before he reluctantly let her go.

"Thank you, Lord Blackthorne, for the invigorating walk around the garden," she said politely, with a shallow curtsy.

"It was my pleasure, Lady Hastings, it was most simulating. I hope I will have the honor of escorting you again." He bowed and left the group.

Rhea looked back to the gentleman waiting and extended her hand. She couldn't remember his name and it would be rude to refer to her dance card now. He took her hand and started to lead her to the dance floor. She felt no excitement at his touch. It was not firm like Sy's, nor did she feel any heat through her glove. In fact, she was repulsed.

"I believe Lord Blackthorne has taken an interest in you," her dance partner suggested, as he led her to the floor.

"He is a very good friend of my brother's," she explained. "I'm sure he just felt obligated to act in his stead."

"That is very good news," he said, with enthusiasm. "Very good news indeed."

Bile threatened to rise in her throat. How much longer must she endure this? She looked over her shoulder at her aunt and gave a pleading look. Titan caught it and chuckled. Then he leaned over to Sy and said something. Sy looked her way and she could tell whatever Titan said had annoyed him. He stood, walked into the crowd and disappeared. It was if the breath had left her body.

∾

SY NEEDED A DRINK. That was the hardest thing he had to do in his life thus far. Hand Rhea over to another man. After their interlude in the garden he was holding on by a thin thread. Titan's constant comments on the merits if Rhea's suitors weren't helping. A man could only take so much. He decided to retreat to the gentlemen's parlor for a while and calm his nerves. He was just about to enter the smoky room when a shrilly voice came from behind him making him stop.

"I was told that you were lost at sea. I'm glad to see that rumor was untrue." Penelope Verny Blackthorne said sarcastically to his back.

Sy didn't try to keep the disgusted expression from his face as he turned to her. He groaned annoyed, Penelope wore a blood red dress more appropriate for a harlot than a Lady. No surprise there, it must've cost a fortune to have the thousands of black beads sewn onto every inch. He was ashamed this woman carried his family name.

"Sorry to disappoint you." he answered, refusing to greet her or use her title in his address.

"No bow or kiss for your mother?" she said, taking a step forward expectantly.

"You are not my mother." He hissed. "Nor should you ever expect me to bow to you." he replied, disdain dripping from his statement.

"Can you not find a way for us to be friends? Your father won't be here forever. We must deal with each other eventually, we are family after all," she said, false sweetness dripping in her voice.

"Enjoy your time as my father's wife, for when my father's time comes to an end, you will see no favor from me. I suggest you treat your husband with the utmost respect and hope he lives a long and healthy life," he replied, the threat clear. He turned without a farewell, leaving her with her mouth gaping open. A portly man came to Penelope's side.

"That didn't go very well, now did it," the gentlemen stated.

"He's going to be a problem. Why couldn't he have died at sea like the rumors said! That would have served us well." Disdain of her own dripped from her voice. "We will just have to find a way to get to him. Everyone has a weakness, we just need to find his. Have him followed and report back to me. I want every detail of what he does and who he talks to, you never know what could be important."

"And the plans for his father?"

"Too risky, let those lie for the moment."

"And if an opportunity arises for Lord Blackthorne to have an accident while he's being followed?" he asked, hopefully.

"Take it." She dismissed him, straightened her dress, and scanned the crowd. Time to set herself up with a new husband. She intended to be a widow soon.

RHEA BARELY HAD time to take a breath for the next hour. As soon as she was lead off the dance floor she was escorted back on. The night seemed to drag. She didn't see Sy until it was time for their waltz. She tried not to stare as he approached. He was a head taller than the other gentlemen. The familiar heat was forming in her loins as he crossed the ballroom to escort her to the dance floor. His hands felt warm and firm while they waited for the waltz to begin. He gave her the rakish smile that was becoming familiar. She smiled back. It surprised her how gracefully he danced, considering his size. At times, she didn't think her feet were touching the floor as they glided to the music. It felt like the shortest dance of the evening and she was disappointed when the music ended. He escorted her back to her aunt and bid her goodnight. As he walked away, a wave of sadness hit her. She realized that she had no idea when she would see him again.

It wasn't long before Titan came for the final dance. To her relief, he escorted her and her aunt to their carriage immediately afterward. She did not want to linger in the ballroom like so many others did. Aunt Magda looked as exhausted as she felt. In the carriage, she closed her eyes, sighed, and relived her time in the garden with Sy. Would she ever be able to be around him without craving his kisses? How will she ever be able to walk away from him?

CHAPTER 13

*R*hea was relieved to rid herself of her gown and corset. She sat at her vanity and savored the feeling of her hair being brushed out from the elaborate hairstyle she was forced to wear all evening. Liana was gently brushing and mumbling about all the tangles these English styles made. Rhea was only half listening, lost in yet another daydream about Sy and the feel of his fingers as they grazed her nipple, his lips on hers, among other erotic memories. She shivered. She knew she was torturing herself. It was going to be difficult falling asleep with this feeling of, she didn't exactly know what, longing? Hunger? Dissatisfaction? She sighed for the tenth time since leaving the ballroom.

"I can finish Liana, thank you so much for everything." Rhea said, needing to be alone with her thoughts.

Rhea opened the window, hoping for a breeze to cool her skin. No such luck, she left it open hoping the heat would escape the room. She pulled her bed covering back. It was just too hot this evening for anything more than a sheet. While she slid the coverlet down, she heard a sound behind her. Trying not to flinch, she slowly reached under her pillow for her knife. Hoping to catch whomever off guard, she swung around quickly, her knife in front of her. She stopped short and sucked in a sharp breath of surprise. It was Sy!

He was dressed completely in black; black pants, polished black boots and a black shirt that was open to his navel, exposing a large portion of his sculpted chest and abdomen. He looked like a pirate, barbaric and unbelievably handsome. He was just standing there, rooted to his spot, staring at her, waiting.

She stood frozen herself. Realization hit her hard. He came to her. He was longing for her as much as she was him or he wouldn't be here, right? She dropped her knife. It made a loud clanking noise as it bounced, then rattled in place as it settled on the floor. Their eyes locked. She searched for clarity in his gaze. Why was he here? Lust? Challenge, because she said she wouldn't come to him? She could see only vulnerability and longing. Her heart warmed, and tears came to her eyes. Without thinking, she launched herself at him, jumping onto his chest, putting her arms around his neck and her legs around his waist. She covered his lips with hers with urgency, as he had done to her so many times.

SY KNEW he had risked everything slipping into her room after he promised that he would wait. After he returned home from the ball he paced his parlor, trying to get the urge to go to her to dissipate. Rhea had said no, she wouldn't come to him, he was moving too fast. He felt like a caged animal. The pacing wasn't working. He thought of calling on Smith or going to the club, but he knew that wouldn't satisfy his need to see her. Rhea was his wife, damn it, he had to see her! The decision made, he dressed quickly and verily ran to her Aunt's townhouse. He stood below her window, indecisive, and paced again. What had this little Minx done to him? He was her husband, damn it, he reminded himself. If he wanted to see her he should march through the front door, get her, and bring her home. It was his right.

Instead, he climbed the trellis. He watched as she dismissed her lady's maid and opened her window. He took the opportunity, and jumped through.

He was ready accept whatever the outcome of his rash behavior, but he had to see her tonight, even if she asked him to leave. Relief flooded him as she jumped on his chest. He caught her, one hand on her thigh, the other around her back, crushing her to his chest, wanting, needing, to feel her body against his. He kissed her with all the longing he had felt since he let her hand go at the ball. She smelled divine, jasmine and Rhea. He breathed her in, and relished the sensation. Her body was soft but firm. Her legs were strong as they gripped his waist tight. Her tongue slipped over his again and again, filling him with the taste of her. She slid her fingers into his hair and found the leather tie of his queue. She released it, then ran her fingers though his unbound hair, pulling in her urgency to get him closer. He went instantly hard when he realized her eagerness to touch him equaled his. He reached up and grabbed a large amount of her hair and pulled her head back gently to give him access to her neck. She moaned in pleasure as he paid homage to her sensitive skin. He lifted his head, still holding her head in place by her hair and looked at her.

"Rhea, you are mine," he whispered, he slammed his mouth on hers as gently as he could manage, and kissed her with all the pent-up frustration he needed to release.

He walked them over to the bed and laid her down, coming down over her without breaking contact. He continued to kiss and suck on her neck as he untied the ribbon at the top of her chemise. He pulled one side down over her shoulder and exposed her breast. Her rosy nipple was hard and waiting for him. He immediately put his mouth on it and sucked it gently. She squeezed her legs around his waist and arched up against him in response.

Fueled by desire, everything started happening fast. He wanted her chemise off so her could see her. He reached down, grabbed the hem and slowly started to pull it up, giving her the opportunity to stop him. When she didn't protest he put his hand under her back and lifted her enough that he could pull the chemise off in one swift movement. Rhea lifted her arms to assist. She pulled at his shirt trying to remove it. He stopped and quickly pulled it over his head before laying back on her. When her bare breasts touched his chest, he had to stop himself from crying out, it felt so erotic. He had to taste her. Starting at her neck, he licked and sucked his way down to her collarbone. Rhea moaned, the sexy little sound encouraged him as he slid his hand down her flat belly into her triangle of hair. She gasped, when he slid his fingers in to the folds of her womanhood searching for her nub. He was pleased that she was wet and ready for him. He knew he found her nub when she bucked up against him, exhaling sharply. She closed her eyes and bit her lip as he softly circled her the sensitive spot with his thumb. He worked her nub until it was hard and her womanhood was weeping with need. He put his mouth on hers to absorb her cries of surprise when he slowly inserted a finger into her entry. He inserted a second finger, she was tight, too tight to accept him. He thrust his tongue in her mouth matching the slow rhythm he was thrusting his fingers into her. She made sweet little moaning sounds in his mouth and ground her hips against his hand. He circled her nub one more time with his thumb. Sy knew Rhea was close to climaxing, she was barely responding to his kiss anymore, lost in ecstasy. He didn't want her orgasm yet, he wasn't done exploring her.

He started kissing his way down between her breasts. He wanted to touch every inch of her, to possess her body. He circled his tongue around her naval at the same his thumb circled her nub.

She threaded her fingers into his hair as a moan escaped

and she circled her hips. He needed to taste her. He moved down her body and removed his hand from her slick warmth.

"Sy?" she whispered.

"Open for me Rhea," he pleaded.

He pushed on her legs gently and they spread apart for him timidly, then opened wider still as she tried to relax. He ran his hands down her inner thighs, closing in to her most intimate place. He kissed all along her inner thigh and felt her shiver in response. As he parted her intimate folds, she twisted her hips hesitantly. This was all new to her, he wanted to show her the heights of pleasure, make it special for her. He brought one of his arms around her leg and braced it across her belly so she could not move. Then ran his tongue down her soft pink skin, circled once before he plunged his tongue into her entry. She took a sharp intake of breath and slammed her palms on the bed clenching the sheets between her fingers. When he ran his tongue up and circled her nub she let out a moan that spurred him on. He started flicking her nub with the end of his tongue, and after a few flicks, he sucked her nub in his mouth and messaged it gently with his tongue. Rhea cried out and her body convulsed as she was consumed by her climax.

She tasted so good he wasn't ready for her to let go. He wanted to taste her longer but pleased she was so passionate. He could see the evidence of her climax and his arousal throbbed painfully. He had to make her his now. He pressed two fingers inside her and tried to stretch her a little so it would be easier to accept him. She tried to arch her back, held her down, he loved how responsive she was to his touch. He stood to unbutton his pants but stopped when he looked down at her. She was incredibly beautiful laying naked, spread open for him, her body quivering from the aftermath of her orgasm. Her hair was fanning the sheets around her head and her hooded eyes were full of passion. For the first time, he noticed the mark on her thigh, he recognized his coordinates on the outer ring that made her his, forever. He rubbed his fingers over the mark. A feeling of possessiveness consumed him. She was his.

"You're mine now and forever more Rhea," he said, his voice gruff with emotion.

She held her arms up to invite him into her embrace and he lost all rational thought. He freed his erection, lowered himself on top of her and kissed her passionately with the primal urge that consumed him. He took his arousal in his hand and rubbed the tip up and down her intimate folds. He groaned, she felt so soft against his tip, hot, wet and ready for him. He hovered at her entry, then pressed into her gently. She gasped at the invasion as the tip of his shaft entered her. He closed his eyes, straining, as tried to control himself. He wanted to thrust into her but she was so tight he didn't want to hurt her. She tensed, so he pulled out a little, vowing himself that he would go slowly. He pressed into her again gently, and slid in a fraction more. Good God, she was tight. Rhea closed her eyes. Her fingers squeezed his shoulders, arched her back moaning with pleasure. He lost control, he pulled out and was about to thrust into her when two soft knocks sounded on her door.

"Rhea dear? Are you still awake?" Aunt Magda asked softly through the door.

～

RHEA'S EYES SPRANG OPEN. It was like a bucket of cold water was tossed on her. Oh, my God, was her door locked? If her Aunt came through the door and saw them like this what would she think? She tried to sit up but he held her down in an iron grip. She looked into Sy's face. He was livid. He motioned to her to tell her aunt to go away.

'I can't,' she mouthed back.

He grabbed her hips and pushed further into her. It felt so good, he was stretching her skin in the most delicious way!She dropped her head back and tried not to moan at the sheer pleasure of it. She bit her lip to stop any sound from escaping. She looked at Sy again. He was wearing an arrogant smile that immediately irritated her. If Aunt Magda walked in...

"Just a moment Aunt Magda, I need to find my wrapper," she called out, and gave him a pleading look.

She immediately regretted it. He pulled out of her, then stood and pulled up his pants. She wanted him back instantly, wanted to reach out, but he walked away too fast. He walked to the side of the door and positioned himself so he would be hidden when she opened it. She grabbed her wrapper off the chair and slipped into it as fast as she could, haphazardly tying it in the front. She ran her hands over her hair hoping to tame it a little. She opened the door just enough so that she and her aunt could see each other.

"Is something wrong Aunt Magda?" she asked, trying to keep her voice even.

"My legs are paining me something awful after the ball this evening. I was going to get a cup of tea when I saw your light. You looked flush dear. Are you well?" she asked. Concern and sincerity laced her voice.

Rhea immediately felt guilty.

"I am fine Aunt Magda, I have more of the cream Doc made, it seemed to help you a little last time. Shall I fetch it for you?" she said, trying to not act guilty. Sy pulled her hair in objection. She tried not to make a face.

"That would be wonderful dear. Why don't you meet me down in the kitchen for tea? We can sit and talk about the ball while the cream takes effect," she offered sweetly.

Sy grabbed Rhea's hand from behind the door and put it on his erection. Her eyes widened in shock. He curled her fingers around his shaft. It was firm and soft, she had never touched that part of a man's anatomy before, she resisted the urge to look as he ran her hand up and down his shaft. It was so soft and hard at the same time. She squeezed it tighter and Sy put his other hand on her wrist. She could hear his soft groan at her boldness.

"If you don't want tea we can make chocolate," Aunt Magda suggested, misjudging Rhea's reaction.

She was trying to concentrate on an answer when he took her hand from his shaft and started sliding his hand up her leg under her wrapper. It felt like heaven. Her skin was so sensitive and his strong, rough hands titillated her skin. Once he got to the juncture of her sex he slid one finger back and forth between her folds. She bit her lip and knew she must have a silly look on her face.

"Are you sure you're well, Rhea?" her Aunt asked, concerned.

"Why yes, just tired from tonight. I'll see you downstairs in a few minutes. I have to locate the cream. It'll take me a minute to find it," she said, while closing the door.

"Alright dear, I'll see you in a few min…. Oh!" she said, shocked when the door shut in her face.

"I'll be right down." Rhea called through the door and put her back against it.

Sy moved closer and knelt in front of her. He picked up one of her legs and put it over his shoulder. He untied her wrapper, moved it out of his way, then he put her other leg over his other shoulder. He plunged his tongue into the creases of her sex. She arched to give him better access. He worked his magic, licking her into a frenzy in just a few short seconds. What was she doing? Falling under his spell again. She pushed at his shoulders but he didn't budge an inch. He grabbed her derriere to hold her in place. She surrendered to the pleasure for a moment, it felt so good. A warm sensation started to grow again as his tongue worked his magic. She threaded her fingers through his hair, pulling him closer. She didn't want him to stop but knew they had to.

She tried to speak several times and finally managed to squeak out. "She'll just come back and check on me when I don't go downstairs."

He pulled back growling, angrily. He reluctantly put her back on her feet.

"You are my wife, damn it, and she well knows it. I will go and talk with her," he said, getting to his feet.

"Please don't." she said in a whisper, and looked at the floor. Sy lifted her chin, forcing her to look at him. "I couldn't stand it if my aunt thought I was wanton, behaving like a hussy. She's such a sweet lady and she's done so much for me. I'd die of embarrassment if you talked to her right now." She could feel tears welling in her eyes.

The tension that had gripped Sy's shoulders eased.

"Fine, but this torment ends tomorrow. I will be here to escort you and your aunt to the opera. I will make it clear to all that I am interested in a match with you. A couple dinners parties or events will solidify our relationship, you can choose which. I will post bans next week. No arguments," he said, sternly. Then he dropped his forehead to hers and sighed. He rubbed the back of his fingers down the side of her cheek. "I cannot guarantee that I will be able to wait that long to make you mine, Rhea. Not being able to have you is driving me mad. I need to be inside you, know that you are mine in every way once and for all."

"Oh Sy," she said in a whisper. Her heart was beating rapidly.

She put her hands on the sides of his face and drew him to her. It was short kiss, one meant to seal their new arrangement. He growled low in the back of his throat before he stepped away. He picked up his shirt and, without breaking his stride, jumped out the window. She ran over to be sure he didn't fall and break his neck. A shadowy figure was making its way down the trellis and she relaxed.

She donned her chemise and made herself look presentable, then quickly grabbed the cream and proceeded downstairs. As soon as she sat down, she felt the throbbing between her legs. This was going to be another long night, filled with longing for Sy.

CHAPTER 14

"*J*t's an aquamarine silk off the shoulder gown, my lord. It has touches of chain with silver beads at the shoulders and a wide silver belt encrusted with the same silver beads and chain as the sleeves," Syers informed Sy as he sat behind his desk going over yet another bundle of paperwork on the Blackthorne estate.

"You are a marvel Syers. May I ask how you acquired that information so quickly?" Sy asked, curious since he had asked Syers to find out the color of Rhea's dress for the opera less than an hour ago. He was shocked that he had already obtained the information.

"I am extremely good at my position, my lord," Syers said, proudly and threw his nose in the air and shoulders back to validate his statement.

"You're tupping one of Lady Chamberlain's staff," Sy stated, returning his attention to his paperwork.

"And I'm tupping one of Lady Chamberlain's staff," he confirmed stoically.

"Nonetheless, good job Syers, please send for Mr. Smithington. Tell him to bring me all he has with aquamarine stones. Spare no expense. Tell him I need him here within the hour," he said, without looking up.

"As you wish, my lord," he looked at Sy and smiled. *It's about time*, Syers thought to himself. He walked to the kitchen to find Tommy and send a missive to Mr. Smithington, the most exclusive jeweler in London.

Forty-five minutes later, Mr. Smithington arrived with two henchmen carrying a large leather box. Syers showed them into Sy's office. He opened the leather box in front of Sy and presented the first array of aquamarine jewelry. Sy studied the tray as if looking for something in particular.

"These are too green. I need stones that are bluer. These stones are too small. I'm thinking of a necklace or choker, something that makes a statement. It should have silver metal and diamonds," he explained.

"Ah, a gentleman who knows what he wants. Rare indeed, my lord. Most usually pick something from the selection," he said, impressed.

"I would have had something custom made but I need a piece for the opera this evening," Sy explained.

"Can you describe or draw the piece you would like? I may have a piece that is similar to your needs," Mr. Smithington asked.

Sy took paper and ink and drew a crude picture of what

he would like to see around Rhea's neck. It had to be simple and elegant but unique to match her. Society may not know that she is already the Marchioness of Blackthorne but he did, and she must dress as one. He handed the drawing to the jeweler, whose eyes widened.

"My lord, I have a similar piece in my collection but currently it has a sapphire as the center stone. I could replace it with this aquamarine." He rifled through his box for a moment and pulled out a small black velvet bag. "But I warn you, my lord, the size of this aquamarine is rare, unique in fact. Why I know of only two others in existence. The price may not be favorable." He slid the stone from the bag and placed it on Sy's desk. Sy's heart leapt in his throat. It was the exact color of Rhea's eyes. Sitting on the black velvet it mirrored the black ring around her irises. This was the stone for his Marchioness.

"How much?" Sy asked. The jeweler named his price. "Done. Pending my approval of the necklace and that I can have it by five o'clock this afternoon."

The jeweler called over his henchman and said something quietly to him. The man bowed at Sy and turned to leave.

"The necklace will be here in fifteen minutes, my lord," Smithington said, enthusiastically. "I will need every minute to make your timeline, my lord. Can you wait and approve it? Replacing the stone can be completed in time if you approve the piece now"

"Fifteen minutes you say? Show me what you have for rings..."

RHEA SAT in front of the mirror trying to concentrate on the conversation happening around her. It was no use. She was going to see Sy in less than hour and that's all she could think about. His words resonated with her and she was conflicted. He intended to post the banns in just a few weeks. If she could manage to control her desire they might get free of this situation yet. She was just not sure she felt a strong resolve to do that anymore. She was falling in love with Sy. The words he said to her last night melted her heart. Could she really find love with Sy? What about the island and all she had built there? What about Otis and the *New Star*? Would she be able to live in society and stomach the town life? This wasn't her. Would Sy let her be captain of the *Star* and understand her work? What a mess. She didn't know what to do. Her heart and body were following different paths than her mind. Her mind started to wander to their love play last night. She could still feel his tongue on her and squirmed in her seat. Liana tugged at her hair pinning it into a new coif.

"Rhea, a package came for you. It was escorted by two burly looking guards. I had to sign for it. How exciting!" Aunt Magda said, thrilled. She placed a black leather box on the vanity table.

She looked at the box, afraid to touch it. Everyone stopped what they were doing, waiting for her to open it. She moved the box to her lap and opened it slowly, her hands shaking. She gasped at the contents. It contained the most beautiful choker she had ever seen. It had a large blue-green stone surrounded by small diamonds. It was connected to chain straps that had several bars of the same sized diamonds running vertically connected together by silver chains. It was simple, elegant, and stunning. There was a small handwritten card sitting in the middle of the necklace. She took the card and turned the box around for everyone to see its contents. There was a collective gasp.

"It's glorious!" Aunt Magda exclaimed, her hands flying to her chest. "It's almost the exact color of your eyes. My heavens, it must've cost a fortune. It's perfect to wear with your dress tonight!" she continued, with enthusiasm.

Everyone was hovering around the box, talking about the necklace. Rhea opened the note and read it.

Minx,

For your first opera.

Sy

She put the note in the pocket of her robe and walked to the window to get some air. Would he be giving her these gifts if he knew the truth about her? Guilt overwhelmed her. She should tell him, confess who she was and that this could not continue as he planned. Tears welled in her eyes and she felt like someone had stabbed her in the heart. She jumped when her aunt called her name.

"Rhea, we must finish dressing. Lord Blackthorne and Titan will be here in a half an hour! We must hurry. Liana, finish her hair. Hilda, see to her dress. The least we can do is make her the most beautiful woman he's ever set eyes on after such a generous gift. My heavens, I must get dressed myself. Lucy please assist me..." Aunt Magda left the room in a tizzy, barking orders to everyone. Rhea returned to her seat at the vanity table to let Liana finish her hair. Liana set the open box in front of her. She fingered the stone of the necklace. Any woman would be overwhelmed with a gift such as this. In truth, she was too, even if it was given to the woman he thought he knew, not her.

Within twenty minutes, she was dressed. She stood in front of the mirror, studying her reflection, as Hilda placed the choker around her neck. She felt like and looked like someone else. Sy would be here any moment. Butterflies fluttered at the thought, would she ever be able to think of the man without her body betraying her in some way? Time to get a grip on herself.

She thanked Hilda and Liana, she suggested they to go help her Aunt so she could have a moment alone. Once they had left, tears threatened. This isn't her, she felt off kilter. This life wasn't for her, she had to tell him that she couldn't stay. This was getting too far out of hand. It wasn't fair to Sy for him to think her a lady in the traditional sense, worthy of a title such as his. She removed the knife from under her pillow and slipped it into the belt behind her back, making her feel more like herself. She checked the mirror again to be sure that it was fully concealed behind her hair. She had to tell him the truth, tonight. Feeling a little better, she looked around for her gloves. Just as she located them there was a knock on her door. Hilda poked her head in.

"Your callers are here, my lady," she said.

"Thank you, Hilda,"

With one last look at herself, and with a determined resolve, she walked out the door to meet her fate.

SY WAITED IMPATIENTLY in the foyer with Titan. He paced, slapping his gloves against his thigh. Did she like the necklace? Maybe he should have waited until he posted the banns to give her gifts. What the hell was wrong with him? He was like a schoolboy going to his first ball. Titan leaned jauntily against the door jamb watching him wearing his signature cat who ate the canary smile. Could the man be any more irritating?

"Anxious to see the opera, Sy? Didn't take you for an opera lover," he said sarcastically.

"Shut up, Titan." Sy snapped, irritated.

Aunt Magda came floating down the staircase.

"Good evening gentlemen. I hope you haven't been waiting long," she said, politely.

"No aunt, not at all. We have just arrived. Is Rhea ready?" Titan looked at Sy, who was staring at the top of the staircase. Rhea stood there, staring down at him.

"Titan dear, will you please help me retrieve my wrap? I

believe it's in the parlor," Aunt Magda said, in a hushed tone as she grabbed Titan's arm and pulled him along.

Sy walked to the bottom step of the staircase as Rhea descended.

"You look incredible, Minx," he said, with a rakish smile, and extended his hand to help her down the last few steps.

"Anyone would look incredible with such adornments, my lord. You are most generous," she said sincerely, locking eyes with his.

Rhea looked unbelievably beautiful making his heart race. As she reached the bottom of the stairs, she stepped so close he could see her pulse in her throat. He wanted to kiss the spot, feel the flutter on his lips.

"Not true. You are not just anyone." He leaned in closer and took in her scent, good lord, he could not get enough of this woman.

"Shall we go?" Titan said, much louder than necessary once he took in the scene between Rhea and Sy.

RHEA HAD to tear her eyes away from Sy's. He tucked her hand in his arm to escort her out the door. Once outside the men helped the ladies into the carriage. Titan sat next to Rhea and Sy tried to squeeze himself next to Aunt Magda. Titan and Sy's knees wouldn't fit sitting across from each other. Aunt Magda suggested that Sy sit across from Rhea and Titan across from her to maximize foot space. Sy jumped out of the carriage and helped Aunt Magda out, followed by Titan. Sy climbed back in, followed by Aunt Magda then Titan. Magda was appalled by how her and Rhea's dresses were being crushed.

"This is ridiculous! We will just have to take two carriages or we will all arrive a wrinkled mess. Titan help me out of this contraption!" she said, in irritation. Titan jumped down and helped his aunt from the carriage. Once she was out, she poked her head into the door.

"You two go ahead, Titan and I will catch up in a moment." She closed the door and instructed the driver to leave. The carriage took off.

"You did that on purpose," Titan stated to his aunt. "People will talk when they arrive without a chaperone."

"It's time that we talk Titan. I have much to tell you." The Chamberlain carriage was trotting towards them. It would have taken several minutes to order her carriage readied. Titan narrowed his eyes at his aunt.

"You did plan that!" Titan exclaimed, surprised he was actually right.

"Just help an old woman into the carriage," Aunt Magda said, sardonically, as the carriage came to a stop in front of them.

~

RHEA COULD BARELY SEE Sy in the shadows of the

carriage but she could certainly could feel his presence. She had the overwhelming urge to touch his leg.

"How long will it take to get to the opera house?" she asked, instead. Time to get this awkward conversation over with.

"It's a short distance, about five to seven minutes at the most," he answered. Not enough time for the conversation they needed to have. It would have to wait.

"My lord...Sy, I mean. Why did you buy me this necklace?" she asked.

"You are my Marchioness. You should dress like one," he replied, flatly. She couldn't see his face to read his reaction. He leaned forward into the light. "It's a tradition for a Marquess to adorn his wife with jewels. Don't you like it?" he asked.

"It's beautiful," she replied, truthfully, fingering the necklace but she was disappointed with his answer.

"I wasn't going to do this till later but since we are conveniently alone...the necklace was a gift from the Marquess to his Marchioness, but this is a gift from me, to you. It just seemed to suit you better somehow." He produced a velvet pouch from his breast pocket and handed it to her. She took it, untied the string and let the object slide into her hand. It was a knife. It had an ivory handle with carvings on it. The handle curved into a small face of an animal she didn't recognize. The animal's eyes were aquamarine stones. She looked at the knife and tears welled in her eyes, then she looked at his face. He was looking at the knife and didn't notice.

"I had it made for you. Look here." He turned the knife into the little bit of candlelight in the carriage. "On this side, our intertwined initials are carved." He turned the knife over. "On the other side is the Blackthorne B. It's a good weight for you and totally balanced in case you need to throw it. I had the knife curved at the end so it cannot easily slip from your hand. I wager you your new necklace that you can't guess what the animal's face is though..." When he looked at her his sentence drifted off. "Rhea, why are you crying?" he asked, alarmed. He leaned forward and wiped away her tears.

"It's just...it's just that..." say it Rhea. *I think I love you.* He really did know her, at least on some level. But she couldn't get the words out, she was too frightened. She decided to show him instead. "You please me so much." She whispered and lunged at him. He had to scramble to keep from cutting her with the knife. He dropped it on the seat and caught her. She kissed him with all the love that she felt. She pulled away to look at his face. "Thank you," she said, looking in his eyes, grateful the carriage was dark and he couldn't see her expression. She sat on his lap instead of returning to her seat. "You were saying something about a wager?"

SY SAT STUNNED FOR A MOMENT. What just happened? He wanted to kiss her again, he hugged her close. It felt good having her on his lap, right, as it should be. As she leaned over to picked up the knife from the seat, her breast rubbed his arm. His member immediately started to thicken. Good God, this woman was going to be the death of him. She examined the knife closer under the light.

"What animal's face is that? A cat?" she asked, as she turned it at different angles examining it. He watched her face in the candlelight. He could see her eyes sparkling with excitement. His heart skipped a beat.

"It's a Minx, with aquamarine eyes," he stated.

"Oh Sy, its beautiful!"

"You're beautiful Rhea. And you're mine." He pulled her in for a kiss. It started gently then quickly grew feverish. The carriage jolted to a halt. They had arrived at the opera house. Rhea quickly discarded her old knife between the cushions and put her new knife in her belt. Sy chuckled.

"What?" she asked innocently.

"My little Minx," he said, gave her a quick kiss, and set her back on her own seat. He exited and helped Rhea down. They stood outside looking at each other for a brief moment.

"Are you ready for this?" he asked, her searching her face.

"Are you sure this is what you want? It's not too late to change your mind," she asked, feeling insecure.

"I don't think I've wanted anything more in my life," he said with sincerity, as he rubbed the back of his fingers down her cheek. He lifted her hand, gave it a lingering kiss, then tucked it into the crook of his arm. "We are in this together till the end. Shall we?" He didn't wait for her answer and started walking up the steps of the opera house. The carriage rolled away and the next rolled up.

"Rhea, Sy, wait for your old aunt!" Aunt Magda called from her carriage window. The door opened and Titan climbed out to assist her. They caught up the few steps to Rhea and Sy so they could enter the opera house together.

"Well done," Titan said to his aunt, who gave him a knowing smile in return. His expression changed when he locked eyes with Sy. Anger radiated from Titan.

The opera house lobby was full of members of the *Ton*, all dressed in their finery. A hush rolled over the crowd when the two couples walked into the lobby. All eyes turned to stare at Sy and Rhea. Within seconds the noise returned to its previous level. Sy gave Rhea's hand a reassuring squeeze as they entered the lobby. They were immediately surrounded. Sy greeted everyone politely and switched his hand to the small of Rhea's back to guide her through the throng. They stopped to talk to another couple but he did not remove his hand. Instead, he slipped it further around her waist and gently pulled her closer. The couple noticed this immediately, excused themselves quickly, and scurried off to another group to report what they have seen.

"That should do it," Sy leaned in closer than was proper to whisper in her ear. "If not, then this certainly will," he whispered, his voice a low baritone. His hot breath on the side of her face and neck made her shiver. She resisted the urge to close her eyes and lean into his lips for more. She turned her head slightly towards his.

"If you keep up these ministrations, my lord, I will lose my composure and there will be no doubt of our intentions for each other. As it is, I am holding on by a thread," she whispered back. She did not just say that! Did she?

He gave her a low sensual growl. "Minx!" he whispered before he straightened up to his full height and looked down at her with his rakish smile.

"Aren't you going to introduce me Sy?" A female voice came from in front of them.

~

RHEA FELT Sy's muscles tense and alarm bells went off in her head. She looked at the woman. She was a beautiful brunette with large brown eyes and creamy pale skin. The woman was older than Rhea by a few years which was evident by her stature and confidence. She ignored Rhea completely as she looked at Sy. It was apparent that she knew him intimately since she used his given name. A young, tall, gentleman with blonde hair and bright blue eyes escorted her. He was devilishly handsome and it was obvious that he knew it, too. He gave them a sly smile as he waited for Sy to answer. Sy slid his hand to Rhea's lower back once again. Rhea could sense that this time it was not just a show for the audience but an instinctual move of possessiveness. The hairs on the back of her neck went up. She slowly moved her arm to her back and rested it on top of Sy's, close to her knife.

"May I present Lady Rhea Hastings," Sy said, in a cautious voice. "Lady Hastings, may I present Lady Amelia

Willoboughy and her stepson Lord William Willoboughy," he continued, in a tight voice. Rhea made a small curtsy, and Sy's hand tightened at her waist. Rhea didn't think Sy was even aware of what he was doing.

"Lady Hastings? *The* Lady Hastings?" Lady Willoboughy's head snapped to Rhea's face. "You are the little island girl that everyone is talking about? My, my…" she raked her eyes from the top of Rhea's head down to her toes. "You aren't at all what I expected." She said it in a sweet tone but it was evident that it was a cut to Rhea. Sy tensed and Rhea could see his anger as he clenched his jaw in reaction. She squeezed his arm.

"Why thank you for the compliment Lady Willoboughy. I pride myself on being unexpected. You do me an honor," she cut back, just as sweetly with another small curtsy. William chuckled, but quickly caught himself and tried to disguise it as a cough.

"*Sy*, do you think there's enough time for a glass of champagne before we have to go to our box?" Rhea asked, looking at his face adoringly. Before Sy could answer Lord Willoboughy chimed into the conversation.

"Well, I certainly can see what all the talk is about. Lady Hastings you truly are unique, not only in beauty but also in wit, as well. It is no surprise that you have made an impression on these starchy members of the *Ton*. You are a breath of fresh air sorely needed." William bowed and took Rhea's hand even though she did not present it. He kissed it while keeping his eyes on her, and lingered longer than necessary.

He held out his arm next. "It would be my honor to escort you to the champagne table."

Rhea could feel anger bubbling in Sy. His jaw was clenched and a muscle was ticking on the side of his face. She was sure Lord Willoboughy could see the raw anger he was evoking, and enjoying it.

"That won't be necessary, Lord Willoboughy," Sy said through clenched teeth.

"Come now Blackthorne, you have her for the whole evening, certainly you can spare her for a stroll across the room," he said, ignoring Sy's anger and staring at Rhea.

"That's a wonderful idea. It will give us a moment to catch up. It's been a long time since we last saw each other. I would love to hear of your adventures Sy," Lady Willoboughy interjected.

SY WAS SEETHING. They were backed into a corner. It would be rude for Rhea not to take Lord Willoboughy's arm. The thought of that bastard touching or spending time with Rhea made his blood boil. Get ahold of yourself man. It's just a walk across the room. He couldn't make a scene. Not tonight. They had to get through the evening to lay the foundation of their match. Causing a scene would result in a scandal and that needed to be avoided at all costs. He was forced to relent. He gave Rhea a reluctant nod. She gave him an understanding smile and squeezed his arm behind her back. As he slowly released her, he felt her put her hand on the hilt of her knife. Good girl. It was torture to see her take Willoboughy's hand and let him lead her away. Sy watched him escort her to the table laden with glasses of champagne. He felt a physical pain in his heart as they separated. He felt a slap of a fan on the side of his arm.

"Sy are you listening to me?" Lady Willoboughy said in a pouty voice.

"Apologies, what were you saying?" he answered, obviously annoyed. He looked at Amelia. He once thought her beautiful, now she paled in comparison to Rhea.

"How long have you been back?" she asked again, now that she had his attention, and gave him a coquettish look he recognized from before.

"A little over three weeks."

"Three weeks! Why have you not come to see me?" she asked, shocked.

"That's over Amelia, and you know it," he replied flatly.

"It doesn't have to be Sy," she said softly, and discreetly rubbed her fan on his arm. He stepped back out of her reach. A clear message. She looked disappointed and angry.

"Well, when you tire of babysitting the *Ton's* new 'on dit,' let me know," she said angrily and stormed off in a huff. He could hear a few giggles from the lookie-loos nearby. Good, another step in the right direction. Hmmm, he's married to the *Ton's* new 'on dit'? This night just kept getting better and better. He looked over at Rhea. When William took a flirtatious step in her direction, she immediately countered with at step back. He could see her hand behind her hair, reaching for her knife. Anger surged and he started toward them.

"YOU REALLY ARE exquisite Lady Hastings. You eye color is most unusual." He took another step closer. She'd had enough of this cad. In one swift move, she withdrew her knife and placed it in the folds of her skirt. Come closer, you bastard, and I'll surely give you a night to remember, she thought to herself. Sure enough, he took another step toward her. She quickly turned and wedged her knife at his groin. He looked down and his eyes widened in surprise.

"You overstep, my lord. You mistake me for a different type of lady. I would appreciate that you keep a respectable distance in the future or we will surely cause a scene," she hissed.

He looked down at the knife and then into her eyes. His eyes instantly changed from surprise to lust.

"Well, aren't you full of delightful surprises. Shall we meet later then?" he whispered. He pressed his hip forward slightly and twisted so he brushed his genitals against her hand. Bile rose in her throat.

"You are a dead man." A deep menacing voice came from behind Rhea, igniting the telltale shivers and butterflies. She lowered her knife discreetly and replaced it in her belt. She looked at Willoboughy's pants and there was a small cut in the fabric.

"That won't be necessary, my lord, Lord Willoboughy needs to go home and tend to his trousers," she said, with a sweet smile. "Come, my lord, please take me to our box. I feel slightly ill to my stomach." She tugged discreetly on Sy's arm but he didn't budge. He was staring down Willoboughy, livid. "Please, my lord, all is well," she pleaded softly.

"This isn't over Willoboughy," Sy threatened. Willoboughy's eyes widened. Sy took Rhea's hand, put his arm around her waist, and started to walk away when she stopped him and turned back to Lord Willoboughy.

"Oh, and Lord Willoboughy, may I suggest that the tailor take in your trousers, they are far too big for such a small... offering," she said clearly for all within earshot, then retook Sy's hand as they walked toward the theater. Lord Willoboughy turned three shades of red at her comment and turned to leave the building, ignoring the snickers coming from around him.

"I'm sorry, my lord, I shouldn't have said that. My apologies, I let my temper get the best of me." She sounded contrite, even embarrassed.

"No apologies necessary, my lady. I'm proud of you." He gave her a sincere smile. Then the smile left his face. "You will not leave my side for the rest of the evening understood?" he said, sternly.

"I never wanted to in the first place," she stated softly. That earned her the rakish smile that she was falling in love with and made her heart race. Damn, she wished she could kiss him right now. They turned to walk into the box.

"Thank you again for my gift. It has already proven to be very useful," she said, before they entered. Sy chuckled. Titan and her aunt were already seated.

"It was my pleasure, I assure you," he replied, holding the chair for her. He sat her next to her aunt, then took the seat behind her next to Titan. He looked at Titan and got a scowl for his effort. Who put a bee in his bonnet?

"You missed all the fun." He leaned close to Titan and spoke softly. "I need to talk to you later, if you don't have plans for the evening. There's been trouble with Willoboughy."

"It seems I've been missing quite a lot, lately. I wish to have a word with you, too." Titan said angrily.

CHAPTER 15

*T*he opera was boring. Sy was reminded why he never attended. Rhea seemed to enjoy the music, giving a hearty applause at the end. Aunt Magda asked to go home at intermission, pleading leg pain. Titan reluctantly offered to escort her, Rhea insisted they all leave together. The never-ending stream of people stopping by the box during intermission for an introduction to the new sweetheart of the *Ton* prevented their departure in any case. It seemed the scene in the lobby had only served to elevate her position. Many were happy that she had called out the notorious rake Lord William Willoboughy. His little Minx was not only a beauty, but a force to be reckoned with. After the performance, Sy could tell she was exhausted, even though she tried to hide her yawns. She leaned heavily on his arm as they tried to exit the opera house, but many stopped them for either an introduction or to issue an invitation. Rhea greeted each person with grace and charm, a stark contrast to her treatment of the infamous rake Willoboughy. Sy finally pushed his way through the throng and put her into their carriage.

Once inside, she sighed and leaned her head against the wall. Three late nights in a row were catching up with her. She looked so adorable sitting there, trying to keep her eyes open for his sake. He couldn't take it another moment. He reached over, pulled her into his lap, and cuddled her against his chest. She felt so right there. When she sighed, and snuggled against his neck, a sense of satisfaction and contentment washed over him.

"You were sensational tonight, a natural Marchioness. No one will be surprised when I post the banns next week," he said softly, and kissed the top of her head.

"Uh hum…" she said sleepily. She nuzzled her nose under his chin and gave him a soft kiss.

"I will talk to your brother tonight and make my formal offer but, by his attitude earlier, I have a suspicion that your aunt has already informed him of our situation," he continued. She reached her hand up lazily, and slowly untied his cravat. He acted as if he didn't notice.

"Maybe," she said softly.

"We should attend at least one dinner and one other public event. I could escort you to the museum if there isn't a party you'd like to attend. Then we will be done with this business," he said, flatly.

Rhea removed her gloves and undid his buttons at his

collar. His heart started pounding with the memories of their first evening at the Wessex's. His breath caught as her fingers skimmed his skin when she pulled his collar apart. His arm tightened around her reflexively. He groaned when her lips connected with his now tingling skin. She licked and sucked from his collar bone to his chin.

"Mmmm, I've been waiting to do that all night," she said softly in his ear. Her hot breath wreaked havoc on his senses. She reached down, lifted her dress past her thighs, turned, and straddled his lap. His member turned rock hard at the sight of her shapely legs. He got a glimpse of his mark on her thigh. All the possibilities this new position came to mind. "But mostly I have been waiting to do this..." She gently licked the crevasse of his lips, opened his mouth with her fingers on his chin and sucked his lower lip into her mouth. He lost all control at that point. He took her possessively, thrusting his tongue into her mouth feverishly. He put his hand at the back of her neck to hold her captive. Then he kissed his way down her neck sucking the tender spot where he could feel her heartbeat. She put her head back to give him better access, arching her breasts into his chest. He ravished her collar bone before he worked his way down to cleavage of her breasts. One strong tug at her sleeves and her breasts were exposed to him.

"Beautiful," he whispered, then circled one of her nipples with his tongue. She moaned and arched her back putting her hands on his shoulders, as she did her sex brushed against his erection. White hot heat surged, leaving him throbbing. A groan escaped from deep in his throat and he sucked her nipple into his mouth, she arched against him again. He repeated the sweet torment with her other nipple.

"Sy...," she pleaded, her voice ragged with ecstasy as the carriage swayed to a stop.

"Damn it!" Sy exclaimed. He growled in frustration and took her nipple in his mouth one more time and suckled it. She groaned and arched against him again. Then he let her go and pulled her dress back into place. He buttoned his collar and with jerky frustrated motions, then loosely tied his cravat. He looked into her eyes and pulled her hips against his arousal. She circled her hips against his hardness and arched her back to increase the pressure on the pleasurable sensation. Oh my, it felt so good!

"Sy!" she moaned.

He stopped her, and growled in frustration again, he was tired of this torture.

"I have to get you out of this carriage, right now," he said, coarsely. He saw her recoil from him. Sy lifted her off his lap and set her roughly on the other seat and exited the carriage. Once outside, he bent over as if in pain. He rested his hands on his knees and took a several deep breaths. Rhea leaned forward and peeked out the door to see what was keeping him.

"Sy? Is all well?" she asked, innocently, embarrassed.

He laughed and tried to stand up. Once composed, as much as he could be, he adjusted himself, hoping he wasn't too vulgar, and offered his hand to help her out of the carriage. As she climbed down he got a good look at her cleavage and groaned as his arousal throbbed again. He walked her up the steps of her aunt's townhouse. Once there, he lifted her chin.

"I regret that I am unable to see you inside this evening, Minx," he stated. Tears welled in her eyes, it was like a stab to his heart.

"Did I do something wrong?" she asked, in a sheepish voice. This was killing him. Damn, this stupid farce they had to play. She should be going home with him right now so they could continue what they started. Now she felt insecure.

"No love, you were perfect. It wouldn't be decent for me to greet your aunt or anybody in my current condition, understand?" He tried to be reassuring, but he knew she didn't have a full understanding. Standing on the front stoop was not the place to educate her. "I'll come and visit you tomorrow."

"As you wish, my lord." She looked at her feet embarrassed, defeated. Damn it, she was back to 'my lord.'

"Rhea, promise me you won't read into this, you must trust me," he said firmly.

"As you wish, my lord."

Damn, damn, damn. She opened the door and went in. "Goodnight, my lord," she said, forlornly.

"Good night Rhea." He watched as she closed the door softly.

Damn it to hell! Where was her infernal brother? He needed to get this conversation over with so he could get back here, to her. He would explain, show her that he loved her touch. He bounded to the carriage and barked orders to the driver. Once inside he banged his head on the back wall and relished the pain. He handled that horribly. She is innocent of men, not some hussy from the brothel that would be pleased by his condition, he could see that now. She was so full of passion and desire, so responsive. He loved that. He never meant for her to feel as if she couldn't be herself with him. Damn it! The coach rolled up to his townhouse and he opened the door before it came to a complete halt.

"Stay here," he yelled up to the driver, before taking the steps two at a time and bursting through the door.

"Syers!" he bellowed. "Syers!" he bellowed again, impatiently. The startled butler came running down the hallway, putting his night wrapper on as he went.

"Yes, my lord, is there a fire?" he asked, scanning the room for an emergency. Sy immediately felt guilty.

"Apologies, Syers, I have an urgent matter to discuss with Lord Huntington. He is expecting a message that I have returned. Please send someone to fetch him. Whomever can take the carriage. Tell them to do what it takes but bring him to me immediately." He rushed out.

"I will see to it myself, my lord." He bowed and rushed out of the room.

Sy walked into his study and poured himself a healthy portion of brandy. He drank the entire glass in one gulp. Damn. Damn. Damn. He poured another glass. Someone started pounding the front door, followed by another impatient round of pounding. He could hear Syers running to answer. Next came Titan's bellow. Sy smiled, *he definitely knows.* He suddenly felt leagues better, he didn't have to be the one to break the news.

"Lord Huntington requests an audience, my lord," Syers announced, at his study door, trying to sound formal despite Titan's anger.

"Damn right I do!" Titan shouted, as he barged past the staunch butler.

"It's alright Syers, please bring more brandy and dismiss the coach," he said, calmly.

"And just when were you going to inform me about this arrangement between you and Rhea?" he said, angrily. "Here I thought you were taking a genuine interest in her, but now I find out it's all a ruse for business! I won't have it, Sy, my sister is not to be a pawn for seats in the House of Lords, do you hear me!" He was getting angrier with each sentence.

"May I remind you that I am not the mastermind behind this. Our fathers are. I am just as much a pawn as Rhea," he said, defensively.

"Don't play coy with me, Sy," he said, seething. "Aunt Magda, with a little persuasion, told me everything. I will not have it, damned the seat, we will find another way to do business, if needed."

"I'm afraid it's much more complicated than that, Titan," he said, calmly. He respected Titan's protectiveness. "I'm afraid the contract is binding and the marks have been made. She is my wife. I intend to fulfill my end of the agreement."

"You don't understand, Sy. She is not like other women. I know she seems like it here, all dressed up for London life, but you have to trust me when I tell you she's...she's..." Titan struggled to find the words, "she's different."

"I don't understand Titan, you said your parents sent her here to make the match?" he asked. This could be a problem. What if Titan were to disapprove, it could cause a problem with Rhea. He never considered that Titan would object to the match. His heart dropped at the possibility.

"I WOULD NOT OBJECT if it weren't for other circum-stances that complicate the matter." Titan gave as a feeble explanation. How could Titan possibly expound without giving up her identity and his own breaking their oath in the process? Originally, he thought Sy was the perfect match for her, but truthfully, he never thought it would amount to anything since they were to leave soon. Then he found out about the arrangement. He half expected Sy to want out, he should have known better. He saw how Sy reacted to Rhea at the ball and in the days since. He ran his hand through his hair and sat down next to the fireplace, dejected, not knowing how to proceed. "Truthfully, I thought she would come here and attend a few functions, maybe the opera, to appease my parents. Then we would go back."

"Do you disapprove of me as a match for your sister?

That is really the only issue here," Sy asked firmly, unconsciously holding his breath waiting for Titan's reply.

Titan dropped his head into his hands and spoke softly.

"Actually, you are perfect for her, in almost every way."

Sy released the pent-up breath as relief washed over him.

"Then I don't understand, Titan. Why are you so distraught? I have come to accept it and I believe Rhea is showing signs of accepting it too," he pointed out, a rakish smile lifting his lips.

"Do you love her?" Titan looked him straight in the face and searched his eyes for the truth. "Or could you love her in time at least?"

For a moment, Sy went completely still. Titan could see he had surprised him with the question. He watched Sy consider the question carefully, one he clearly had not considered before. He knew the moment Sy had come to a decision.

"With all that I am," Sy answered, confidently. Titan relaxed.

Sy realized he had just passed a test of some kind.

"You will need to love her. That will be the only way to get to the end of this thing. There are things about my family that may be hard for you to accept," he confessed.

"What things?" he asked, confused.

"It is not for me to say. Trust me, you will find out soon enough. Are you willing to blindly take on the challenge? If you aren't, let her go now. Annul the marriage and walk away. I'll not have her hurt," Titan threatened.

~

THE THOUGHT of never seeing Rhea again twisted his stomach. He wanted her, needed her, lusted for her, and had to see her every day since she came to his room that night. No, it was before that. It began when they met in his father's parlor. He was enchanted with her ever since. He thought of their time in the carriage, when holding her on his lap would've been enough, the feeling of contentment he felt when she was with him, of his overwhelming possessiveness of her. The thought of her with another man gave him physical pain. He looked into Titan's eyes.

"Nothing will ever take Rhea from me! Whatever it is that you speak of makes no difference. Rhea is mine and I will fight to the death before I let anyone take what is mine! Even you Titan." Sy was practically shouting. He could see tears welling in Titan's eyes, his love for his sister evident.

"Well then, welcome to the family." He extended his hand. Sy slapped Titan's forearm in a healthy handshake. Titan returned it in equal measure. "Good luck, you are going to have your hands full!" Titan teased, belying a grain of truth.

"I wouldn't have it any other way," he replied. "Now out. I have somewhere important to be."

"Goodbye *brother*," he said, sardonically, laughing in relief.

Sy ran up the stairs two at a time, shedding his formals as he went. He pulled out his black shirt and boots donned them as quickly as he could. He was about to go to Rhea's townhouse when he smelled the faintest hint of jasmine. He turned, and there she was, in the same dark cloak she wore the first time she came. She looked like a nymph, with her hood covering her hair and only her beautiful face visible. Only black slippers were peeking out from under her cloak everything else was concealed. She stepped forward , close the door to his room and pushed her hood back. He was mesmerized and couldn't move a muscle. She reached up and untied her cloak, her hands shook as she pulled the ribbons. It fluttered to the floor. She stood there completely naked, except for her slippers.

She was perfect. Her long blond tresses surrounded her beautiful face and cascaded down in waves well past her breasts. She had a long slender neck, full round breasts with rosy nipples, a perfect curve to her waist and flat belly, and a light brown triangle of hair at the juncture of long shapely legs. His mouth went dry seeing her in all her glory. He knew she was beautiful but he underestimated her greatly. She blushed delightfully under his scrutiny.

"I can do better if you will allow me to try. I just need for you to teach me," she said, her voice cracking, tears welling in her eyes.

He was jolted out of his stupor. He caused this, and he was going to damn well fix it.

"Rhea, if you get any better, you will kill me," he stated light heartily. "You misunderstood my actions tonight. I could barely walk with the arousal you caused, much less face your aunt if she was awake. Do you understand?" Her eyes widened for a moment then he could see her features relax, and a small smile lift her lips. Thank God.

"I'm relieved to hear it, my lord. I was willing to practice until I got it right. I can see you are preparing to leave. I don't wish to disturb...." She started to reach for her cloak but didn't get close to touching it before he was upon her. In two long strides, he scooped her up in his arms.

"Oh, no you don't."

His mouth descended on hers before she could say another word. She threw her arms around his neck and pulled him to her with all her strength. He melted into her warmth as he plundered her mouth. A feeling of gratification warmed him. He walked over to the bed, laid her down gently, and propped himself up above her.

"YOU HAVE ME AT A DISADVANTAGE, sir. I believe you have too many clothes on," she teased, looking into his eyes. Without a word, he stood, took off his boots, and quickly divested himself of the rest of his clothing. He was about to lay back down when she sat up and pressed her hand on his belly to stop him.

"Wait," she said. She looked up at his eyes, then to his chest. She stood in of front him and shyly pressed her hands to his chest. He closed his eyes briefly when her hands made contact with his skin. She needed to touch him, explore his body, to know him everywhere as he did her. She rubbed her hands up to his neck. She stood on tip toes to reach behind his neck and untie the piece of leather that held his queue. He moaned when her breasts rubbed against him. She ran her fingers through the thick black mass of hair languishing in its silky softness. She bought handfuls around to frame his face as she lowered from her toes. He looked down at her with his piercing blue eyes, desire evident in his stare, but continued to stand still to let her explore. He was even more handsome with his hair unbound, giving him a wild barbaric appearance. Her heart skipped a beat when he reached up and lovingly traced the back of his fingers down the side of her face. She closed her eyes and leaned into the caress. She stopped his hand and placed it back at his side her message clear. It was her turn.

She caressed his chest again, feeling the sinew of his hard muscle under his soft skin then turned her hand over and ran the back of it down his sculpted abdomen. He sucked in his breath when her hand brushed his hair and the base of his shaft. She eyed his nipple and decided to taste it. She rose up on her toes slightly to reach it and was rewarded with a sensual groan when she licked it gently with her tongue, then sucked it into her mouth, it turned into a hard peek. He threw his head back when she circled it with her tongue one more time. She licked her way across to the other nipple and gave it equal attention while she slid her hands around to his back feeling his muscles quiver there and pulled him closer. Relishing in the taste of him, she ran her tongue down to his naval, while sliding her hands lower down his back at the same pace. Once at his naval, she plunged her tongue in and swirled it around a few times. She sat back on the bed as she moved even lower, nuzzled her nose in the trail of hair that lead down from his navel as she slid her hands over his buttocks squeezing his firm flesh. She moaned at the delicious feel of him and the musky smell of his skin. Her hot breath on his belly made his muscles tremble He moaned. She smiled with satisfaction.

"Rhea you must stop… It's not a…" he whispered.

She grabbed his hips firmly so he couldn't step away. She could feel the tip of his erection hitting her chest. She looked down and put her hand around it just under its pillowy head. He sucked in his breath.

"Rhea you have no idea what…oh God…"

She slid her hand down to the bottom of his shaft. It was soft but hard and she loved the feel of it, then slowly slid her hand back up to the head again enjoying herself playing as she went twisting slightly and pulling the skin gently. A bead of liquid escaped the end. She licked the bead to taste it. It was salty, she put her mouth over the head and suckled to get a little more.

"GOOD GOD, Rhea… you have to stop… I can't…" Sy was losing his ability to concentrate, her mouth was so hot and moist. It felt so good he was going to spill his seed in her mouth any second. She took more of his shaft into her mouth and her soft tongue rubbed against the sensitive spot just below its head as she sucked harder. Oh God, he wanted to grab her head and thrust into her hot moist mouth. He'd be damned if that was going to be her first experience. He reached down and took her hand off him and put his hands under her arm pits and lifted her off the bed, completely off her feet.

"Good God, Rhea, have you done that before?" he asked, looking into her eyes.

"Never, my lord, did you not like it?" she asked, concerned. Her brows furrowed in confusion.

"Like it?" he asked incredulously. He brought his mouth to hers and showed her how much he liked it. "You are incredible, my delicious Minx."

She put her legs around his waist and melted into his kiss. Once she was holding on he lowered her back down to the bed. They kissed as if they had no more time together, feverishly, manically. He moved to the side of her face and sucked on her earlobe. She moaned when his hot breath warmed her ear. He moved down her neck and chest to take her nipple in his mouth, circled each one with his tongue till they were rosy peaks, then sucked them into his mouth slowly deliberately. She gasped and thrust her hips up to show her pleasure.

He moved down her belly and smiled as reached her belly button. He gave it the same attention she gave his mimicking her every move as he slid his hand down into her triangle of hair. She was wet and ready. He could wait not longer to taste her. He moved down the bed, kneeling on the floor. He spread her legs, separated her folds then ran his tongue up and down her sensitive skin. She rocked her hips back and forth with the pleasure he was giving her. He plunged his tongue as far as he could into her entry. Then in a slow tortuous pace he ran the flat of his tongue up to her nub and sucked it into his mouth. He took pleasure in her quivering muscles as he worked her nub into a hard pebble. She moaned, thrashing her head side to side clenching the sheets, close to climaxing, he could feel it. He put a finger inside her and she gasped at the invasion. He added a second trying to prepare her for his engorged member. He spread his fingers a few times then he sucked her nub into his mouth again and flicked it with his tongue as he pumped his fingers into her. She grabbed the top of his head and pulled his hair gently as her climax built. He couldn't wait any longer. He raised himself up and guided the tip of his erection to her entry. He slid the tip in. Oh. My. God. She was hot, wet and oh so tight as she encased him. She put her feet flat on the bed, thrust her hips forward and pushed him in deeper. He put his head back and groaned at the sheer pleasure. He had to make her his now. He took her legs and put them around his hips. He slid in as far as he could, until he hit the membrane that was her virginity. Satisfaction poured over him that he was to be her first, her only. He pulled back and thrust into her hard, ripping the membrane. She cried out in pain and he stopped.

"You are truly mine now Rhea, now and forever. The pain

will pass, I promise," he soothed. He kissed her with tenderness and the love he was feeling at this special moment. "Are you well?"

"It wasn't that bad really." She stared at his neck.

"Rhea, look at me." She met his eyes and he saw confusion there.

"Um, are we done then?" she asked shyly.

He chuckled. "No Rhea. We are far from done." He pushed up onto his elbows and looked down at her as he said it. He pulled out slightly then pushed back into her gently. She gasped in surprise, closed her eyes and arched against him. "Does that hurt?"

"No, no, do it again." She squeezed her legs and tried to pull him in deeper.

That was all the encouragement he needed, he lost all rational thought at her words and movements. He got to his knees and grabbed her hips and plunged into her. She felt so good, so tight, so wet. He couldn't stop himself, he thrust harder and faster chasing his orgasm. She met him thrust for thrust, arching her back in pleasure, rocking her hips side to side to take him deeper. When he was close, he put his thumb on her nub and let the rhythm of their love making take her to the edge. She was turning her head side to side as her ecstasy built. Then she stopped thrashing and he could feel her pulsating around his erection as her orgasm came. It was his undoing, his seed burst into her violently. He threw his head back as his body was racked with an orgasm of his own.

He fell to her side knowing she couldn't bear his weight and brought her limp body with him. He wasn't ready to leave her yet. Incredible, that was incredible, was all he could think. He kissed the top of Rhea's head and she gave him a weak hug in return. He chuckled. Simply perfect.

"When can we do that again?" she asked.

CHAPTER 16

*R*hea couldn't move her arms or legs. Her head was pinned down, too. She tried to open her eyes, but her lids were too heavy. What was that delicious smell? She inhaled deeply, it was familiar. She smiled, it was Sy's smell, musky and wonderful. She turned her head toward the soft breathing next to her ear and cracked one eye open. Sy was sound asleep next to her. Memories came flooding back. They made love for hours and they must've fallen asleep. They fell asleep! What time was it? She needed to get back to the townhouse before they discovered she was gone! She looked out the window. The dawn was lighting the sky but it was still early. She had to hurry.

She looked over at Sy again. He looked so peaceful in his repose. His face was relaxed and his black lashes fanned his cheeks. They were quite long and curly for a man's lashes she noticed. His skin was shiny with a lite sheen of sweat covering his brow and several tendrils of his black hair were clinging to his wet neck. Oh, how she loved that neck. She sighed and tried to move her arm. She was completely trapped laying on her back with one of his massive arms under her breasts pinning her upper body and a heavy leg thrown over hers. To further complicate things most of her hair was trapped under his head. She would rather just sneak away while he was sleeping but that was not going to be possible. She tried again to move his arm gently. It wouldn't budge.

"Where are you going, Minx?" he said, sleepily, and pulled her closer to him. He didn't open his eyes and turned his nose into her hair and inhaled. He smiled, a boyish smile that made her smile in return. She tried again to free one arm and he lifted his slightly to accommodate her. She ran her fingers along his hairline to brush the loose tendrils off his face and neck. She couldn't resist rubbing the back of her fingers up and down his neck.

"Hmmm," she sighed with pleasure. "I have to go. It's almost dawn."

"I don't care. You're mine. You stay." He lifted his arm from her chest, ran his hand down her belly and into the triangle of hair. He cupped her sex and stuck a finger inside her. She sucked in her breath and arched against his hand, her skin still sensitive from long hours of love play.

"Are you tender?" He put his thumb on her nub and started making lazy circles. A look of pure satisfaction was on his face when her eyes became hooded and her hips started grinding against his hand. He repeated his question. "Are you tender?"

"No... yes...no...ah, a little," she moaned, in reply.

"You're so wet and ready for me." He removed his leg and lifted her up to straddle him. "Let's do this right this time." Her eyes widened in remembrance of the first time she strad-dled him. He lifted her to hover above his erection. Then he slowly guided her hips down as he entered her.

"Oh my," she sighed, as she impaled him. "This is sooo much better." He lifted her up and let her slide down at her own pace. She took over from there, increasing the rhythm faster and faster as she chased her fulfillment. He kept his hands on her hips only because he wanted to touch her, she set the pace. She put her hands on his chest to steady herself. He watched her as she made love to him, her hair swung about and her breasts bounced with the rhythm she set. Then to his surprise she arched her back and put her hands behind her, straddling his legs. Her hair pooled on his thighs as she started grinding her hips against his erection. Good God, he was so deep. She was fully impaled on him. She ground her hips harder and moved them side to side then in circles. It was so erotic watching her taking him with abandon. White hot heat shot through him as his orgasm threatened. Suddenly she shot back forward, her hands slapping against his chest squeezing the muscles there. He lost control.

"God damn," he whispered and thrust his hips up and pulled her back and forth on his erection with his hands on her hips. She let out a long groan and he could feel the spasms of her orgasm gripping his shaft. He let go and exploded inside her. White light came from behind his eyes as he spilled his seed in her. Then she collapsed on his chest, her hair like a curtain around them, the scent of jasmine assaulting his senses. She was gasping for breath, completely spent, lying there limp.

"That was my favorite so far," she stated, between breaths.

He couldn't speak, he was so overwhelmed. He knew he had to say something but words were just not forming in his brain. It was as if she sucked all rational thought from his mind. He was still hard inside her. He flipped her over and looked at her face. He pushed into her slightly to feel the closeness he could only feel when he was inside her.

"Rhea, I...I..." he paused, then kissed her passionately, trying to convey what he couldn't articulate. She kissed him back in understanding.

"Sy, I really have to go."

She was right. He didn't want to let her go but she needed to get back. He had thought that once they joined, it would be easier to be separated from her. That couldn't be further from the truth, now it was worse. He growled in frustration for the umpteenth time and rolled off her. She sat up and he saw her wince and smiled in satisfaction. She'll be thinking of him for the rest of the day, whether they were together or not. That pleased him very much. She stood up naked and he remembered she wasn't wearing anything under her cloak.

"Do you have clothes stashed somewhere? Tell me you did not walk over here naked under your cloak!"

"Of course not," she said, standing at the edge of the bed combing out her hair with her fingers. She looked utterly feminine and infinitely beautiful. His heart swelled at the vision. "I had my slippers," she said sarcastically, with a devilish smile.

"You can't be serious!" He grabbed her around the waist and threw her back down on the bed. He hair fanned out and she gave him the most wonderful giggle. She slapped him on the shoulder playfully.

"I'm joking. My clothes are in your study. I may be crazy for you but I'm not crazy." She leaned up and gave him a chaste kiss then wiggled out from under him. She grabbed her cloak, put it around her, then picked up her slippers. When she opened the door, she looked both ways before she slipped into the hallway.

This is ridiculous, he thought, technically she was sneaking around her own house. He got up and dressed quickly to walk her back. Now he was going to have to climb out his own window. This is absurd. Other arrangements would have to be made. He would not sleep another night without his wife. Period. He walked into his study. She was dressed and was pulling on her slippers.

"I'll be fine. You don't have to go with me, go back to bed."

"Not a chance in hell, Minx."

She harrumphed and crawled out the window.

"I can take care of myself you know," she told him, before her head disappeared.

He walked over to the window, jumped down to a lower branch, then to the ground and looked up. She struggled down the first branch then attempted to jump to the ground but her cloak got caught so when she hit the ground it looked like it was hanging her. Sy reached up casually and detangled it for her.

"Don't you dare say a word," she hissed, narrowing her eyes in warning. "You try climbing a tree in a dress and see how you fare." Sy struggled to hold back his chuckle. He found her utterly delightful. They started walking towards her aunt's townhouse.

"You know, you could use the front door, it is your house too." He gave her a sideways glance. "I'm going to talk to your aunt and see what can be done. I don't like you walking the streets at night by yourself. It's dangerous."

"I never thought of it like that," she said.

"It's very dangerous in the city at night, even in a neighborhood such as this."

"No. Not that. That your house is technically my home now too." She looked at him. "How do you feel about that'?"

"Like I want to take you back there right now. That it's absurd that I have to sneak in and out of my own window to see my own wife." Irritation laced his voice. She giggled, then started laughing. He looked down at her and started laughing too.

"It's quite funny once you say it like that." She giggled again. They reached the gate to her aunt's garden. He opened it and let her through then followed. He walked her over to the trellis and turned her to face him.

"It might be amusing but it's not funny to me. Something must be done Rhea. I can't live like this." He pulled her in a tight embrace.

"I don't like it either. It won't be much longer." She stood on her toes and kissed his neck. He groaned, leaned down and took her lips. He reluctantly pulled away.

"Ok, up you go." He helped her onto the trellis and watched her until she made it safely in the window. He felt like a Shakespearian character standing there when she poked her head out and waved goodbye. This situation was getting more comical by the moment.

Once he exited the gate he noticed a shadowy figure lurking in a shallow alcove of the building on the other side of the street. Was someone following them? He'd find out soon enough. He walked along as if he hadn't noticed. Once he approached the building, the man jumped out in front of him, wielding a knife. He threw the knife from hand to hand in a menacing fashion and was crouched down ready for a fight. Was he serious? Without breaking his stride, Sy walked up to him, kicked the knife from his hand and punched him in the face. The man crumpled to the ground. Sy stepped over him and proceeded on his way.

That's it! Arrangements would have to be made, he did not want Rhea on these streets alone. He couldn't live with himself if something were to happen to her. He reached the tree and started to climb. What the hell was he doing? He jumped down, turned the corner, and went through the front door. He went back up to his bedroom, removed his boots and went back to bed. That's when he noticed the red stain on the sheets. Proof that he took her virginity. He took the bloody sheet off the bed, rolled it up and put it at the very bottom of his sea truck under his shirts. He wasn't sure why he was keeping it other than he wanted it. After getting a clean sheet from the closet then haphazardly placing it on the bed, he laid down and brought the pillow under his head. He could smell her. Yes, something would have to be arranged immediately.

RHEA STRIPPED down to her chemise. She hugged herself and turned in circles then plopped down on her bed. She grabbed her knees and rolled back and forth a few times before she flopped spread eagled with a big sigh. That was the most wonderful, erotic night of her life. She was sure that Sy was about to tell her that he loved her too. Fear started to creep in. No! She was not going to let anything ruin this moment for her.

She wanted to relive the night over and over. He was wonderful, gentle but passionate, firm but erotic. Nothing and no one would ever take it from her. She was giddy. She needed to get some sleep though. She had promised Jat she would check the manifests in the morning. The *Star* had arrived and was safely hidden. It needed to be restocked for her return trip to the island. The crew needed some well-deserved time in town. They wanted to shop for themselves and bring back gifts to *Paradiso*. She was excited to see them. It had been months since she'd seen her crew and she was excited to get caught up on news from home. She wanted to hear about Otis, too. She was so excited she couldn't sleep. She would have to calm her racing heart.

She wished she could find a way to combine these two worlds. She didn't want to give up either of them, but so far, it seemed inevitable that she would have to. How would she ever be able to make that choice? Give up Sy? The mere thought made her nauseous. She loved him so much, even more after last night. She never felt so cherished in her life. As Captain, she was respected, she had worked hard for that honor. She didn't want to let that go, either. Then, there was her work. Would Sy let her continue? She didn't know what to do. She rolled over, and punched her pillow. She needed to be honest with Sy. Lay everything out for him. Trust him. She wanted to talk to him at the opera but that didn't work. He was so distracting, with his handsome face and penetrating blue eyes. She just couldn't control herself when he was near, it would be even worse now. Now that she knew the ecstasy his kisses promised.

She would make an appointment with him. That's what

she would do. Keep it business. Some of her designs could help his company. If she could contribute, then maybe he'd let her continue her work. At least she could be on the sea some of the time. First, she would talk with Titan, get his opinion. She felt better having a plan of action, when she closed her eyes she fell asleep immediately.

SY SAT AT THE TABLE, drinking coffee and reading the paper. He fell in love with coffee on his travels. Now he drank it every morning, instead of the traditional tea. Four months until the House of Lords convened. Titan needed to be immersed into society's social circle by then. That meant more social engagements. Rhea may need a larger wardrobe. He should have asked her aunt about that earlier. Dress-makers take time, he would address that today. The jeweler too, if needed. He chuckled. He had already slipped right into the role of husband. After having the choice made for him, he was angry but Rhea has changed all that. Now he couldn't imagine not being married to his little Minx, society's sweet-heart. How his life had changed in a few short weeks.

"Message for you, my lord." Syers walked in with a missive on a silver tray.

Sy opened it and read it.

"Thank you Syers, please have the carriage brought around." His father needed to see him urgently. This couldn't be good, wanted to see Rhea and discuss living arrangements with her aunt. He wanted them to move in here once he posted the banns, which would be tomorrow. His solicitor was expected this afternoon. He couldn't bear being away from Rhea any longer. He's hoping she would agree. There had to be a suitable reason for the move. Whatever happened, he didn't want Rhea traversing the streets at night, especially after his encounter the previous morning.

"Your carriage is ready, my lord," Syers informed him.

"I may be having guests and would like to be prepared. Please be sure that two rooms are ready."

"As you wish, my lord. When can we expect your guests?" he asked, stoically.

"I'm not sure yet, ready them immediately nonetheless."

Just the thought of Rhea living in the walls of his house brought a smile to his lips as he jumped into the carriage. How ironic it was that the last time he took this ride he was angry and beyond irritated. Now he was the happiest he'd ever been in his life, looking forward to his future. Both situations were due directly to decisions made by his father. He wasn't sure how to feel about that.

The short ride had him conflicted and concerned because of the urgency of his father's missive. He knocked once, and the door opened abruptly. Watson looked relieved to see him and opened the door wider for him to enter. Sy could tell something was wrong.

"What is wrong Watson?" he asked, as he entered the foyer. "And don't give me that 'All is well my lord,' I can see the worry on your face."

"I am relieved to see you, my lord. Your father is ill and refuses to see a physician. I am worried, my lord. Something is not right," he confessed.

"Call the physician immediately. I will be responsible for the outcome. Do you know why he called me here so urgently?" he asked, concerned.

"Sorry, my lord, but I cannot say."

"See to the physician then. Where is he?"

"As you wish. He is currently in his study, he's expecting you."

"Thank you, Watson." Sy put his hand on Watson's shoulder. "Thank you," he repeated, in a serious tone. Watson gave him an understanding nod.

He walked into the study a moment later. When Sy saw his father, he was shocked, he was gaunt and pale. He was ill.

"Hello, father. This is twice in a month that I have had to come because of an urgent missive." He sat in the chair facing his father's desk. "I'm frightened to know the outcome of this meeting. Do I have a child I was unaware of, perhaps?"

"No son, one less ship in our fleet." he said, matching his sarcastic tone. "Oh, and someone set the *Breakneck* on fire. That constitutes a little urgency wouldn't you say?"

"What! Bloody hell! What is going on?"

"We are under attack. I know Verny is behind this somehow. My life has been a living hell since I attended that infernal soiree. Now I'm living my life in damage control. Son, I need your help. I have some kind of stomach virus and cannot travel. I need you to go to the Blackthorne shipyard and investigate. We have a mole or a saboteur at the offices. We can't afford another loss with you and Huntington new to the seats next session. We must rectify these issues before the sessions begin or Blackthorne Shipping could be in serious jeopardy."

"Of course, father, I am at your disposal. I will take care of the matter immediately. Right now, I am concerned for your health. I have called the physician. I am not leaving until you have been examined to determine if treatment is warranted," he said, in a commanding tone. His father gulped back the emotion he felt at his son's affectionate attitude.

"I'm sure it's just a virus, son. If I could wait it out and go myself I would, but too many catastrophes are happening in short order to ignore." He tried to convey the importance of the matter at hand and distract from his illness, which he was sure would pass.

"Nevertheless, I will wait for the doctor's diagnosis before I depart," he said, with finality. "On another subject, I would like to inform you that I will be posting banns for my engagement with Lady Hastings this week. We plan to have the wedding as soon as possible," he said, matter of fact. He might be grateful to his father for his match with Rhea but he was not ready to talk about it.

"That is good news. Even though you are legally covered, it will be good for society to see you as a solid match. I heard she's made quite an impression on the *Ton*. Something about rebuffing Lord Willoboughy in pubic? Is that true?" he asked.

"It is. Willoboughy is lucky. I would have called him out for the insults that lecher made towards Rhea, if it wouldn't have caused a scandal. He's lucky to be breathing," Sy said, with venom. His father studied him for a moment.

"You have taken a liking to the lady I take it?" he asked.

"You could say that," he replied, holding back a smile.

"Nothing would make me happier, son. I loved your mother with all my heart and miss her still. If you could have a fraction of the happiness we shared, you would live a content life. That is my greatest wish for you and your sister," he said, full of emotion and sincerity.

"Excuse me, my lords, the physician is here," Watson interrupted, saving Sy from having to reply to his father's statement. It didn't save him from the stab to his heart. He waited for his father to pass and walked out behind him.

"I will wait in the parlor for the physician. Please send him to me before he departs regardless of any orders from my father. Is that clear?" Sy whispered to Watson. "Father, I will attend to the matters we discussed as soon as I have spoken to the physician," he called.

He walked in to the parlor and started pacing in front of the fireplace. Damn. This will change all his plans. It was at least a three-day ride to the shipyard, longer by carriage. He needed Smith, he had a keen mind and would see things he missed, in regards to the fire. Where was Smith? He'd been so preoccupied with Rhea he hadn't noticed Smith's absence till now. He would go by his townhouse on the way home and let him know he needed him.

What about Rhea? He could take her along. No, he didn't know if what he was headed into was dangerous. Besides, that would mean her aunt would be forced to chaperone and that would slow the process down considerably. It would be better if she were to stay behind and take Titan as her escort to all the functions so he could continue to foster connections. They were running out of time as it was.

He smiled, he was sure she was sitting on a mountain of invitations to choose from, his little Minx. Damn it to bloody hell. This couldn't have come at a worse time. He wanted to be the one to escort his beautiful wife. The thought of being separated from her was a like a stab to his stomach. He was a lovesick fool. He chuckled to himself. It took a little Minx to steal his heart. The doctor walked into the parlor breaking into his reverie.

"Good morning, my lord, it is good to see you again, although I wish it was under other circumstances," Dr. Williamson greeted him.

"I agree whole heartedly, doctor, thank you for coming so quickly. Tell me, how is my father?" he asked, with concern. It wasn't easy to see the doctor again. He was the same physician that had treated his mother till her death. A feeling of dread washed over him. What if he lost his father too? They might have their differences, but he was still his father.

"It is curious, my lord, I'm afraid I do not have a clear diagnosis of the problem. He has the symptoms of a stomach virus, yet he does not," he said, stitching his brows together.

"I don't understand doctor. Is it or is it not a virus?" Sy asked, confused.

"It acts like a virus but it is escalating instead of the typical dissipation. Many things can cause this. It could be intestinal issues, food allergies, or something else entirely. I will need to investigate further to get to the bottom of it. With your permission, I would like to consult with a colleague who specializes in this area. I would also like to monitor his diet," he replied.

"Of course, anything you need. Treat him as you see fit, regardless of what he says. He can be quite stubborn when it comes to matters of his health. You are under my orders, doctor. If he should be uncooperative, you can tell him that. I will have Watson assemble the kitchen staff for questioning before I depart. Unfortunately, I must leave on urgent business. I can be reached through my man, Syers. Please contact me immediately with any results or changes."

"Certainly. For now, I will give him something to settle his stomach and make him drowsy. This will force him to get the rest he requires. I promise you, my lord, he will receive the best of care. I will send you progress reports regularly."

"I should be back in two weeks' time. Thank you doctor." He shook the doctor's hand firmly to convey his confidence, and departed.

Once in his carriage he was able to let his guard down. What if he should lose his father? Fear gripped him. He should send for his sister, Raven. His father needed family with him, besides, she should be here for the wedding regardless. He would make arrangements for her return as soon as he arrived at the shipping office. The last thing he wanted was to put her in harm's way, especially with a possible saboteur on the loose, he would have to take extra precautions for her trip home.

His thoughts drifted to Rhea. How would Rhea like his little sister? Raven was too young to make the voyage when he went to the island to visit long ago. Raven was a beautiful young girl, if not a little flighty and distracted. She had an uncanny ability to answer a question before anyone had the chance to ask. It was a little disconcerting at times. He swore she could read his mind, but then she would do or say something silly which made him dismiss that possibility. He missed his little sister. Had she changed much since going to finishing school? It had been years since he'd seen her. It was hard to imagine the woman she has become.

The carriage rolled to a stop in in front of Smith's townhouse. He stepped out.

"I'll be just a moment," he told the driver. He knocked loudly on the door and waited. A prickly butler cracked the door.

"Pardon me for coming unannounced, I am Lord Blackthorne, an acquaintance of Lord Smith," he told the cautious butler.

"Of course, my lord, please enter." He opened the door.

"Thank you, I must speak with Lord Smith about an urgent matter."

"I'm sorry, my lord, but Lord Smith is not at home. He is

visiting in the country at the moment," the butler informed him. Bloody hell, another damn inconvenience.

"It is a matter of some urgency. Do you know where in the country he is visiting?" he asked, hoping Smith had been forthcoming with his whereabouts. If not, he would have to go it alone.

"Yes, my lord, he is visiting the Waterford estate in Kent. Shall I send a missive to him for you?"

"As in Miss Maisy Waterford?" he asked, surprised.

"I'm sure I don't know, my lord," the protective butler replied. "Shall I send a missive for you?" he repeated, this time in a more insulted tone. He was obviously very guarded with his employer's business.

"That won't be necessary. Thank you." He gave the butler a knowing smile and turned to leave. The butler cut him off to reach for the door.

"My lord, Lord Smith talks highly of you, as if you were his brother. It is obvious that he is loyal to you beyond measure." The butler said hesitantly. Where was this going?

"And I to him, you can be assured," he replied, curious.

"That is also obvious, my lord. I..." Sy could tell he wanted to say something but felt it wasn't his place to speak.

"You may speak freely, anything you say will be kept in my confidence." He could see the butler relax a fraction.

"Thank you, my lord. Lord Smith was gone for a long time in your service. His family is just now getting reacquainted. Now that Miss Waterford has caught his eye, his family and staff are pleased at the possibility of him settling down. But if you were to ask...." The genuine concern for his friend moved him.

"I assure you, I am not here to ask Lord Smith to join me on a long voyage. I have reason to settle myself. His happiness is of upmost priority to me as well." He winked, and slapped the butler's shoulder. The butler opened the door.

"If there is anything I can do for you, my lord, I am at your disposal," he said, sincerely.

"Thank you," he called over his shoulder as he departed. He instructed the driver to go the Chamberlain townhouse. No wonder he hadn't seen his friend. He'd been courting little Miss Waterford. How curious. When did that happen? What a selfish friend he had become, so preoccupied with his little Minx, he hadn't noticed his best friend had possibly lost his heart. Did Rhea know? Probably not, since she'd been just as preoccupied. Suddenly, he couldn't wait to see her.

CHAPTER 17

*R*hea was walking around on a cloud. Titan was looking over the last of the cargo to be loaded on the *Rogue* while she tried to concentrate on the manifests. Jat had done an excellent job acquiring the cargo and had it organized for approval. He never ceased to amaze her, despite the fact that he couldn't talk he could still manage everything efficiently. Spending time with him made her realize how much she had missed him. She understood him so much better, now that she was also in love. Now, she could sympathize with his hurry to get back to the island to be with Liana. She could understand why he jumped off the ship and sprinted to his hut. And, the lingering looks he gave his wife when he thought no one was looking. she used to think they were cute, but silly, all made sense now. It made her long to see Sy, sneak off for a long passionate kiss, or more. Just thinking about what she wanted to do, starting with her obsession with his neck, shot white hot heat to her loins. Concentrate, she told herself, or this will never get done. She shook her head.

"According to the manifests, everything seems to be in order. The only item I don't see is the crate of fuses Otis needs," she shouted to Titan and Otis. Jat motioned something in her direction. "Tomorrow? Fine, I'll check it off as long as you promise to confirm the crate made it aboard." He nodded, and went back to what he was doing.

A crude whistle came from behind her. She was used to the cat calls and wolf whistles while on the docks and had learned to pay them no attention. She hadn't had a problem so far, mostly because either Jat or Titan had been with her to deter any trouble. But this whistle was too close for comfort. Jat and Titan were on the other side of the dock, too far to be of assistance. She reached for her knife.

"Well don't you look the tasty morsel in that dress... Captain," someone sneered, from behind her. Wait, she knew that voice. She whipped out her knife, twirled around, and placed it at the man's throat.

"Not a morsel a dead man can taste," she sneered back, pressing the knife to his skin. Then she smiled. "Hello, Timbo."

She pulled her knife away and gave him a big hug. He twirled her around. He put his hands on her shoulders and pushed her back.

"You haven't lost your touch, I see. But woo wee, you look bonny in a dress, lass. Jat and Titan must be having a hell've a time keepin' them gents off you," he exclaimed. She slapped his shoulder.

"Oh stop, that's so silly." She looked behind him, and saw the rest of her crew. They looked too shy to approach. Timbo must've been the elected representative, she guessed. Tears came to her eyes at the sight of her brethren. She opened her arms in invitation.

"Get over here now, and give a lady a hug. That's an order," she barked.

They started tussling with each other to get to her. She gave each and every one of them a long hug that had them blushing. Then, she had them all sit on crates as they told her about their voyage on the *Star*. They told her about the squall they hit and that the *Star* was as sturdy as ever. She got caught up on the happenings on the island and the new construction that had been finished in her absence. Now, it seemed everyone had a permanent home, and there'd been a competition to see who could build the biggest and sturdiest. She settled a few disputes that had happened on the voyage over, one over bunk space, and the other over rum rations. Then, Little Hand Larry asked permission to bring home a wife if could find himself one while he was here.

Little Hand Larry got his name for his left hand, which was underdeveloped at birth. Rhea gave him his name when she found him working in the galley of the *Rogue*. After a few conversations, she found out that he was an outcast her brother picked up at the last port and employed despite his disability. He longed to work on deck, not be in the galley for months on end. She told him he should have pride in his little hand and gave him his 'pirate name.' She took him up on deck and started him as a deck boy, from there he had worked his way up. Now, no one paid attention to his little hand and he'd become a valuable part of the crew. She missed these men so much. She was so glad they were all faring well. They made her homesick for her island. She dismissed them for a week. They were to check in with Jat on the fourth day to get their orders for departure. With a bunch of hoots, hollers and jeering about whorehouses, they dispersed.

Unbeknownst to her, lurking in the shadows between the buildings, someone was watching.

"Is that her?" Penelope asked a gentleman sporting two black eyes and a swollen nose.

"Yep, at's her. Told yer she's a beauty, ain't I right?" he answered.

"You saw *her* climbing up a tree and into the window of the Lord Blackthorne's residence? You're absolutely positive about that?" she asked again, surprised.

"Yes ma'am, weren't no good at it either. Just 'bout fell to 'er 'eath twice. I was feelin' the urge to go 'elp her a little, she's so bonny, she is. Next morn' both of 'em climb down and walked to an'ther house down the way. Let 'er in the gate like a real gent 'e did and 'elped her climb up ter an'ther window. Watched 'er real protec've like. I tried to dispa'tch 'im right there but 'e's a big one 'at Blackthorne, yes 'e is. It were a real battle 'fore 'e got the best o' me." he answered.

"Could you hear any part of their conversation?" she pressed.

"No' a lot o' it. He were upset 'bot climin' out the winder ter see 'is wife er somethin' like 'at and she giggled all purty like. And er..." he scratched his head in thought. "Oh and 'e said 'e couldn' live like this no mo'. She didn' seem upset none tho'. Gave 'im a real nice hug she did, real nice." He smiled an almost toothless smile at her. She handed him a small bag of coins.

"Follow her now, instead of him, and there will be more where that came from. Do not talk to her understand?" she instructed. "Report back to me in two days."

"Yes ma'am," he replied, and walked over between the buildings to take up his post. Once out of earshot, she turned to her companion.

"Wife? Do you think he took a wife? That would be a major complication." She was so angry her voice was shrill.

"He's only been back for a month. That's not enough time to get no wife. You can't take no guttersnipe's half heard conversation as truth. All we know for sure is that he likes the lady more than friend," he responded.

"We have to find out for sure. Do you know who that is? That's Lady Hastings, the current sweetheart of the *Ton*. It's no wonder he's dallying with her. We need to get rid of her. She could ruin everything," she said, clearly agitated.

Jealously surged through her veins. There is no way she was going to let this chit take away the title she had worked so hard for. She was the current Marchioness of Blackthorne.

The name opened doors. If old man Blackthorne would've just tupped her until she had a child, she wouldn't have to go to these measures. He would barely talk to her, much less tup her. The fake pregnancy didn't work. Damn him. He dropped her off at the Blackthorne dowager house straight from the church, and had her watched till she had no choice but to fake a miscarriage. The old man wasn't one bit surprised. The allowance he gave her barely covered the expenses of the house and staff much less her wardrobe. If it wasn't for the income from the information she sold on his trade routes and the percentage of the cargo they pirated, she'd have next to nothing.

Damn her stupid father and his idiotic plan to take over Blackthorne Shipping. It didn't work out the way he'd planned and now he was in his cups all day, no help whatsoever. He'd left everything up to her to figure out. He had lost ninety percent of Verny Trading to the Red Dragon in a card game. Upon her insistence, the Dragon had sent one small frigate to help the failing company. How was she supposed to be competitive with that?

The only asset in the situation was that the captain of that frigate was an angry ex-royal navy man with a chip on his shoulder. He'd been successful in pirating everyone that she assigned. He was ruthless in his pursuit, killing the entire crew at a whim. At least he saw reason this last time and kept ship and crew if they swore fealty to him. Now they had a better chance to advance at *'privateering'* as long as she could keep the inside information coming or manage to take over the company completely.

Sy was a big problem. Timing would be everything. The old man would have to die after Sy disappeared. It had to look like he died of despair over the loss of his son. The old man could not die first. That stupid maid had better not be going overboard with the potion she gave her. Penelope didn't trust anyone working in desperation. She looked over at Frankie Two Toes, her necessary evil. She'd acted like she was in love with him to gain his cooperation. He was a foul man with bad breath, but he was connected and had more money than her father ever had. He wanted to be seen as a legitimate businessman. Currently, he peddled blackmail and larceny, and had markers due him all over the city. He could get information on anyone, anytime, which made him very useful and he was not bad at tupping, if she closed her eyes and held her breath.

"Who do you have at the Chamberlain house?" she asked.

He pulled a small black book from his breast pocket and thumbed through the pages.

"Millie, she's a chambermaid, owes money she borrowed when her mum was sick. Bitch died anyway. Ain't called her marker yet."

"'I haven't, I haven't called her marker yet.'" she corrected him. "How are you ever going to sound like a legitimate businessman if you talk like a common guttersnipe?" she scolded, annoyed. He stepped closer, jammed his hand down the top of her dress and pinched her nipple hard. She moaned with pleasure and arched into his hand.

~

"YOU LIKE that I'm a common guttersnipe when I'm chewin' on your puss and slappin' your ass, now don't ya," he hissed in her ear. Frankie knew what she liked. He twisted her nipple hard to prove it and was rewarded with her putting her hand on his crotch for a caress of encouragement. He knew what ladies like her wanted. He was giving it to this one for free, for now, because she had something he wanted. Respectability. He would slap her ass and puss red and raw to get it, too. Then he'd throw her in the streets to fend for herself. "If ya don't need my services anymore, I *ain't* got no problem moving on." He twisted her nipple again, and she squeezed his crotch hard.

"No, no Frankie. I was just trying to help you. Let's go back to my townhouse and I'll show you how much I need you." she pleaded.

"Not now. I'm gonna call for Millie. Are you sure Blackthorne will be leaving?"

"Positive. He has no choice. He has to see to the problems at the shipyard. His father is ill and can't go. He needs to leave tonight. Is all in place when he gets there?" she asked, breathlessly. Frankie slid his hand inside her dress to the other nipple. He toyed with it for a moment.

"Have I ever let you down, darlin'?" he hissed in her ear,

then twisted her other nipple hard. She moaned in pleasure and she squeezed his crotch again.

"Are you sure there isn't enough time to stop by the town house for a…" she pleaded, but he cut her off.

"No. But if you're a good lass I'll chew yer puss in the coach. Now quit yer whinin' and let's go."

He yanked his hand out of her dress, letting go of her nipple at the last second, pinching it painfully. He abruptly walked away to her coach. There are certain things she would definitely miss about this foul man when this was done. Penelope straightened her bodice, her nipples tingling. She was looking forward to this coach ride.

TITAN WAS READING the manifest of the *Annabelle* on the coach ride home. Rhea was dying to ask his opinion about Sy, but was frightened. Problem was, she had no one else to ask, so she'd just have to be brave and hope for the best.

"Titan?"

"Hmmm?"

"I need to ask you a question," she asked, shyly.

That got his attention. "Yes?" He looked at her expectantly, but she couldn't meet his gaze. Instead she looked at her clenched hands. "What is it Rhe? This is not like you. What's bothering you?"

"I need your advice, but I'm afraid you might be mad at me."

"I'm always mad at you, so what's new?" he joked.

"I'm serious Titan. This is important," she scolded.

"There she is, I knew you were in there somewhere, I'm all ears Rhe Rhe." He gave her a smile, and she felt instantly lighter. They would figure this out together.

"Now that you know about me and Sy, how do you feel?" She looked at him to judge his reaction.

"Took your sweet time getting around to asking me, now didn't you?" He held up his hand to stop her talking. "I understand Rhe, the fact that nobody told me stings a little, but I understand the reasoning behind it. Being in town these last few weeks, I can see why secrecy was so important. In truth, I would've been too nervous about the whole thing and probably mucked it up for you if I knew. You seem happy Rhe, that's all that matters to me." Tears welled in her eyes at his kind and understanding words. "But make no mistake. If he hurts you, he's a dead man. Husband or not," he said, in a serious tone. She reached across the carriage and gave him a long loving hug. He squeezed her back in kind. When they separated, he looked at her. "Feel better?" he asked.

"Of course, yes, but I have another question. Should I tell him about the *Star* and *Paradiso*? I would never do so without your agreement," she rushed on to explain before he could comment. "I really don't want to give up my work. Do you think Sy would ever see his way to letting me continue? Maybe if I could contribute to the expansion of the company? Timbo says the *New Star* is ready. The new cannon design is also ready for testing on water. The land testing is complete.

It worked Titan, Otis doubled the range! We can mount one in the bow and one in the stern and the *New Star* will be invincible. I just need to test and configure the mounts with Otis." Titan's eyes widened at her announcement. "I want to give the *New Star* to Sy as a wedding present, so you both can use the designs to improve Blackthorne Shipping. What do you think?" she asked, contritely.

"It's yours to give, Rhe. Only you can make that decision. Have you considered that telling him about the *Star* means revealing that you are the White Lyon he's been chasing all over the Caribbean? It would also be revealing my identity as well. With his support, I am due to take a seat in the House of Lords in four months. How much do you trust him Rhe? This could crumble the entire plan and take Blackthorne Shipping with it. Reputation is everything. That is why father has distanced himself as he has. To serve as the protector anonymously."

"Why can't we stay anonymous? He has nothing to gain by revealing us. It would be better for him to maintain the relationship just as his father has with our father."

"That was because Uncle Harry was the Black Lyon back then. He never came to England and he certainly did not have a seat at the House of Lords!" he exclaimed. "I'm supposed to retire, pass on the roll to Pax. No one was to know that I was the Black Lyon. Pax would continue my work while I was in England, then no one could accuse me of being the Black Lyon if he was still sailing a half a world away. If you reveal yourself, then you reveal me, and Sy is in the position of collusion with the Black Lyon and the mythical White Lyon. We would have to trust him to keep that secret for all time. So, I ask you again. How much do you trust him?"

She put her hands over her eyes in the hope of clearing the confusion. So much was at stake. Did she trust him? Her heart did. Her instincts did. What kind of marriage would she have if she kept this secret from him? What if he found out in another way? He would never trust *her* again. She had to tell him and hope that she was right.

"I trust him Titan, he's my husband and I... I have fallen in love with him. I could never live with myself if I based my marriage on a lie. I have to tell him and then, come what may," she said, lifting her chin in finality.

"Well, I'll be damned." he smiled. "Then we'll tell him together. Besides, I don't think he'd believe you're the White Lyon without a little back up," he teased. She giggled and slapped his knee.

"I want to tell him before he posts the banns. Then he can change his mind if he wants," she stated.

"He won't." Titan said with confidence.

CHAPTER 18

*S*y bounded up the steps of the Chamberlain townhouse two at a time. He was excited to see Rhea. He had so much to discuss with her and needed to get on the road as quickly as possible. Now he had to make a detour to get Smith. He wanted to get his fill of her before he left. Just thinking about leaving made him miss her. He was a lovesick fool and he didn't care. He knocked on the door.

A young maid answered the door. Her eyes widened to large saucers when she saw him.

"Lord Blackthorne," she said, in shock, and gave him a polite curtsy.

"Where's the butler?" he asked, confused.

"He's entertaining the gentlemen that refuse to leave, my lord. He asked me to answer the door and turn away anyone else that asked to see Lady Hastings," she replied, in a small voice.

"May I come in?"

"Oh, of course, my lord." She curtsied again and let him in.

"I take it Lady Hastings is not in?"

"No, my lord."

"Then please announce me to Lady Chamberlain," he requested.

"As you wish, my lord." She scurried away quickly.

He looked around the foyer. It was full of flower bouquets of all shapes and sizes. They were everywhere, even on the floor, since all the tables were full. One of the reception tables was full of correspondence, all unopened. Good God, she really was the sweetheart of the *Ton*. It irritated him to know she was still being pursued despite the fact he made his intentions clear at the opera. There were going to be a lot of disappointed gentlemen when the banns were posted tomorrow. He smiled in satisfaction. The sound of Aunt Magda chastising the little maid filled the foyer.

"You left him standing in the foyer? That is unacceptable Millie. My heavens!" She appeared at the top of the stairway. "Hello, Lord Blackthorne, I'm so sorry to leave you standing in the foyer. Please let us retire to my husband's study, I would show you into the parlor but it is currently occupied."

"That won't be necessary. I take it Lady Rhea is not here."

"Unfortunately, no, she is with Titan and Jat. They had family business to attend to today."

"When do you expect them back?"

"I don't know, my lord. Would you like to leave Rhea a

message?" she asked.

"There's been a change in our circumstances, I need to leave town. I was hoping to explain before I went," he stated. He couldn't help but be disappointed; he was looking forward to seeing her.

"Oh, I hope all is well?" she asked, hoping he would explain further.

"Me too, madam, me too. I will try to stop by again before I depart. Until then. Thank you." He bowed and turned to leave.

"Are you sure you don't want to leave her a message, my lord, so she won't worry?" she queried.

"I will be back, my lady, it's a message I want to relay myself." The truth was he needed to see her, if he left a message he'd have no reason to come back. He'd go home and gather the belongings he needed, meet with his solicitor, then come back to see Rhea before he departed for Kent. "Thank you again, Lady Chamberlain."

"My pleasure, Lord Blackthorne."

SHE WATCHED him see himself out. He seemed so despondent. She couldn't help but worry. Was he upset over the callers or the flowers? It had to be irritating to have your wife pursued by other gentlemen. Maybe she should have told him that Rhea had refused to see any of the gentlemen or open the cards and letters. She should clear this foyer so it wasn't uncomfortable for him to visit. She'd get rid of the visitors too, it was ridiculous they refused to leave. She'd had it with this farce. It was obvious that Rhea and Sy had affection for each other, which she couldn't be more pleased about. She walked over to the parlor and opened the door. Eight or nine gentlemen were sitting and standing around the room conversing. Her butler, Stanley was walking about filling teacups and there were several trays of refreshments, which she was positive were encouraging them to stay. She needed to starve them out.

"Gentlemen, I just got word that Lady Hastings has been delayed and will not be returning until late. She will unable to receive visitors today," she announced. There was an audible groan. "I suggest you send a request for an audience and wait for a response before returning. Thank you, gentlemen. Stanley will see you all out." None of them made a move to leave.

"Now!" she shouted, harsher than she intended.

Stanley picked up his tray and started gathering teacups quickly, some right from their hands. Grumbles started and some of them reluctantly made their way to the door. All of them were bowing in Aunt Magda's direction as they passed. When the last one left, Stanley closed the door and leaned against it.

"No one gets in for the rest of the day, no one, only Lord Blackthorne. Is that clear Stanley?"

"As you wish my lady, it would be my pleasure." He wiped his brow with his handkerchief.

"And clear this foyer, you can put the flowers in a guest room or, better yet, give them away. Remove the letters too. Also prepare the parlor for Lord Blackthorn's return."

"Yes, my lady, right away," he answered.

"Thank you, Stanley. This ridiculousness is almost at an end," she told him.

"Glad to hear it my lady, I'm afraid I'm getting too old and too impatient to entertain young lovesick fools," he stated, wiping his brow once again. She laughed.

"Me too," she agreed. "Me too."

Rhea, Titan and Jat opened the front door and walked in, conversing jovially.

"Hello Aunt Magda," Titan greeted her, brightly.

"Hello," Rhea greeted. "My goodness, have more flowers come while we were gone? We can barely walk in here!"

"Yes, you have had a steady stream of gifts and callers all day," she said, somewhat irritated.

"I'm so sorry Aunt Magda. I never meant to be a bother," Rhea apologized, embarrassed. Titan laughed.

"You have always had this effect on people, or I should say men. What did you think was going to happen?" he teased.

"I'm just not used to it in such...high volume, I guess," her cheeks turning pink. Titan chuckled again and hugged his sister's shoulders.

"You just missed Lord Blackthorne," Aunt Magda stated.

"I did? Did he leave a message for me?" she asked, excitedly.

"He said he was going to return later. He seemed somewhat out of sorts. He said there had been a change in your circumstances, that he was leaving town. He wanted to explain it to you himself. He seemed upset Rhea. Do you know what he's talking about?" she asked. Concern laced her tone. Rhea went pale and looked at Titan.

"Now don't read into things like you usually do. It could be anything, Rhe. Wait and see what he has to say," he reasoned.

"You're right, of course. Will you wait with me? I want this over with today. If I had been honest with him earlier this would not be happening," she answered, unable to keep the worry from her tone.

"Honest? Told him what?" Aunt Magda asked, confused.

"I'm starving," Titan stated. "Could we have something to eat? We will explain all over a meal. If he just left, then he might not be back for hours. Let's eat and explain everything to Aunt Magda. We will all feel better." Rhea still looked concerned. "Come on Rhe, all will be well." He gave her another hug and a playful bump with his hip. He clapped his hands together and started towards the parlor. "Let's eat!"

SY DROPPED a small satchel in the hallway by the study door. He walked in to wait for his solicitor and poured himself some brandy. It was going to be a long ride, especially since he'd had an extra hour tacked on to track down

Smith. He smiled when he imagined Smith and Maisy Waterford together. Smith would tell her one of his silly jokes and she would giggle enthusiastically. He was happy for his friend and was hoping this wouldn't be too much of an intrusion. He heard the knock on the door, then footsteps.

"Mr. Sanford has arrived, my lord," Syers announced.

"Show him in Syers."

Mr. Sanford had been the Blackthorne solicitor since his grandfather had retained him. He was getting on in years, and Sy was surprised when the elderly gentleman shuffled in to the room and shook his hand.

"Lord Blackthorne, a pleasure to greet you after such a long time. I am happy and relieved to see that you are not lost at sea, as the rumors proposed," he stated. "Never believed that hogwash anyway. Blackthornes have been sailing the seas for five generations, none have died at sea. I knew they weren't going to start with you. Just look at the size of you, my lord, it's going to take more than Neptune's trident to take you."

"Thank you, Mr. Sanford, I am honored that you came yourself. One of your barristers would have been sufficient for this meeting," he said, motioning for the elderly gentleman to sit in the chair facing his desk. Sy walked around and sat.

"Actually, I have been meaning to contact you. I have several documents in regards to your title that need your signature. Since your father abdicated while you were away, the transfer was done by proxy. To make it official, I will need your signature. A matter of this importance, I would never leave to a barrister. I've taken care of the Blackthorne family affairs since I was a barrister myself and will continue until the breath leaves my body." He pulled a stack of papers from his satchel and put them in front of Sy. "The top ten papers are copies for your personal records." He pulled those aside. "I will need your signature here, my lord." Sy signed where he pointed. "And here." He took the signed documents and put them back into his satchel. "These forms will be recorded in the House of Lords official records. Congratulations. You are now officially the Marquess of Blackthorne, amongst other titles. And may I add, that was a brave move by your father to protect the estate and title from that awful woman. It is unfortunate he got caught up with those people. As a solicitor, I am bound to privilege with my clients but I don't think it is a breach of my oath to tell you that she tried this once before with another client of my firm. She wasn't successful that time, thrown out on her arse she was, and rightly so. If we could find the proof, the union with your father could be annulled and the Blackthornes could be rid of that scum. She's legally bound to the family by a very thin thread.

Proof of entrapment or duplicity, can be proved with one witness, my lord. Your father has been searching for a witness since this treachery happened. It's been my experience that there is always someone willing to talk. They must have this person under lock and key somewhere," he stated, clearly agitated.

Penelope had tried this before? With whom, Sy wondered. He may have let his anger get in the way of better judgment in this situation. If his father was an innocent victim, he deserved his help, not his indignation.

"I will see what I can do Mr. Sanford. Thank you for that information. Now, I called you here to post banns for me. I would like to post them tomorrow so the wedding can take place as soon as possible," he said with a smile.

"This is wonderful news. Congratulations, my boy! May I ask who the lucky lady may be?" he asked.

"Lady Rhea Hastings," he answered. Mr. Sanders whistled.

"The sweetheart of the *ton*. Do you have her consent for the union?" he asked.

What an odd question.

"Actually, we were married by proxy at the same time my father abdicated. We have decided to formally marry in front of society to make it official. I would say that is consent enough but if you are asking if the lady consents, then, I would say yes. Why?" he queried.

"My office has been very busy writing up offers for the young lady. I will have to thank her one day for all the business I have received on her behalf. Married by proxy you say? I don't believe my office prepared that paperwork. Do you have a copy of the contract?"

"And just how many offers have been written for my wife?" he asked, irritated.

"At my office alone? Seventeen, but I heard offers have

been written at other firms as well. She's quite the buzz amongst the legal community. She must be some lady," he replied.

Seventeen! His anger flared with that information. He wanted this done, immediately!

"Well then, you can see my urgency to post the banns and stop this nonsense. I will send someone to your office with the proxy agreement this afternoon. I believe that her father's solicitor drew it up. What else will you need to post the banns tomorrow?"

"My lord, even with all the information, it takes four to five days to fill and file the paperwork before you can post the banns. Let's see." He rubbed his chin and looked at the ceiling. "Today is Tuesday, or is it Monday?"

"It's Tuesday," Sy replied, getting impatient and annoyed that the answers weren't what he wanted. Seventeen! His mind was spinning with that news.

"Tuesday. Need two days for the forms and it'll take another two days to record it if they aren't backlogged. Twenty-four hours' notice to post he banns. Sunday, yes Sunday will be the soonest to make it public. That is unless you need a special license. They are hard to get, but not impossible, and would cause a lot of speculation as to the reason," he informed Sy.

What a nightmare. Another week of this hell.

"No need for a special license. Post the banns as soon as feasible. I need to leave town for the week. My father can act in my stead if anything else is needed to accomplish the task. I will send someone over for the paperwork this afternoon."

"That won't be necessary. I will stop by on my way back to the office and talk to your father. I will get the process going right away. Is there anything else you need ,my lord?" he asked, standing slowly to depart.

"Not at this time, Mr. Sanford. Again, I appreciate you coming yourself to handle this matter."

"Momentous day, yes, a very momentous day! You've gained two titles today, Marquess and husband. Congratulations, my lord, congratulations." He gave Sy a hearty handshake. "Tell me. Is this announcement to be kept confidential till the banns are officially posted? I won't lie and say don't I love the business but if you want the gentlemen to stop pursuing the lady, I can leak the news unofficially," he suggested.

"Tell everyone about the banns, keep the marriage by proxy confidential. I don't want anything released that can potentially embarrass my wife, understood?"

"Perfectly, my lord. This is going to be the biggest story of the season and it has just begun. Thank you, my lord." He exited, with a spring in his step. As soon as he cleared the doorway Syers appeared.

"There's a messenger for you, my lord." Syers announced.

"Show him in."

A young man entered the study. He looked tired and dusty. He stood in front of Sy's desk, spinning his hat in his hands meekly.

"I have a message for you, my lord. I was sent to your father's house first, but they sent me to you." He started "There's been another fire at the shipyard. I am to bring you back with me, post haste. I am not to leave your side until we are there."

Damn it to bloody hell!

"I am ready to depart. I need to pen a note, then we can be off. Give me one moment. Go to the kitchen and get a bite to eat and a cup of ale. I'll send for you when I am finished," he told the messenger.

"Thank you, my lord." The boy said relieved to get a short break.

Sy wasn't sure what he was more disappointed about; the banns not being posted for a full week or not having the time to visit Rhea before he departed. Now he wouldn't have time to stop in Kent for Smith either. He would have to send a messenger and hope he will come. He sat at his desk to pen the missives. The one to Smith was easy and quick. He summarized the situation, the urgency and asked if he could come to the shipyard to help. He added he would understand if he was otherwise occupied. His missive to Rhea wasn't as easy to compose. He wasn't used to expressing emotion in writing and or otherwise. He wanted her to know how much he was going to miss her. He felt silly writing his feelings down but he penned it anyway.

Rhea,

I am sorry that I missed you earlier. I wished to see you before I departed. I have to go to Blackthorne Shipyard to investigate possible sabotage to our ships and offices. I fear there may be trouble and want you to stay in town under your brother's protection. Please be cautious when you travel about and do not go anywhere alone. I mean it Rhea, please obey me on this.

If this trip weren't of the utmost importance, nothing could've have ripped me from your side. I think of you every moment of the day. You have captured my heart and own my soul. The banns will be posted this Sunday. I would like to exchange vows in the next fortnight. I cannot bear to be apart from you any longer. Tell your aunt to start planning our wedding. I'm sure this news will give her pleasure.

I wish I could've told you this in person. I desperately wanted a goodbye kiss and to hold you before I left. Unfortunately, the situation has escalated and I have to leave immediately. Please take care, my love.

Tell Titan not to follow. I will send a report once I investigate. He is to stay and escort you where you need to go. I place your safety in his hands.

Your Finance/Husband,

Sy

HE FOLDED BOTH MISSIVES, sealed them with wax and the Blackthorne crest. He called Syers, instructed him to send the missive to Smith at the Waterford's country estate, and the other to the Chamberlain townhouse. With a heavy heart, he went to the kitchen to inform the messenger that he was ready to depart. He was on the road a scant ten minutes later.

illie's hands shook as she handed Sy's missive to Frankie Two Toes less than an hour later. He grabbed the paper.

"Go wait in the kitchen till I call ya girl," he ordered. He sat behind the desk in Penelope's town house study as if he belonged there.

"Will this fulfill my marker, sir? I need to get back before I'm missed or I will lose my position. I need this job sir," she asked, panicked that she might have to wait and be missed. When the missive addressed to Lady Hastings arrived, she answered the door. Stanley was busy serving the family supper and didn't hear the knock. She knew this was the opportunity to free herself of Frankie Two Toes. How bad could it be to steal a message they were not expecting? It was probably unimportant, perhaps simply telling Lady Hasting he was running late. What harm could it do? Then she would be clear of her marker. It was better than some of the things they made other girls do. At least she didn't have to slip something in someone's drink. She heard bad things always happened to those people.

"I said wait in the kitchen! Don't ya even think of leavin' gel before I call fer ya understand?" he threatened. She jumped and ran from the room.

"Let me have it!" Penelope said as soon as Millie scurried away. She grabbed the missive and slid a knife under the wax seal so as not to break it. She read it out loud so Frankie could hear. "Damn it! I knew it! He's going to marry that chit and take my title," she pouted. "All will be lost if our plan goes awry at the shipyard. I don't trust those buffoons you sent to overpower a mammoth like Sy. The man is a force to be reckoned with. I've had my plans go wrong before," she whined. Her voice was shrill and her face contorted.

"Calm yerself now," he said, and walked to the door. "Tommy!" he bellowed. "Go fetch me Freddy the Forger. I want him here in ten minutes or I'm not going ta be the only gent with missin' toes. Got it?" He turned and locked the door behind him.

There were certain things he loved about his work. One was to manipulate these desperate upper crust bitches. He got a rush from the feeling of power it gave him, bending them to his will. They usually shunned him, hoped and prayed that no one would find out their dirty little secrets. Having the power to bend them to his whim excited him. He craved that excitement, needed it, was addicted to it. Like now, he would comfort his little lady, take a little more of her dignity, and make it his. Right now, she needed him to survive and he would suck her dry. He had to be very careful not to get carried away like last time. It cost too many markers to cover up that mess. It wasn't easy to make a lady of title disappear. He knew what his mistake was, he wouldn't make it again.

Penelope was the highest titled lady he'd ever had. He needed to make sure his plan was complete before he discarded her. She was a twisted one alright, and was good at it too. He loved it and was going to miss her when this was over. If she was a good gel, then maybe he'd put her in one of his houses where the gents would pay good money to do things to her. She'd like that, he thought. Probably wouldn't even put up much of a fuss. He removed his belt and walked over to her.

"That stupid chit is the sweetheart of the *Ton*." Penelope whined. "Now she's going to marry one of the handsomest highest ranked bachelors. They are going to accept her with open arms, you watch!" she screeched getting more agitated as she continued. "No one did that for me! Oh, they put up a false front to my face and snubbed me behind my back. I was going to show them all! Now he's going to marry her and I will be dowager!" she whined.

Frankie walked up behind her and put his hand around her waist then guided her to the front of the desk.

"Don't ya fret none now, Frankie's gonna take care of it. Nobody ain't gonna marry nobody." he said, soothingly.

"Here now, bend over lass. Frankie's gonna make you feel better." He pressed his hand to her back and she bent over and laid her chest on the desk. "That's a good gel. Now put yer hands flat on the desk and lift up fer me a little." She complied. He slipped the belt around her neck and through the buckle. He could see a faint bruise from the last time they played this game. He'd have to be gentler this time. He reached down, pulled her skirt up and pooled the excess fabric on her back, exposing her derriere. He rubbed his hand slowly from her hip down the curve of her arse and slid his fingers into the folds of her sex but did not enter her. She moaned. He slapped her ass hard and pulled on the belt, squeezing her neck.

"Open fer me gel." He wrapped his hand around the belt. She opened her legs wider. He slapped her again. "I said open for me," he hissed. When she spread her legs more he let go of some of the tension on the belt.

"That's a good gel." He ran three fingers up and down her sex to get them wet. Then, without warning, he jammed those three fingers into her and tightened the belt around her neck at the same time. She half gasped, half gagged, so he loosened the belt while he pumped her hard with his fingers, jamming his fist against her sex. She moaned and pushed back to receive more of his hand and rotated her hips from side to side enjoying the pleasure he was giving her.

"You like that don'tcha gel."

He cinched the belt tighter around his hand grinding his fist on her, feeling the power surge through him, making his erection hard and throbbing. It was time to push her harder. He put his thumb on her anus and did circles to test her reaction. She moaned and pushed back against his hand. He knew she was a twisted nut job. The feeling of power surged through him again. He loosened the belt a fraction. He pressed the tip of his thumb inside.

"Ya want me in there don't ya gel." She pressed back to answer his question. "Answer me gel, I want to hear ya beg."

"Please," she coughed out. He removed his fingers from her and slapped her ass again.

"What was that gel?"

"Yes, please, please Frank..." he retightened the belt before she finished. He lined himself up with her, excited about how good this was going to feel. He grabbed her hip with his free hand and rammed himself into her and pulled back on the belt. Ah, that felt fucking good. He pulled out and slammed into her again. He let go of the belt, grabbed both of her hips, and thrust into her wildly. Once he was about to climax, he grabbed the belt and tugged slightly. Her legs started quivering. He pulled it just tight enough to restrict her air flow as she had her orgasm. Her body shook as her climax came and pulsed around his erection. He let his seed spill into her, feeling that telltale power rush at the same time. He let go of the belt and she collapsed on the desk, panting for air. He pulled out of her and let her go. Her knees went limp leaving the desk the only thing holding her up. He took one of her petticoats to wipe himself, reached over and slid the belt from her neck. He slapped her ass one more time to get her attention.

"Get yerself together gel, Freddie the Forger will be here in a minute and ya got a missive ta write."

~

TITAN HAD everyone laughing at Rhea's expense. It was fine with her, she was laughing too. It helped to relieve her anxiety that Sy still had not returned. She was worried that he was upset about something, but more nervous to tell him that she was the White Lyon. There was no way to predict his reaction.

"Then there was the one time she tried to swing down a line from the mainsail. She forgot to tighten the line to take out the slack before she jumped. She came falling down so hard the line jerked out of her hand. Thank God, Pax, Jimbo and Jat were paying attention. They all came running to catch her but ended up running into each other. Knocked Jimbo right out!" he said, laughing so hard he couldn't continue.

"Well their three bodies did make a nice pillow to land on, I must say," Rhea giggled.

"My heavens Rhea, why would you want to continue after all those mishaps?" Aunt Magda asked, fanning herself from laughing so hard.

"Actually aunt, Rhea is an excellent seaman, better than most, she was voted Captain by her crew. She deserved it too. Still does. When they were here today, you could see the admiration and respect they have for her. Don't let that dress fool you." He put his hand on hers reassuringly.

"Thank you, Titan, that means a lot coming from you," she said, softly.

"A missive came for you Lady Hastings." Millie stood behind her holding a silver tray with a message on it.

"Put it with the others Millie." Aunt Magda instructed.

"Pardon me my lady, it bears the Blackthorne seal, I thought it might be important since he's the only gent let in the house now," she said, her voice shook with fear. Rhea thought she was nervous for daring to speak back to Aunt Magda. She took the missive from Millie's shaky tray.

"It's alright Millie, you did the right thing. Thank you." She gave her a sincere smile.

"Thank you, my lady, you have always been so kind to me." When she said it, it almost sounded like an apology and quickly left the room.

"My heavens, what has gotten into that girl? For the last few days she's been so jumpy and emotional. I'm going to have to have a talk with her." Aunt Magda said, annoyed.

"If you'll excuse me, I'm going to the parlor to read this," Rhea said.

"Why of course dear." Aunt Magda looked concerned. "Call us if you need us."

"Thank you." She stood and Jat and Titan stood too. She walked as slowly as she could till she reached the foyer and ripped the missive open.

Rhea,

I am sorry that I missed you earlier. I wished to see you before I departed. I wanted to tell you this in person but was unable to wait for you to return. I have had some time to reflect on our relationship. I cannot live like this anymore. I regret to inform you that I will not be able to marry you and will be terminating this relationship. Please don't try to contact me in the future. I mean it Rhea, please obey me on this. It will be too painful for both of us.

I have decided to voyage to the West Indies and set up trade routes there so we will have some distance from each other. I hope in time you will be able to move on as I have. I wish you well. Please take care.

Regards,

Sy

She read the message three times. Each time her heart cracked wider until finally it shattered into a million pieces. She let the missive flutter to the ground. The world started to spin, her knees became weak, then everything went black.

"STOP PACING TITAN, that's not helping anything." Aunt Magda chastised. "And Jat you're going to rub the skin off her face, here let me do that." She took the rag and dipped it in the bowl of cold water, wrung it out and put it on Rhea's forehead.

"I'm going to kill the son of a bitch! I'm going to hunt him down and slice him from gullet to gut. I swear to you I will," Titan said angrily. Jat reached for the cutlass in his waistband, nodding vigorously.

"Come now. Let's be sensible, this doesn't make any sense, now does it. I think there's something amiss. Wait till you talk to the man before you head off halfcocked," Aunt Magda reasoned.

"Nobody is going to talk to him, or it'll be me cutting someone from gullet to gut," Rhea said, in a soft whisper, sitting up from the settee. "I mean it. This is my problem."

"Rhea!" all of them said in unison. Titan was at her side in two strides helping her to stand.

"There has to be a reasonable explanation. We just...," Aunt Magda started, but Rhea held up her hand.

"If you will excuse me, I wish to retire." Without waiting for anyone to say anything, she left.

Once she got to the stairs she picked up her skirts, ran to her bedroom and closed the door. She ripped off her dress and her corset and threw them on the ground. She started on her hair next, ripping out the pins and the hair attached to them. Oh, my God, the pain in her chest was overwhelming, consuming her, making it hard to take a breath. She held her stomach and doubled over. She stumbled over to her bed and fell onto it. She reached under her pillow and hit the knife Sy had given her. She took it out and went to throw it, but couldn't. Instead, she hugged it to her chest in desperation to hold onto something that was connected to him. It nicked her arm, but she didn't care. She relished the pain. That's when the tears came, wracking her body. She rolled back and forth, hugging the knife to her chest. Oh, my God, what had she done.

～

"GIVE her a few minutes of privacy, Titan. And stop that infernal pacing! You're driving me to distraction! Sit down, please! You too Jat." They looked at each other, then obeyed. "Thank goodness," she sighed.

"Aunt Magda, I need to go to his townhouse to see if the rat bastard is still in town," Titan said, trying to keep the anger from his voice so she would let him go.

"I have already sent someone to see if he's at home. I did it the moment we found Rhea collapsed in the parlor. He is not at home, he left hours ago. He is on his way to Black-thorne Shipyards. He left immediately after he met with his solicitor this afternoon. He took only a small satchel. Now does that sound like a man leaving to go on a long sea voyage? What does he mean he can't marry her? They're already married. None of the makes any sense, I tell you, something's amiss. That man is crazy in love with Rhea, I could feel it. Nothing would keep him from her and he would not be sending a note like a coward to break it off." Aunt Magda reasoned.

"You have no proof of that, and nothing you said convinces me that the note is not true. He could have met with the solicitor to annul the marriage. He could've sent his trunk ahead to the ship. He also could've lost his nerve to face her since he's been leading her on this whole time, making it public too. I see that as a good reason to slink off to the shipyard to get a ship to the West Indies. The rat bastard! I'm going to kill him!" Titan was getting worked up just reasoning it through for himself, he started pacing again.

"Go home, Titan. There's nothing that can be done tonight," Aunt Magda stated. She would never be able to reason with him while was is so angry. "Get some rest. Your sister will need you tomorrow."

"I'm spending the night, just in case that rat bastard decides to show up. Besides, Rhea may need me tonight," he stated emphatically. Aunt Magda smiled. His love for his sister was endearing.

"Of course, she does, and of course you can stay as long as you like. I will tell Stanley to send someone for your things."

"Thank you, Aunt Magda." he said, relaxing a little.

"I will send for some brandy as well. I know I could use a nibble myself." she confessed.

CHAPTER 20

*S*y was beyond tired when he reached the Blackthorne Shipyard. It was too late to find lodgings for the night, so he decided to bunk in the office. The quartermaster was a very kind gentleman who offered a room at his home, but the thought of getting back on his horse for another hour after a two-and-a-half-day ride was enough to dissuade him, even from a comfortable bed. At this point, the office settee seemed adequate. Besides, he wanted to get this situation settled and back to London as soon as possible. He missed Rhea, her smell, her touch, her lips on his neck. He had nothing else to think about on his way here. Lord help him, he was bewitched by this woman and glad for it. He never realized how empty his life was until Rhea filled it.

He laid his head down on the settee. His feet hung well over the edge, but anything was better than that infernal horse. He put his hands behind his head and tried to get comfortable. He wondered what Rhea was doing right now. Was she thinking about him? What a lovesick fool he was. He chuckled at himself.

When he heard footsteps outside, he sat up and reached for his knife. The window rattled, someone was checking to see if it was locked. He knew the door was next. Grateful that he had removed his boots, he padded over to the door, unlocked it, then backed into the shadows. Sure enough, the footsteps rounded the building toward the office door. Only one set of footsteps, good, hand to hand combat he was comfortable with. The door knob started to turn, then opened slowly. A black shadowy head poked in and looked around, then stepped in and turned to close it. Sy attacked. He jumped from the shadows and slammed the intruder into the door. He heard a loud 'huh' as he knocked the wind from his lungs. Then he slid the knife to the man's throat. Just as he did, the intruder stomped on his toe with his boot. Pain shot up his leg. Distracted, his opponent was able to push the knife from his neck and threw his head back which connected with his chin. Pain shot through his jaw and he stepped back reflexively. His opponent spun around to attack then stopped suddenly.

"Sy?" he called out.

"Smith?" Sy answered, surprised. "I could've killed you! Good God, what the hell are you doing sneaking around the offices like that?"

"Kill me? I believe I was just about to slice you through!

What the hell are *you* doing in the offices this late?" he said, insulted.

"I just got here. I didn't expect you till tomorrow. How did you get here so fast?"

"At the suggestion of Mr. Waterford, I took the route through Penbury and cut my time by half a day. I was going to crash in the office and wait for you to come here tomorrow," Smith answered.

As the adrenaline subsided, Sy started to laugh. Smith chuckled too. Happy to see his friend, he felt an overwhelming sense of brotherhood. He grabbed the front of his shirt, brought him in for a short embrace and slapped his back repeatedly. He could feel his friend relax and return his affection.

"Let me light the lantern. There's a settee behind you if you want to sit." Sy walked over to the desk and lit the lantern. He grabbed a chair and sat backward on it facing his friend. Smith groaned and arched his back to stretch before taking a seat.

"I haven't been on the back of a horse for that long in my entire life. I am not looking forward the trip back."

"Me either, I think I'm much more suited for the sea," Sy replied. After Smith got settled, he looked at his friend and smiled. "So...Waterford?"

Smith's head jerked up and he stared at Sy, searching to see if he was teasing him or not. Then, with a sigh, he dropped his shoulders. He raked his hands through his hair and looked at his lap. Sy had never seen his friend act like this before, especially about a woman.

"I don't know what happened, one moment I was admiring Lady Hastings as the epitome of beauty and grace, then the next I was staring into the most beautiful brown eyes I've ever seen. I swear, my heart stopped. I asked her to take a stroll in the garden. I just wanted a moment alone with her, but the next thing I knew, I was kissing her in an alcove. Never in my life, with all the women I've kissed, even the ladies of experience, have I felt like I did the moment her lips touched mine. I don't know what's wrong with me, she occupies my every thought. I feel lost and distracted when I'm not around her. She giggles, and it brightens my heart. She's like my own personal sunshine." He looked at Sy. "Please don't laugh at me, I couldn't bare it." When he saw no judgment on Sy's expression, he was relieved. "I blame this all on you, you know."

"Me? What did I do?" he asked, astonished.

"Three years in your dower company, I needed a little sunshine," Smith teased. Sy chuckled and slapped his arm.

"Welcome to the club, my friend. Thank God, I thought I was going to have to muddle through this love business alone," he confessed.

"Lady Hastings?" he asked.

"Yes," he said, surprised. "How did you know?"

"The dance card," Smith chuckled.

"In retrospect, that was silly. I had good reason though. I

have a confession to make. But first, I need your word of confidence on the matter," he said, seriously.

"You know you have it," Smith said, putting his hand over his heart.

"Lady Hastings and I are already married. Have been for some time. Our parents married us by proxy years ago." He waited for Smith to react.

He just sat there with his mouth open for a moment before he spoke.

"You, lucky son of a barnacle! Geez, I cannot believe your luck! Your parents married you to that gorgeous thing and you're not shouting it from the rooftops?" he exclaimed, in surprise, and genuine happiness for his friend.

"It's a little more complicated than that. I wasn't sure it was going to work. She's been reluctant and I have been trying to respect her wishes to get to know each other. She was willing to come out in society together, act the part of the courtship and marriage, but she wanted an annulment after a year. I had to change her mind. It took some work but banns will be posted Sunday."

"You, lucky son of a barnacle!" he repeated. "Congratulations my friend. Congratulations!" It was his turn to slap Sy on the arm. It warmed Sy's heart, the genuine reaction from his friend, but he only wished he could be as happy with Miss Waterford.

"So, will you be offering for Miss Waterford then?" he asked jovially, expecting a resounding yes. He was surprised when Smith lost his smile and looked away. "What's wrong?"

"Her father wants a solid match for her, one that will see her secure. I cannot offer her that. I'm a third son of an earl. I will never inherit. I have no residence to offer. Now that you are to marry it looks as though I'm out of a job. If I get another commission, I will be away for a year or more. Her father would never agree to the match no matter how we feel about each other," he replied solemnly. Sy's heart broke for his friend. Something must be done. He thought for a moment before he knew exactly what to do.

"Well that is just not acceptable. I owe you for two years' commission correct?"

"Yes, but…"

"And you have the salary from our first commission together, correct?"

"Yes, but…"

"Then this is what is to be done. You will buy the Blackthorne dowager townhouse until the time you can afford something bigger. You will, in three years' time, pay for the Blackthorne country seat that just happens to be conveniently located in Kent close to Miss Waterford's parents. When the time comes to dowager the next Marchioness, you will sell back both properties at the price you bought them for. Since Rhea is the next Marchioness to be dowered, I think that should give sufficient time to relocate. Agreed?" Smith looked at him, assonished by his friend's generosity.

"Sy, of course I would agree but you seem to forget that I have no source of income at the moment."

"Your income as chief engineer at the new Blackthorne

Ship Building Company should provide a more than adequate income for you and your hopefully growing family. You practically built the *Breakneck*, it wouldn't exist if it weren't for you, so I feel you are qualified for the position. The *Breakneck* has fire damage from the saboteur, it will need to be repaired. You can assess the damage tomorrow to start repairs. I also need you to help with the investigation to catch this saboteur. I insist you start immediately." he stated, nonchalantly.

"I...I don't know what to say," he said, stunned. Sy smiled.

"You are a good friend, more like a brother to me. Your happiness is my priority." He put his hand on his friend's shoulder and squeezed. He could see the wetness forming in Smith's eyes. He instantly felt good about his decision.

"One question... isn't the Blackthorne dowager townhouse currently occupied by your mother in law?" he asked, confused.

"It is, but I know that she is behind this treachery and I intend to prove it. That is why I wanted you here. I know your keen mind will find the key that will tie her into everything. Too many mishaps have occurred and she's the only person that would profit from the outcome. She has a reputation of deception, but her ruses are not always successful. We need to be sure that is the case this time as well," he stated emphatically.

"I would've helped you no matter what. Now I'm motivated more than ever!" Smith smiled, and Sy could see the sparkle of intrigue in his eyes.

"Great, let's purge the hull of rats then. This is what I know so far..." he told him what he had learned and what he suspected. Both men had a hard time falling asleep, their minds whirling with the intrigue, sabotage and their futures.

Come morning, Smith went to investigate and assess the *Breakneck*. Sy looked over the remnants of the office fire and the records of the *Dogwind*, to see if anything stood out as unusual. He was so distracted he almost forgot to make arrangements for his sister.

"Quartermaster, I need to retrieve my sister from her finishing school in France. With everything that is happening here and at home, I cannot go myself. I need someone trust-worthy to bring her to London as soon as possible. With a saboteur on the loose, I need someone worthy of protecting her. Do we have anyone that you could recommend for the job? The compensation would be handsome."

"Actually, my lord, I have the perfect man for the job. Captain Cullen McLanister. He arrived yesterday and is unloading his payload now. He is the most honest captain I have had the pleasure of working with. On several occasions, he has negotiated deals that have brought a higher profit than expected. He turns over every shilling when others would not. Interesting fellow too, my lord. He is actually a Baron in Scotland. According to his story, part of his estate burned, killing his mother. His father never rebuilt and the estate went into ruin. He has been rebuilding the place himself since he became of age. He wouldn't take an elevated rank due to his title, either. He worked his way up from the bottom. He was voted Captain by his crew, an astonishing accomplishment in three years. I liked the fellow immediately; big brute of a fellow, one hell of a fighter too. He's not quite as large as your lordship, but a formidable opponent nonetheless. He would be the best we have for the job. I must tell you, my lord, he is already commissioned to go to France. He volunteered for the voyage so he could pick up materials needed for his estate on the return. He paid in advance for the use of the ship and I already gave him permission to stop in Scotland on his return to offload his cargo. I don't think he will consider taking on your task unless he could complete that part of the journey," the quartermaster explained.

"Can you please call him to the office so I may speak with him?" Sy asked.

"Aye, right away, my lord."

It took a few minutes to locate Captain McLanister. Sy poured over the manifests as he waited. Finally, the quartermaster returned with the captain in tow. Sy smiled as the captain ducked through the door to enter the room. He was a large man like himself, slimmer, but no less muscular. As expected, he had the auburn hair of a Scotsman and emerald green eyes that looked at him straight on. He stood tall and made no hint that he felt the need to regard Sy as anyone other than just another man in the room, not as the owner of Blackthorne or a Lord in England. Sy liked him right off. He extended his hand.

"Captain McLanister, I presume? I am Captain Sy Black."

"Pleased to make yer acquaintance Cap." McLanister took his arm at the elbow and gave him a hearty handshake. His Scottish accent was pleasing.

"I understand that you are already commissioned to France on your next assignment?" Sy asked.

"Aye, Captain, got some business there meself, I made prior arrangements. Ye can ask the quartermaster, I paid ye in full." he answered honestly, obviously curious why the infamous Captain Black was inquiring.

"I have no doubt of your honesty Captain. I have a task of the upmost importance that I need done. I can guarantee you generous compensation if you will consider the inconvenience."

"Exactly what would this task be, Captain?"

"I need my sister transported from her finishing school in the south of France back to London post haste. Our father is ill, but more importantly, we have a saboteur setting fires at the shipping company and I feel she may be in danger. I need someone to retrieve her from her school, insure her protection during the journey, and bring her to me in London. I understand that you have a stop in Scotland and I am happy to honor that delay if you can guarantee her safety while she is there. To compensate you for your troubles, I would be happy to refund the amount you paid to transport your cargo and an additional two thousand pounds, plus expenses."

Captain McLanister stared at Sy for a second, obviously undecided.

"Why would ye no' go yerself Captain?" he asked.

Sy respected his question, it meant he was not taking on the task for monetary gain alone.

"As I said, my father is ill. We have a saboteur in our midst. I would go if these emergencies didn't take precedence. I need to secure my sister's safety immediately. You have come highly recommended from the quartermaster. Besides, if you were to take the task and fail, there is nowhere on this earth that you could escape my wrath," he said, in an ominous tone.

Captain McLanister smiled. "I can tell ye are a fair 'nd generous man, Captain. I accept," he said, and held his hand out. Sy took it and the deal was sealed.

"I will send you with the proper document for the school to release her into your care. Do you have others worthy of the task?" Sy asked, concerned.

"Aye, Cap, I 'ave Mongo and Skipper. They 'ave worked fer me fer years. De ye need te meet them, then? They be right outside," he offered.

"It would ease my mind, thank you," he replied.

Cullen walked to the door and waved the fellows in. Mongo was bigger than Sy and Cullen put together. He was Samoan and as big as a house. Skipper was the smallest of all of them but Sy could tell he was wily and not new to the art of fighting, by the look of his nose. Sy was satisfied.

"Thank you, gents, your captain will explain why you were summoned once we are done with our meeting," Sy explained.

Mongo grunted and Skipper nodded, and they left. Sy smiled at Cullen.

"Interesting crew mates you have Captain. I will compensate them five hundred pounds each once my sister is safely delivered. Agreed?" Sy offered.

"Aye, Captain, agreed." he said, emphatically.

"I will have the proper paperwork prepared by this afternoon. I need for you to leave post haste as there may be a chance my sister is in danger. When can you be ready to leave, Captain?" Sy asked, concern on his face.

"We can leave with the evenin' tide Cap," McLanister replied. "I will go 'nd prepare me ship then," he said, with a salute.

"Captain." Sy halted him before he got to the door. "I...um...must warn you. My sister, she can be...confusing at times. Please don't let her rattle you," he said, cryptically.

"Aye, Captain," Cullen said, and issued another salute.

Sy quickly penned a letter for Cullen. With that task behind him, he felt free to concentrate on the problem at hand. As planned, Sy and Smith met back at the office to go over the information compiled. The quartermaster's wife brought a tray of meat and cheeses for their midday meal.

"It's curious Sy, the damage to the *Breakneck* was extensive, but it was mostly to your quarters and the poop deck above but nothing critical was damaged. Arson to be sure, but the fire was set in a place where the least amount of damage would be done. It makes no sense," he stated, perplexed.

"What do you mean?"

"If you're going to set a ship on fire, then why not set it on the gunnery deck? That's where the most damage would be done. The *Breakneck* would have burnt to the waterline. Whoever set this fire did it so there wouldn't be very much damage, so what was the point?" Smith asked.

"The office fire was the same. It was set outside, doing minimal damage as well. The wall was scorched and that's all. No real loss. Also, I compared the manifests. The ships we lost had cargo that would be easy to disburse, but not very valuable, so the loss was also minimal. If you had access to inside information, why would you not target the most profitable cargo?" Sy asked.

"It's almost as if the saboteur was reluctant. What do you make of that?" Smith questioned.

"This is all very bizarre. It has to be someone who has an attachment to Blackthorne Shipping, otherwise why would they care?" Sy inquired. The quartermaster walked in with two cups of ale.

"Thank you," Sy said. "Tell me, who, besides yourself, has access to the manifests?" he asked.

"Only myself and Cyrus. Is there a problem with the entries Lord Blackthorne?" He sincerely seemed concerned.

"No. It's just we have reason to believe that the information has been leaked outside the office. I will need to talk with you and this Cyrus immediately," he ordered. "Is he at work today?"

"Yes, my lord, I will go get him." He left the office.

"What about the quartermaster? Do you think he could be responsible?" Smith asked, once he was gone.

"My father would be heartbroken. He has been with the company for decades. My father bought him a residence in the area to relocate his family when we bought the shipyard. He has proven to be a loyal employee. I have never met this Cyrus. At this point, I don't rule anyone out," Sy said. The quartermaster returned with a very tall thin gentleman who looked at his feet as he walked. He didn't make eye contact with Sy or Smith as they were introduced. Sy was immediately suspicious.

"Mr. Cyrus, how long have you worked for Blackthorne Shipping?" he asked, as an ice breaker. Maybe he was nervous to talk to him because of who he was.

"Going on a year and a half, my lord," he said, still looking at his feet.

"Do you value your job here?" he pushed. His head snapped up at that question.

"Yes, my lord, am I losing my position?" he asked, panic in his voice.

"That is to be determined. Honesty and loyalty are expected from Blackthorne employees. As you have seen, there is someone, an employee we suspect, that has been setting fires. From what my investigation has revealed, information from the manifests has been leaked from this office. Since you and the quartermaster are the only two employees that have access to the manifests, it would seem that one of you is responsible for these leaks."

Insulted by the accusation, the quartermaster jumped in. "I can assure you, my lord, my reputation with the company is beyond the pale, and your father can vouch for my work. I am unaware of information leaving this office. Cyrus, do you know anything about these leaks?"

Cyrus paled and started backing toward the door. Smith blocked his exit.

"Cyrus?" The quartermaster looked shocked at his behavior. "Do you know something about these events? If you do, you need to tell these gentlemen everything!" He yelled at his employee.

"I had no choice, I swear, they would've killed me or my wife if I didn't do it!" he rushed out.

"No one is threatening you here. Please relax, Mr. Cyrus, we only want the truth." Sy said, in an even tone. "Please be seated and tell us what happened." He put a chair in the center of the room. Smith casually leaned against the door jamb, continuing to block the only way out of the office. The quartermaster was visibly angry but he held his tongue. Cyrus sat, resigned.

"I don't know where to start, my lord," he said, looking at his feet again.

"Start with who is going to kill you," Sy suggested.

"Frankie Two Toes. I lost money at his club last month. I don't gamble much, my lord, I swear. I was hoping to make a few extra quid for my wife's birthday, you see. When I lost all my money, he gave me a credit so I could try to recover. I lost my head, my lord, I should've walked away, but I really thought I could win it back. I should've known better. He said I could make payments for the credit and I was, but then he came and told me he wanted information from the manifests instead. He wanted to know the destinations of the ships which had the best cargo loads. That's when I knew I was set up, my lord. I knew it!" he confessed.

"But you didn't give him the most profitable ship information?" Sy stated.

"NO! My lord! Blackthorne shipping has been good to me. The quartermaster too. I figured I'd give him information that wouldn't impact your business, then he'd give up and go away. I even kept making payments, trying to pay off the marker. I was hoping I could pay it off before they realized I was I duping them. I was wrong, he sent his thugs to my house and threatened me and my wife. They held her down on our bed, my lord, with a knife at her throat," he said. His voice broke and his shoulders slumped. "They said they would have their way with her while they forced me to watch, then kill her in front of me." Sy felt for the man, if that had been Rhea he would've done anything to save her. He looked at Smith, knew he was thinking the same.

"I told them I would do anything they wanted, my lord, I had to save my Bessie. She was so scared. It broke my heart to see her like that, it was all my fault." Sy could see the sincerity in the man's eyes. "They said I had to set the *Breakneck* on fire to lure you to the shipyard office as soon as possible. You didn't come, my lord, so I had to set the fire behind the office to make it urgent. I sent James to get you with instructions not to come back without you. I didn't want to take the chance of having to destroy any more property. It was the only thing I could think to do," he continued.

"Do you know why they wanted me here?" Sy asked.

"No, my lord. I want you to know that I did my best to not do a lot of damage to your ship. It would've been even less but the men were slower to respond with the water buckets than I thought," he pleaded.

"That is evident Mr. Cyrus. I will take that fact into consideration," he confirmed.

"I love my job here my lord. Like I said, the quartermaster has been good to me. If they hadn't threatened my Bessie, I would lay my life down for you and Blackthorne Shipping," he pleaded again.

"Thank you for your honesty Mr. Cyrus, please wait in the other room. If you run, I will know that you are being dishonest and you will be tracked down with no mercy. You do not want to face the Blackthorne wrath, I assure you," he threatened. Cyrus' face paled at the threat.

"Of course, my lord, I wouldn't think of it." He turned to go, waiting for Smith who menacingly move out of the way as emphasis. Smith was clearly conveying that he was to obey Sy's orders unconditionally. He was almost out the door when he turned.

"My lord, there is something else," he stated.

"Yes?" Sy answered.

"I overheard them thugs talking about you. I couldn't hear all they were saying, but the gist was that they have a plan for you. You need to watch your back, my lord. They are up to no good, I tell you," he said.

"Thank you, Mr. Cyrus. Anything else?" he asked.

"They said something that made no sense too. Something about the sweetheart and that they wished their wives were as pretty. They said they couldn't wait to get you gone so they could have a go at her. Does that mean anything to you?" he asked. Sy paled and looked at Smith, who straightened at the statement. "I truly want to make amends, my lord, I truly do," he said sincerely.

"Thank you, Mr. Cyrus. Please wait in the other room." Sy was trying not to panic but Rhea being mentioned was gave him anxiety. He waited until Cyrus was gone.

"What the hell!" he shouted. "Was this a distraction to get me out of town so they could get to Rhea? Good God, I need to leave right now!"

"I'm going with you," Smith said, looking for his things.

"Thank you, Smith." He grabbed his satchel and threw in the manifests. "Quartermaster, can you please have our horses brought around?" he asked, as nicely as he could.

"Of course. What should I do about Cyrus, my lord?" he asked.

Sy stopped and tried to think on the situation, but he could hardly concentrate, feeling that Rhea may be in danger. He couldn't fault Cyrus for protecting his wife, but couldn't allow the sabotage either.

"Demote him for now. He's not to be around any sensitive material. He could still be useful in catching this Frankie

Two Toes. If he's willing to help and the result is favorable, we will reconsider his position. He seemed sincere to me. What do you gentlemen think?" he asked. He needed validation, as he knew he wasn't thinking clearly.

"He seemed sincere to me too. He didn't have to give up the extra information," Smith confirmed.

"He's always been an upstanding man. I know he's had some financial problems lately. He asked for more hours at work to compensate. It could be because he was trying to get out from under his marker. I will double the guards patrolling the yard and put him in a position where I can keep an eye on him." The quartermaster left the room.

"Do you really think this is about Rhea?" Smith asked.

"If Penelope is behind this it would make sense. She would lose her title and influence if Rhea was my Marchioness. She's vindictive enough, that much is proven. Either way, I'm not taking any chances," Sy replied.

"True. At least Titan and Jat are there to protect her," Smith pointed out.

"Yes, as long as Rhea relayed the message to them. I can't take the chance that she didn't, she is always rattling on that she can take care of herself, they won't be looking for trouble. Damn it, why didn't I go by and deliver the message in person? If anything happens to her..." Sy couldn't continue.

"Nothing's going to happen to her. We can take the shortcut I took to get here. It saved half a day. Let's go."

"Right behind you."

CHAPTER 21

*S*y would have galloped all the way to London. He was frustrated when they had to let the horses rest. Time seemed to drag as they traveled. They hadn't made it as far as he wanted and soon they would be forced to stop for the night.

"We are almost to the cut across," Smith said, trying to reassure Sy. "We will reach it in the morning and it will save us a half a day at least. If we can get new mounts at the inn we could push a little harder and save even more time," he reasoned.

"Good thinking, I will ask around once we get there." Thank God for Smith, he always helped him keep his head. The stress of the possibilities grated his nerves. The anticipation was killing him! Smith tried to lighten the mood.

"Wouldn't it be funny if we were racing across the countryside to get to Rhea and she was just sitting in the parlor at her aunt's house drinking tea and eating cakes?" Smith joked, trying to ease the tension.

"Wouldn't be the first time I made a fool of myself in front of her," he pointed out. They both chuckled.

Suddenly, two masked men jumped from the forest. One had a pistol trained on Sy, the other held a sword.

"Get off yer horses or I'll shoot you through, I will," the man holding the pistol threatened. "Roy, Mickey, get yer asses out here!" he yelled to someone in the bushes. Two other masked men came out behind them. Both were holding knives.

"Don't use me name, ya ass," one of the men exclaimed.

"Oh, shut up, what difference do it make anyway?" he answered. He looked at Sy, waved his pistol as he commanded, "I said get down, now! Both of ya!"

Calmly, Sy dismounted his horse. He couldn't reach for his knife without notice. In his haste to leave, he hadn't loaded his pistol. He and Smith were going to have to use their fists. He gave Smith a look that he knew he could read. Smith nodded discreetly. Was this a robbery or was this what Cyrus warned him about?

"Just take my money, we won't fight you. You can have the horses too," Sy said, in a tone that clearly meant neither was going to happen. He didn't have time for this. He needed to get to Rhea.

"Sorry Cap, ain't that easy, wish it were, but it ain't," he replied. Sy had his answer, and anger surged through his veins. Cyrus' warning was true. They knew who he was, they were there for him. "Now get down on your knees, nice and easy like," he ordered.

"Someone get the rope. Tie 'im up real tight, 'e's a big one alright. Get 'is friend too."

"Let him go, he has nothing to do with this, I'm the one you want," Sy said.

"Not to worry Cap'n. We took a vote and we ain't gonna kill ya 'ike they asked us. No worry 'bout that. We're just gonna send ya away for a while, 'at way we can get clear of this mess. We 'ave respect fer a man 'ike ya, it's no right what they're trying to do. We need ter fake yer death. So, don't give us no fuss an' this 'ill be over quick like," he reasoned.

Acting like he was going to comply, Sy went down on one knee and Smith did the same. As the assailant came close, Sy grabbed his ankle and pulled. The man landed flat on his back, knocking the wind out of him. He grabbed a handful of dirt and threw it in the other man's face. Smith kicked his assailant in the stomach, knocking him off his feet. He lunged toward the sword-wielding man and tripped him before he could attack Sy. Sy jumped up, kicked the pistol from the other man's hand and punched him in the nose. As he crumpled to the ground, Sy picked up the pistol and swung around to the others.

"Halt! Or I will shoot first and worry over it later," he commanded. The other three froze. Smith was livid and couldn't help but punch his opponent one more time.

"Now sit down right there. Smith, if you could divest them of their weapons please."

"It would be my pleasure," Smith said, sardonically. He retrieved their sword and knives, then dragged the unconscious man, dropping him next to the others. He patted him down for weapons, then removed the identity papers from the unconscious man's pocket and did the same to the others.

"Who sent you?" Sy asked, to confirm his suspicions.

"Frankie Two Toes," one of them blurted out. He got an elbow in the rib for his effort. "I ain't gonna lie no more. I'm only here cuz my brother-in-law got his self in trouble. I ain't gonna die or kill nobody fer nothin'. Look mister, we all voted an' we weren't gonna go through with it. We were just gonna put ya on a boat fer the Americas. We figured ya'd make yer way back soon enough. Ask them, they'll tell ya." He nodded his head towards the rest of his crew. "Yer were supposed to be by yerself. We meant no 'arm to yer friend. We're just tryin' to get clear of our markers 'ats all."

"So, it would seem to be the case with everyone lately. You said 'them,' who is Frankie working with?" he asked.

"Don't rightly know her name. Know she's upper crust though. Awful lady, whinin' all the time. Cryin' bout her title an' money ta Frankie. Don't know how 'e does it, couldn't stand to be around the lady me self." The others nodded in agreement.

"Could you identify her if you saw her again?" he asked.

"Yes sir, would never forget that lady," he answered.

"Do you know anything else about their plans? Why do they want me killed?" he questioned.

"Don't rightly know sir, she was whinin' 'bout her title an' that you was getting' married or somethin'. Swear that's all I know." He put his hand up as if he swearing before a court of law.

Sy looked at Smith and jerked his head to signal, "Let's go." Sy returned to his horse as Smith addressed the ruffians.

"We have your papers. I will be calling on you, so go back to London and wait. If you cooperate in identifying this lady and Frankie Two Toes you will be rewarded. Now, if you don't mind, I will be restraining you before we go. I'm sure that you can understand why." Smith said. Smith and Sy tied their hands and feet, then tied them together. They gathered all the weapons and departed.

"So much for tea and cakes," Sy said. "We need to find new mounts and ride through the night!"

"Agreed!"

TITAN LET himself into his aunt's townhouse without knocking. He found her in the parlor looking over Sy's note for the thousandth time. It irritated him that she couldn't accept what Sy had done and he was through trying to convince her. It had been three days and Rhea hadn't left her bed. Something needed to be done and rereading that stupid note wasn't helping anything.

"Burn that infernal thing, Aunt Magda. I don't want Rhea seeing it. Did she come down for breakfast today?" he asked, irritated.

"Hello, Titan. No, she hasn't come down. A broken heart is a hard thing to overcome, you must give her time. I still can't believe it." she whispered the last part and folded the note to put it in her pocket. "She just needs time, she'll recover, she's a strong woman," she stated, optimistically.

"Humph! She'll recover when I kill that son of a bitch," he said, under his breath.

"I heard that," Aunt Magda stated.

"I want to go home," Rhea said from the doorway. Both her aunt and brother were startled at the sound of her voice. She looked gaunt. She had on a light blue day dress and her hair was pulled back into a simple ponytail. Her eyes were red rimmed from crying and had black circles around them. She was holding a black leather box.

"Alright Rhe, I will take you home. I know being with mother and father will be the best place for you right now," he agreed.

"No, I want to go home, to *Paradiso*. That's where I belong," she stated, and walked over to her aunt. "Thank you, Aunt Magda for all you've done for me. Can you please see that this is returned to the Blackthornes? I don't feel right keeping it." She solemnly handed the box to her aunt.

"Dear, I am..." Titan gave Magda a look of warning. "I will see it done," she said, resigned.

"The *Star* will be stocked and ready to travel in two days,

289

Rhe. We can leave then," Titan stated. A panicked look came over Rhea's face. She went to her knees in front of him, grabbing his hands.

"Titan please, I need to go home. I...I can't stay here another moment. Everything reminds me of him. I'm going insane, I can't take it any longer, I'm losing my mind." She squeezed his hands in her panic, her eyes were filled with tears. "I have to go now. The *Rogue* is ready to go. You can catch me with the *Star* in a day or two. Jat can stay and finish preparing the *Star*. Liana can bring my things when she comes. I'll take Pax and Tom for protection. Please Titan, I can't stay here another moment." Tears welled and threatened to fall as she begged. It broke his heart to see her like this. Her face was filled with hurt and misery. She belonged to the sea and *Paradiso*. He sighed. He'd let her go home. He could catch her easily in the *Star*, that much was true. He had no choice, he had to let her go.

"Alright, Rhe," he said, and cupped the side of her face. "Get your things, high tide is in three hours. If you hurry, you can make it." He wiped a tear from her cheek. He saw a brief moment of joy and relief before she stood and ran up the stairs.

"Are you sure this is a good idea, Titan?" Aunt Magda asked, with concern.

"We would leave in two days' time anyway. I can see no reason to delay her misery. I can catch up with her. Let the sea and fresh air heal her, it's what she knows," he stated, sad for his little sister.

"This is not right, they deserve to be together. They were meant for each other," she said, in disbelief.

"Tell that to the rat bastard when he returns." Titan said. "Please send her to the docks when she's ready. I will go ahead to be sure everything is prepared. Thank you, Aunt Magda for all you tried to do for us. I mean it," he added.

"I will see you at the docks, I want to say goodbye to Rhea before she goes," she said, sadly.

IN HER ROOM, Rhea grabbed a small satchel from the wardrobe.

"There's really no reason to bring any of these gowns, Liana. I have no use for them. Just bring the day dresses for when I visit my parents," she stated, as she packed her leather pants, shirt, belt, and boots. She would change on the ship once they left port. The garments seemed foreign to her now, even though she had worn them just a month ago. She couldn't wait to feel the sea breeze on her face, in her hair and rid herself of dresses. She'd feel like herself again then, wouldn't she? She put her pistols and cutlass in the satchel. She pulled the knife Sy had given her out from under her pillow. She wasn't going to give it up. It once represented hope that he would accept her for who she was, but now it was a reminder to never trust anyone. She knew she was lying to herself. It was a piece of him. When she looked at it, she could see his face as he explained the markings to her.

She could feel his touch and his lips on hers when she held it. She hugged it close and it comforted her somehow. She had several nicks in her skin because of it. She threw it in her satchel, refusing to think about it. No more crying. She would go home and return to her work. She would continue to build *Paradiso* where she was loved, respected and accepted for who she was, pants and all.

"Bring only three of the day dresses," she told Liana. "Leave the rest behind, I don't want them," she stated. She hugged Liana, and then patted her rounding belly. "See you at home. Travel safe. Thank you for everything." She smiled at her, and then left for the last time.

Titan had everything ready at the docks. He looked down at his sister with concern.

"I don't know Rhe, maybe this isn't such a good idea after all." She panicked a little; she could not go back to her aunt's house. It was too painful to even contemplate. She had to convince him to let her go ahead.

"What are you saying? You can't captain the *Star* as well as me? Afraid you won't catch me in the *Rogue* because I will out maneuver you?" she challenged, with a sassy smile. "Let Jat captain then, he can catch me," she teased.

"Why you little minx!" he teased back, not knowing Sy used the nickname. It was like a stab to her heart but she didn't let her smile falter. She would fall apart on the ship once it left port.

"Give me a hug, Captain." She leaned in and he scooped her up in a comforting brotherly hug.

"Smooth sailing, Captain, take care of my ship. Remember she is full of cargo so she's going to be a little sluggish. Not like the *Star*," he told her. She rolled her eyes.

"Take care of my ship, too. Have fun and open her up a bit. She loves to fly." She kissed his cheek and went to Aunt Magda.

"There are no words for everything you've done for me aunt," Rhea said sincerely. "I hope it won't be too long before we see each other again."

"It'll be sooner than you think, I'm sure," Aunt Magda reassured her. "Have a safe journey dear."

Rhea walked up the gangway and greeted the crew. She looked back at her family on the dock, and had a feeling of unease as the gangway was removed. She stood and stared at Titan. He looked so worried. Pax came and stood beside her.

"Captain?" he asked, in a low voice. Without taking her eyes off her brother she shouted her orders.

"Weigh anchor!" she shouted for all to hear. The crew was bustling, getting the ship underway. "Pax, you have the helm, see her out of the bay. I need to get out of this infernal dress. Call me when we are at sea," she told him, in a commanding tone.

"Aye, Captain! You heard her boys, heave to!" he shouted.

Rhea walked to her brother's cabin and closed the door. She immediately ran to her satchel and retrieved the knife. She sank to the floor and let the tears flow. It was as if part of her had died. Would the pain ever go away? Would she ever feel herself again?

CHAPTER 22

*S*y and Smith arrived in London in less than two days. They were able to change mounts twice for a hefty price. Smith's shortcut helped as well. They were bone tired and covered in dust when they arrived at Rhea's aunt's townhouse. Sy was never more relieved. He needed to see Rhea and be sure she was safe before he could rest. Smith felt the same way, bounding up to the door step for step with Sy. He pounded loudly. The butler opened the door and immediately recognized him.

"I'm sorry, my lord, but Lady Chamberlain is not receiving visitors," he said, in a rejecting tone.

"She will damn well receive me!" He pushed his way through the door. "Where is Lady Hastings, I need to see her at once!" he yelled.

"I must insist, my lord, you must..." he tried to usher them out.

"It's alright, Stanley." Aunt Magda came floating down the staircase. "Lord Blackthorne, my heavens, you look horrible! What is going on?"

"Where is Rhea? I must see her at once. Is she well?" he asked, feeling like bellowing up the stairs for her. Aunt Magda looked at him confused.

"I don't know how that is possible, my lord, after the missive you sent," she stated. "Stanley, have someone send for Lord Huntington, let him know that Lord Blackthorne has returned."

Sy was confused, tired and frustrated. All he wanted to do was throw Rhea over his shoulder and take her home.

"Gentlemen, shall we retire to the parlor, you both look exhausted. Brandy?"

Sy allowed himself to led towards the parlor, "Please, madam, if you will just tell me where Rhea is, I will go to her."

"I do enjoy being correct," she said, under her breath as she poured the brandies. Sy was about to ask what she meant when she met his gaze and said, "I believe you are in for an insurmountable challenge, Lord Blackthorne."

"Lady Chamberlain," he said, trying to keep his patience in check. "My colleague and I have ridden for two days with no rest or food because we have good information that Rhea may be in imminent danger. So, you will forgive my bad manners. Where is my wife!" he yelled.

"Danger?" Her hand flew to her chest. "What do you

mean danger?" Sy lost his patience. He opened his mouth and Smith put a hand on his chest to calm him.

"Lady Chamberlain, if you could just have Lady Rhea come down, I think..." he couldn't finish his sentence. Titan came barreling into the room straight for Sy.

"You son of a bitch!" Before Sy had a chance to process that Titan was going to hit him, his fist flew and clocked him across the chin. Stunned, he flew backward a few steps, his hand going to his chin.

"What the hell was that for?!?" Sy yelled, confused.

"Titan stop!" Aunt Magda bellowed, as Titan lunged for Sy again, only to be stopped by Smith. Then Jat ran into the room, cutlass in hand. Aunt Magda was alarmed by the weapon. This was getting out of hand by the second. She needed to do something quick.

"Gentlemen stop this right now!" she bellowed, again.

Jat readied himself to come to Titan's defense. Smith, who was exhausted, was losing his grip on Titan. Sy took a defensive stance. Jat advanced on Smith to defend Titan. This was definitely getting out of hand. Aunt Magda looked around for something to get their attention. She grabbed a vase. She sighed, it was one of her favorites. Without further hesitation, she threw it at the fireplace. Everyone suddenly stopped fighting and looked towards the crash. She pounced.

"GENTLEMEN STOP THIS AT ONCE!" she yelled, at the top of her lungs. "Sit down, all of you, and we will get to the bottom of this!" They were stunned, staring at her like statutes. "SIT DOWN, NOW!"

Slowly, they separated. Smith took a seat next to Sy. Titan barely perched on the settee directly across from them. Jat stood behind Titan, refusing to sit. Aunt Magda walked over and took Jat's cutlass in two fingers.

"Stanley!" she yelled. He appeared instantly. He had most certainly been eavesdropping, "Take this and bring more brandy right away!" she whispered.

"Now. Let's get to the bottom of this without bloodshed, shall we? Lord Blackthorne, why do you think Rhea's in danger?" she started.

"He's the only one in danger here aunt." Titan said, venom dripping from his statement.

"What the bloody hell is going on here? Where is Rhea? Is she well?" Sy said, concern obvious.

"What the hell do you care you bastard? She is gone. To a place where you can never find her or hurt her again," Titan spat. Jat crossed his arms and nodded. Sy looked from Titan to Jat, and back again, confused. Aunt Magda intervened. She handed the missive to Sy.

"Did you write this message to Rhea, my lord?" she asked.

The blood drained from his face as he read it.

"She believed this?" he asked, incredulous. "I didn't write this. I love Rhea. She is mine, the love of my life, my wife, my responsibility, I would never hurt her. Oh, my God! Where is she! I have to tell her none of this is true." Dread filled him and his heart sank. He was suddenly lightheaded. He put his head between his hands trying regain his composure. Smith took the missive and read it. Anger surged through him.

"Titan, you bastard, you've known Sy since Eton. You believe he would send this cowardly note?" He looked Titan directly in the eye. Anger radiated in defense of his friend. He could see Titan change, shame coming to the forefront, and become embarrassed as he realized the truth.

"Rhea believed it. She was devastated and didn't eat or leave her room for three days. I guess I was so engrossed with my anger and her suffering that I didn't think it through. Sy look at me. Did you write this note to my sister?" He need to hear it from Sy's lips. In his heart, he knew the answer, but he needed to hear Sy say it.

Sy, face still in his hands, shook his head no. Then it struck him. Someone had switched the notes. That's how Frankie and Penelope knew they were getting married and not that they were already married. He had to find Rhea, she was in danger, and to do that he needed Titan to believe him.

"I most definitely did not. I did send a note but it said that I had go to the Blackthorne shipyard to investigate sabotage. I told her she owned my heart and soul and I would miss her desperately. It said that the banns would be posted on Sunday and to tell her aunt to start planning our wedding. I told her to be careful and to tell YOU that I placed her in YOUR protection. So, tell me, Titan. Where the hell is my wife!"

∾

TITAN LOOKED AT HIS AUNT, who gave him an 'I told you so' look. Titan, dreading the reaction, told Sy the truth.

"She went home, Sy. She took the *Rogue* and went ahead. She couldn't take the pain another day, she was going mad, so I let her go," he said, sheepishly, knowing that whatever came from Sy's mouth next would sting. He braced himself.

"Let me see if I understand this correctly. You let Rhea, by herself, take the *Rogue* into open waters with no gunship to protect her?" He stood slowly. "Are you insane? How long has she been gone?"

"Two days," Titan said. He watched the blood drain from Sy's face for the second time. This time he sank to his knees in despair. It was heart breaking to see, Sy crumple to the ground defeated.

"Oh, my God." He whispered. "Without the *Breakneck* I can't catch her." Smith put a hand on his friend's shoulder, feeling his pain. Titan immediately felt contrite. Smith tried to explain.

"Someone's been watching Lady Rhea and wishes to do her harm. We believe it to be the Marchioness Blackthorne trying to protect her title, with the help of a criminal named Frankie Two Toes. She has been pirating ships from Blackthorne with the Red Dragon's help. They set fire to the *Breakneck* and the Blackthorne offices. We were attacked trying to get back here to Lady Rhea. They had orders to kill us," Smith relayed, so they could understand the gravity of the situation. "Who in this house could've intercepted Sy's missive? They may have information that may help us," Smith asked.

"Millie delivered the missive. I will call for her." Aunt Magda left to call for Millie.

"I had no idea, sweet Jesus. We need to get to Rhea!" Titan said panic setting in, and looked at Jat. Jat nodded, and manually communicated to Titan. "Agreed, but they will need to agree to say the words and walk the line."

"What the hell are you jabbering on about? Haven't you done enough?" Sy said, coming to his feet with Smith's help. "You bastard, you may just have killed my wife, your sister." Sorrow and anger dripped from his words. Titan looked at Jat, then back to Sy and Smith, and gave them his 'cat that ate the canary' smile.

"Maybe not. We can catch her. Be at the docks in an hour," he said, with no explanation. Aunt Magda came rushing in with Millie, who looked distressed. Sy was beginning to recognize that look. It looked like Frankie Two Toes had his fingers in a lot of pies. He had no time for this, he needed to get to Rhea.

"Here is Millie, my lord," Aunt Magda announced. Sy walked up to her in his most intimidating pose.

"Who wrote the letter you delivered to Lady Hastings? I know it wasn't Frankie Two Toes, he couldn't write a message such as that. Tell me who it was girl. Now!" He had no patience left for politeness. She jumped and started crying.

"The Marchioness Blackthorne, my lord. I swear. I heard

her say the words to Freddie the Forger, I did. They made me wait so I could deliver it. I felt awful bad I did," she stammered.

"Yeah, yeah, you had no choice," he continued for her.

"I didn't want to have to poison no one like Tammy is doing, my lord, I thought it would do no harm," she sobbed.

"What?" Dread hit him for the third time this evening. "Who is Tammy poisoning? Speak up girl!" Sy shouted.

"She's done it twice before and she ain't got caught. So, they sent her over to do it again. She drugged yer father, my lord, once a long time ago, now they are tryin' to make him look sick, poisonin' him real slow like, so he'll die without nobody being the wiser. I heard her talking about it today. She's real proud of her work, she is. Puts the stuff in his tea so no one can tell," she confessed.

"Good God! They'll stop at nothing." He looked at Smith. "Lady Chamberlain do you think you could…"

"I will take care of your father. You gentlemen go save our girl. Go!" she said, pushing Titan's and Sy's shoulders.

Sy turned to Titan and punched him as hard as he could. Titan, taken by surprise, flew back and landed hard on the settee. Millie screamed and Aunt Magda stepped back.

"What was that for? I'm on your side!" Titan asked, rubbing his jaw.

"That's for leaving my wife unprotected and believing I sent that message. Be at the docks in an hour. You'd better have some miracle that can catch her or you will be receiving several of those." He walked out without looking back.

Smith looked around at the stunned faces.

"Lady Chamberlain. Can I bother you for paper and ink? I need to send a message to the Waterford estate before I depart. It is very important," Smith asked.

Within the hour, Sy took a quick bath, grabbed his sea trunk, and took his carriage to the dock. He should have been too exhausted to move but he couldn't stop worrying about Rhea. He had an overwhelming feeling of dread. If they were willing to go to the lengths they had with the sabotage, poison and assault then there was no predicting what they would do in pursuit of Rhea. He was pleased to see that Titan and Jat were there. Smith rolled up in a carriage a moment later.

"Smith, you don't have to go. Go, see to Miss Waterford," he suggested.

"I sent her a note explaining the situation. I told her I loved her too. Sounded like a sap, I'm sure, but I wanted her to know. How could I face her with her friend in jeopardy? I would feel like a coward. Besides, if it were Maisy instead of Rhea you would be at my side," he stated.

"You're damn right I would." He slapped Smith on the shoulder. Smith slapped him back.

"Let's go get your wife. I'm beyond curious what miracle Titan has to catch her. I'm also looking forward to getting some sleep. I've always slept better underway," he announced, and strode over to Titan. Sy looked at his friend's retreating back. He was very fortunate indeed, to have such a loyal friend.

He instructed the drivers what to do with the trunks, then walked over to Titan.

"Which vessel, Titan?" he queried, looking around the docks for a ship that might be worthy of the task.

"We have to take a short jaunt on the *Booty Taker* here, then we will be on our way." Sy looked at the small fishing boat that was barely sea worthy. He grabbed the front of Titan's shirt and lifted him off the ground.

"What the bloody hell, Titan! This is no time for jests!" he threatened.

"Whoa, whoa big guy. I need a little blind faith right now. I told you, warned you, that you would have to have it if you were to stay married to Rhea. This is one of those times," Titan recited. Jat walked up calmly and put his hand on Sy's shoulder. Once Sy made eye contact with him, he nodded. Sy slowly let Titan back down to his feet.

"Well, I for one, am intrigued. Let us be on our way gentlemen." Smith said, light heartedly. He walked over to the boat and jumped on its deck. Their trunks were loaded quickly. Titan and Jat jumped in next, followed by Sy after he had pushed them off.

Once out of port, they rounded the peninsula. Sy was quickly losing patience with Titan's shenanigans. Time seemed to be ticking by slowly as they sailed out to the open water. Titan was conferring with Jat, who was pointing to the sea. Didn't they know that Rhea was in danger? Where was their sense of urgency? How could he leave her vulnerable like that? Sy felt helpless, powerless. These were feelings he was unaccustomed to. Now he was in a small, less than seaworthy boat, barely able to make it across the bay, much less catch a fast-moving frigate in the open sea. He was just about to express his frustration when Titan and Jat came to him and Smith with serious expressions.

"Gentlemen, for us to proceed, I will need for you to swear your oath fealty to our brethren. I cannot allow you aboard without it. The crew will not stand for it. Jat will serve as witness until the marks can be made and you can walk the line before the Captain. Do you agree?" Titan announced.

"Aboard what?" Smith asked, scanning the sea.

Titan looked Sy squarely in the eyes.

"I know you love my sister, Sy. I see that clearly now. I did you a disservice when I didn't question the note as false, even when my aunt tried to convince me. I shouldn't have let Rhea go off on the *Rogue* ahead of me, unprotected. Truth is, she's special and she's has had me wrapped around her little finger for a long time. I wasn't thinking clearly. I was blinded by anger at the hurt I saw in her eyes. For that, I apologize. Please believe me, I would never intentionally put my sister in danger." He put his hand on Sy's shoulder in solidarity. Sy nodded in acceptance. "With that said, I cannot break my oath to our brethren. Not even for Rhea. You will have to swear yourself in to continue. I need just a little more of that blind faith I warned you about. I swear to you on my life that we will get Rhea back or die trying. Do you agree?" Sy looked at Smith. At their nods, he proceeded.

"As Captain of the *Rogue* I accept you as a brother. From this moment on I will give my life for yours if needed. You will be given no favor. You must follow orders without objection and with haste. You will never steal from your brothers. You will never be a traitor to *any* ship in our fleet or its crew even if you must give your life. You will treat all women and men of association with honor and respect and protect them as your own. From this moment on you will never abandon your brothers unless life has left their body, or yours, for they will do the same for you. To these terms do you pledge yourself?"

"Yes, we do." Sy and Smith said in unison. Titan clapped Sy's hand and shook it. He did the same to Smith. Jat was next.

"Jat, note the coordinates. They will receive their mark and walk the line underway, but we will have to go get her Captain first." Titan said.

"What? You are not the Captain?" Smith asked, perplexed.

"No. I am Captain of the *Rogue*, not this ship. Fly my colors Jat," he ordered. Jat climbed the mast and unfurled the flag of the Black Lyon.

Sy and Smith looked at each other in shock.

"You're the Black Lyon!" Sy exclaimed in shock. "If you're not the Captain then who the bloody hell did we just swear fealty too?"

They looked at the sea, expecting a ship come into view over the horizon. The white blinding light caught them by surprise. They both covered their eyes till the light dissipated. Just ahead, a ship appeared as if from nowhere. What?

"You swore fealty to the White Lyon." he said, sporting his usual irritating grin.

"What!" Smith said, shocked. "If you are the Black Lyon then who is the White Lyon?" he asked, confused.

They pulled up beside the ship and ropes came down for them. Shouts of greeting rained down. Titan leaned forward so he wouldn't have to repeat his answer. He looked Sy straight in the eye and said.

"Rhea. Rhea is the Captain of the *Star*. Rhea is the White Lyon."

CHAPTER 23

*J*at immediately took the ropes and hooked up the trunks. With a signal to the ship, they quickly shot up to the crew waiting to receive them. The process was repeated until all the trunks had been loaded. Then they lowered a line with a loop at the bottom, Jat put his foot in it, signaled, and shot up the side of the ship.

"What the hell?" Smith gasped. "How are they doing that?" he asked Sy, in a whisper.

"I have no idea," Sy replied, looking up trying to figure it out.

"Come on gentlemen, it's fun, Rhea and Otis invented it. Cuts loading and unloading time by half," Titan said, as he reached for the rope. "Smith you're up. Put your foot in the loop and hold on."

Smith put his foot in the loop. Titan signaled, and Smith shot up the side of the ship.

"Rhea invented that?" Sy asked Titan, with awe and surprise.

"Rhea designed the entire ship, Sy. Otis helped her with a lot of the mechanical engineering and added a few things, but Rhea was the mastermind behind the *Star's* design. She's special, I keep telling you. Here, go aboard and see for yourself." Titan handed Sy the rope.

In shock, Sy put his foot in the loop, and his stomach plunged as he shot up the side quickly. Once at the top of the rail he jumped to the deck. The crew was lined to up meet him with curious, but skeptical, looks. So, this was Rhea's crew? He wondered how they were going to take the news that he was her husband. Smith stepped to him excitedly.

"Wasn't that fun? I want to do it again. It's ingenious really, so simple, it's done with a counterweight. Can't believe someone hasn't thought of it..." Sy watched over Smith's shoulder while a big menacing-looking man walked toward them rapidly.

"Later Smith," Sy said, in a warning tone. Sy heard the line whiz as Titan was hoisted up. All the while, he kept his eye on the menacing looking gentlemen headed their way. He didn't seem to have a weapon on him but he didn't trust he wouldn't pull a knife.

"Ho, ho there, Timbo." Titan moved forward blocking his path. "Didn't Jat explain what's going on?" he asked, putting his hand out to stop the giant.

"He were tryin' to, till I saw these scallawags board. Then I come over here to tend to business, if you know what I mean, Cap," Timbo answered, looking directly at Sy, the threat clear in his eyes.

"No need for that Timbo, they said the words. Jat was the witness. Shorty will give them their marks when we are underway," Titan explained.

"Captain weren't lookin' fer no new crew to my knowin', why are they here?" he asked, still not happy with Sy and Smith's intrusion.

"I can vouch for them and assure you that your Captain will approve their oath. Let me introduce them. This is Lord Smith, first mate to this gentleman..." he motioned to Sy, "The Marquess of Blackthorne, owner of Blackthorne Shipping, Captain of the *Breakneck*. Known to you gents as Captain Sy Black and also...," he paused, to prepare himself, "Captain Rhea's husband." He rushed out. The crew surged forward. Questions started flying. Some were astonished, others angry, others questioning the truth of it. Sy had his work cut out for him with this crew. Their loyalty to Rhea was apparent. He didn't blame them for their reaction, but he needed their help.

"Halt!" he bellowed, in a commanding voice. "I will be happy to address all your questions and concerns, but this is not the time. Your Captain, my wife, is in danger. She is three days ahead of us in the *Rogue* with no gun ship. I have reason to believe that she is being pursued by those associated with the Red Dragon. They mean to overtake her and do her harm!" He turned to Titan. "Captain, can we please get underway?" He gave Titan a pleading look.

"He's right. Weigh anchor!" he ordered. "We'll deal with this underway. Jat you have the coordinates. Heave ho, gents! It's time to see how fast the *Star* can fly."

"Your order for the *Booty Taker,* Captain?" Timbo asked.

"Set her adrift. We have no time to deal with her now," Titan replied.

"How can we help, Captain?" Sy and Smith stood next to Titan.

"Go below and try to get some sleep. You both look about to drop. You're no good to me like you are. I need able bodies to keep this vessel at top speed. You can take the second watch," he told them both. "Sy, we'll catch her," he tried to reassure him. "Get some sleep. I need you at your best." Titan put his hand on Sy's shoulder again. "Take Rhea's cabin. It has the biggest bed. Smith, you bunk with Jat in the first mate's cabin. I'll see you when the first bell tolls."

"Aye, Captain," they replied, in unison.

"Larry, show Captain Black to the Captain's quarters and Smith to the first mate's. See that their trunks are delivered." A young boy with a deformed hand led the way. He opened the door to the Captain's cabin and let Sy pass.

"This is you, Captain. I'm Larry Little Hand, they call me that cuz'n I got a little hand see." He showed him his deformed hand. "Do you think they will hurt her, sir? I couldn't abide anything ta happen ta her, ya know," he asked, with concern.

"Not if I can help it son," Sy replied, with authority. "You just get me to her and I'll keep anything from happening to her. I swear it on my life."

"If she's only three days 'afore us, we'll catch her. The *Star* is fast as the wind, sir. Ya wait and see," he said, with pride. "Your *Breakneck* almost caught us tho', we were all impressed with ye that day, fer sure we were. Still talk 'bout you from time to time. Yer kinda a legend on this ship," he exclaimed.

"Is that so?" he said, surprised.

"Well, I'll leave you be, sir. You look dead tired if I do say so myself. With the Captain gone they're sure gonna need you gents to help with the relief. This way Smith, yer down the hall a spell." With that, they walked away and Sy closed the door.

He looked at the cabin. Jasmine assaulted his senses. He walked over to where the wash station was. Her soap was in a bowl next to a pitcher. He picked it up and smelled it. Pain radiated in his chest as memories flooded in. My God, she must have been so hurt to flee like she did. Anger immediately replaced the pain. How could she believe that message after all they were to each other? After all the things he said to her? After they made love? He should have told her he loved her. When he found her, he was going to wring her neck. First, he was going to kiss her for days and make love to her till she couldn't walk, then he was going to wring her neck. He wanted her back. He sat on the bed and pulled off his boots. He was still holding the soap in his hand when he laid down. As soon as his head hit the pillow, he was asleep.

Hours later, Sy went on deck to look for Titan. He had his spyglass in his hand. He walked to the bow of the ship and scanned the horizon with his glass. Nothing but the horizon and the setting sun came into view.

"We probably won't intercept her till late tomorrow if we catch good wind." Titan said, coming up behind him. "I can show you on the charts, maybe you'll see something I don't. That's quite a spyglass you have there. Mind if I have a go?" he asked, impressed. Sy handed it to him with one hand. Titan took it from Sy with one of his but wasn't quite prepared for its weight and quickly grabbed it with both. "Whoa! It's heavy. You hold this up to your eye?"

"I'm used to it, I had it custom made. It can see ten leagues, but the price for that range is the weight. Brace your elbow on the rail to steady it. I warn you though, if you drop it in the sea, you'll be swimming after it," Sy said, gruffly. Titan did as he suggested. He scanned the horizon, getting used to the spyglass.

"This is amazing, a very useful tool. Can't wait for Rhea to see it. I should warn you though, she'll tear it apart to see how it works. She'll probably figure out how to make a better one too," he stated, with a chuckle. Sy gave him a stern look.

"How is it that you aren't out of your mind with worry? I can hardly breathe; my chest is so constricted. I can't stand this anticipation," Sy stated bluntly.

"I have to be myself around the crew. They love her

beyond reason. If I start to show my panic, then they will panic too," he pointed out. "Trust me, I'm not as put together as I act. I've never been in love with someone like you are with my sister. I can see that it's more difficult for you."

"You have no idea," Sy said, solemnly. He just wanted to punch everything. "Let's take a look at those charts. I feel better when I'm busy," he stated. They walked back to the Captain's quarters and looked at the charts.

"I'm guessing she's probably about here," Titan pointed to a location on the map. "We are somewhere here. The *Rogue* is fully loaded and therefore going to have a lot of drag. She won't push it either and will stay away from the normal shipping routes until we join her. She'll probably slow down, too, if she doesn't catch sight of us by tomorrow midday. She knows not to go in these waters unprotected." He circled a part of the charts with his finger. "Rhea would never put her crew at risk. Besides, Pax, my first mate, wouldn't let her," he explained.

"Does she always do what you tell her to?" he asked, curious. Titan chuckled.

"She never does what I say, but I know she would never put her ship or crew in harm's way," he said, seriously. Smith came into the room, looking for Sy.

"Sy! This ship is a marvel. I've been looking around, as much as the crew will let me, you will not believe the innovations. It's incredible. There are things here that will revolutionize the ship building industry." He looked at Titan. "I can understand why you have been keeping her hidden. It's unbelievable."

"Have Shorty give you your marks. The crew is superstitious and suspicious. They will never trust you until that is done. Then I'll have someone take you around and show you everything. She really is worth the look," Titan relayed. "I have to get back on deck. Come see me when it's done. Here Sy." He handed him the spyglass.

"Keep it for now. It may be of some use later."

"Did he threaten to make you swim for it if you dropped it in the sea?" Smith asked Titan.

"Yes, he did. Why?" Titan answered.

"Good. I wanted to be sure it wasn't just me he didn't trust with that Goliath of thing." He sounded satisfied. "Come Sy, let's go find this Shorty. I want a better look at the ship before we get distracted." He walked out of the room, expecting Sy to follow.

Shorty was an older fellow with somewhat shaky hands. Smith looked nervous, so Sy went first. He was pleased to see that Shorty used rum as an antiseptic before he started. He was done in quick order, doing a surprisingly excellent job, despite the quiver in his hands. Sy couldn't see the whole mark on his shoulder but took Smith's word that it looked good. He stood by with a rum soaked rag over his new mark and watched Smith get his. He wondered what Maisy would think of this whole business? Her future husband being in league with a band of mythical pirates. He guessed she might never know, would Smith keep it from her? Could he keep it from her? This was all new territory for him. He's never had to figure out what to do with a wife before.

"Yer finished. Tell me young Mister Smith. Do yer intend to steal all my *Star's* secrets now that you've seen her?" Shorty looked into Smith's eyes.

"Certainly not!" Smith said, affronted. "I admire the innovations and may make a suggestion or two to improve them. But I am not a thief, sir. I certainly would not steal from the brethren!" he replied, sincerely. Shorty stared at him, taking his measure.

"I believe ya boy," he said, and slapped Smith's mark. Smith flinched but didn't cry out. "Welcome to the *Star*. Better get used te it boy. Yer gonna get a question from each of us now. Better hope all yer answers earn ya a slap or you'll be swimming home, ya will. It'll be worse when ya walk the line of acceptance. If you ain't bright red and bleedin' then yer in trouble. Means they don't trust ya boy. Same goes fer you Cap'n Black. I'm thinkin' you got it worse comin'. Ya really married her son?" he asked Sy.

"We were married by proxy but we will be married properly once we return. I have made all the arrangements," he answered. Shorty stood up and looked him in the eye just as he had Smith.

"Do ya love her son?" he asked, seriously.

"With all that I am, I would die for her." He answered quickly and looked Shorty straight in the eye to prove his sincerity.

"I believe ya too, son. Let me see it." Sy pulled the rag away. He examined the mark for a minute then gave it a resounding slap. "She needs a strong man that loves her deep. She's unique, that one. She can twist any man around her finger easy as a knife through butter. I envy yer and don't envy yer at the same time. If yer knowin' my meanin'. They don't call her the White Lyon cuz of her hair ya know." He made that statement and walked out the cabin.

"What the hell did we get ourselves into?" Smith asked, after Shorty left.

"Not sure yet. It could be heaven or it could be hell. But this I know, that will depend on if we get Rhea back," he answered.

Smith and Sy walked to the bridge, where Titan was discussing something with Jat. Sy was intrigued with their silent language. He would like to have known what the signs meant. He remembered Rhea talked to Jat the same way when she was a girl. He would like to learn more about Rhea's world. To be honest, he never thought about her past, only about their time together and the future he planned. Now he realized he hadn't taken into consideration what she would be leaving behind to be his Marchioness. He also realized he knew very little about what she did before they met in London. He wouldn't make that mistake again. He would use this time to learn everything he could about her.

"Everything going as planned?" he asked Titan timidly, trying not to pry in his ship's business.

"You can ask anything you want Sy. Please feel free to join

in any conversation. Technically, this ship belongs to you. I'm only Captain until you get up to speed with her mechanics and what she can do. Are your marks done then?" he asked. When they showed him and he smiled. "Well then, let's get started, shall we? But first, I'm starving. Let's go to the galley and get something to eat. I'm sure you're full of questions that need answers. I will endeavor to answer them while we eat."

"Shouldn't we eat in the Captain's cabin, for privacy?" Smith pointed out.

"No need. The galley will do." He walked down the stairs. They noticed that even when they went down below the waterline, natural light lit the stairwell. The galley opened up to a bright room with rows of tables. The last shift was taking their afternoon meal. Everyone had a pensive attitude. Smith was trying to figure out the light source, since there were no candles. He walked over to a light well and peered up the hole. Then he scanned the room a second time, staring intently at the walls. When he returned, he was scratching his head. Titan sat at a table away from the rest of the men. He motioned for Sy and Smith to come sit with him.

"What is the light source for this room?" Smith asked. "I don't see a single candle," he asked Titan.

"Right now, it's sunlight. This ship is full of mirrors. Mirrors were the inspiration for the *Star*. Rhea was looking at one, playing with the light it reflected and got an inspiration. It exploded from there. She built light wells around the perimeter of each room. As the sun rises and sets, the mirrors are adjusted to reflect down the wells. Genius really, the system lights all four floors of the ship. A few strategically placed mirrors in the stairwells pick up the light from the rooms. They act as a defense mechanism as well. You can see who is coming and going if you know where the mirrors are. Also, they reduce the risk of fire, and are brighter than candles.

The chickens love the light, too. We get a large bounty of eggs because of all the light in the store room. They don't even know they're on a ship. No hard tack for the *Star*. We get fresh baked goods using real eggs. Can't you smell it? Ah, here comes our food. You'll get to taste the difference right now." A large potbellied gentleman brought three bowls of delicious smelling stew and a basket of freshly baked buns. Titan reached for one. "Thank you, Philippe."

Sy and Smith looked at each other and heartily dug into the food. Between racing to London and leaving hastily for the ship, they hadn't had a decent meal in days. The rolls were right out of the oven and were divine. After a few good bites, Smith went back to his questions.

"What about at night, when there no sunlight?" he queried, his mouth full. Titan didn't look up from his food to answer.

"Oil lamps in the same light wells, not as bright, but good enough. Also, serves a dual purpose. They light the lower floors and the deck. The lamps are below the rail and very faint, but enough to walk around at night. There are no lanterns, making the *Star* indiscernible at night. It's actually quite beautiful on deck, wait and see," he explained.

"How does the *Star* disappear?" Smith inquired.

"Now that explanation is more complicated. I'll let Rhea and Otis fill you in on the details. Basically, we use mirrors again. We have a screen that covers either the front or the rear of the ship and reflects the sky and sea at the horizon. It effectively makes it seem like the ship disappears. Only drawback is that we can't fire the rear cannons when the cloaking device is deployed. If someone spots us they can fire and we are defenseless. That's why we never let the *Star* get close. She was only a diversion. She got very good at the deception. She was skilled at sneaking up behind ships and disabling their rudders. Sy, you're the only one that gave chase and had even the smallest chance of catching her. Personally, I think she slowed down to get a look at you and the *Breakneck*. I had to admit, I was curious myself. Is your ship as fast as they claim?" he asked, leaning in for the answer. By this time, some of the other members of the crew came over to sit and listen.

"Does she really have two rudders? I heard she has one that you use and one that can be pushed out in case the main one is taken out?" someone said.

"I heard she has four guns in the bow and three aft. If that is so, how do you keep her from divin' in the rough seas?" someone else asked.

More questions came, one after the other. Sy nodded permission for Smith to answer. They were sworn to each other now. They had been forthcoming with information about the *Star*. He guessed Titan was right, technically the *Star* was his and Rhea's, but he felt no ownership. This crew knew the ship better than he could in the short time he'd been aboard. He would never take away Rhea's accomplishments or claim her rank. But, he was very curious how she had gotten here. He looked over to Titan. He nodded his head toward the door in a signal for him to follow. They left Smith to answer the crowd's questions.

"Can I speak to you alone? Smith can answer these questions, he helped design the *Breakneck*," Sy said.

"Lead the way," Titan said, following Sy up the stairs to the Captain's cabin. He closed the door.

"I had no idea. I would've never suspected Rhea would be involved something like this. How did all this start?" Sy started the conversation.

"It's about time you asked. I was thinking your reaction to this was quite...quite...stoic," Titan remarked.

"Tell me then, what is the proper reaction when you find out that your wife is the mythical White Lyon, a pirate that you have been pursuing for months, to whom you were married by proxy? Oh, before you answer, please take into account that I have fallen in love with her, raced across the English countryside for two days and am now racing across the seas to save her because she's in eminent danger." He looked at Titan. After a short pause, Titan answered.

"Point taken. I'll tell you everything you want to know. Ask me anything." He sat down and settled in.

"Just give me a summary from the time I left that summer."

"Alright, let's see...where to begin? Rhea, with Jat in tow, followed me everywhere, trying to show me the little boats she built, toys mainly. I thought it annoying little sister stuff, trying to get attention. One day, she must've been fourteen or so, I challenged her to a boat race, hoping she would get disenchanted with sailing once and for all. I bet her that when she lost, she would give it up and go to finishing school like my mother had begged. She bet that if she won, I would let her earn her mark on the *Rogue* as one of my crew. I thought I had her. Even if I lost, I didn't think she'd want to spend her time doing grunt work on my ship with a bunch of gruff gents."

"So, what happened?" Sy asked.

"She beat me, good and sound! It wasn't even close. She and Jat built a little sailboat that flew across the water. It was humiliating. I had no choice but to bring her aboard the *Rogue*. She earned her spurs with no complaints, and wrapped that burly crew around her finger in a flash. One day, the deck boy slipped and fell overboard. Before anyone could react, she had a line tied around her waist and dove overboard in a flash. She saved that boy. We pulled them both out, alive and well. It was unbelievable. Her judgment was unselfish and her reflexes fast. She won the crew over that day. She was no longer the little sister of the Captain but a man of her own. To my surprise, my parents agreed to let her get her mark. She has a mark on her leg, and walked the line like everyone. Our parents wouldn't let her be gone more than a week at a time though, so she was only allowed to take the local voyages. The men looked forward to her voyages, and, truth be told, so did I. I never had so much fun in my life.

When she matured a little, she started to get attention from the officers in port. The crew was not having any of it, which made it difficult for her. There was one lieutenant that stood out, and he offered for her, but my father turned him down. He tried to take her. Crawled in her window one night and tried to ruin her, rape her. She almost killed him with a knife," he said, deep in memory. Sy looked away. Jealousy and anger hitting him hard.

"What happened to this lieutenant?" he asked, harshly.

"We dispatched him directly. I doubt he could ever pleasure a woman again. Pax and Tom, they kicked him in the crotch over and over on the way back to his ship. I doubt his pecker would ever work again," he recalled.

"Where is he now?" Sy asked, still perturbed.

"Don't know. We left it for the Royal Navy to deal with on the orders of my father. Never saw him again."

"What happened after that?" Sy asked.

"Rhea threw herself into ship design and working on the *Rogue*. Then we met Otis and they eventually built the *Star*. She assembled her own crew and started to assist me with running off the Red Dragon. Finally, my parents said we needed to go to England to fulfill our duties. Truly, I think they just wanted us to stop before someone caught us or one of us got hurt. You know the story from there." He sat back in his chair, spent.

Sy could tell there were a lot of details missing. He wouldn't push his brother-in-law today. But it did explain some things about Rhea, such as the bargain, her tepid response to the necklace and the enthusiastic response to the knife. It also explained her reluctance to the marriage, once he found her he would make it clear he didn't care about any of that. They would decide together how their future would go.

The alarm bell rang. Sy and Titan were out the door in a flash. They could hear the call long before they reached the deck. Sy's heart leapt in his throat.

"Sail ho! Larboard!" the shout came from above.

"Where's my spyglass!" Sy shouted. Titan retrieved it from a nook where he had stowed it. Sy ran to the front left of the ship. Everyone jumped out of his way. He raised the spyglass. His heart dropped. Two ships were grappled together, one had a large smoking hole in its stern, on the other, the foremast was down, laying across the length of the ship. Oh, my God. He tried to identify the ships. The Blackthorne crest was still visible on the ship with the smoking hole. He handed the spyglass to Titan.

"I believe the ship larboard is the *Bounty*," he said. "Can you identify the other? There was a battle. The foremast is down."

"Oh, my God, it's the *Rogue!*" he said, with terror. "Prepare for battle, gents! Shoot the *Star*, now, before they spot us!" Titan bellowed. The ship was a flurry of men running to their stations. Sy stood stunned and anxious, staying out of the way as the crew manned their stations. Dread filled his body and his knees went weak at the thought of Rhea being on that ship. *Get it together Sy, it's no time for you to fall apart.* Smith ran up to hand him his cutlass and pistols. He looked at the trepidation on Sy's face.

"What are your orders, Captain?" Smith asked, in an attempt to bring him back to the present. "Captain! What. Are. Your. Orders. Sir!" he shouted. Sy shook his head.

"Prepare to board. Find Rhea first, let the crew dispatch the others. They would've taken her below deck." Sy shouted over the sound of the rigging hissing as they launched the cloaking device. Smith looked around in awe as a screen came up and the tell-tale white light flashed. The screen was covered in a sparkling silvery substance. They could see the ships they were approaching through the screen.

"What are they doing?" Smith called out, over the noise.

"Prepare to fire bow cannons!" Titan bellowed.

The order was echoed over and over until it reached below. Sy grabbed his spyglass and looked at the men scurrying around on the *Rogue*. What were they doing? They were trying to untangle something, working frantically at it, a flag maybe? Why would they be trying to fly a flag unless....

"Hold that order, Captain!" he shouted. The crew waited for orders from Titan.

"Hold!" he shouted. It echoed to the men down below. Titan ran to Sy.

"What do you see?" he shouted, anxious.

"Three men, one frantically waving in our direction, the other two fighting with a piece of cloth, a flag I think. They may be trying to show us their colors," he replied.

"Is it white? Are they trying to surrender?" he shouted. The flag unfurled at the stern of the *Rogue*. It was the flag of the Black Lyon. Relief washed over him. Rhea had won the battle.

"It's your colors, the Black Lyon!" He looked at Titan, relief visible between them.

"Thank God!"

CHAPTER 24

*S*y didn't wait for the Star to pull up and be grappled to the *Rogue*. He cut a line from the mainmast and swung on to the deck as soon as they were close enough.

"Where's your Captain?" he asked, to everyone. Titan followed his lead and swung himself to the deck.

"They took her, sir," a man rushed out. Sy saw stars and his heart dropped into his stomach. He grabbed the man's shirt with one hand and lifted him off his feet.

"What do you mean they took her! Who took her?" he shouted. Titan came up behind him and put a hand on his shoulder.

"We know this man, Sy. This is Tom, remember? He's a brother and loyal to me and my sister. Put him down so he can tell us what happened," Titan cajoled. Sy dropped the man. Tom stood up and gave a wary glance Sy's way then faced Titan.

"We did all that we could Cap, I swear. It was that lieutenant we beat some time ago. When he saw her, he walked right up and punched her, knocked her right out. They dragged her away. Charlie took a knife to the gut tryin' to save her. Don't think he's gonna make it. We were outmanned. We surrendered, hopin' they would let her go. He just dragged her off to the other ship, not listen' to nobody," Tom rushed out, his fear and anxiety evident.

"How'd you re-gain control of the *Rogue?*" Smith asked. When did he get here? Sy thought. He didn't even notice, all he could concentrate on was that Rhea was missing.

"They tied us up. That other Captain was in a big hurry to get underway. He didn't even look at the cargo. He left the other crew to clean up this mess. It weren't an hour after the other ship left that this gentleman here came and untied us." He pointed to a man standing next to him. "Said he was loyal to Blackthorne, not that sadistic Captain Riley. We joined together with the others loyal to Blackthorne, took the ship back and defeated the crew. Threw 'em overboard we did. Let 'em live at the bottom of the sea for all we care. We were trying to repair the ship when we saw the light of the White Lyon. We knew it was you."

"Where's Pax?" Titan asked, dreading the answer.

"He's down with doc, took a knife to the leg, needed to be stitched up," he answered. Titan's relief was palatable. Sy could tell he had the same kinship with this Pax as he did with Smith, but he had to interrupt. They were wasting time.

"How long ago did they leave?" he asked. Tom took a step back warily.

"Four hours, maybe more," he replied, cringing, waiting for Sy to hit him.

"Which direction? Did he say where they were going?" Sy asked, trying not to scare the man.

"South by southeast. The man likes a brothel in New Haven. He will head there. I'd stake my life on it!" came a voice from behind them. They both turned around. Pax stood there, his anger for the situation palatable.

"I suggest we get underway Captain. He has our girl and he got a chip on his shoulder for what we did to 'im." Pax said, in an angry protective voice. "If he laid one finger on her, I'm killin' him Cap and there's nothing you can say to stop me this time."

"Not if I get to him first," Sy stated, and turned to re-board the *Star*. "If you aren't on this ship in one minute, I'm leaving without you." The crew had already started readying for their departure.

"I'll stay here and get one of these vessels seaworthy. I will get them back to the Blackthorne shipyard and wait for you there. Go get your girl, Sy!" Smith knew he was more help here than on the *Star*. Pax, Titan, Tom, and two large burly seamen boarded the *Star* behind Sy. Sy took his cutlass and cut the mooring lines to free the ship. He looked at Smith and nodded his head in appreciation. He nodded back.

"Smith has the helm!" Titan called to his crew. "His orders are as if I said them myself. We will return as soon as possible," he called out, as the *Star* started to move. Smith then turned and started barking orders. They took long boards and helped the *Star* cast off. They were underway in minutes.

It was getting dark fast. Sy and Titan consulted with Jat about the *Stars'* capability of maneuvering at night. Jat pantomimed that it had never been tested above five knots. Sy didn't care. He pushed it to eight knots for two and a half hours before he slowed down. The deck lights were a godsend. So was the half-moon they had that evening, at least they could see across the bow for obstacles but they were still pushing it. Jat navigated by the stars. Titan consulted the charts with Pax and Tom. Sy's arms were shaking from holding his spyglass to his eye looking for any sign of the other ship. Where was his Rhea? Were was his wife?

～

"SHE AIN'T WAKE up yet, Cap? Ya must've clocked her real good," someone said.

"That's not all she's gonna get," the captain said with a sneer. "If she doesn't wake up soon, I'm gonna wake her up. I just wanted to get my distance from the other ships before I started. Once I do, I don't want to be interrupted understand?" He issued the order as if he were talking to a simpleton.

"Aye, Cap. You just let ol' Lenny know when yer ready to start yer business. I'll guard yer door just like last time," he responded. "I likes to hear the noises. Makes me feel funny in my stomach it does, I likes it," he replied happily. "I likes that you let me touch 'em some when yer done too. It don't matter none that they don't move no more, I still likes it," he said excitedly, in anticipation.

"This one is special Lenny. If I don't get too carried away, you may get to play with her while she's still moving. Would you like that?" Nigel asked him, like a parent talking to a child. "No promises but I'll try. Ok?"

"Yes Cap! Please try. Oh, yes please try to control yerself!" Lenny exclaimed, running in place and clapping his hands. He laughed a childish laugh.

"Then go fetch me a pail of water and we'll wake her up," he commanded, feeling excited himself.

Nigel looked over at Rhea, slumped against his wall. How many women had he tied there, in that exact spot, fantasizing it was her? Now, she was really here. He was nervous. What would she think of him now? She was captain of that ship, much to his surprise. The other women had been intimidated by the fact that he was the captain, but Rhea was a captain herself. Would she cower like the others? She had bested him that night, long ago. He could still feel her knife at his throat. She would've killed him if her brother hadn't run in the room when he did. Now he could never pleasure a woman, thanks to those thugs who took him back to the docks. It had taken months for him to recover. And the pain! There were times he'd wished they'd killed him instead. Anger surged through his veins at the thought. He couldn't remember their faces but he could remember hers. He had dreamed of her, the last woman to get his member hard. Now he had to make do with a wooden replacement. He hated it. It embarrassed him to his core, he would shove it into them until they screamed in pain, the same pain he felt every time that he had to use it. He couldn't stand the screaming. The pillow worked best for him; muffled the sound while he finished his task. Lenny took over after that, God knows what he did to them. He didn't care. Lenny always discarded the leftovers to the sea, so he didn't have to deal with it.

He lifted Rhea's head. She was more beautiful than he remembered, even with the bruise forming on her chin where he had hit her. He gently moved some of the hair that covered her features. God help him, he still loved her. She was to be his forever. If it hadn't been for her stupid father, everything would have been different. He dropped her chin and poured himself a glass of rum. This wasn't going to be as easy as he had thought. He knew she was on that ship, Frankie Two Toes had sent him after her, and he jumped at the chance. He was to hold her and wait for instructions, but that scum was never getting her back. She was finally his, and he was never letting her go. After all these years of thinking about revenge, what he would do to her, what he would say to her, now she was here. He wished she would wake up so he could talk to her.

Lenny returned with the bucket of water.

"Here ya go Cap. Do yer want me to pour it on her?" he said, with anticipation.

"No Lenny, put it down and go get something to eat. By the time you get back, your favorite noises will be coming through the door. You go eat a *full* meal first, then come back, understand?" he instructed. He had things to say to her that he didn't want anyone to hear. Not even Lenny.

"I understand Cap. I'll eat and then stand by the door till yer done, right?" he asked. At the captain's nod, he continued. "Then it'll be me turn, right? You'll try to keep her movin' some fer me this time, right?" he asked.

"I'll try, now go on Lenny," he ordered.

"Aye, Cap, I be goin' right now." Lenny left. Nigel followed him and locked the door.

RHEA HEARD him turn the lock. The sound made her stomach drop. She had no choice now, God help her. Rhea had pretended to be unconscious, trying to bide her time till she was left alone. She couldn't believe Nigel Riley was captain of this ship. How could this be? She peeked under hooded eyelids and tried to survey the room. What kind of captain never left his cabin for Christ sake? She'd faked that she was unconscious for hours, waiting for him to leave. Her neck was cramped. Her shoulders ached from being tied to an iron ring bolted to the wall. She didn't know if she could keep up this ruse much longer. Her knife was on his desk. If he would just leave, she might be able to kick it off and cut the ties binding her hands.

Now, she had no choice, she would have to talk to him and try to stall. She prayed that Titan had found the *Rogue* and was on his way in the *Star*. It was a long shot but it was all she had to cling to. She would have to try and subdue him. Without a weapon, that would mean she would have to let him in close, very close.

She started to moan and move her head from side to side, as if she were coming to. She heard his footsteps, then the noise of something dunking in water. He lifted her chin gently. She felt a cold wet cloth wiping her face. She opened her eyes and looked at Nigel. He sucked in his breath when their eyes met.

"Feeling better Rhea?" he asked, nervous. She jerked her head out of his hand.

"Why did you hit me Nigel? It wasn't necessary, I would have gone with you." She acted indigent.

"You would?" he replied, surprised. "Your ship disabled the *Bounty* and your men threatened me when I tried to talk to you."

"What did you expect? The *Bounty* attacked first. I didn't know it was you until you boarded us. You didn't even let me get over the surprise of seeing you again." At least that much was true. What was he doing on a Red Dragon ship? How

333

did he become a captain? "Why am I tied to this bed?" she asked, hoping he would untie her hands.

"What were you doing on the *Rogue* acting as Captain?" he asked, his eyes narrowed with suspicion.

"It's my brother's ship. The crew knows it belongs to my father, so I convinced them to take me home. I didn't want to stay in London anymore. Why did you attack us?" She feigned innocence. She knew perfectly well that they wanted the cargo.

"What's the hurry to get home Rhea?" he asked, she had the feeling he was testing her.

"My mother is ill," she lied, hoping to gain sympathy. He slapped her across the face, knocking her head to the side. Pain shot up the side of her face to her ear as tears involuntarily welled in her eyes.

"Liar!" he yelled in her face. He walked over and leaned on his desk, closed his eyes, and took a deep breath. "Now Rhea, if we are to get along you must be honest with me, understand?" he said, as if he were addressing a child.

Fear crept up the back of her spine.

"What do you want from me?" she asked, her voice shaking. She had to be patient, wait for him to get closer. She couldn't provoke him, give him reason to knock her unconscious.

He laughed a sinister laugh, one laced with insanity.

"What do I want from you? I want everything from you, just like you took everything from me."

He ran to the bed and grabbed her face, pinching her

cheeks together painfully against her teeth, and put his face a few inches from hers. She tried to inch her legs around closer, looking for an opportunity to defend herself.

"You were my world, Rhea. You were to be my wife, my future. Now everything is ruined! Ruined because of you!" He slapped her again. White stars bounced around in her vision.

"Do you want to see what they did to me because of you?" He jerked at his belt, unable to unfasten it in his anger. He struggled, finally getting it undone, and dropped his pants so she could see his deformed genitals. She looked away. Guilt stabbed her. She had no idea they beat him that badly. He reached for his pants and pulled them up quickly, embarrassed.

"Nigel, I had no idea...I...," She didn't know what to say.

"Loss for words, are you? Well I have a few for you. Eye for an eye, I say, eye for an eye." He had an insane, faraway look. His anger was building. He reached for her belt and started to undo it. Panic spiked in her. She had to talk to him, get him to understand she didn't know.

"Nigel, it doesn't have to be like this, we can..." He cut her off.

"We can what Rhea? We can marry? Start a family? What Rhea? What! You bitch, don't you know you stole everything from me!" His eyes were glassed over and he had a crazed look on his face. "Shut up!" He slapped her again. She felt herself blacking out.

A loud cracking sound filled the air, and the ship lurched

to one side. Cannon fire! She jerked herself out of her daze. Someone was firing on them! Another boom came, followed by a splash. A miss or a warning? It had to be Titan. She looked over at Nigel. He looked confused.

"Damn and blast. What was that?" He looked at her, indecision clear. Should he go or stay here and finish? Then there was a crashing sound outside the door followed by a loud thud. A second of silence followed. Rhea stared at the door. Nigel lunged for his cutlass. Just as he was about to reach it, the door flew off its hinges and dropped to the floor. Sy stepped inside, ducking his head to make it through the frame. He quickly scanned the room, his eyes settling on Rhea. She could read fury in his eyes, pure fury.

"She mine!" Nigel yelled, and lunged for his cutlass again. Sy reached him in three long steps. He picked him up by the front of his shirt, swung him in a circle, and threw him against the wall. Nigel crumpled to the floor. Sy ran to Rhea and took his knife out of his boot to cut her free. Rhea could see Nigel rise from the ground in a rage, grab his cutlass, and come running to stab Sy in the back. Her eyes widened in horror.

"Behind you!" she yelled at Sy.

Sy reacted in an instant. He spun, kicking the cutlass from Nigel's hand. In the same motion, he took his knife and sliced his throat. Nigel grabbed his neck in surprise, then fell to his knees. He gurgled for a moment, then fell forward, blood pooling around him as he lay motionless. Sy stepped over his body and ran to Rhea.

"Rhea." He reached up with his knife to cut the ropes. "Are you hurt?" he asked her, concern in his tone.

She was afraid to look in his eyes. Was he really here? Was she imagining this? Dreaming? If she was, she didn't want to break the spell by looking into his face. Her bottom lip quivered. Did he come for her? She could feel his fingers on her wrists, removing the rope and rubbing her reddened skin.

"Rhea look at me. Are you hurt?" he said, softly, she could hear the underlying panic in his tone. She gulped, and looked at him, waiting for him to dissolve as he had in her dreams so many times in the past week. She could read the relief in his eyes. He closed his eyes for a second longer than needed, then cupped her face.

"Where are you hurt?" he asked again, rubbing his thumbs on her cheeks, still red from Nigel's slaps. His eyes were full of concern.

Titan burst through the door. Relief engulfed him when he saw Sy attending Rhea.

"Rhea, thank God! Sy, we must go, carry her if you must, but we have to go now! We are about to be overtaken." Panic was in his voice. He ran back out to help the others.

"Rhea, we have to fight our way out of here, we are outnumbered two to one, we cannot let them take the *Star*. Can you walk?" he asked, frantic.

Take the *Star*? That brought her back to her senses. She started to stand, pushing Sy's hands from her face.

"I'm fine, let's go," she said, coming back to reality. Titan and Sy were together on the *Star*? How did this happen? Sy grabbed her hand and started pulling her from the room.

"Wait!" she said, in a panic, pulling her hand from his grip. She ran to the desk, where she had last seen her knife. It wasn't there, so she moved some of the mess on the floor to search for it. Relief washed over her when she saw a bit of the hilt. She grabbed the knife and ran for the door. Sy raised his eyebrows. She shrugged. He grabbed her hand again.

"Stay close!" he ordered.

Rhea looked at the body right outside the door. Lenny. Dead. It was true then, they used women for their sick fetishes then discarded them like trash. She felt no remorse for Nigel or Lenny or the crew. As captain, she knew what was happening on her ship at all times. She didn't believe this crew didn't know what their captain did to women. Anger surged through her. She bent down and took the cutlass from Lenny's belt.

"I can fight!" she exclaimed, with all the emotion she was feeling. Sy stopped short. She couldn't stop her momentum and ran into his back. He turned and grabbed her shoulders.

"Rhea, I cannot take the chance of something happening to you. I won't survive losing you again. Do not argue with me, just climb on my back and I will get you out of here." His eyes were filled with such emotion. Her heart skipped a beat. There was no time for this, she was fine, she could help. She remembered that he didn't know this about her. She reached up and cupped his face.

"Sy, I will stay at your back the whole time. There is no

time to explain, but you must trust me, I can fight. I will press against you the whole time so you will know that I am there." They locked eyes for a second.

"Fine," he said, resigned. "But, if you leave me for a second, I am carrying you out of here." He turned and pulled her to his back forcefully, all the while holding Nigel's cutlass in front of him.

"Ready?" he asked. She nodded against his back. She felt his hand reach between them and retrieve a pistol from his belt. She wished she had had time to braid her hair. It was getting in her face. She could hear the battle raging outside, steel against steel, men crying out in pain as they were wounded. This was it, all that she trained for, she needed to do her part, not be a burden. What was he waiting for? The anticipation was becoming worse than the fight.

"Sy?" she asked, pressing against his back, nudging him to go.

WHAT THE HELL was he doing! He needed to carry her across the deck and throw her onto the *Star*. This was insanity thinking that she could fight at his back. He couldn't step out in the fray. He couldn't lose her again, no matter if she could fight or not. He could feel her warmth through his shirt. She was pressing against him, ready to go. He scanned the deck quickly, looking for Titan. If he could get to him, he would help keep her safe. He was there, waving for him. God help him, he was going to have to do this. He shot the first man running toward them, and dropped the pistol. He reached back and drew her closer as he stepped into the fray. He parried a cutlass coming from his right. He could feel Rhea swinging and the clang of steel as she came in contact with a sword. He could feel her body moving against his back as she rocked from side to side with each swing. He parried forward against another attacker, who went down under the strength of Sy's blow. He kicked the man in the head. He surged closer to Titan. They were almost there. Titan moved in to help defend Rhea. He could feel her defending them from behind. Someone screamed as she stabbed them through. She dropped her sword when they fell back.

"Behind you Pax!" she yelled, over the fray. He knew then that the crew was starting to rally around them to protect her. He tightened his grip on her as he surged forward toward the rail. Once there, he let her go, to climb to the top. He held his hand down to her to lift her over to the *Star*. Titan whistled to the crew signaling to abandon the fight and board the *Star*. The entire dynamic of the fight changed. Last blows were given, the crew ran to the rail, and jumped on the *Star*. The crew on the *Star* took axes and cut the lines keeping the ships together. Simultaneously, long boards came from the cannon ports to push the *Star* away from the ship.

Sy had his hand out for Rhea. She reached for him but someone grabbed her hair from behind and pulled her down to the deck. He heard her scream and watched as she reached up to her head in pain. She hit the deck hard.

"Noooo!" Sy cried out. He looked to jump but it was too late. The long boards had pushed the *Star* too far from the other ship. Panic seized him. He looked back at Rhea. She had already jumped up and had her knife in front of her ready to fight. He looked up, searching for the right rope. He spied it and prayed it would be long enough.

"Make a hole!" he screamed, as he cut the line with his cutlass, ran across the deck, jumped the rail, and swung toward Rhea. He kicked the closest man to her in the face.

"Jump!" he yelled, as he swung in her direction. She looked up and read the situation immediately. When he approached, she grabbed him around his waist and ran along the deck to keep their momentum. He grabbed under shoulders to lift her above the rail as she jumped to clear it. The crew on the *Star* was ready for them and grabbed the rope as soon as they swung onto the deck. The couple fell on the deck together. Sy rolled to his back, taking most of the impact, Rhea ending up on top of him. Once they came to a stop, they looked in each other, locking eyes. Rhea started to smile, Sy smiled back as the crew hooped and hollered in celebration.

"Heave ho gents! Let's get out of here! We aren't clear of this yet!" Titan called, as Rhea crawled off Sy and extended her hand to help him up. He took it, not because he needed a hand, but because he wanted to touch her.

Titan walked the deck, shouting orders as sails were raised. Sy and Rhea stood staring at each other, still holding hands.

"Get ready to shoot the *Star* gents! It's time to get the hell outa here!" Titan shouted .

Rhea's eyes widened at that order. She let go of Sy's hand and turned from him in a panic.

"Delay that order!" she shouted, as she turned in a flurry of hair and ran to the aft deck. "Jat!" she shouted, and motioned to him as she ran up the stairs. He took off running. Following behind her, he ran to a cubby at the side of the poop deck, retrieved something, and tossed it to her. She looked through it at the retreating ship.

"Prepare aft cannons one and two!" she shouted. Without hesitation, the crew repeated the order, echoing to the decks below. She continued to look through the device as she waited for them to call they were ready. A moment later the voices relayed they were 'standing by'.

"Cannon one, five degrees up angle, ten degrees' port! Fire when ready!" she commanded. Again, it echoed through the ship. The cannon fired and the ship lurched. She lowered the device to watch. A large explosion of wood and smoke filled the air, she hit her target. Her crew erupted with cheers. She raised the device to her eye again. The crew immediately quieted, each of them elbowing the other to be silent.

"Cannon two, fifteen degrees up angle, twenty-two degrees' port, fire when ready!" she commanded, with finality.

Sy watched Rhea as a Captain. She was confident, calm and in control. Her crew hung on her every word, their trust in her evident. He watched her body language. He knew she had just relayed the deathblow to the other ship. The White Lyon had never sunk a ship to his knowledge. She was not enjoying this moment, merely doing what had to be done. She lowered the device slowly and watched. The cannon ball flew and hit its mark. Once it was over, she turned to face her crew.

"It's over. Thank you for saving me," she said, simply. "Shoot the *Star* gents!" She turned back to watch the retreating ship as it started to sink. A resounding cheer went up. Sy could see she took no pleasure in it. Timbo started issuing orders in a commanding voice as he walked the deck. The deck was a flurry of motion as they all went to their stations and launched the cloaking device.

RHEA WATCHED THE SINKING VESSEL, knowing that she left the crew no choice but to abandon ship. She had sent not one but two cannonballs into the hull at the waterline. There would be no recovery, it would sink to the bottom of the sea. She had never thought to sink a ship before, but she couldn't live with herself if she didn't sink this one. How many innocent women had Nigel tortured and killed? And all of those men aboard could've helped them but had just let him do it. The sea would be their judge and jury. If they survived then they deserved to live. She turned her back on it, resigned. So be it.

"Rhea!" Titan called out, bounding up the steps. He picked her up and spun her around in a brotherly hug. "Thank God you're alright!" he said, relieved.

"I'm fine Titan," she responded, cupping the side of his face reassuringly. "I'm fine. Another adventure for you to tease me about later," she said, sarcastically.

"Oh, ha ha! No more of these adventures, promise me Rhe? You're making me an old man before my time!" he said seriously, giving her another tight hug.

"Alright, if you insist," she said, jokingly, giving him a small smile. She looked around the deck for Sy. He was staring at her from below, he hadn't moved. She gave him a tight smile, not sure what he was thinking. Now he knew everything.

All of a sudden, he started running. She watched as he bounded up the stairs two at a time, then across the deck where she was standing. He didn't stop his urgent stride till he was right in front of her. Without warning, he reached down, picked her up and unceremoniously threw her over his shoulder. The next thing she knew, she was upside down being carried down the steps. When he reached the main deck, the shock had worn off the crew and they started hooting and hollering at Sy's display. His long strides were purposeful and everyone stepped out of his way to let him pass. When he reached the captain's cabin he ducked through the door and slammed it shut.

He bent down and set her on her feet. She backed away, using her arm to push her hair out of her face. They stared at each other for a moment. She'd missed his handsome face and those piercing blue eyes. She looked into them, waiting for him to say something. He knew everything about her now; she was frightened to know how he felt. Would reject her?

"I didn't write that missive Rhea," he said softly, and took a hesitant step toward her. "Why did you believe it? After all that happened between us, why would you think I would ever leave you?" he asked. She could hear the hurt in his voice.

Tears welled in her eyes. He didn't write the missive? He didn't leave her, reject her once and for all? He came for her! It all started to sink in. A warm feeling started in her belly and her muscles started to ease. She could see the apprehension in his face as he waited for her to say something.

"I didn't at first, but there were things in the missive that were said between us, in private. Nobody could've known you said those things. I thought that I may have misunderstood their meaning the first time and read into them. The longer you were gone, the easier it was to convince myself. Besides, I wasn't what you thought... I was... you didn't know I was the..." she stammered and looked down, unable to say it out loud, unsure how he felt about her.

"You mean, I didn't know were the White Lyon, the mythical pirate I chased for months? That you are Captain of your own ship, one that you designed and built yourself? Not exactly what is expected or accepted by the upper crust of English society, correct?" He closed the distance between them. He put his hand under her chin and gently lifted it. "I want to show you something." He untucked his shirt and pulled it over his head in one swift movement. She sucked in her breath at the sight of his muscular chest and abdomen. He turned sideways slightly so she could see the mark at the top of his arm. Her eyes widened in recognition. He bore her mark, the mark of the White Lyon.

"I am yours, Captain Rhea, Lady Rhea, Marchioness Blackthorne. I care not for the titles you bear. I have died a thousand deaths these past weeks thinking I lost you," he said, with all the love he felt for her. "I love you and will follow you anywhere. Make no mistake, I will not be separated from you again. Ever."

Rhea reached up and gently ran her fingers over the mark on his arm in disbelief. He closed his eyes briefly at her soft touch. He was part of her crew. He was willing to give up everything and had sworn fealty to her. She was overwhelmed. She looked back at his face, tears streaming down her cheeks. He loved her. She jumped in his arms.

"Oh Sy! I love you too!" She put her lips on his and kissed him with all the love she had pent up inside her.

He reached down and put her legs around his waist, then pulled her against him, wanting, needing her closer. Then he took possession of her mouth. The hot moist heat of her lips welcomed him, making him feel as though he was melting into her, becoming one with her. He was losing control, every time their tongues touched it was a tempest was brewing, threatening to overtake him. He was squeezing her hard against his chest. He had to ease back so he wouldn't crush her.

"Sy," she said, breathlessly. "I need you inside of me. Now."

"Aye, Captain," he replied, and walked them over to the bed.

He set her on her feet. She hastily kicked of her boots and pants. He did the same. He reached for the hem of her shirt. Slowly, he raised it, rubbing the back of his fingers on her skin as he went. She shivered as he grazed the sensitive skin on the sides of her breasts. She felt her nipples harden immediately. Heat and desire shot to her loins. She raised her arms to aid in getting the shirt over her head. He removed it completely, then let it flutter to the floor. He looked down at her naked body hungrily. Rhea placed her hands on his chest. She rubbed slowly over his nipples feeling them harden under her touch. She slid one hand up to the back on his neck, pulling his lips down to hers. Once they touched she slid the other hand down his belly passing his navel into the dark patch below. She could feel his muscles quivering under her hand. She put her hand around his hard shaft and rubbed her thumb over the tip. He groaned in her mouth and pushed his hips forward into her touch.

"I want you inside me, please," she begged, in a whisper. "I've missed you so much."

Sy lost the last thread of control he had. He picked her up and threw her gently down on the bed, following her, crawling between her legs. He put her legs around his hips and guided his erection to her entry. He pushed the tip in slightly to test her wetness. He closed his eyes at the sheer pleasure wracking his body at the feeling. She was ready for him, she raised her hips impatient for him to enter.

"I love you Rhea," he said, as he thrust into her, hard. She gasped and grabbed his hips pulling them forward. She moaned and rotated her hips side to side. He pulled out and thrust into her again. Then again and again. Her moans of pleasure spurred him on. He thrust into her hard, possessing her. He wanted to be deeper, consumed by her. He rolled them over never losing their connection. Her hair was a cloud of white as it settled around her face and shoulders. Once she was straddled above him she arched her back and circled her hips in pure desire, wanting more of him. She raised off him slightly then slammed herself down on him hard. The end of his shaft hit the core of her. He let out a sharp breath at the intense pleasure it invoked. She lifted and slammed hard on him again. Good God, he could spill his seed into her right then. She arched her back and braced her arms behind her and ground herself on him. Her hair pooled on his thighs, soft and erotic, intensifying his pleasure. He grabbed her hips and thrust into her further. A guttural moan escaped her lips and her head rolled in a circle showing her pleasure. He did it again.

"Oh Sy!" she said his name in an erotic haze, her voice shaky.

He thrust his hips upward again and slid her hips back and forth across his erection. Sweet Jesus, she felt good, he couldn't stop. He quickened the pace, moving her hips back and forth faster and faster thrusting against the core of her. He could tell she was close. She started to cry out, he put his thumb on her nub and made circles around it. It was hard and wet from their passion. She cried out again, clenching the sheets with her hands as her orgasm wracked her body. He felt her sheath tighten and pulsate around him. His seed exploded violently inside her. He pulled her hips forward hard as he spilled his seed in waves inside her, his orgasm intensified by her pulses.

He could feel her starting to relax, spent, and he reached up and pulled her against his chest to lay on top of him. Her heartbeat was slamming in her chest, matching his own. Contentment washed over him. He put his arms around her and squeezed in a not so gentle hug.

"I love you wife, you are mine, now and forever," he whispered to the top of her head, then kissed it gently. She raised herself on her elbows and looked into his eyes. She kissed his lips softly.

"Now and forever," she repeated, whispering against his lips. "I love you too, husband." She put her head back down on his chest. She sighed, taking pleasure in the sound of his heartbeat.

"As your Captain, I order you to do that to me at least twice a day," she said, in a mock commanding voice.

"Aye, Captain," he answered, resoundingly. "As you wish, I'm at your command."

CHAPTER 25

*S*y and Rhea did not emerge from their cabin for hours. They made love slowly next, cherishing each other, then falling into a relaxed sleep. They woke with a start when the bells chimed, alerting the crew to the sight of another ship. They rushed to dress but had to stop to kiss more than once. Rhea tried her best to tame her rumpled hair with no success. She finally took the tie from Sy's hair and used it on her own. He chuckled.

"I don't like yours tied back anyway," she stated.

"Aye, Captain, duly noted," he said, and opened the door for her.

Up on deck, Titan was struggling to hold up Sy's spyglass without the use of the rail. Sy laughed at his bravado.

"Here, let me see," he said, teasing, as he took it from Titan with one hand.

He held it up to his eye and looked at the ships. It was

the *Rogue*. She was underway and towing the *Bounty*. Sy was impressed with Smith, he had taken the situation under control and was on his way back to port within hours.

"It's Smith and the *Rogue*. They are underway with the *Bounty* in tow," he relayed to Titan and Rhea.

"Really? Already? Now that's impressive." Titan said, echoing Sy's thoughts exactly.

"That's why I hired him as chief engineer of Blackthorne Ship Builders," he stated, proud of his most trusted friend.

"Blackthorne has a ship building company?" Rhea asked, surprised.

"We've had a shipyard for years. For the most part, my father used it as storage and a loading dock. I claimed a small portion of it to build the *Breakneck*. But now, I have reason to expand the building part of Blackthorne," he said, looking down at Rhea.

"For Smith to build more ships for you?" Rhea asked, tentatively.

"Smith is good man and a good engineer, but I know someone better. She needs space for her work," he stated, nonchalantly. Rhea wanted to cry; he was going to let her continue her work! She launched herself into his arms. She kissed him quickly before he let her down.

"Thank you," she said, quietly. He took her hand and squeezed it.

It took four days to sail back to London. It was slow going with two ships disabled. Those four days were the happiest days of Rhea's life. Titan and Jat made sure that Rhea and Sy could have the same relief time, which they spent in her cabin. They made love for hours, getting to know each other's bodies. They talked about everything. Their hopes and dreams. Rhea told Sy all about *Paradiso* and the people who lived there. She didn't tell him about the *New Star* though, wanting to keep her gift a surprise. Sy filled her in about everything he discovered about Penelope and what he intended to do once they returned. He also told her how worried he was about his father.

Despite being on a ship, Sy was still feeling overprotective of Rhea. Not an hour went by that he wasn't checking on her. Smith asked her to look at the broken rudder shaft of the *Bounty*. As she deliberated with Smith on a fix, Sy constantly checked on her. Rhea recognized his unease about being separated for long periods of time, since she often felt the same anxiety. When she saw him checking on her, she felt the same sense of relief. Since they obviously felt better being around each other, she kept him busy helping repair the rudder shaft, using his brawn to her advantage. Together, they devised a patch for the shaft that would hold long enough to get the ship to Blackthorne Shipyard for repairs.

~

SMITH AND SY sat in the galley of the *Star* eating fresh baked biscuits, "These are the best biscuits I've ever tasted," Smith grabbed another from the bowl. "Still can't get over the innovations on this ship. She really is intelligent Sy, you lucky son of a barnacle."

Sy felt his chest puff with pride. He looked around the brightly lit room at the seamen that were so devoted to his amazing wife. He was damn lucky, indeed.

"At the risk of being punched in the face, I have to ask you a question."

"You have my attention, ask away." Sy said, intrigued.

"There are times she looks at me, waiting for me to answer a question or say something, and I swear I look in those eyes of hers and lose my train of thought. She's so damn beautiful. She probably thinks I'm a simpleton, I'm sure. How do you keep your wits about you when you're with her?" he asked honestly.

Sy chuckled. "I don't, probably never will. Her beauty scares me to death, has from the beginning. Why do you think I'm always checking on her like a love-sick fool? To be perfectly honest Smith, after what happened, I don't think I will ever be at ease unless she's by my side," Sy confessed, lowering his voice. "Even now, I am having anxiety that she is not with me. I know she's taking her shift at the helm and is fine, but soon I will give in to my fear and go see her. Do you think I will ever get over this?" he asked.

"You've both been through a lot. And we have yet to settle this matter with Lady Blackthorne and this Frankie Two Toes menace. You will feel better once that is done. Even so, it may take some time for you to trust people with her. I know how consuming love can be. Maisy is never far from my thoughts. I cannot wait to see her again. I have no idea if she shares my depth of feeling. This love business is nerve wracking!" Smith confessed.

"How could she not? We will be back at port tomorrow. Your wait is almost over. I am extremely worried about my father. We need to stop in London before we take the ships to Blackthorne for repairs. I want this business settled immediately. The *Star* will need to be hidden until all is settled. Then we will have to see what Rhea wants to do with her."

"I agree. This would be a very dangerous ship in the wrong hands. It must be protected at all costs."

Sy slapped his thighs and stood.

"Well, here I go to lay eyes on my wife to keep my protective instincts at bay. I'm a love-struck fool, but the happiest I've ever been. I hope your Maisy will make you feel the same as I, as inconvenient as it may be," he joked to his friend.

Up on the deck, he saw his wife standing with Jat next to the wheel. She looked up and made eye contact. He could see her relief at seeing him. He smiled. She motioned something to Jat and came down the stairs. Smith was right. His heart skipped a beat and he was speechless as she looked up at him.

"Can I speak with you in private for a moment?" she said, in a commanding voice. She turned and walked into the Captain's cabin. He followed her in and when he passed, she closed the door and jumped into his arms. This had become their way and he loved it. She would jump in his arms and he would catch her. He loved the way her legs would wrap around his waist so he could hold her derriere with her breasts crushed against his chest. She was firm but soft, and her hair brushed against his arms. It felt so intimate. Everything about her was soft, moist and sensual. Her lips covered his urgently, kissing him feverishly, frantically, almost in desperation. Sy pulled her back and looked in her face.

"Rhea," he said, breathing heavily. "What's wrong?"

"I missed you," she said, breathlessly.

He could see the passion in her eyes, which drifted down to his neck. His pulse sped up and he started to get hard with the thought of her lips on his sensitive skin. Her head slowly followed her eyes, placing her lips on his neck, sucking at the spot where her lips landed. She ran her tongue up to his chin, at the same time she slid her hand down between their bodies and came to rest on his arousal. She squeezed him as she sucked the spot where his pulse beat. He moaned at the pleasure she was giving him, hardening in her hand. He walked over to the wall, resting her back against it, while squeezing her derriere to show how much he liked her ministrations.

He took her mouth again, loving the taste of her. She kissed him back, taking her other hand and slipping it behind his neck to hold him to her. He let her legs drop and she immediately started kicking off her boots. He started undoing her belt and she undid his pants. He took over his pants and pushed them down to his knees while she wiggled out of hers, kicking them out of the way. He lifted her and put her legs around his waist again, and bracing her against the wall, as he guided his hard member into her. She moaned and arched into him, her head against the wall, closing her eyes in sheer ecstasy. Tears started falling from her eyes and she grabbed the back of his neck and kissed him feverishly again. He stopped, something *was* wrong. He pulled back from her again and looked in her face.

"What's wrong Rhea?" he said, holding her in place. "I know something is wrong love, talk to me," he said, lovingly. He kissed her cheek and rubbed his against hers to wipe her tears.

"I love you so much it hurts Sy. I need you, I really need you," she said, in a frightened voice. She rotated her hips against him, moaning at the pleasure it invoked.

"Ahhh," he moaned. "I love you and need you too. What can be wrong with that love?" He thrust into her, then pulled out and thrust into her again.

"We are almost back and...I can't...I don't want...oh God. I need you so much." She could hardly get the words out as he thrust into her again and again. He stopped, understanding donning on him about what was bothering her.

"Rhea. Look at me. Look at me love," he said, sternly. When she was focused on him, he continued. "No one is going to separate us again, no one, not for one night, or one minute. I won't have it. Understand?" He could see some of the tension fade from her features but there was still some uncertainty. He kissed her.

"But my aunt will surely..." she started.

"Understand that I won't have it. She has no choice in the

matter. You are mine, my wife in every way, I will not have us parted again, ever. We will make it work, or we will pretend to run off to Gretna Green, or I will ruin you in public. I don't care about propriety or society. You are my world Rhea. We will not be apart ever again." This time she was crying, but they were tears of joy.

She grabbed his face with both hands and kissed him tenderly. He started to thrust into her again, she moaned in his mouth.

"Look at me Rhea," he asked. He watched her face as he thrust into her again and again until they both found fulfillment. Her face was beautiful and glowing when he reluctantly pulled out of her.

"I have to go back on deck," she said, wishing they could lay down together. He rubbed her legs before he let them down. He slapped her backside affectionately.

"Then get back to work, Captain."

The next afternoon, The Star was carefully hidden with Timbo in charge of her safety. They boarded the *Rogue* and limped to port. They sent Titan to Blackthorne Shipyards with both the disabled boats. Sy sent Smith home, though he suspected his friend would soon be heading to the Waterford Estate.

The hack they hired rolled up in front of Aunt Magda's townhouse. There was a flurry of excitement at the Chamberlain townhouse. People were carrying boxes in and out. Stanley was directing traffic and issuing orders. When Rhea and Sy ascended the stairs he almost didn't notice. Once he recognized them, he gave them a warm, yet excited greeting.

"Hello my lord and lady, may I take the liberty of being the first to congratulate the both of you. I will see you to the parlor and tell Lady Chamberlain you have returned. Would you like refreshments? Of course, you would, what a silly question. I will see to it right away," he rambled, as he saw them to the parlor.

"Uh, Stanley, what is happening around here?" Sy asked, confused, looking around at all the boxes and packages stacked throughout the foyer and parlor.

"It's very exciting, my lord, very exciting indeed! I will let Lady Chamberlain explain." He bowed and left, presumably to get Aunt Magda.

Sy walked over to the stack of letters piled on one of the tables. The top one was addressed to Rhea and Sy. He opened and read the missive and looked up at Rhea in shock.

"The banns must've posted as I directed. This is a request from the Duke of Wellington to attend the wedding. Why would the Duke of Wellington request to come to our wedding? I don't know the Wellingtons." he asked, confused.

"Because the Prince Regent has requested that you be married at his country estate and will be attending. Anyone who's anyone is clambering an invitation. They have been sending gifts of congratulations to win your favor, my lord," Aunt Magda answered. She ran to Rhea and gave her a big hug. "I'm so glad to see that you are back safe, my dear. You gave us a fright you did! Are you well?" she asked, with genuine concern.

"Yes, Aunt Magda, I am well," she answered, stunned. "Why does the Prince Regent want us to be married at his country estate?"

"Mostly because I declined to have it at the palace. I knew you wouldn't want all that opulence. The pomp and circumstance didn't seem to suit you, so I took the liberty of suggesting a garden wedding at his country estate. One does not say no to the Prince after all, but it was not hard to convince his advisors that this was the better option."

"I don't understand, I am not connected to the Prince? Why would he want to host our wedding at all?" Sy asked, confused.

"Everyone would love to host your wedding, my lord, both of you have become quite the celebrities since your departure. Someone leaked the details of your pending rescue of Rhea after the banns were posted. The romance of it all, you and Titan, sailing off to save Rhea from danger. The tale has completely captured the interest of society of every rank. The story has monopolized the papers. *'The Sweetheart of the Ton being recused by her handsome sea captain.'* The Prince feels it is just what England needs right now, a love story for the masses. There are wagers at White's over the outcome of the rescue. Once the Prince took interest in your story everyone started demanding to be a part of the wedding. It's been mayhem around here," she explained.

"Who leaked the story, Aunt Magda?" Sy asked, narrowing his eyes at her.

"Why I did, of course. I had to say something regarding both of your hasty departures. We can't afford a scandal, after all!" she said, as if it was the most natural thing to do.

"How is my father?" Sy asked, remembering suddenly that he had become distracted.

"Oh, he is well, my lord. Almost fully recovered. He has been a tremendous help with all of this. Once we knew that poison was the cause of his illness, it was simple to discern that his tea had been laced. We discovered that a friend of one of the kitchen maids planted it. We have since tracked her down and she is in the custody of the magistrate. She has confessed to her crime along with other crimes she had committed because of blackmail some street thug was using against her.

Lord Blackthorne, she admitted to drugging your father at the Verny estate. Your father is seeking an annulment from Lady Verny as we speak. The utmost secrecy has been placed on this case. Your father doesn't want Lady Verny to know until the annulment has been granted. You and Rhea being in favor with the Prince should be a tremendous help to his cause," she explained.

Sy had to sit down to process everything. Rhea walked over to him and put a supportive hand on his shoulder.

"Why don't you go to your father, Sy. I'm sure he's dying to see you've returned safely," Rhea said.

"I have already sent for him," Aunt Magda said. "He should be here momentarily."

Stanley walked in with a tray of tea and biscuits. He barely had time to put the try down when someone pounded on the front door. He ran to answer it but it flew open and the senior Lord Blackthorne walked into the foyer.

"Where is my son?" he demanded.

Sy stood, feeling like a child in trouble, and faced the door waiting for his father to enter. Rhea slipped her hand into his, squeezing. He looked down at her and gave her a shy smile.

A moment later his father ducked through the doorway. He looked himself again, strong and virile, with the color returned to his skin. He looked at Sy and relief softened the concern in his expression. He walked straight over to Sy, ignoring everyone else, put his hands on Sy's shoulders and examined him for a short second before drawing him in for a tight hug. Sy hesitated for a split second, then let go of Rhea's hand and hugged his father back. A warm feeling surrounded his heart and he could feel the last bit of anger fade way. He squeezed his father harder, then they stepped back.

"I was worried sick about you, son. If that bitch willing to poison me, I had no idea what she had planned for you. Thank God you have returned to me safely. Your mother was looking over you. I know she was, son. She has been watching over both of us. I'm sure of it," he said.

"I'm sure she was, father. Lady Verny did make an

attempt on my life but it backfired. I will fill you in on the details later. First I want you to formally meet my wife." He turned to Rhea, who had stepped back to let the men reunite. She put her hand back in Sy's when he extended it to her. "This is Lady Rhea Hastings, the new Marchioness Blackthorne," he announced with pride. Rhea curtsied to his father, and gave him a shy smile.

"It's a pleasure to meet you, my lord," she said, softly.

He looked at her with a stunned expression, then looked at Sy.

"Well, I can certainly see what the fuss is about. Come here girl and give your father-in-law a hug!" He opened his arms in invitation. She walked into them and put her arms around his waist as he hugged her. He looked at Sy over her head and mouthed *'gorgeous'* and gave him a wink. Sy gave him a knowing smile in return. Rhea had charmed his father with one sentence and a smile. He let her go and she went back to Sy and slid her hand into his again.

"I am relieved that you are both back safe. Sy, once you have settled your wife, I need to meet with you immediately," he stated, urgency in his tone.

"Yes father, I agree. On that subject," he turned to Aunt Magda, "Rhea will be staying with me. I don't care what the implications will be, I will not allow us be separated," he said, emphatically.

Aunt Magda smiled.

"Rhea's belongings are already at your townhouse, my lord. Mine as well. While you were gone, the upper floors of my house were infested with some kind of vile animal, mice or something, I have been forced to move out while the exterminators remove the unsanitary beasts. Since so many packages and correspondence have been coming for you, it seemed the most efficient thing to do was to move into your residence. I hope I didn't overstep, my lord," she said, with a knowing smile and a wink.

He smiled back. The lady was a marvel. Maybe she could help Smith with Maisy?

"Of course not. I would have suggested it if you hadn't thought of it first," he answered. He wished he could hug her, he was so relieved. "Lady Chamberlain, you have done so much for us, thank you. I wonder if you might do me one last favor?"

"Anything, my lord, how can I be of service?" she asked, standing straighter from his praise. It was obvious that she was enjoying herself.

"Could you please invite Rhea's friend, Miss Waterford, to come and stay with us until the wedding? Rhea will need attendants and she is one of Rhea's closest friends," he asked.

"My lord, Miss Waterford is already in residence at your house along with Lady Lily Belfort. I was drowning in correspondence, as you can see, so I enlisted their help. They were more than happy to come," she said, with that knowing smile again. Sy couldn't help staring at her. He had déjà vu, it was like talking to his sister. He shook off the feeling for the moment.

"Thank you, Lady Chamberlain," he replied, in a tight voice. He looked at Rhea. She shrugged, and tightened the grip on his hand.

"Oh, and my lord, Miss Waterford seems to have developed feelings for your friend, Lord Smith. She has been going on and on to Lady Lily about him, driving her a tad bit crazy. I was forced to separate the girls. I took the liberty of setting a bed up in your study. It has the loveliest tree outside the window, which I'm sure will be of comfort for Miss Maisy, since it's not truly a bedroom and trees being a rare commodity on this side of town and all. She doesn't seem to mind one bit. She stays up late working on the correspondence at your desk. She's such a lovely, enthusiastic young woman. Do you think Lord Smith might come by for dinner one evening? I'm sure that Miss Maisy would enjoy that immensely."

There was that knowing smile again. He looked at Rhea. Her eyes were as wide as saucers and her cheeks slightly pink. No, she couldn't know, could she?

"Whatever you feel is best, Lady Chamberlain," he answered. Aunt Magda leaned in closer to Sy and Rhea.

"Windows with trees always seem to work well with budding romances also, don't you think?" she whispered. She turned and started to walk way away before they could react.

"I'll have the carriage brought around. I'm sure you are anxious to get home. The girls are going to be so excited to see that Rhea has returned safely. They've been very worried.

I'm sure you are both dying to bathe after your adventure too. Stanley!"

"Well, all seems to be under control here. I will return to my house and wait for you to come." Sy's father walked over to Sy and Rhea. He took Rhea's free hand. "Welcome to the family, Lady Rhea. You are a beautiful addition to be sure. I look forward to getting to know you better," he said, sincerely, then put his hand on Sy's shoulder. "I'm glad you're back safely son, we have much to do. I will see you in a while." He let himself out. Sy looked at Rhea.

"Let's go home."

CHAPTER 26

Sy's townhouse was just as overrun as Aunt Magda's and just as full of packages. Rhea was overwhelmed with all the activity surrounding her wedding. Thank goodness her aunt was in charge of the details. Lily and Maisy came running down the stairs when she arrived genuinely relieved that she was safe, and demanded that she tell them everything. Sy gave Rhea a sweet kiss on the cheek and excused himself so she could visit with her friends.

"You have to tell us everything, every detail, leave nothing out," Lily said, perching on the settee in Sy's parlor. "It is all so romantic!"

"Everybody is talking about it. All the ladies want to be you. Everyone has been imitating your dresses and hairstyle. It's gotten past the point of ridiculous, if you ask me, but it is very entertaining watching them mimic you," Maisy exclaimed, settling next to Lily. "Tell me Rhea, is Lord Smith well? I have been on pins and needles waiting for some word of him."

"Lord Smith is very well, Maisy." She put her hand over Maisy's. "He is a hero. He saved Sy's life and helped to rescue me. He is the reason we were able to get back here so quickly. If it wasn't for his ability to repair Titan's ship, we would be drifting at sea this very moment," she explained.

"You exaggerate your description of me, my lady. I believe it was a team effort," Smith said, from the doorway. He looked the perfect gentleman. He had bathed and put on clean clothes and was holding a bundle of papers in his hand. It was clear that he was not expecting, but was delighted, to see ladies sitting in the parlor. At the sound of his voice, Maisy rose. They locked eyes, in silence. Rhea looked at Lily, who rolled her eyes, teasingly. Rhea nodded her head toward the door.

"I assure you Lord Smith, I'm not embellishing one bit. You will always be a hero to me," Rhea said, sincerely. "I will tell Lord Blackthorne you are here. Is he expecting you?" she asked. He tore his gaze away from Maisy and looked at Rhea. She gave him a knowing smile and started for the door, dragging Lily with her.

"No, he is unaware that I was coming, please don't let me disturb your visit. I can see to myself. Is he in his study?"

"I believe he is." She looked at Maisy, who was visibly disappointed that he was leaving. Her heart went out to her friend. She understood, and tried again. "It's no bother, my lord, I'm happy to tell Sy that you are here. Then you may have a... moment to...ah...as I was saying, it's no bother."

She stumbled over her words. She wasn't good at this at all. Where was her aunt when she needed her?

"Thank you, but I'll be on my way. Excuse me ladies," he said, and bowed politely.

~

SMITH TOOK the stairs two at a time, toward Sy's study. The door was open so he went in, plopped himself down in a chair, and put his head in his hands.

"Smith?" Sy asked, concerned, looking up from his paperwork. "What's wrong? What are you doing here?"

"I just made a buffoon of myself in front of Maisy. I wasn't expecting to see her, you see, and there she was. I lost my composure. Oh, my God, what an idiot I am." He buried his face in his hands again, shaking his head. Sy chuckled. He went to the side bar to pour Smith a brandy.

"Here, drink this. I'm glad you're here. I was going to see if you could come by anyway. I have to go to my father's and I was hoping you would stay with our ladies while I'm gone. I don't trust this Frankie Two Toes or Lady Verny. I want Rhea protected till this situation is resolved. I would feel better if you were with them," he asked, with a smile.

"Of course, I'm at your disposal. I agree, he tried to get to her once, we should be cautious. Do you have a pistol I can get easy access to?" He gulped down the brandy Sy gave him.

"Here, it's loaded." He took the pistol from the back of his waistband and put it on the desk. "Now, what happened? It can't be all that bad. Just go back down there and claim your lady, Smith," he stated, emphatically. "If that doesn't work, I would like to point out, that is her bed behind you and there is a very convenient tree right outside the window," he said, waving his hand in the direction of the window. He gave Smith a rakish smile.

Smith looked at the bed, and then the window, his eyes widening.

"Good lord," he whispered, under his breath. "How'd you manage that?"

"I didn't, Lady Chamberlain is responsible for this arrangement. It seems Miss Waterford has been mooning over you. Let me say this, that tree and window were instrumental in the development of Rhea's and my relationship. I highly recommend the use of it," he said, with a chuckle.

"Ah, duly noted," he replied, smiling in understanding.

"Why are you here? Since you didn't know that Miss Waterford was here, I assume you needed to see me?"

"Oh, yes. Here." He set the stack of papers in front of Sy. "Here are the identification papers of the ruffians that attacked us on the way back to London. I took them once we had them subdued. I thought they would be of use to you and your father."

"Smith, you're a genius! I didn't think we would be able to use that incident against Penelope because we had no physical proof. This will tie her to it. I don't know what to say," he proclaimed. "I have the magistrate and my solicitor meeting at my father's in an hour. This just might be the last thing I need to end this nightmare."

"Bow Street should be able to round up these men. They didn't exactly seem resolute to their task, or particularly loyal to Frankie Two Toes. I'm sure they will confess everything for the reward you offered. It shouldn't be difficult to rid yourself of that Verny scum now," Smith pointed out.

"This is good news, good news indeed. Let's go find our beautiful ladies. I could use a moment with mine before I go. I need to be sure she will stay with you until I return," Sy said, happy, but with concern.

"I won't let her out of my sight till you do. I give you my word." Smith paused, then asked. "Could you help me orchestrate a moment alone with Maisy before you leave? I need to make up for my earlier behavior."

"Let me see what I can do," Sy said, with a smile.

A moment later, they entered the parlor to find Rhea and Lily consoling Maisy, who sat hunched over on the settee. Smith's heart dropped when he saw how upset she was.

"He must've had an urgent matter to discuss with Lord Blackthorne, that is all. Try not to read anything into it before you speak to him," said Lily, trying to reason with her.

"Thank you for being so nice Lily, I know I've driving you crazy talking about him all the time. But it's obvious, now that he has seen me again, his feelings have changed." she said, forlornly. "I should go home."

Smith panicked at the thought of Maisy leaving.

"They certainly have not!" Smith interrupted, and swiftly walked over to the settee. He grabbed her hands and helped her up so he could look her in the eyes. "It is my unwavering resolve to make you my wife that had me nervous. I'm sorry about how I acted earlier, I wasn't expecting you to be here. I panicked and acted like a buffoon. I'm new to this love business, please forgive me." He lovingly ran the back of his fingers down the side of her face.

"Oh Lionel, of course I forgive you!" She put her arms around his neck. "I've been so worried about you."

RHEA AND LILY SCURRIED OUT, unnoticed by the couple. Rhea grabbed Sy's hand and pulled him after her.

"Thank God." Lily said, once they were in the foyer. "Maisy would have been inconsolable for months otherwise. I could hardly stand her mooning all the time, I can't imagine if she were heartbroken!" she joked. Rhea and Sy laughed.

"Well, they will need a moment. I guess I'll return to my mountain of correspondence. Now that you're back, can we set a date for the nuptials? It would be so much easier to send out the invitations," she asked.

"You may set them for the earliest possible date." Sy said, emphatically.

"Wonderful, I will consult with Lady Chamberlain as soon as she arrives. How exciting! Two weddings!" Lily did a small curtsy and headed upstairs.

Sy looked at Rhea. She looked very happy for her friend. He stared at her beautiful face and felt fortunate that he would get to see it every day from now on. He hoped she would always look this happy.

"What?" she asked, after a moment passed.

"You look so beautiful and happy," he confessed. She slipped her arms around his waist and leaned into him.

"I am happy. I hope you are happy too," she said, giving him a hug, pressing her cheek against his chest.

"The happiest I've ever been in my life," he said, sincerely, then pushed her back so he could look at her with a serious expression. "And I'd like to keep it that way. I need your promise that you will stay here with Smith. I have to go to my father's to see about his soon to be ex-wife and this Frankie Two Toes. They have been ruthless and I don't want you taking any chances. I want your word of honor, Rhea. No matter what, you'll stay with Smith."

"I promise. But, if Smith is going to stay here and Titan and Pax are sailing the Rogue to the shipyard, who will have your back?" she asked, concerned.

"My father and the magistrate. We have enough evidence to charge them with a number of crimes. I will see them hauled off to Newgate prison. Then I can relax. Until then, take no chances, understand?" He put his finger under her chin and looked into her eyes.

"Aye, Captain," she answered.

"Minx."

He leaned down and kissed her soft lips, but before they could get carried away he pulled back.

"Ahem." Aunt Magda walked through the door. "Sorry to interrupt," she said, apologetically.

"No worries, my lady, I was just leaving. Can you please lock the door behind me and deliver Rhea to Lord Smith? He's in the parlor with Miss Waterford. Also, there's to be no more package deliveries until I say so. I need to secure the house. Hopefully this business will be over by this evening," he stated.

"Certainly, my lord. Please be careful," Aunt Magda said, concern in her voice. He nodded and took one last look at Rhea before he left the house.

"Well, shall we go see what the new lovebirds are up to then?" Aunt Magda said, as she walked to the parlor. "Come along Rhea dear, shall we ring for some tea?" she asked, louder than necessary. Undoubtedly, to give warning of their approach. Rhea smiled. Was there anything her Aunt Magda didn't know how to do?

WITHIN THE HOUR, Sy and his father were in the carriage on their way to the Blackthorne dowager townhouse. Mr. Sanford insisted on tagging along to talk about other business matters. Despite the protests Sy delivered, he was seated across from the man, whose smile was starting to grate his nerves.

"Mr. Sanford, may I ask why you seem so happy? This situation hardly calls for that big smile you are sporting," he pointed out, wishing the man had stayed behind.

"Quite the contrary, my lord. I have waited a long time to see something done about Lady Verny. I wouldn't miss this for the world. Although that is not the reason for my smile. It's the other matter I wish to speak to you about that has me smiling. It's not often that I get to be bearer of good news. Unexpected good news at that," he eluded.

"What good news?" Sy's father asked, before Sy had the chance.

"Lady Blackthorne's asset list came from her father. It's most unexpected. According to the marriage contract, all of Lady Hasting's assets are to be transferred to the Blackthorne estate, except for *Paradiso*. It was to remain her sole separate property until her death, then to pass directly to her children."

"*Paradiso*? What is *Paradiso*?" his father asked.

"It's a small island she inherited from her uncle Harry Hastings," Sy explained. "I would never have expected to receive what is considered a family property."

"I have checked on this *Paradiso*. Until recently, it had remained an uncharted island. It is by no means a small island, my lord. Further, it is in a very strategic location. You might want to talk to your wife about developing it and using it as a port to restock ships if the natural resources are abundant. I believe that's what her uncle used it for. It's very valuable, very valuable indeed. It would triple your trade route abilities."

"I will consider it Mr. Sanford. Right now, I have decided to use any extra resources to invest in the ship building side of Blackthorne Shipping. We intend to be on the cutting edge of the industry," he said with a smile, in anticipation of the challenge. Mr. Sanford was smiling again, almost giddy.

"Resources," he laughed. "I am happy to inform you that you have the recourses to fund two shipping companies and develop the island if you should so wish, and then some. The dowry Lady Hastings is bringing to your estate is sizable. Very sizable," he stated.

"How sizable?" Sy's father asked.

"Three hundred and fifty thousand pounds to start. She also receives twenty five thousand a year from her mother's estate. Once her mother passes she will receive a controlling interest in several overseas manufacturing companies that build parts for the shipping industry. Lady Hastings is in the process of building yet another manufacturing plant that will make weaponry. Cannons, I believe. She is a very industrious businesswoman it seems." He paused, waiting for Sy's and his father's reaction. Both sat stunned. "You are a very wealthy man, my lord, one of the wealthiest in the country. Are you not pleased?"

"Did you say three hundred and fifty thousand pounds?" Sy asked, coming out of his stupor.

"And twenty five thousand a year currently. That number will rise as her mother's estate grows."

"Good God. Where did she get all that money?" Sy asked.

"I'm sure I don't know, my lord. All I know is that arrangements are being made for you to receive the funds by the end of the month."

Sy looked at his father. His faced changed from shocked to concerned.

"I don't want the money. Send it back to where it came," he said, emphatically.

"What?" his father and solicitor said in unison.

"You can't mean that, son. Why would you do that?" he asked.

"Because father, I love Rhea, I don't want her or anybody else to think I married her for money. Ever. No one will believe that I didn't know about it. I won't see her hurt, not for one second, we've been through enough." he stated.

"Son, nobody knew about this. She knows that, and, she knows that you love her. She would never believe otherwise. Besides, one would have to be blind not to notice that you are head over heels for the lady. Talk to her before you make any decisions. See what she wishes you to do."

"Alright, I will talk with her. You two will keep this in confidence until I decide."

"As you wish, my lord, it will be kept strictly private, of course," Mr. Sanford assured Sy.

The carriage started to slow. Sy could see the townhouse. There was a wagon parked in front. Men were loading it with trunks and furniture.

"What the hell? Is she trying to steal things from the

house?" Sy exclaimed, and started to jump out of the carriage.

His father did the same. Sy ran up the steps, his father right behind him. He could hear Penelope screeching orders from down the hall and went toward the sound.

"Take that and that," she said, pointing at various objects. "Hurry, I want to be gone within the hour," she ordered.

"What do you think you are doing?" Sy's father demanded.

Sy stepped aside and let his father into the room. Penelope jumped at the sound of his voice.

"And why is there a wagon full of Blackthorne property in front of the house?" he bellowed.

"My goodness, my lord, you gave me a start!" she said, putting her hand to her chest. "I am thinking of doing some redecorating and was cleaning out the things I am giving to charity. It should go a long way to help repair the Blackthorne image, since your son here made a spectacle of himself running after his little slut. I suppose a special marriage license will be required."

Sy was seething with anger, and took a step forward. His father put a hand on his chest.

"That is no longer any of your concern, Penelope."

"How can it no longer be my concern? I am the Marchioness and the Blackthorne reputation is my primary responsibility."

Sy's father stepped to within a foot of her. Anger radiated from him. Fear crossed Penelope's face.

"You have never been the Marchioness of Blackthorne and you never will be. I know you had my brandy drugged that night. I never touched you, not then, not ever. This sham of a marriage is over. You will leave this house with what you came with, nothing."

"You'd love to get rid of me, wouldn't you? Pitch me right in the gutter. But you can't, we are married, till death do us part," she screeched, a twisted look on her face.

"You tried that too didn't you. Poison for me, and an ambush for Sy. You tried to kill both of us, you, sociopathic bitch. I will see you hang for touching my family."

"So what if I did, you can't prove it, it's your word against mine," she said, confidently. "Everyone knows you've been an abusive husband. Why even last night you hit me. Look, I have the bruises to prove it." She pulled down her collar to reveal a string of bruises around her neck. "I will go to the magistrate and show him what you've done. You're the one that should be arrested."

Sy's father laughed, a joyless laugh.

"Fine, let's talk with him right now. We stayed up all night together, compiling the evidence against you. I'm sure he'll be interested to learn when I had time to slip away," he said, resolutely. Sy waved his hand. The magistrate walked in, a young girl on each arm.

"Is that her?" He asked them simply, no introductions. "Be certain before you answer."

"Yes sir, that is her. I sat in the kitchen of this very house while she wrote the letter to Lady Hastings," Millie said, without hesitation. The other girl was looking at her feet. The magistrate gave her arm a shake.

"Look at her, girl. You're in enough trouble already, don't make it worse for yourself," he commanded.

The girl looked at Penelope. She nodded, and resumed studying her feet. The magistrate gently shook her arm again.

"You have to say the words girl or it doesn't count," he stated.

"It's her, the lady I told yer about. Her father gave me the stuff to put in his brandy at the party but it were her that gave me the stuff to put in his Lordship's tea. Showed me how much and everything. She wanted me to do it right. Threatened to turn me in for druggin' his Lordship if I didn't. Said no one believe me if I told the truth," she rushed out in fear. "They're going to kill me now. Nobody crosses Frankie Two Toes and lives to talk about it."

"You are safe with us girl. I'm not going to let anything happen to you." The Magistrate nodded at two uniformed officers, who escorted the girls out.

"You are going to believe two guttersnipes over a Marchioness?" Penelope asked the magistrate.

"You were never the Marchioness of Blackthorne, Lady Verny. Because of the preponderance of the evidence and the testimony of those two 'guttersnipes', your marriage has been annulled," Mr. Sanford announced, as he handed her a document from the court, proof of the annulment. "In the case of annulment because of fraud, you now owe the Blackthornes for all expenses incurred during the time of the fraud. Over the last four years, this is how much you have spent." He handed her another document. "As you can see, we have seized your share of Verny Shipping and Trading to help offset your debt. Unfortunately, the value of your portion doesn't come near to satisfying the total. How would you like to pay the balance, Lady Verny?" he asked.

"You can't do this," she said, stunned.

"She will have to satisfy her debts once she has paid for her crimes," the Magistrate said. "Lady Verny, you are under arrest for attempted murder, larceny, blackmail, and fraud. You will have to come with me." He shackled her hands behind her back. Panic set in, and she started to struggle and scream.

"You can't do this. Frankie! Frankie! Get in here! Frankie!" she screeched, as the officer forced her out the door.

Realization quickly sank in. Sy started searching around the house. They should have searched it immediately when they arrived. He ran through the bottom floor as the other uniformed men checked upstairs. Everyone came up empty handed.

"Not to worry, we know where to find Frankie Two Toes. He couldn't have gotten far. You go home and let us handle it from here. He would be crazy to bother you or yours now, Lord Blackthorne. But I will station two officers in front of your houses until he's caught."

"Thank you, Lord Magistrate. We will be on our way once the house and property is secured."

"As you wish." He exited the house, relaying orders as he left.

Sy looked at his father.

"It's over, father, she's gone from your life forever."

"Well, that calls for a drink now, doesn't it?"

CHAPTER 27

*R*hea jumped into Sy's arms upon his return. His heart swelled at his favorite greeting as they kissed. He needed a moment alone with her, not only because his arousal came to attention, but to discuss her dowry.

"Is everything settled then?" Smith asked.

"Frankie Two Toes is on the run but they expect to catch up with him quickly, if they haven't already. You are officially off duty my friend," he said, without putting Rhea down.

"Mind if I stay for dinner? I'm starving," he asked, his excuse was weak but clearly he didn't want to leave Maisy. Sy smiled.

"I'm sure you are, my friend, I'm sure you are." He slapped Smith's shoulder affectionately. "I need to talk to my beautiful wife before dinner, can you make excuses for us?"

"No problem, see you at dinner." He walked back to the ladies.

Sy carried Rhea up the stairs. She looked disappointed when he steered her into the study instead of his bedroom. He set her down once they entered the room.

"What's wrong?" she asked.

"Nothing really, why do you think something is wrong?"

"Because we are in the wrong room," she said, starting to untie his cravat. He stopped her, groaning, reluctant to give up what her actions promised. He gave her a peck on the lips instead.

"That is exactly why we are in *this* room. If we went to our room, there would be no way I could concentrate on this conversation." He sat at his desk. She sighed, and lowered herself into the chair on the other side, like a child in trouble.

"What is it we need to converse about?" she asked. She licked her lips and bit the bottom one seductively as he stared at her. He gulped and shook his head to concentrate.

"Why didn't you tell me about the money Rhea?" he asked. He saw her flinch just a little.

"What money?" She feigned innocence.

"Rhea," he said, sternly.

"Oh, my dowry money? Well, I didn't think it was important. It was your money, so I ignored it really." She stood up and kicked off her slippers.

"Three hundred and fifty thousand pounds and twenty five thousand a year?" he asked, incredulously.

"Is it that much now? I have no use for money on *Paradiso*. We don't use currency, so I just told my solicitor to save it as part of my dowry. It seemed the easiest way to handle the influx at the time." She leaned over the desk, propping herself on her elbows, giving him a good view of her cleavage. "Is that a lot of money?" she asked. When he didn't answer, distracted by her display, she brought her elbows in, pinching her breasts together, teasing, and enjoying her power over him.

"Sy? Is that a lot of money?" she asked again, and stood up.

That brought him back to the conversation. This woman was going to drive him mad. He shifted in his chair, adjusting for his arousal.

"Rhea, that's an incredible amount of money. You are one of the richest people in England!"

"Surely you mean, *you* are one of the richest people in England. The money is yours. I don't need it, I'm sure you will do the proper thing with it." She plopped back down in the chair.

"Where did it come from, all that money?" he asked, curious.

She bent over and began to run her hands from her ankle to her thigh, gathering her dress as she went, giving him a generous peek of her leg. She stopped at the top of her stocking and untied it, she put her foot on the edge of his desk, and slowly rolled her stocking down, explaining as she went.

"Well, it was Otis' idea really. He suggested that I register some of my designs under an assumed name since women are not allowed to. I had several, you see. My mother helped me with this idea and handled the paperwork for me. One day, someone from a manufacturing plant asked if he could buy one of the designs, but my mother said no, she wouldn't sell anything without asking me first. Then, he offered her fifty percent of the profit of every piece sold instead and she said yes."

She put her other foot on the desk and repeated the ritual, rubbing her hand up her leg seductively, then rolling her stocking down slowly.

"It wasn't long before he was back, offering to manufacture other designs, too. Soon they were only making the things Otis and I designed. My mother, the hardline businessperson she is, said she would pull the two best sellers and manufacture them herself unless she could be fifty percent owner of the plant. After that was a success, she bought another plant on her own, and now she's setting up a new one for Otis' new cannon design. I just need to get back to *Paradiso* and figure out the *mounting* system," she said, in a seductive voice, as if she were describing what she wanted to do to his body instead of explaining the history of her dowry.

Once both stockings were removed, she ran her hands slowly up her legs, pooling her dress in her lap. She removed her drawers next, one side at a time. Sy was mesmerized. He was staring at her hands as she removed each piece of clothing. Then, she rubbed her hands up her inner thighs, spreading her legs slowly. "That's what happened. Now, apparently, you're rich." She touched herself, put her head back, and moaned. Sy came unglued.

He quickly threw Rhea over his shoulder, marched down to his room, and locked the door. He threw her on the bed. He discarded his belt and pulled his pants down, freeing his erection. He threw up her dress, covering her face, grabbed her hips and pushed the tip of his erection in her. Thank God, she was wet. He feverishly thrust into her over and over. She arched her hips to match his rhythm. He put his thumb on her nub and made circles. She cried out with pleasure. Soon, he felt her pulsing with her orgasm and he let his come. When her legs relaxed, he let them go and laid on top of her. He moved the dress and kissed her.

"You drive me mad, Minx," he said, and kissed her again. She smiled but didn't open her eyes. He sighed, and lay next to her.

"If anyone finds out about the money they will think I married you because of it. But I only want you, Rhea. I could care less about your dowry."

"Then don't tell anyone. I've never spent a schilling of it. I want you to have it. Spend it on Blackthorne Shipping, if it'll help. I have so many ideas. I just want to work on them and see them come to life. It's the one thing that makes me happy." She rolled on her side and put her hand on his face. "Except you, of course. You are my world now, Sy. Take the money, I know you will put it to good use. Give some to Smith and Maisy so they can have a beautiful wedding."

He put his hand over hers and kissed her palm.

"You are an amazing woman, my little Minx. I love you."

"I love you too."

∼

TWO WEEKS LATER, they were married in front three hundred guests at the Prince Regent's summer home. Aunt Magda outdid herself. The outdoor wedding was simple, but elegant, just like Rhea.

Rhea's dress was the star of the day. It was made of silver silk, with aquamarine and sea blue glass beads which adorned the waist, then faded as they went up the bodice and down to the bottom of the skirt. The gown was accentuated by her signature wide belt, adorned with aquamarine beads. She wore her aquamarine choker, which Aunt Magda had returned to her without Sy's knowledge. Rhea was grateful that her aunt hadn't returned it to Sy, he would have been hurt that she tried to return it. Rhea was glad Aunt Magda had the foresight to spare him that sorrow.

Sy and Rhea escaped the reverie for a moment, hiding in an alcove.

"My love, I have no idea what to get you as a wedding gift. I have thought on it for some time and I can't think of a thing that would fit such a unique woman as you. So instead, I have decided to ask you what you would like," Sy said, as he kissed her neck, wishing they didn't have to go back to the celebration.

"I am not one for gifts, my husband, as you well know, but I am very excited to give you your wedding gift. Take me home to *Paradiso*, Sy. I wish to share this last bit of my life with you. Also, your wedding gift from me happens to be there. Please, my love, take me home. Liana wants to have her baby there. The *Star* and her crew should return to their families and the *Rogue* is full of supplies for the island. That would be the best wedding gift you could ever give me," she pleaded.

"Leave it to my wife to ask for a gift that gives more to others than to herself." He looked at her beautiful face. "I can deny you nothing, my Minx, I would love to see your *Paradiso*," he said, kissing her passionately. "We sail as soon as the *Rogue* is repaired."

EPILOGUE

One Month Later

SY COULDN'T BELIEVE what he was seeing. It looked as though they were sailing in to the rocky shore of the island she called 'Paradiso.' It was a nerve wracking experience to watch her maneuver the *Star* into the bay through an indiscernible channel. No wonder the *Star* remained hidden, and not a soul could ever figure out where she was moored. He doubted he could have navigated the *Breakneck* with the precision Rhea and her crew did.

Once they entered the bay, Sy couldn't find words. The beauty of the cove was indescribable. They had created a small world of their own in the most beautiful place on the face of God's earth.

"*Paradiso*," Rhea whispered. He could hear her joy and pride. "It means paradise. A fitting name, don't you think?"

"It's beautiful, there are no words to describe its beauty, Rhea," he said. "It's just like you. Too unworldly to describe."

She blushed at his complement.

"Now, you can see your wedding gift." She pointed to a ship that was ready to be launched. "I built a better version of the *Star*. At Titan's urging, I left off the cloaking device so it could be moored anywhere. But, if you want the device installed, we can add it. It's my greatest masterpiece. Now, it is yours. I named it the *Black Star*." He stared at the most elegant ship he had ever seen. The sleek lines of the hull practically vibrated with energy even while moored.

Rhea continued, "It has many new innovations that I have not released. I thought it might help with Blackthorne Shipping, with the ship building division, that is." Sy thought about the extraordinary ingenuity that had gone into the *Star's* many innovations and could not imagine that what marvels of engineering she still had in that beautiful brain of hers. He was in awe, utterly speechless. "You don't have to use my ideas if you don't want to. I understand." She said quietly when he didn't say anything.

He looked at Rhea, finally breaking his gaze from the *Black Star*. Was she crying?

"My love, look at me," he said, putting his hand under her chin. "You astound me, shock me speechless. It's the most incredible vessel I have ever seen. It's not every day your wife gives you the ship of ships. Please excuse my bad manners. Although you are the greatest gift of my life, this," he waved his hand at the bay, "and that," he waved his hand toward the *Black Star*, "should render a man speechless, don't you think?" he asked.

She smiled. He bent down and kissed her, a loving kiss, one anyone would give their life to have just once.

"There's more," she said.

"I'm not sure I can take much more," Sy said, honestly.

As the *Star* docked, a large crowd gathered on the pier. Once the gangway was lowered, Sy and Rhea descended. The crowd clapped and cheered. Rhea was overwhelmed by the community's response. With tears in her eyes, she greeted each one, and introduced them to Sy proudly. There were a few suspicious looks from the gentlemen. Finally, Sy took his shirt off so all could see that he wore the mark of the White Lyon. Some of the women swooned, but the men relaxed and slapped his mark as they made their way through the crowd.

He was overwhelmed by their love for Rhea. He felt unworthy, yet protective at the same time. He needed to prove his worthiness to this community. His worthiness of her. Understanding dawned. This was the plight of ladies in English society. Men have all the power, ladies have none. They can only hope for a good match, yet still have no control over their lives. How often had he thought of Rhea as "his"? Nevertheless, she always gave him respect, gave herself freely, even when he thought of her as a possession. It was his turn to be worthy of *her*. It was no wonder that she didn't want to leave this world where she could flourish and be herself.

"Sy, I would like to introduce you to Otis." She presented an older gentleman, wearing modest clothes and no shoes. He had a kind face and wore spectacles with one cracked lens. This is the gentleman he had been jealous of? He felt a fool.

"I have heard much about you, sir. It is a pleasure to meet you," he said sincerely, taking Otis' hand for a hearty shake. "I am a great admirer of your work."

Otis grinned, showing a few gaps in his teeth.

"Why thank you, son. Aren't you a mountain of a man! You are just what our Rhea needed, by God yes, exactly what she needed!" He winked at Rhea. "Are you a fan of cold ale son?" he asked.

"Cold ale?" Sy asked, confused.

"Ahh, the best thing I've ever invented! Let me introduce you to the one thing that will revolutionize the world of liquor. You don't mind if we borrow him for a while do you Rhea?" he said, as he pushed Sy towards to village. "Come along, your life is about to change," he said, pulling Sy along. Sy looked at Rhea, questioning whether he should resist. She just waved him on with a smile. Several of the men joined in Otis' enthusiasm. Before he could protest, he had twenty or so gentlemen whisking him off to try something called cold ale.

At Maggie's, Sy engulfed the room. The ceiling was short and the chair was small, making him feel awkward. The cold ale was wonderful, though the questions hurled at him were not.

"Are you really the one they talk about, that Cap'n Sy Black?" one of the gents asked.

"I am," he said, taking a long pull from his cup. How long does this ale stay cold? He felt as though he should drink it fast so it wouldn't get warm.

"You almost caught us once, you're a legend here," another gent said.

"I didn't though, isn't that the point?" Sy said, to Rhea's favor.

"True, 'tis true, but now yer married to the gel," he pointed out. "No one could get close to her, 'ccept ya, now yer married to the gel. That's somethin' ain't it?" another gent said in awe.

"Sorry gents, I may be fast at sea, thanks to my ship, but it has nothing to do with my love for your Rhea," he replied, knowing this was a test of some kind.

"It don't?" several of them said, in unison.

"Nope, she owns my heart and soul, gents. I'd give my life for her. Makes no difference to me how fast she is. I'd follow her anywhere, no matter how fast or slow she goes," he said. He raised his glass. "To the White Lyon, long may she live!"

"Long may she live!" everyone said, in unison.

He spent the next twenty minutes having his mark slapped by every man and woman in the bar. He could have sworn some of the women slapped him twice.

He spent the next hour sipping ale, even though his eagerness to see Rhea was playing havoc with his nerves. Just when he thought he was going to have to leave and search the village for her, she walked in. He relaxed instantly. She fit right in, in her pants and peasant shirt, as she sauntered over to him.

"Are you done with him yet?" she asked the room in general.

"Long may she live!" a few shouted, while others chuckled.

She walked over to Sy and extended her hand. He let her help him up, pretending he needed it. He swerved and leaned heavily on her shoulders as they walked toward the door.

"Thanks a lot, everyone. He's useless to me now!" The room burst into laughter.

Once outside, she cursed and repositioned his arm over her shoulders.

"Everyone loves you here," he said, trying to sound besotted.

"Well, it is my island," she said, in a matter a fact tone.

"That's not why they love you," he tried to slur. "That's not why I love you," he drawled, leaning more of his weight on her shoulders.

"God in heaven, how am I ever going to get you up the path?" she groaned. He sat down, knowing she could never pick him up.

"How could I ever take you from this place?" he said, looking forlornly to the ground. "This is your home," he said, with the genuine sadness he felt, letting his head fall forward heavily.

After a long pause, she knelt in front of him. She lifted his head. Her eyes were full of tears.

"You may not understand me right now Sy, but you are my home. Where you are, I am home, whether it be on a ship, in London or here. You are my home, understand?" She kissed his lips gently, as if he was a child.

He grabbed her waist and pulled her down. He deepened the kiss with all the love he felt for her. She was right. Home was wherever they were together.

"I love you Rhea. You are my home too," he said. He picked her up as he stood. "Now, where do you live?" he asked, promise in his voice.

"You're not drunk?" she asked.

"I thought it was expected, so I let them think so. I need to make love to my wife. I'm not crazy," he said, putting her down.

"This way." she said, and started pulling him toward her cottage.

They couldn't get their clothes off fast enough. He did pause for one second when he saw the massive size of her bed, startled. They made good use of it for the next few hours. Once sated, they talked about their future.

"We can come back here as much as you want. Can we please make a larger cottage though? I can't stand up in the kitchen," he asked.

She giggled as she ran her hand down his neck and chest. She rolled over and sighed in contentment.

"Of course. Where would you like to have our baby? Here or in London?" she asked, as if she were inquiring about the weather.

"You mean when we have a baby? Right?" he asked, sitting up to look at her, thinking he misunderstood her question.

"Since it will happen seven months from now, we need to plan. We won't be able to sail once the winter months come," she said, nonchalantly. "Since it will be your first year in the House of Lords, I think we need to be in London for this one. I would like to have the next one here, though. We will need to pick up my mother on our way back to London, she will want to be there for the birth."

"Wha...what?" he said shocked. As she watched, she could see his expression turn to understanding, then joy.

It was the happiest moment of her life, so far...

Made in the USA
San Bernardino, CA
28 November 2018